I0726754

ADV
Your Choice for Fiction Variety & Reading Pleasure

ISBN: (PAPERBACK) 978-1-950464-84-5
ISBN: (EBOOK) 978-1-950464-96-8

ADV

Your Choice for Fiction Variety & Reading Pleasure

WINTER 2025   **ISSUE #18**

WHAT

WHERE

In Remembrance of
Bonnie Hawkins
1938-2025

**Though you live on in eternal peace, rest, and happiness,
you will be sorely missed.**

Notes from the Editor

We're in a festive mood here at ADV because we think we have found the perfect stories to get you into the holiday spirit.

In this issue we have a sweet Thanksgiving story by the author of "Anne of Green Gables," a story about Santa Claus by the author of "The Wizard of Oz," an original tale about Christmas written by Ashley K. Frantik, and a classic ghost story. Hold on a minute, you say - a ghost story? How is that festive? Allow me to elaborate.

Remember "A Christmas Carol" by Charles Dickens? That might be the most famous secular Christmas story of all time, and, guess what - it's a ghost story! It's the perfect example of a trend in Victorian literature to tell ghost stories around the winter solstice. According to a story on History.com about the subject, "The long midwinter nights meant folks had to stop working early, and they spent their leisure hours huddled close to the fire [and told ghost stories]. Plus, you didn't need to be literate to retell the local ghost story." And the stories didn't have to be about Christmas; in fact, most weren't.

So with this in mind, we chose to add "The Castle of Otranto" by Horace Walpole to this edition. It's considered the first Gothic story - it was written in 1764! - and is one of the most influential books in Gothic/horror culture. We think you'll enjoy reading it. We also have "The Meditations of the Emperor Marcus Aurelius Antoninus" in case you want to start the new year off with a deeper, somewhat philosophical read. And we have the usual fun things you find in ADV - photos, games, Retro Rewind, and more.

We hope you have a great holiday season, and our fondest wish is that 2026 is a great year for you personally.

See you in the spring!

Michael Brian

Michael Brian

Letters to the editor:
Comments/Questions accepted.
Put *Letter to Editor* in Subject
and send to:
AdventuresBookzine@proton.me
*Name and Email content could
be published in a future Issue.

AUNT SUSANNA'S THANKSGIVING DINNER

BY L.M. MONTGOMERY

"Here's Aunt Susanna, girls," said Laura who was sitting by the north window—nothing but north light does for Laura who is the artist of our talented family.

Each of us has a little pet new-fledged talent which we are faithfully cultivating in the hope that it will amount to something and soar highly some day. But it is difficult to cultivate four talents on our tiny income. If Laura wasn't such a good manager we never could do it.

Laura's words were a signal for Kate to hang up her violin and for me to push my pen and portfolio out of sight. Laura had hidden her brushes and water colors as she spoke. Only Margaret continued to bend serenely over her Latin grammar. Aunt Susanna frowns on musical and literary and artistic ambitions but she accords a faint approval to Margaret's desire for an education. A college course, with a tangible diploma at the end, and a sensible pedagogic aspiration is something Aunt Susanna can understand when she tries hard. But she cannot understand messing with paints, fiddling, or scribbling, and she has only unmeasured contempt for messers, fiddlers, and scribblers. Time was when we had paid no attention to Aunt Susanna's views on these points; but ever since she had, on one incautious day when she was in high good humor, dropped a pale, anemic little hint that she might send Margaret to college if she were a good girl we had been bending all our energies towards securing Aunt Susanna's approval. It was not enough that Aunt Susanna should approve of Margaret; she must approve of the whole four of us or she would not help Margaret. That is Aunt Susanna's way. Of late we had been growing a little discouraged. Aunt Susanna had recently read a magazine article which stated that the higher education of women was ruining our country and that a woman who was a B.A. couldn't, in the very nature of things, ever be a housewifely, cookly creature. Consequently, Margaret's chances looked a little foggy; but we hadn't quite given up hope. A very little thing might sway Aunt Susanna one way or the other, so that we walked very softly and tried to mingle serpents' wisdom and doves' harmlessness in practical portions.

When Aunt Susanna came in Laura was crocheting, Kate was sewing, and I was poring over a recipe book. That was not deception at all, since we did all these things frequently—much more frequently, in fact, than we painted or fiddled or wrote. But Aunt Susanna would never believe it. Nor did she believe it now.

She threw back her lovely new sealskin cape, looked around the sitting-room and then smiled—a truly Aunt Susannian smile.

"What a pity you forgot to wipe that smudge of paint off your nose, Laura," she said sarcastically. "You don't seem to get on very fast with your lace. How long is it since you began it? Over three months, isn't it?"

"This is the third piece of the same pattern I've done in three months, Aunt Susanna," said Laura presently. Laura is an old duck. She never gets cross and snaps back. I do; and it's so hard not to with Aunt Susanna sometimes. But I generally manage it for I'd do anything for Margaret. Laura did not tell Aunt Susanna that she sold her lace at the Women's Exchange in town and made enough to buy her new hats. She makes enough out of her water colors to dress herself.

Aunt Susanna took a second breath and started in again.

"I notice your violin hasn't quite as much dust on it as the rest of the things in this room, Kate. It's a pity you stopped playing just as I came in. I don't enjoy fiddling much but I'd prefer it to seeing anyone using a needle who isn't accustomed to it."

Kate is really a most dainty needlewoman and does all the fine sewing in our family. She colored and said nothing—that being the highest pitch of virtue to which our Katie, like myself, can attain.

"And there's Margaret ruining her eyes over books," went on Aunt Susanna severely. "Will you kindly tell me, Margaret Thorne, what good you ever expect Latin to do you?"

"Well, you see, Aunt Susanna," said Margaret gently—Magsie and Laura are birds of a feather—"I want to be a teacher if I can manage to get through, and I shall need Latin for that."

All the girls except me had now got their accustomed rap, but I knew better than to hope I should escape.

"So you're reading a recipe book, Agnes? Well, that's better than poring over a novel. I'm afraid you haven't been at it very long though. People generally don't read recipes upside down—and besides, you didn't quite cover up your portfolio. I see a corner of it sticking out. Was genius burning before I came in? It's too bad if I quenched the flame."

"A cookery book isn't such a novelty to me as you seem to think, Aunt Susanna," I said, as meekly as it was possible for me. "Why I'm a real good cook—'if I do say it as hadn't orter.'"

I am, too.

"Well, I'm glad to hear it," said Aunt Susanna skeptically, "because that has to do with my errand her to-day. I'm in a peck of troubles. Firstly, Miranda Mary's mother has had to go and get sick and Miranda Mary must go home to wait on her. Secondly, I've just had a telegram from my sister-in-law who has been ordered west for her health, and I'll have to leave on to-night's train to see her before she goes. I can't get back until the noon train Thursday, and that is Thanksgiving, and I've invited Mr. and Mrs. Gilbert to dinner that day. They'll come on the same train. I'm dreadfully worried. There doesn't seem to be anything I can do except get on of you girls to go up to the Pinery Thursday morning and cook the dinner for us. Do you think you can manage it?"

We all felt rather dismayed, and nobody volunteered with a rush. But as I had just boasted that I could cook it was plainly my duty to step into the breach, and I did it with fear and trembling.

"I'll go, Aunt Susanna," I said.

"And I'll help you," said Kate.

"Well, I suppose I'll have to try you," said Aunt Susanna with the air of a woman determined to make the best of a bad business. "Here is the key of the kitchen door. You'll find everything in the pantry, turkey and all. The mince pies are all ready made so you'll only have to warm them up. I want dinner sharp at twelve for the train is due at 11:50. Mr. and Mrs. Gilbert are very particular and I do hope you will have things right. Oh, if I could only be home myself! Why will people get sick at such inconvenient times?"

"Don't worry, Aunt Susanna," I said comfortingly. "Kate and I will have your Thanksgiving dinner ready for you in tiptop style."

"Well I'm sure I hope so. Don't get to mooning over a story, Agnes. I'll lock the library up and fortunately there are no fiddles at the Pinery. Above all, don't let any of the McGinnises in. They'll be sure to be prowling around when I'm not home. Don't give that dog of theirs any scraps either. That is Miranda Mary's one fault. She will feed that dog in spite of all I can do and I can't walk out of my own back door without falling over him."

We promise to eschew the McGinnises and all their works, including the dog, and when Aunt Susanna had gone we looked at each other with mingled hope and fear.

"Girls, this is the chance of your lives," said Laura. "If you can only please Aunt Susanna with this dinner it will convince her that you are good cooks in spite of your nefarious bent for music and literature. I consider the illness of Miranda Mary's mother a Providential interposition—that is, if she isn't too sick."

"It's all very well for you to be pleased, Lolla," I said dolefully. "But I don't feel jubilant over the prospect at all. Something will probably go wrong. And then there's our own nice little Thanksgiving celebration we've planned, and pinched and economized for weeks to provide. That is half spoiled now."

"Oh, what is that compared to Margaret's chance of going to college?" exclaimed Kate. "Cheer up, Aggie. You know we can cook. I feel that it is now or never with Aunt Susanna."

I cheered up accordingly. We are not given to pessimism which is fortunate. Ever since father died four years ago we have struggled on here, content to give up a good deal just to keep our home and be together. This little gray house—oh, how we do love it and its apple trees—is ours and we have, as aforesaid, a tiny income and our ambitions; not very big ambitions but big enough to give zest to our lives and hope to the future. We've been very happy as a rule. Aunt Susanna has a big house and lots of money but she isn't as happy as we are. She nags us a good deal—just as she used to nag father—but we don't mind it very much after all. Indeed, I sometimes suspect that we really like Aunt Susanna tremendously if she'd only leave us alone long enough to find it out.

Thursday morning was an ideal Thanksgiving morning—bright, crisp and sparkling. There had been a white frost in the night, and the orchard and the white birch wood behind it looked like fairyland. We were all up early. None of us had slept well, and both Kate and I had had the most fearful dreams of spoiling Aunt Susanna's Thanksgiving dinner.

"Never mind, dreams always go by contraries, you know," said Laura cheerfully. "You'd better go up to the Pinery early and get the fires on, for the house will be cold. Remember the McGinnises and the dog. Weigh the turkey so that you'll know exactly how long to cook it. Put the pies in the oven in time to get piping hot—lukewarm mince pies are an abomination. Be sure—"

"Laura, don't confuse us with any more cautions," I groaned, "or we shall get hopelessly fuddled. Come on, Kate, before she has time to."

It wasn't very far up to the Pinery—just ten minutes' walk, and such a delightful walk on that delightful morning. We went through the orchard and then through the white birch wood where the loveliness of the frosted boughs awed us. Beyond that there was a lane between ranks of young, balsamy, white-misted firs and then an open pasture field, sere and crispy. Just across it was the Pinery, a lovely old house with dormer windows in the roof, surrounded by pines that were dark and glorious against the silvery morning sky.

The McGinnis dog was sitting on the back-door steps when we arrived. He wagged his tail ingratiatingly, but we ruthlessly pushed him off, went in and shut the door in his face. All the little McGinnises were sitting in a row on their fence, and they whooped derisively. The McGinnis manners are not those which appertain to the caste of Vere de Vere; but we rather like the urchins—there are eight of them—and we would probably have gone over to talk to them if we had not had the fear of Aunt Susanna before our eyes.

We kindled the fires, weighed the turkey, put it in the oven and prepared the vegetables. Then we set the dining-room table and decorated it with Aunt Susanna's potted ferns and dishes of lovely red apples. Everything went so smoothly that we soon forgot to be nervous. When the turkey was done, we took it out, set it on the back of the range to keep warm and put the mince pies in. The potatoes, cabbage and turnips were bubbling away cheerfully, and everything was going as merrily as a marriage bell. Then, all at once, things happened.

In an evil hour we went to the yard window and looked out. We saw a quiet scene. The McGinnis dog was still sitting on his haunches by the steps, just as he had been sitting all the morning. Down in the McGinnis yard everything wore an unusually peaceful aspect. Only one McGinnis was in sight—Tony, aged eight, who was perched up on the edge of the well box, swinging his legs and singing at the top of his melodious Irish voice. All at once, just as we were looking at him, Tony went over backward and apparently tumbled head foremost down his father's well.

Kate and I screamed simultaneously. We tore across the kitchen, flung open the door, plunged down over Aunt Susanna's yard, scrambled over the fence and flew to the well. Just as we reached it, Tony's red head appeared as he climbed serenely out over the box. I don't know whether I felt more relieved or furious. He had merely fallen on the blank guard inside the box: and there are times when I am tempted to think he fell on purpose because he saw Kate and me looking out at the window. At least he didn't seem at all frightened, and grinned most impishly at us.

Kate and I turned on our heels and marched back in as dignified a manner as was possible under the circumstances. Half way up Aunt Susanna's yard we forgot dignity and broke into a run. We had left the door open and the McGinnis dog had disappeared.

Never shall I forget the sight we saw or the smell we smelled when we burst into that kitchen. There on the floor was the McGinnis dog and what was left of Aunt Susanna's Thanksgiving turkey. As for the smell, imagine a commingled odor of scorching turnips and burning mince pies, and you have it.

The dog fled out with a guilty yelp. I groaned and snatched the turnips off. Kate threw open the oven door and dragged out the pies. Pies and turnips were ruined as irretrievably as the turkey.

"Oh, what shall we do?" I cried miserably. I knew Margaret's chance of college was gone forever.

"Do!" Kate was superb. She didn't lose her wits for a second. "We'll go home and borrow the girls' dinner. Quick—there's just ten minutes before train time. Throw those pies and turnips into this basket—the turkey too— we'll carry them with us to hide them."

I might not be able to evolve an idea like that on the spur of the moment, but I can at least act up to it when it is presented. Without a moment's delay we shut the door and ran. As we went I saw the McGinnis dog licking his chops over in their yard. I have been ashamed ever since of my feelings toward that dog. They were murderous. Fortunately I had no time to indulge them.

It is ten minutes walk from the Pinery to our house, but you can run it in five. Kate and I burst into the kitchen just as Laura and Margaret were sitting down to dinner. We had neither time nor breath for explanations. Without a word I grasped the turkey platter and the turnip tureen. Kate caught one hot mince pie from the oven and whisked a cold one out of the pantry.

"We've—got—to have—them," was all she said.

I've always said that Laura and Magsie would rise to any occasion. They saw us carry their Thanksgiving dinner off under their very eyes and they never interfered by word or motion. They didn't even worry us with questions. They realized that something desperate had happened and that the emergency called for deed not words.

"Aggie," gasped Kate behind me as we tore through the birch wood, "the border—of these pies—is crimped—differently—from Aunt Susanna's."

"She—won't know—the difference," I panted. "Miranda—Mary— crimps them."

We got back to the Pinery just as the train whistle blew. We had ten minutes to transfer turkey and turnips to Aunt Susanna's dishes, hide our own, air the kitchen, and get back our breath. We accomplished it. When Aunt Susanna and her guests came we were prepared for them: we were calm—outwardly—and the second mince pie was getting hot in the oven. It was ready by the time it was needed. Fortunately our turkey was the same size as Aunt Susanna's, and Laura had cooked a double supply of turnips, intending to warm them up the next day. Still, all things considered, Kate and I didn't enjoy that dinner much. We kept thinking of poor Laura and Magsie at home, dining off potatoes on Thanksgiving!

But at least Aunt Susanna was satisfied. When Kate and I were washing the dishes she came out quite beamingly.

"Well, my dears, I must admit that you made a very good job of the dinner, indeed. The turkey was done to perfection. As for the mince pies— well, of course Miranda Mary made them, but she must have had extra good luck with them, for they were excellent and heated to just the right degree. You didn't give anything to the McGinnis dog, I hope?"

"No, we didn't give him anything," said Kate.

Aunt Susanna did not notice the emphasis.

When we had finished the dishes we smuggled our platter and tureen out of the house and went home. Laura and Margaret were busy painting and studying and were just as sweet-tempered as if we hadn't robbed them of their dinner. But we had to tell them the whole story before we even took off our hats.

"There is a special Providence for children and idiots," said Laura gently. We didn't ask her whether she meant us or Tony McGinnis or both. There are some things better left in obscurity. I'd have probably said something much sharper than that if anybody had made off with my Thanksgiving turkey so unceremoniously.

Aunt Susanna came down the next day and told Margaret that she would send her to college. Also she commissioned Laura to paint her a water-color for her dining-room and said she'd pay her five dollars for it.

Kate and I were rather left out in the cold in this distribution of favors, but when you come to reflect that Laura and Magsie had really cooked that dinner, it was only just.

Anyway, Aunt Susanna has never since insinuated that we can't cook, and that is as much as we deserve.

The End.

SILENT FILM ACTRESS RUTH HELMS

Southwest Scenarios

COMMENTARIES FROM RURAL ARIZONA
BY DARRYLE PURCELL

Fad of the past could be a holiday blessing

From Nov. 7, 1997

FADS ARE FLEETING, AND IT SEEMS THE ONCE TRENDY VIETNAMESE POTBELLIED pigs have gone the way of the pet rock and Nehru jacket.

A few years ago, these immigrant porkers were touted as more intelligent and cleaner than dogs, and destined to remain small, cute house pets. According to a Scripps Howard news story, house-pig buyers were told the little beasts wouldn't grow to be over 50 pounds. After a couple of years, those people, some of whom paid more than $1,500 per pig, are waking up to 250-pound wallowers in their homes.

And, according to Patty Williams, bureau manager of the local animal shelter, people are losing their once welcome house pets at an alarming rate. Last week the shelter picked up five conveniently lost potbellied pigs.

Only 60 percent of animal shelters will even take in the pigs, according to the Scripps Howard story. The shelters are designed for dogs and cats, not livestock. What's a humane society to do?

Well, folks, the holidays are coming. And the Salvation Army and community service clubs will be doing their best to feed the homeless and less fortunate during those special days.

It seems to me that a lot of poor folks would be pleased to have "the other white meat" for Thanksgiving and Christmas. I'll just bet the shelter would be happy to donate these creatures, which have overgrown their welcome, to any service club willing to "prepare" them for holiday services.

Think how happy this will make our hungry transients this holiday season, as well as how thankful it will make many turkeys.

Southwest Scenarios

The commentaries here and in future issues were originally published by *The Mohave Valley Daily News between 1993 & 2013*--and in many ways they apply to today.
We are grateful to republish these commentaries written by Darryle Purcell in full and unedited. His own brand of humor and style can deliver insight, provoke thought, and even boil blood.

MARCUS AURELIUS ANTONINUS

Rendering based on the Foulis translation of 1742
by George W. Chrystal

BOOK I

1. I learned from my grandfather, Verus, to use good manners, and to put restraint on anger.

2. In the famous memory of my father I had a pattern of modesty and manliness.

3. Of my mother I learned to be pious and generous; to keep myself not only from evil deeds, but even from evil thoughts; and to live with a simplicity which is far from customary among the rich.

4. I owe it to my great-grandfather that I did not attend public lectures and discussions, but had good and able teachers at home; and I owe him also the knowledge that for things of this nature a man should count no expense too great.

5. My tutor taught me not to favour either green or blue at the chariot races, nor, in the contests of gladiators, to be a supporter either of light or heavy armed. He taught me also to endure labour; not to need many things; to serve myself without troubling others; not to intermeddle in the affairs of others, and not easily to listen to slanders against them.

6. Of Diognetus I had the lesson not to busy myself about vain things; not to credit the great professions of such as pretend to work wonders, or of sorcerers about their charms, and their expelling of Demons and the like; not to keep quails (for fighting or divination), nor to run after such things; to suffer freedom of speech in others, and to apply myself heartily to philosophy. Him also I must thank for my hearing first Bacchius, then Tandasis and Marcianus; that I wrote dialogues in my youth, and took a liking to the philosopher's pallet and skins, and to the other things which, by the Grecian discipline, belong to that profession.

7. To Rusticus I owe my first apprehensions that my nature needed reform and cure; and that I did not fall into the ambition of the common Sophists, either by composing speculative writings or by declaiming harangues of exhortation in public; further, that I never strove to be admired by ostentation of great patience in an ascetic life, or by display of activity and application; that I gave over the study of rhetoric, poetry, and the graces of language; and that I did not pace my house in my senatorial robes, or practise any similar affectation. I observed also the simplicity of style in his letters, particularly in that which he wrote to my mother from Sinuessa. I learned from him to be easily appeased, and to be readily reconciled with those who had displeased me or given cause of offence, so soon as they inclined to make their peace; to read with care; not to rest satisfied with a slight and superficial knowledge; nor quickly to assent to great talkers. I have him to thank that I met with the discourses of Epictetus, which he furnished me from his own library.

8. From Apollonius I learned true liberty, and tenacity of purpose; to regard nothing else, even in the smallest degree, but reason always; and always to remain unaltered in the agonies of pain, in the losses of children, or in long diseases. He afforded me a living example of how the same man can, upon occasion, be most yielding and most inflexible. He was patient in exposition; and, as might well be seen, esteemed his fine skill and ability in teaching others the principles of philosophy as the least of his endowments. It was from him that I learned how to receive from friends what are thought favours without seeming humbled by the giver or insensible to the gift.

9. Sextus was my pattern of a benign temper, and his family the model of a household governed by true paternal affection, and a steadfast purpose of living according to nature. Here I could learn to be grave without affectation, to observe sagaciously the several dispositions and inclinations of my friends, to tolerate the ignorant and those who follow current opinions without examination. His conversation showed how a man may accommodate himself to all men and to all companies; for though companionship with him was sweeter and more pleasing than any sort of flattery, yet he was at the same time highly respected and reverenced. No man was ever more happy than he in comprehending, finding out, and arranging in exact order the great maxims necessary for the conduct of life. His example taught me to suppress even the least appearance of anger or any other passion; but still, with all this perfect tranquillity, to possess the tenderest and most affectionate heart; to be apt to approve others yet without noise; to have much learning and little ostentation.

10. I learned from Alexander the Grammarian to avoid censuring others, to refrain from flouting them for a barbarism, solecism, or any false pronunciation. Rather was I dexterously to pronounce the words rightly in my answer, confining approval or objection to the matter itself, and avoiding discussion of the expression, or to use some other form of courteous suggestion.

11. Fronto made me sensible how much of envy, deceit and hypocrisy surrounds princes; and that generally those whom we account nobly born have somehow less natural affection.

12. I learned from Alexander the Platonist not often nor without great necessity to say, or write to any man in a letter, that I am not at leisure; nor thus, under pretext of urgent affairs, to make a practice of excusing myself from the duties which, according to our various ties, we owe to those with whom we live.

13. Of Catulus I learned not to condemn any friend's expostulation even though it were unjust, but to try to recall him to his former disposition; to stint no praise in speaking of my masters, as is recounted of Domitius and Athenodorus; and to love my children with true affection.

14. Of Severus, my brother, I learned to love my kinsmen, to love truth, to love justice. Through him I came to know Thrasea, Helvidius, Cato, Dion, and Brutus. He gave me my first conception of a Commonwealth founded upon equitable laws and administered with equality of right; and of a Monarchy whose chief concern is the freedom of its subjects. Of him I learned likewise a constant and harmonious devotion to Philosophy; to be ready to do good, to be generous with all my heart. He taught me to be of good hope and trustful of the affection of my friends. I observed in him candour in declaring what he condemned in the conduct of others; and so frank and open was his behaviour, that his friends might easily see without the trouble of conjecture what he liked or disliked.

15. The counsels of Maximus taught me to command myself, to judge clearly, to be of good courage in sickness and other misfortunes, to be moderate, gentle, yet serious in disposition, and to accomplish my appointed task without repining. All men believed that he spoke as he thought; and whatever he did, they knew it was done with good intent. I never found him surprised or astonished at anything. He was never in a hurry, never shrank from his purpose, was never at a loss or dejected. He was no facile smiler, but neither was he passionate or suspicious. He was ready to do good, to forgive, and to speak the truth, and gave the impression of unperverted rectitude rather than of a reformed character. No man could ever think himself despised by Maximus, and no one ever ventured to think himself his superior. He had also a good gift of humour.

16. I learned from my father gentleness and undeviating constancy in judgments formed after due reflection; not to be puffed up with glory as men understand it; to be laborious and assiduous. He taught me to give ready hearing to any man who offered anything tending to the common good; to mete out impartial justice to every one; to apprehend rightly when severity and when clemency should be used; to abstain from all impure lusts; and to use humanity towards all men. Thus he left his friends at liberty to sup with him or not, to go abroad with him or not, exactly as they inclined; and they found him still the same if some urgent business had prevented them from obeying his commands. I learned of him accuracy and patience in council, for he never quitted an enquiry satisfied with first impressions. I observed his zeal to retain his friends without being fickle or over fond; his contentment in every condition; his cheerfulness; his forethought about very distant events; his unostentatious attention to the smallest details; his restraint of all popular applause and flattery. Ever watchful of the needs of the Empire, a careful steward of the public revenue, he was tolerant of the censure of others in affairs of that kind. He was neither a superstitious worshipper of the Gods, nor an ambitious pleaser of men, nor studious of popularity, but in all things sober and steadfast, well skilled in what was honourable, never affecting novelties. As to the things which make the ease of life, and which fortune can supply in such abundance, he used them without pride, and yet with all freedom: enjoyed them without affectation when they were present, and when absent he found no want of them. No man could call him sophist, buffoon, or pedant. He was a man of ripe experience, a full man, one who could not be flattered, and who could govern himself as well as others. I further observed that he honoured all who were true philosophers, without upbraiding the rest, and without being led astray by any. His manners were easy, his conversation delightful, but not cloying. He took regular but moderate care of his body, neither as one over fond of life or of the adornment of his person, nor as one who despised these things. Thus, through his own care, he seldom needed any medicines, whether salves or potions. It was his special merit to yield without envy to any who had acquired any special faculty, as either eloquence, or learning in the Law, in ancient customs, or the like; and he aided such men strenuously, so that every one of them might be regarded and esteemed for his special excellence. He observed carefully the ancient customs of his forefathers, and preserved, without appearance of affectation, the ways of his native land. He was not fickle and capricious, and loved not change of place or employment. After his violent fits of headache he would return fresh and vigorous to his wonted affairs. Of secrets he had few, and these seldom, and such only as concerned public matters. He displayed discretion and moderation in exhibiting shows for the entertainment of the people, in his public works, in largesses and the like; and in all those things he acted like one who regarded only what was right and becoming in the things themselves, and not the reputation that might follow after. He never bathed at unseasonable hours, had no vanity in building, was never solicitous either about his food or about the make or colour of his clothes, or about the beauty of his servants. His dress came from Lorium—his villa on the coast—and was of Lanuvian wool for the most part. It is remembered how he used the tax-collector at Tusculum who asked his pardon, and all his behaviour was of a piece with that. He was far from being inhuman, or implacable, or violent; never doing anything with such keenness that one could say he was sweating about it, in all things he reasoned distinctly, as one at leisure, calmly, regularly, resolutely, and consistently. A man might fairly apply that to him which is recorded of

Socrates: that he could both abstain from and enjoy these things, in want whereof many show themselves weak, and, in the possession, intemperate. To be strong in abstinence and temperate in enjoyment, to be sober in both—these are qualities of a man of perfect and invincible soul, as was shown in the sickness of Maximus.

17. To the Gods I owe it that I had good grandfathers and parents, a good sister, good teachers, good servants, good kinsmen, and friends, good almost all of them. I have to thank them that I never through haste and rashness offended any of them; though my temper was such as might have led me to it had occasion offered. But by their goodness no such concurrence of circumstances happened as could discover my weakness. I am further thankful that I was not longer brought up with my grandfather's concubine, that I retained my modesty, and refrained even longer than need have been from the pleasures of love. To the Gods it is due that I lived under the government of such a prince and father as could take from me all vain glory, and convince me that it was not impossible for a prince to live in a court without guards, gorgeous robes, torches, statues, or such pieces of state and magnificence; but that he may reduce himself almost to the state of a private man, and yet not become more mean or remiss in those public affairs wherein power and authority are requisite. I thank the Gods that I have had such a brother as by his disposition might stir me to take care of myself, while at the same time he delighted me by his respect and love. I thank them that my children neither wanted good natural dispositions nor were deformed in body. I owe it to their good guidance that I made no greater progress in rhetoric and poetry, and in other studies which might have engrossed my mind had I found myself successful in them. By the Gods' grace I forestalled the wishes of those by whom I was brought up, in promoting them to the dignities they seemed most to desire; and I did not put them off with the hope that, since they were but young, I would do it hereafter. I owe to the Gods that I ever knew Apollonius, Rusticus and Maximus; that I have had occasion often and effectually to meditate with myself and enquire what is truly the life according to Nature. And, as far as lies within the dispensation of the Gods to give suggestion, help, or inspiration, there is nothing to prevent my having already realized that life. I have fallen short of it by my own fault, and because I gave no heed to the inward monitions and almost direct instructions of the Gods, to whom be thanks that my body hath so long endured the stress of such a life as I have led. By their goodness I never had to do with either Benedicta or Theodotus; and afterwards, when I fell into some foolish passions, I was soon cured. I give thanks that, having often been displeased with Rusticus, I never did anything to him which afterwards I might have had occasion to repent; that, though my mother was destined to die young, she lived with me all her latter years; that, as often as I inclined to succour any who were either poor or had fallen into some distress, I was never answered that there was not ready money enough to do it, and that I myself never had need of the like succour from another. I must be grateful, too, that I have such a wife, so obedient, so loving, so ingenuous; that I had choice of fit and able men to whom I might commit the education of my children. I have received divine aids in dreams; as in particular, how I might stay my spitting of blood and cure my vertigo; which good fortune happily fell to me at Caieta. The Gods watched over me also when I first applied myself to philosophy. For I fell not into the hands of any Sophist, nor sat poring over many volumes, nor devoted myself to solving syllogisms, or star-gazing. That all these things should so happily fall out there was great need both for the help of fortune and for the aid of the Gods.

in the country of the quadi, by the granua.

END OF THE FIRST BOOK.

BOOK II

1. Say this to yourself in the morning: Today I shall have to do with meddlers, with the ungrateful, with the insolent, with the crafty, with the envious and the selfish. All these vices have beset them, because they know not what is good and what is evil. But I have considered the nature of the good, and found it beautiful: I have beheld the nature of the bad, and found it ugly. I also understand the nature of the evil-doer, and know that he is my brother, not because he shares with me the same blood or the same seed, but because he is a partaker of the same mind and of the same portion of immortality. I therefore cannot be hurt by any of these, since none of them can involve me in any baseness. I cannot be angry with my brother, or sever myself from him, for we are made by nature for mutual assistance, like the feet, the hands, the eyelids, the upper and lower rows of teeth. It is against nature for men to oppose each other; and what else is anger and aversion?

2. All that I am is either flesh, breath, or the ruling part. Cast your books from you; distract yourself no more; for you have not the right to do so. Like one at the point of death despise this flesh, this corruptible bone and blood, this network texture of nerves, veins, and arteries. Consider, too, what breath is—mere air, and that always changing, expelled and inhaled again every moment. The third is the ruling part. As to this, take heed, now that you are old, that it remain no longer in servitude; that it be no more dragged hither and thither like a puppet by every selfish impulse. Repine no more at what fate now sends, nor dread what may befall you hereafter.

3. Whatever the Gods ordain is full of wise forethought. The workings of chance are not apart from nature, and not without connexion and intertexture with the designs of Providence. Providence is the source of all things; and, besides, there is necessity, and the utility of the Universe, of which you are a part. For, to every part of a being, that is good which springs from the nature of the whole and tends to its preservation. Now, the order of Nature is preserved in the changes of elements, just as it is in the changes of things that are compound. Let this suffice you, and be your creed unchangeable. Put from you the thirst of books, that you may not die murmuring, but meekly, and with true and heartfelt gratitude to the Gods.

4. Think of your long procrastination, and of the many opportunities given you by the Gods, but left unused. Surely it is high time to understand the Universe of which you are a part, and the Ruler of that Universe, of whom you are an emanation; that a limit is set to your days, which, if you use them not for your enlightenment, will depart, as you yourself will, and return no more.

5. Hourly and earnestly strive, as a Roman and a man, to do what falls to your hand with perfect unaffected dignity, with kindliness, freedom and justice, and free your soul from every other imagination. This you will accomplish if you perform each action as if it were your last, without wilfulness, or any passionate aversion to what reason approves; without hypocrisy or selfishness, or discontent with the decrees of Providence. You see how few things it is necessary to master in order that a man may live a smooth-flowing, God-fearing life. For of him that holds to these principles the Gods require no more.

6. Go on, go on, O my soul, to affront and dishonour thyself! The time that remains to honour thyself will not be long. Short is the life of every man; and thine is almost spent; spent, not honouring thyself, but seeking thy happiness in the souls of other men.

7. Cares from without distract you: take leisure, then, to add some good thing to your knowledge; have done with vacillation, and avoid the other error. For triflers, too, are they who, by their activities, weary themselves in life, and have no settled aim to which they may direct, once and for all, their every desire and project.

8. Seldom are any found unhappy from not observing what is in the minds of others. But such as observe not well the stirrings of their own souls must of necessity be unhappy.

9. Remember always what the nature of the Universe is, what your own nature is, and how these are related—the one to the other. Remember what part your qualities are of the qualities of the whole, and that no man can prevent you from speaking and acting always in accordance with that nature of which you are a part.

10. In comparing crimes together, as, according to the common idea, they may be compared, Theophrastus makes the true philosophical distinction, that those committed from motives of pleasure are more heinous than those which are due to passion. For he who is a prey to passion is clearly turned away from reason by some spasm and convulsion that takes him unawares. But he who sins from desire is conquered by pleasure, and so seems more incontinent and more effeminate in his vice. Justly then, and in a truly philosophical spirit, he says that sin, for pleasure's sake, is more wicked than sin which is due to pain. For the latter sinner was sinned against, and so driven to passion by his wrongs, while the former set out to sin of his own motion, and was led into ill-doing by his own lust.

11. Do every deed, speak every word, think every thought in the knowledge that you may end your days any moment. To depart from men, if there be really Gods, is nothing terrible. The Gods could bring no evil thing upon you. And if there be no Gods, or if they have no regard to human affairs, why should I desire to live in a world void of Gods and without Providence? But Gods there are, and assuredly they regard human affairs; and they have put it wholly in man's power that he should not fall into what is truly evil. And of other things, had any been bad, they would have made provision also that man should have the power to avoid them altogether. For how can that make a man's life worse which does not corrupt the man himself? Presiding Nature could not in ignorance, or in knowledge impotent, have omitted to prevent or rectify these things. She could not fail us so completely that, either from want of power or want of skill, good and evil should happen promiscuously to good men and to bad alike. Now death and life, glory and reproach, pain and pleasure, riches and poverty— all these happen equally to the good and to the bad. But, as they are neither honourable nor shameful, they are therefore neither good nor evil.

12. It is the office of our rational power to apprehend how swiftly all things vanish; how the corporeal forms are swallowed up in the material world, and the memory of them in the tide of ages. Such are all the things of sense, especially those which ensnare us with pleasure or terrify us with pain, or those things which vanity trumpets in our ears. How mean, how despicable, how sordid, how perishable, how dead are they! What are they whose opinions and whose voices bestow renown? What is it to die? Your mind can tell you that, did a man think of it alone, and, by close consideration, strip it of its ghastly trappings, he would no longer deem it anything but a work of Nature. To dread a work of Nature is a childish thing, and this is, indeed, not only Nature's work, but beneficial to her. Your reason tells you how man reaches God, and through what part, and what is the state of that part, when he has attained unto him.

13. Nothing, says the poet, is more miserable than to range over all things, to spy into the depths of the earth, and search, by conjecture, into the souls of those around us, yet not to perceive that it is enough for a man to devote himself to that divinity which is within him, and to pay it genuine worship. And this worship consists in keeping it pure from every passion and folly, and from repining at anything done by Gods or men. The work of the Gods is to be reverenced for its excellence. The works of men should be dear for the sake of the bond of kinship, or pitied, as we must pity them sometimes, for their lack of the knowledge of good and evil. And men are not less maimed by this defect than by their want of power to know white from black.

14. Though you should live three thousand ears or as many myriads, yet remember that no man loses any other life than that which now lives, nor lives any other than that which he is now losing. The longest and the shortest lives come to one effect. The present moment is the same for all men, and their loss, therefore, is equal, for it is clear that what they lose in death is but a fleeting instant of time. No man can lose either the past or the future, for how can a man be deprived of what he has not? These two things then are to be remembered: First, that all things recur in cycles, and are the same from everlasting, and that, therefore, it matters nothing whether a man shall contemplate these same things for one hundred years, or for two hundred, or for an infinite stretch of time: and, secondly, that he who lives longest and he who dies soonest have an equal loss in death. The present moment is all of which either is deprived, since that is all he has. No man can be robbed of that which he has not.

15. Beyond opinion there is nothing. The objections to this saying of Monimus the Cynic are obvious. But obvious also is the utility of what he said, if one accept his pleasantry as far as truth will warrant it.

16. Man's soul dishonours itself, firstly and chiefly when it does all it can to become an excrescence, and as it were an abscess on the Universe. To fret against any particular event is to revolt against the general law of Nature, which comprehends the order of all events whatsoever. Again it is dishonour for the soul when it has aversion to any man, and opposes him with intention to hurt him, as wrathful men do. Thirdly, it affronts itself when conquered by pleasure or pain; fourthly, when it does or says anything hypocritically, feignedly or falsely; fifthly, when it does not direct to some proper end all its desires and actions, but exerts them inconsiderately and without understanding. For, even the smallest things should be referred to the end, and the end of rational beings is to follow the order and law of the venerable state and polity which comprehends them all.

17. The duration of man's life is but an instant; his substance is fleeting, his senses dull; the structure of his body corruptible; the soul but a vortex. We cannot reckon with fortune, or lay our account with fame. In fine, the life of the body is but a river, and the life of the soul a misty dream. Existence is a warfare, and a journey in a strange land; and the end of fame is to be forgotten. What then avails to guide us? One thing, and one alone—Philosophy. And this consists in keeping the divinity within inviolate and intact; victorious over pain and pleasure; free from temerity, free from falsehood, free from hypocrisy; independent of what others do or fail to do; submissive to hap and lot, which come from the same source as we; and, above all, with equanimity awaiting death, as nothing else than a resolution of the elements of which every being compounded. And, if in their successive interchanges no harm befall the elements, why should one suspect any in the change and dissolution of the whole? It is natural, and nothing natural can be evil.

at carnuntum.

END OF THE SECOND BOOK.

BOOK III

1. Man must consider, not only that each day part of his life is spent, and that less and less remains to him, but also that, even if he live longer, it is very uncertain whether his intelligence will suffice as heretofore for the understanding of his affairs, and for grasping that knowledge which aims at comprehending things human and divine. When dotage begins, breath, nourishment, fancy, impulse, and so forth will not fail him. But self-command, accurate appreciation of duty, power to scrutinize what strikes his senses, or even to decide whether he should take his departure, all powers, indeed, which demand a well-trained understanding, must be extinguished in him. Let him be up and doing then, not only because death comes nearer every day, but because understanding and intelligence often leave us before we die.

2. Observe what grace and charm appear even in the accidents that accompany Nature's work. Thus some parts of a loaf crack and burst in the baking; and this cracking, though in a manner contrary to the design of the baker, looks well and invites the appetite. Figs, too, gape when at their ripest, and in ripe olives the very approach to rotting adds a special beauty to the fruit. The droop of ears of corn, the bent brows of the lion, the foam at a boar's mouth, and many other things, are far from comely in themselves, yet, since they accompany the works of Nature, they make part of her adornment, and rejoice the beholder. Thus, if a man be sensitive to such things, and have a more than common penetration into the constitution of the whole, scarce anything connected with Nature will fail to give him pleasure, as he comes to understand it. Such a man will contemplate in the real world the fierce jaws of wild beasts with no less delight than when sculptors or painters set forth for him their presentments. With like pleasure will his chaste eyes behold the maturity and grace of old age in man or woman, and the inviting charms of youth. Many such things will strike him, things not credible to the many, but which come to him alone who is truly familiar with the works of Nature and near to her own heart.

3. Hippocrates, who had healed many diseases, himself fell sick, and died. The Chaldeans foretold the fatal hours of multitudes, and afterwards fate carried themselves away. Alexander, Pompey, and Gaius Caesar, who so often razed whole cities, and cut off in battle so many myriads of horse and foot, at last departed from this life themselves. Heraclitus, after his many speculations on the conflagration of the world, died, swollen with water and plastered with cow-dung. Vermin destroyed Democritus; Socrates was killed by vermin of another sort. What of all this? You have gone aboard, made your voyage, come to harbour. Disembark: if into another life, there will God be also; if into nothingness, at least you will have done with bearing pain and pleasure, and with your slavery to this vessel so much meaner than its slave. For the soul is intelligence and deity, the body dust and corruption.

4. Waste not what remains of life in consideration about others, when it makes not for the common good. Be sure you are neglecting other work if you busy yourself with what such a one is doing and why, with what he is saying, thinking, or scheming. All such things do but divert you from the steadfast guardianship of your own soul. It behoves you, then, in every train of thought to shun all that is aimless or useless, and, above all, everything officious or malignant. Accustom yourself so, and only so, to think, that, if any one were suddenly to ask you, "Of what are you thinking-now?" you could answer frankly and at once, "Of so and so." Then it will plainly appear that you are all simplicity and kindliness, as befits a social being who takes little thought for enjoyment or any phantom pleasure; who spurns contentiousness, envy, or suspicion; or any passion the harbouring of which one would blush to own. For such a man, who has finally determined to be henceforth among the best, is, as it were, a priest and minister of the Gods, using the spirit within him, which preserves a man unspotted from pleasure, unwounded by any pain, inaccessible to all insult, innocent of all evil; a champion in the noblest of all contests—the contest for victory over every passion. He is penetrated with justice; he welcomes with all his heart whatever befalls, or is appointed by Providence. He troubles not often, or ever without pressing public need, to consider what another may say, or do, or design. Solely intent upon his own conduct, ever mindful of his own concurrent part in the destiny of the Universe, he orders his conduct well, persuaded that his part is good. For the lot appointed to every man is part of the law of all things as well as a law for him. He forgets not that all rational beings are akin, and that the love of all mankind is part of the nature of man; also that we must not think as all men think, but only as those who live a life accordant with nature. As for those who live otherwise, he remembers always how they act at home and abroad, by night and by day, and how and with whom they are found in company. And so he cannot esteem the praise of such, for they enjoy not their own approbation.

5. In action be neither grudging, nor selfish, nor ill-advised, nor constrained. Let not your thought be adorned with overmuch nicety. Be not a babbler or a busybody. Let the God within direct you as a manly being, as an elder, a statesman, a Roman, and a ruler, standing prepared like one who awaits the recall from life, in marching order; requiring neither an oath nor the testimony of any man. And withal, be cheerful, and independent of the assistance and the peace that comes from others; for, it is a man's duty to stand upright, self-supporting, not supported.

6. If in the life of man you find anything better than justice, truth, sobriety, manliness; and, in sum, anything better than the satisfaction of your soul with itself in that wherein it is given to you to follow right reason; and with fate in that which is determined beyond your control; if, I say, you find aught better than this, then turn thereto with all your heart, and enjoy it as the best that is to be found. But if nothing seems to you better than the divinity seated within you, which has conquered all your impulses, which sifts all your thoughts, which, as Socrates said, has detached itself from the promptings of sense, and devoted itself to God and to the love of mankind; if you find every other thing small and worthless compared with this, see that you give place to no other which might turn, divert, or distract you from holding in highest esteem the good which is especially and properly your own. For it is not permitted to us to substitute for that which is good in reason or in fact anything not agreeable thereto, such as the praise of the many, power, riches, or the pursuit of pleasure. All these things may seem admissible for a moment; but presently they get the upper hand, and lead us astray. But do you, I say, frankly and freely choose the best, and keep to it. The best is what is for your advantage. If now you choose what is for your spiritual advantage, hold it fast; if what is for your bodily advantage, admit that it is so chosen, and keep your choice with all modesty. Only see that you make a sure discrimination.

7. Never esteem aught of advantage which will oblige you to break your faith, or to desert your honour; to hate, to suspect, or to execrate any man; to play a part; or to set your mind on anything that needs to be hidden by wall or curtain. He who to all things prefers the soul, the divinity within him, and the sacred cult of its virtues, makes no tragic groan or gesture. He needs neither solitude nor a crowd of spectators; and, best of all, he will live neither seeking nor shunning death. Whether the soul shall use its surrounding body for a longer or shorter space is to him indifferent. Were he to depart this moment he would go as readily as he would do any other seemly and proper action, holding one thing only in life-long avoidance— to find his soul in any case unbefitting an intelligent social being.

8. In the soul of the chastened and purified man you would find nothing putrid, foul, or festering. Fate does not cut off his life before its proper end; as one would say of an actor who left the stage before his part was ended, or he had reached his appointed exit. There remains nothing servile or affected, nothing too conventional or too seclusive, nothing that fears censure or courts concealment.

9. Hold in honour the faculty which forms opinions. It depends on this faculty alone that no opinion your soul entertains be inconsistent with the nature and constitution of the rational being. It ensures that we form no rash judgments, that we are kindly to men, and obedient to the Gods.

10. Cast from you then all other things, retaining these few. Remember also that every man lives only this present moment, which is a fleeting instant: the rest of time is either spent or quite unknown. Short is the time which each of us has to live, and small the corner of the earth he has to live in. Short is the longest posthumous fame, and this preserved through a succession of poor mortals, soon themselves to die; men who knew not themselves, far less those who died long ago.

11. To these maxims add this other. Accurately define or describe every thing that strikes your imagination, so that you may see and distinguish what it is in naked essence, and what it is in its entirety; that you may tell yourself the proper name of the thing itself, and the names of the parts of which it is compounded, and into which it will be resolved. Nothing makes mind greater than the power to enquire into all things that present themselves in life; and, while you examine them, to consider at the same time of what fashion is the Universe, and what is the function in it of these things, of what importance they are to the whole, of what to man who is a citizen of that highest city of which all other cities are but households. Consider what is this thing that now makes an impression on you, of what it is composed, and how long it is destined to endure. Consider also for what virtue it calls; whether it be gentleness, courage, truthfulness, fidelity, simplicity, independence, or any other. Say, therefore, of each event: "This comes from God:" or "This comes from the conjunction and intertexture of the strands of fate, or from some chance or hazard of that kind:" or "This comes from one of my own tribe, from my kinsman, from my friend. He is, indeed, ignorant of what accords with nature; but I am not, and will therefore use him kindly and justly, according to the natural and social law. As to things indifferent, I strive to appraise them at their proper value."

12. If you discharge your present duty with firm and zealous, yet kindly, observance of the laws of reason; if you regard no by-gains, but keep pure within you your immortal part, as if obliged to restore it at once to him who gave it; if you hold to this with no further desires or aversions, and be content with the natural discharge of your present task, and with the heroic sincerity of all you say or utter, you will live well. And herein no man can hinder you.

13. As surgeons have ever their knives and instruments at hand for the sudden emergencies of their art, so do you keep ready the principles requisite for understanding things divine and human, and for doing all things, even the least important, in the remembrance of the bond between the two. For in neglecting this, you will scant your duty both to Gods and men.

14. Cease your wandering, for you are not like to read again your own memoirs, or the deeds of the ancient Greeks and Romans, or those collections from the writings of others that you laid up for your old age. Hasten then to your proper end. Fling away vain hopes, and, if you have any care for yourself, fly to your own succour while yet you may.

15. Men understand not all that is signified by the words—to steal, to sow, to buy, to rest, to see what is to be done. For it is not the bodily eye but another sort of sight that must discern these things.

16. We have body, soul, and intelligence. To the body belong the senses, to the soul the passions, to the intelligence principles. To be affected by the imagery of sense belongs to the beasts of the field no less than to us. To be swayed by gusts of passion is common to us with the wild beasts, with the most effeminate wretches, with Nero and with Phalaris. Moreover, the possession of a mind to guide us to what seems fitting is shared by us, with atheists, with traitors to their country, and with such as shut their doors and sin. If, then, all the rest is common as we have seen, there remains to the good man this special excellence; to welcome with pleasure all that happens or is ordained, not to defile the divinity enthroned in his breast, not to perturb it with a crowd of images, but to preserve it in tranquillity, and obey it as a God: to observe truth in all he says, and justice in his every action. And though others may not believe that he lives thus in simplicity, modesty, and contentment, he neither takes this unbelief amiss from any one, nor quits the road which leads to the true end of life, at which he ought to arrive pure, calm, ready to take his departure, and accommodated without compulsion to his fate.

END OF THE THIRD BOOK.

BOOK IV

1. The power which rules within us, when its state is accordant with nature, so acts in every occurrence as easily to adapt itself to all present or possible situations. It requires no set material to work upon, but, under proper reservation, needs but the incitement to pursue, and makes matter for its activities out of every opposition. Even so a fire masters that which is cast upon it, and though a small flame would have been extinguished, your great blaze quickly makes the added fuel its own, consumes it, and grows mightier therefrom.

2. Let no action be done at random, nor otherwise than in complete accordance with the principles involved.

3. Men seek retirement in the country, on the sea-coast, in the mountains; and you too have frequent longings for such distractions. Yet surely this is great folly, since you may retire into yourself at any hour you please. Nowhere can a man find any retreat more quiet and more full of leisure than in his own soul; especially when there is that within it on which, if he but look, he is straightway quite at rest. And rest I hold to be naught else but perfect order in the soul. Constantly, therefore, allow yourself this retirement, and so renew yourself. Have also at hand thoughts brief and fundamental, which readily may occur; sufficing to shut out the discordant clamour of the world, and to send you back without fretting at the task to which you return. For at what do you fret? At the wickedness of mankind. Recollect the maxim that all reasoning beings are created for one another, that to bear with them is a part of justice, and that they cannot help their sin. Remember how many of those who lived in enmity, suspicion, and hatred, at daggers drawn, have been stretched on their funeral pyres, and turned to ashes. Remember and cease from your complaints. Is it your allotted part in the world's destiny that chagrins you? Be calm, and renew your knowledge of the alternative, that "Either providence directs the world, or there is nothing but unguided atoms;" and recollect the many proofs that the Universe is as it were a state. Do the ills of the body still have power to touch you? Reflect that the mind, once withdrawn within itself, once grown conscious of its own power, has no concern with the motions, rough or smooth, of the breathing body. Remember, too, all that you have heard and assented to concerning pain and pleasure. Are you distracted by the poor thing called fame? Think how swiftly all things are forgotten. Behold the chaos of eternity which besets us on either side. Think how empty is the noisy echo of acclamation; how fickle and how scant of judgment are they who would seem to praise us, and how narrow the bounds within which their praise is confined. All the earth is but a point in the Universe; how small a corner of that little is inhabited, and even there how few are they and of how little worth who are to praise us! Remember then that there ever remains for you retirement into the little field within. And, above all, be neither distraught nor overstrained. Hold fast your freedom: consider all things as a man of courage, as a human being, as a citizen, as a mortal. Readiest among the principles to which you look let there be these two: Firstly, things external do not touch the soul, but remain powerless without; and all trouble comes from what we think of them within. Secondly, all things visible change in a moment, and are gone for ever. Recollect all the changes of which you have yourself been a witness. The world is a succession of changes: life is but thought.

4. If mind be common to us all, the reason in virtue of which we are rational is also common; so too is the power which bids us do or not do. Therefore we have all a common law; and if so, we are fellow-citizens and members of some common polity. The Universe, then, must in a manner be a state, for of what other common polity can all mankind be said to be members? Wherefore it is from this common state that we derive our intellectual power, our reason, and our law; or whence do we derive them? For that which is earthy in me is derived from earth, my moisture from some other element, my breath and what is warm or fiery from their proper sources. And therefore, as nothing can arise from nothing or return thereto, my intellectual part has also a source.

5. Death, like birth, is a mystery of nature; the one a compounding of elements, the other a resolution into the same. In neither is there anything shameful or against the nature of the rational animal, or contrary to the law of its constitution.

6. It is fate that such actions should come from such men. He who would have it otherwise would have figs without juice. This, too, you should remember: that in a very short time both you and he must die; and a little after not even the name of either shall remain.

7. Suppress the thought; and the cry "I am hurt!" is gone. Suppress "I am hurt!" and you suppress the injury.

8. What makes not a man worse than he was, makes not his life worse, nor hurts him without or within.

9. The law of utility must act so.

10. All that happens, happens right: you will find it so if you observe narrowly. I mean not only according to a natural order, but according to our idea of justice, and, as it were, by the action of one who distributes according to merit. Go on then observing this as you have begun, and whatever you do, let your aim be goodness, goodness as it is rightly understood. Hold to this in every action.

11. Think not as your insulter judges or wishes you to judge: but see things as they truly are.

12. For two things be ever ready: First, to do that only which reason, the sovereign and legislative faculty, suggests for the good of mankind: Secondly, to change your course on meeting any one who can correct and alter your opinion. But let the change be made because you really believe it to be in the interest of justice or the public good, or such like, and not with any view to pleasure or glory for yourself.

13. Have you reason? I have. Why then do you not use it? When it performs its proper office what more do you require?

14. You exist as part of a whole. You will disappear again in that which produced you; or rather you will change and be resumed again into the productive intelligence.

15. Many grains of frankincense are laid on the same altar. One falls soon, another later. It makes no difference.

16. Within ten days, if you return to the observance of moral principles and to the cult of reason, you will appear a God to them who now esteem you a wild beast or an ape.

17. Order not your life as though you had ten thousand years to live. Fate hangs over you. While you live, while yet you may, be good.

18. How much he gains in leisure who looks not to what his neighbours say, or do, or intend; but considers only how his own actions may be just and holy, looking not, as Agathon says, to the moral example of others, but running a straight course and never turning therefrom.

19. He who is careful and troubled about the fame which is to live after him considers not that each one of those who remember him must very soon die himself, and thereafter also the succeeding generation, until every memory of him, handed on by excited and ephemeral admirers, dies utterly away. Grant that your memory were immortal, and those immortal who retain it; yet what is that to you? I ask not, what is that to the dead? But to the living what is the profit in praise, except it be in some convenience that it brings? And you now abandon what nature has put in your power in order to set your hopes upon the report of others.

20. Whatever is beautiful at all is beautiful in itself. Its beauty ends there, and praise has no part in it. Nothing is the better or the worse for being praised; and this holds also of what is beautiful in the common estimation: of material forms and works of art. Thus true beauty needs nothing beyond itself, any more than law, or truth, or kindness, or honour. For none of these gets a single grace from praise or one blot from censure. Does the emerald lose its virtue if one praise it not? Can one by scanting praise depreciate gold, ivory, or purple, a lyre or a dagger, a flower or a shrub?

21. If our souls survive us, how, you ask, has the air contained them from eternity? How, I answer, does the earth contain so many bodies buried during so long a time? Just as corpses, after remaining for a while in the earth, change, and are dissipated to make room for others; so also the souls, liberated into air, remain for a little, and then are changed, diffused, rekindled, and resumed into the universal productive spirit; and so give way to others who come to take their places. This may serve for an answer, on the supposition that the soul survives the body. But we have not merely to consider the number of bodies thus buried in the earth. There are also all the living creatures eaten day by day by ourselves and other animals. How great a multitude of them is thus consumed, and as it were buried in the bodies of those who feed upon them. Yet there is ever space to contain them, owing to the changes into blood, air, and fire. What, then, is the key to this enquiry? Discrimination of matter and cause.

22. Swerve not from your path. In every impulse render justice its due, and in all thinking be sure that you understand.

23. I am in tune with all that is of thy harmony, O Nature. For me nothing is too early and nothing is too late that comes in thy good time. All is fruit to me, O Nature, that thy seasons bring. From thee are all things, thou comprehendest all, and all returns to thee. The poet says, "O dear City of Cecrops!" Shall I not say, "Dear City of God!"

24. "Do few things," says the philosopher, "if you would have quiet." This is perhaps a better saying, "Do what is necessary, do what the reason of the being that is social in its nature directs, and do it in the spirit of that direction." By this you will attain the calm that comes from virtuous action, and that calm also which comes from having few things to do. Most things you say and do are not necessary. Have done with them, and you will be more at leisure and less perturbed. On every occasion, then, ask yourself the question, Is this thing not unnecessary? And put away not only unnecessary deeds but unnecessary thoughts, for by so doing you will avoid all superfluous actions.

25. Make trial how the life of a good man succeeds with you, the life of one who is content with the lot appointed him by Providence, and satisfied with the justice of his own actions and the benevolence of his disposition.

26. You have seen the other state, make trial also of this. Avoid perplexity; seek simplicity. Has a man sinned? He bears his own sin. Has aught befallen you? It is well; for all that befalls you is an ordained part in the weaving of the destiny of all things from the beginning. In sum, life is short. Make the best of the present in reason and in justice. Be sober in your relaxation.

27. The Universe is either an ordered whole or a confusion. But, although a mixture of phenomena, it is certainly an ordered whole. Or, do you think that there can be order in you and confusion in the Universe, and that too when all things, though diffused and separated, are all in sympathy, one with another?

28. Consider the deformity of these characters: the black or malicious, the effeminate, the savage, the beastly, the childish, the brutish, the stupid, the false, the ribald, the knavish, the tyrannical.

29. He is a foreigner, and not a citizen of the world, who knows not what the world contains; and he, too, who knows not what happens in it. He is a deserter who flies from the reason that rules this polity. He is blind, whose intellectual eye is closed. He is a beggar, who needs the gifts of others, and has not from himself all that is necessary for life. He is an excrescence on the scheme of things, who withdraws and separates himself from the reasoned constitution of the nature in which he shares, by discontent with what befalls. That same nature which produces this event produced thee. He is the seditious citizen who separates his particular soul from the one soul of all reasonable beings.

30. One acts the philosopher without a coat, another without books, a third half-naked. Says one, "I have not bread, and yet I hold to reason." Says another, "I have not even the spiritual food of instruction, and yet I hold to it."

31. Love the art which you have learned, humble though it be, and in it find your recreation. And spend the remainder of your life as one who with all his heart commits his concerns to the Gods, and neither acts the tyrant nor the slave to any of mankind.

32. Recall, for example, the age of Vespasian. It is as the spectacle of our own time. You will see men marrying, bringing up children, sick and dying, warring and feasting, trading and farming. You will see men flattering, obstinate in their own will, suspecting, plotting, wishing for the death of others, repining at fortune, courting mistresses, hoarding treasure, pursuing consulships and kingdoms. Yet all that life is spent and gone. Come down to Trajan's days. Again all is the same; and again, that life, too, is dead. Consider, likewise, the records of other times and nations, and see how, after their fit of eagerness, all quickly fell, and were resolved into the elements. But most of all, remember those whom you yourself have known, men who were distracted about vain things, men who neglected the course which suited their own nature, neither holding fast to it nor finding their contentment there. And, herein, forget not that care is to be bestowed on any enterprise only in proportion to its proper worth. For if you keep this in mind you will not be disheartened from over concern with things of less account.

33. The familiar phrases of old days are now strange and obsolete; and, likewise, the names of such as were once much celebrated now sound strangely in our ears. Camillus, Caeso, Volesus, Leonnatus; after them Scipio and Cato; lastly, Augustus, Hadrian, and Antonine - all are forgotten. All things hasten to an end, shall speedily seem old fables, and then be buried in oblivion. This I say of those who have shone with the brightness of their fame. The rest of men, as soon as they expire, are unknown and forgotten. What, then, is it to be remembered for ever? A wholly empty thing. For what should we be zealous? For this alone, that our souls be just, our actions unselfish, our speech ever sincere, and our disposition such as may cheerfully embrace whatever happens, seeing it to be inevitable, familiar, and sprung from the same source and origin as we ourselves.

34. Willingly resign yourself to Clotho, permitting her to spin her thread of what yarn she may.

35. All things are for a day, both what remembers and what is remembered.

36. Observe continually that all things exist in change; and keep this thought ever with you, that Nature loves nothing more than changing what things now are, and making others like them. For what now is, is in a manner the seed of what shall be. Therefore, conceive not that that alone is seed which is cast into the earth or the womb, for that is the thought of ignorance.

37. You are presently to die, and yet you have not attained to simplicity or calm, or to disbelief that you can be hurt by things external. You have not learned to be kindly to all men, or to count just dealing the whole of wisdom.

38. Scan closely that which governs men; see what are their cares, and what they pursue or shun.

39. That which is evil for you exists not in the soul of another; nor in any change or alteration of the body which surrounds you. Where, then, is it? It lies in that part of you by which you apprehend what evil is. Stay the apprehension, and all is well. And though the poor body to which it is so closely bound be cut and burned, though it suppurate or mortify, yet let the apprehension remain inactive: that is, let it judge nothing either bad or good which can happen equally to the bad man and to the good. For that which befalls equally him who lives in accord, and him who lives in discord with Nature, can neither be natural nor unnatural.

40. Ever consider this Universe as one living being, with one material substance and one spirit. Observe how all things are referred to the one intelligence of this being; how all things act on one impulse; how all things are concurrent causes of all others; and how all things are connected and intertwined.

41. "Thou art a poor soul, saddled with a corpse," said Epictetus.

42. There is no evil for things which subsist in change; and there can be no good for things which subsist without it.

43. Time is a river, a violent torrent of things coming into being. Each one, as soon as it has appeared, is swept away: it is succeeded by another which is swept away in its turn.

44. All that happens is as natural and familiar as a rose in spring, or fruit in summer. Such are disease and death, calumny and treachery, and all else which gives fools joy or sorrow.

45. Consequents follow antecedents by virtue of a special and necessary connexion. This relation is not that which exists in a mere enumeration of independent things, and depends merely on some arbitrary convention. It is a rational relationship. And just as things now existing are ranged harmoniously together, so those which come into existence display no bare succession, but a wonderful harmony with what preceded.

46. Remember always the sayings of Heraclitus: that the death of earth is to become water, the death of water to become air, and the death of air to become fire; and so conversely. Remember in what a case he is who forgets whither the way leads: that men are frequently at variance with their close and constant companion, the reason which rules all: that men count strange that which they meet every day: that we should neither act nor speak as though in slumber, although even in slumber we seem to act and speak; nor yet like children learning from their parents, with a mere acceptance of everything just as we are told it.

47. If some God were to inform you that you must die tomorrow, or the next day at farthest, you would take little concern whether it was to be tomorrow or the next day; that is if you were not the most miserable of cowards. For how small is the difference? Wherefore, account it of no great moment whether you die after many years or tomorrow.

48. Constantly consider how many physicians are dead and gone, who frequently knitted their brows over their patients; how many astrologers, who foretold the deaths of others with great ostentation of their art; how many philosophers, who wrote endlessly on death and immortality; how many warriors, who slew their thousands; and how many tyrants, who used their power of life and death with cruel wantonness, as though they had been immortal. How many whole cities, if I may so speak, are dead: Helice and Pompeii and Herculaneum, and others past counting. Tell over next all those you have known, one after the other: think how one buried his fellow, then lay dead himself, to be buried by a third. And all this within a little time. In sum, look upon human things, and behold how short-lived and how vile they are; mucus yesterday, tomorrow ashes or pickled carrion. Spend, then, the fleeting remnant of your time in a spirit that accords with Nature, and depart contentedly. So the olive falls when it is grown ripe, blessing the ground from whence it sprung, and thankful to the tree that bore it.

49. Be like a promontory against which the waves are always breaking. It stands fast, and stills the waters that rage around it. "Wretched am I," says one, "that this has befallen me." "Nay," say you, "happy am I who, though this has befallen me, can still remain without sorrow, neither broken by the present nor dreading the future." The like might have befallen any one; but every one would not have endured it unpained. Why, then, should we dwell more on the misfortune of the incident than on the felicity of such strength of mind? Can you call that a misfortune for a man which is not a miscarriage of his nature? And can you call anything a miscarriage of his nature which is not contrary to its purpose? You have learned its purpose, have you not? Then does this accident debar you from justice, magnanimity, prudence, wisdom, caution, truth, honour, freedom, and all else in the possession of which man's nature finds its full estate? Remember, therefore, for the future, upon all occasions of sorrow, to use the maxim: this thing is not misfortune, but to bear it bravely is good fortune.

50. It is a vulgar meditation, and yet very effectual for enabling us to despise death, to consider the fate of those who have been most earnestly tenacious of life, and enjoyed it longest. Wherein is their gain greater than that of those who died before their time? They are all lying dead somewhere or other. Cadicianus, Fabius, Julian, Lepidus, and their fellows, saw the corpses of multitudes carried to the grave, and then themselves were carried thither. In sum, how small was the difference of time, spent painfully amid what troubles, among what worthless men, and in how mean a carcase! Think it not a thing of value. Rather look back into the eternity that gapes behind, and forward into the other abyss of immensity. Compared with such infinity, small is the difference between a life of three days and one of three ages like Nestor's.

51. Run ever the short way. The short way is the way according to Nature. Therefore speak and act according to the soundest rule; for this resolution will free you from much toil and warring, and from all artful management and ostentation.

END OF THE FOURTH BOOK.

BOOK V

1. In the morning, when you find yourself unwilling to rise, have this thought at hand: I arise to the proper business of man, and shall I repine at setting about that work for which I was born and brought into the world? Am I equipped for nothing but to lie among the bed-clothes and keep warm? "But," you say, "it is more pleasant so." Is pleasure, then, the object of your being, and not action, and the exercise of your powers? Do you not see the smallest plants, the little sparrows, the ants, the spiders, the bees, all doing their part, and working for order in the Universe, as far as in them lies? And will you refuse the part in this design which is laid on man? Will you not pursue the course which accords with your own nature? You say, "I must have rest." Assuredly; but nature appoints a measure for rest, just as for eating and drinking. In rest you go beyond these limits, and beyond what is enough; but in action you do not fill the measure, and remain well within your powers. You do not love yourself; if you did, you would love your nature and its purpose. Others, who love the art that they have made their own, exhaust themselves with labouring at it unwashed and unfed. But you honour your own nature less than the carver honours his carving, less than the dancer honours his dancing, the miser his gold, or the vain man his empty fame. These men, when desire takes them, count food and sleep well lost if they can better realize the object of their longings; and shall the pursuit of the common good seem less precious in your eyes and worthy of a lesser zeal?

2. How easy it is to thrust away and blot out each impression that is disturbing and unfit; and forthwith to enjoy perfect tranquillity.

3. Judge no speech or action unworthy of you which is consistent with nature. Be not dissuaded by any consequent criticism or censure from others; but, if the speech or action be honourable, judge yourself worthy to say or do it. Those who criticize you have their own conscience and their own motives. These you are not to regard, but follow a straight course, guided by your own nature and the nature of the Universe, both of which point the same way.

4. I walk the way which is Nature's, until at last I shall fall and be at rest; breathing out my breath into the air wherefrom I daily drew it, falling on that earth whence my father drew his seed, my mother her blood, and my nurse the milk which nourished me; on that earth which has given me my daily food and drink through all these years, which sustains my footsteps, and bears with me—her manifold abuser.

5. Men cannot admire you for your shrewdness. Be it so. But there is many another quality of which you cannot say, "It is not in me." Display these; they are wholly in your power. Be sincere, be dignified, be painstaking; scorn pleasure, repine not at fate, need little; be kind and frank; love not exaggeration and vain talk; strive after greatness. Do you not see how many virtues you might show, of which you are yet content to fall short, though you have not the excuse that they are absent, or that you are unfit for them? Are you driven by some want in your equipment to be querulous, to be miserly, to be a flatterer, to reproach your body with your own faults, to cringe to others, to be vainglorious, to have all this restlessness in your soul? No, by the Gods, you might have escaped these vices long ago. All your fault, then, is that you are somewhat slow and dull of comprehension. This you should strive to correct by exercise; neither neglecting your dulness nor taking a mean pleasure in it.

6. Some men, when they have done you a favour, are very ready to reckon up the obligation they have conferred. Others, again, are not so forward in their claims, but yet in their minds consider you their debtor, and well know the value of what they have done. A third sort seem to be unconscious of their service. They are like the vine, which produces its clusters and is satisfied when it has yielded its proper fruit. The horse when he has run his course, the hound when he has followed the track, the bee when it has made its honey, and the man when he has done good to others, make no noisy boast of it, but set out to do the same once more, as the vine in its season produces its new clusters again. "Should we, then, be among those who in a manner know not what they do?" Assuredly. "But this very thing implies intelligence; for it is a property of the unselfish man to perceive that he is acting unselfishly, and, surely, to wish his fellow also to perceive it." True, but if you misapprehend my saying, you will enter the ranks of those of whom I spoke before. They, too, are led astray by specious reasonings. But if you have the will to understand what my principle truly means, fear not that in following it you will neglect the duty of unselfishness.

7. This is a prayer of the Athenians: "Rain, rain, dear Zeus, on the plains and ploughlands of the Athenians." Man should either not pray at all, or pray after this frank and simple fashion.

8. Just as one says that Aesculapius has prescribed a course of riding for some one, or the cold bath, or walking bare-footed; so it may be said that the guiding Mind prescribes for a man, disease, or mutilation, or losses, or the like. "Prescribed," in the first case, means that such treatment was enjoined on the patient as might coincide with the needs of his health: in the second case it means that each man's fortune is appointed to coincide with the purposes of fate. Now, the very word "coincidence" implies something like that correspondence of squared stones in a wall or pyramid, which workmen speak of when they fit them together in some structure. All things are united in one bond of harmony; and just as all existing bodies go to make the visible world what it is, so destiny, as the general cause, is compounded of all particular causes. The most unphilosophical grasp my meaning, for they say, "Fate gave this to so-and-so: this was appointed or prescribed for him." Let us, then, receive the decrees of Fate as we receive the prescriptions of Aesculapius. He prescribes many things for us, and some of them are harsh medicines. Yet we obey him gladly in the hope of health. Conceive therefore that, for Nature, the doing of her work and the fulfilling of her purposes are, as it were, her health; and welcome all that happens, even should it seem hard fortune, because it tends to the health of the Universe, and to the prosperity and felicity of Zeus. He would not have brought this or that on any man did it not contribute to the good of the whole, nor does any part of Nature's system bring aught to pass which suits not with her government. For two reasons, then, you should content yourself with what befalls you. The first is, that it was created and ordained for you, and was in a manner related to you from the beginning, in the weaving of all destinies from the great first causes. The second is, that even what happens severally to each man contributes to the well-being and prosperity of the Mind which governs all things, and, indeed, even to its continued existence. For the whole is maimed if you break in the slightest degree this continuous connexion, whether of parts or causes. And this you are doing your best to break and to destroy whenever you repine at fate.

9. Fret not, neither despond nor be disheartened, if it be not always possible for you to act according to your principles of perfection. If you are beaten off, return again to the effort, and content yourself that your conduct is generally such as becomes a man. Love the good to which you return; and come back to Philosophy, not as one who comes to a master, but as one whose eyes ache recurs to sponge and egg, as another has recourse to plasters, or a third to fomentation. And thus you will make no empty show of obeying reason; but find that it gives you rest. Remember that Philosophy demands no more than what your nature requires. But you are wont to desire other things which accord not with your nature. "For what," you say, "can be more delightful than such things?" Is not this the very snare which Pleasure sets for us? Yet consider if magnanimity, frankness, simplicity, kindness, and piety be not even greater delights. And what is sweeter than wisdom itself, when you are conscious of security and felicity in your powers of apprehension and reason?

10. The natures of things are so covered up from us, that to many philosophers, and these no mean ones, all things seem incomprehensible. The Stoics themselves own that it is difficult to comprehend anything with certainty. All our assent is inconsistent, for where is the consistent man? Consider, too, the objects of our knowledge: how transitory are they, and how mean! How often they are in the possession of the debauchee, of the harlot, of the robber! Review again the morals of your contemporaries: it is scarcely possible to tolerate the best-mannered among them; not to say that a man can scarcely tolerate himself. Amid such darkness and filth, in this perpetual flux of substance, of time, of motion, and of things moved, I can perceive nothing worthy of esteem or of desire. On the contrary, we should comfort ourselves as we await our natural dissolution, and not be vexed at the delay, but find rest in these thoughts: first, that nothing can befall us which is not in accord with the nature of all things; second, that it is always in our power not to do anything against the divine spirit within us: to this no force can compel us.

11. To what end am I using my soul? Let me examine myself as to this on all occasions, and consider what is passing now in that part of me which men call the ruler of the rest. Let me think, too, whose is the soul that I have. Is it a child's? Is it a youth's, a timorous woman's, or a tyrant's; the soul of a tame beast or of a savage one?

12. Of what value the things are which the many account good you may judge from this: If a man has conceived certain things, such as prudence, temperance, justice, or courage, to be good in the real sense, he cannot, while he is of this mind, readily listen to the traditional gibe about a superabundance of good things. It will not fit the case. But when he has in mind things which seem good in the eyes of the multitude, he is perfectly willing to hear and accept as quite appropriate the raillery of the comic poet. Thus even the ordinary mind perceives the difference. For if this were not so, we would not in the first case repudiate the jest as offensive, nor would we salute it as a happy witticism when applied to wealth or to the opulence which produces luxury and ostentation. Proceed then, and put the question whether these things are to be valued and esteemed good of which we have such an opinion that we may aptly say of their possessor: "He has so many possessions about him that he has no place wherein to ease himself."

13. I consist of a formal and a material element. Neither of these two shall die and fade into nothingness, since neither came into being out of nothing. Every part of me, then, will be transformed and ranged again in some part of the Universe. That part of the Universe will itself be transmuted into another part, and so on for all time coming. By some such change as this I came into being, likewise my progenitors, and so back from all time past. There is no objection to this theory, even though the world be governed by determined cycles of revolution.

14. Reason, and the art of thinking, are powers which are complete in themselves, and in their special processes. They start from their own internal principle, and proceed to their appointed end. Such mental acts are called right, to indicate that the course of thought is right or straight.

15. Nothing should be said to be part of a man which is not part of his human nature. Things that are not part of his essence cannot be required of him, and have no part in the promise or the fulfilment of his nature. Therefore, in such things lies neither the end of man nor the good which crowns that end. Moreover, if anything were really part of a man, it would not be proper for him to despise it or revolt against it, nor would he be praiseworthy who made himself independent thereof. If non-essential things were indeed good, he could be no good man who stinted himself in the use of them; but, as we see, the more a man goes without them, and the more he endures the want of them, the better a man he is.

16. The character of your most frequent impressions will be the character of your mind. The soul takes colour from its impressions, therefore steep it in such thoughts as these:—Wherever a man can live, he can live well. A man can live in a court, therefore he can live well there. Again everything works towards that for which it was created, and that to which anything works is its end; and in the end of everything is to be found the advantage and the good of it. Now, for reasoning beings, Society is the highest good, for it has long since been proved that we were brought into the world to be social. Nay, was it not manifest that the inferior kinds were formed for the superior, and the superior for each other? Now, the animate is superior to the inanimate, and beings that reason to those that only live.

17. To pursue impossibilities is madness; and it is impossible that the wicked should not act in some such way as this.

18. Nothing can befall any man which he is not fitted by nature to bear. The like events befall others, and either through ignorance that the event has happened, or from ostentation of magnanimity, they stand firm and unhurt by them. Strange then that ignorance or ostentation should have more strength than wisdom!

19. Material things cannot touch the soul at all, nor have any access to it: neither can they bend or move it. The soul is bent or moved by itself alone, and remodels all things that present themselves from without in accordance with whatever judgment it adopts within.

20. In one respect man is nearest and dearest to me; in so far, that is, as I must do good to him and bear with him. But in so far as some men obstruct me in my natural activities, man enters the class of things indifferent to me, no less than the sun, the wind, or the wild beast. By these indeed some special action may be impeded, but no interference with my purpose or with my inward disposition can come from them, thanks to my exceptive and modifying powers. For the mind can convert and change everything that impedes its activity into matter for its action; hindrance in its work becomes its real help, and every obstruction makes for its progress.

21. Reverence that which is most excellent in the Universe, and the most excellent is that which employs all things and rules all. Likewise reverence that which is most excellent in yourself. It is of the same nature as the former, for it is that which employs all else that is in you, and that by which your whole life is ordered.

22. That which harms not the city cannot harm the citizen. Apply this rule whenever you have the idea that you are hurt. If the state be not hurt by this, neither am I harmed, and if the state be hurt we should not be wrathful with him who hurt it. Consider where lay his oversight.

23. Consider frequently how swiftly things that exist or are coming into existence are swept by and carried away. Their substance is as a river perpetually flowing; their actions are in continual change, and their causes subject to ten thousand alterations. Scarcely anything is stable, and the vast eternities of past and future in which all things are swallowed up are close upon us on both hands. Is he not then a fool who is puffed up with success in the things of this world, or is distracted, or worried, as if he were in a time of trouble likely to endure for long.

24. Keep in mind the universe of being in which your part is exceeding small, the universe of time of which a brief and fleeting moment is assigned to you; the destiny of things, and how infinitesimal your share therein.

25. Does another wrong me? Let him look to that. His character and his actions are his own. So much is in my present possession as is dispensed to me by the nature of things, and I act as my own nature now bids me.

26. Let the leading and ruling part of your soul stand unmoved by the stirrings of the flesh, whether gentle or rude. Let it not commingle with them, but keep itself apart, and confine these passions to their proper bodily parts; and if they rise into the soul by any sympathy with the body to which it is united, then we must not attempt to resist the sensation, seeing that it is of our nature; but let not the soul, for its part, add thereto the conception that the sensation is good or bad.

27. Live with the Gods. And he lives with the Gods who continually displays to them his soul, living in satisfaction with its lot, and doing the will of the inward spirit, a portion of his own divinity which Zeus has given to every man for a ruler and a guide. This is the intelligence, the reason that abides in us all.

28. Are you angry with one whose armpits smell or whose breath is foul? What is the use? His mouth or his arm-pits are so, and the consequence must follow. But, you say, man is a reasonable being, and could by attention discern in what he offends. Very well, you too have reason. Use your reason to move his; instruct, admonish him. If he listens, you will cure him, and there will be no reason for anger. You are neither actor nor harlot.

29. As you intend to live at your going, so you can live here. But, if men do not permit you, then depart from life, yet so as if no misfortune had befallen you. If my house be smoky, I go out, and where is the great matter? So long as no such trouble drives me out, I remain at my will, and no one will prevent me from acting as I will. And my will is the will of a reasonable and social being.

30. The intelligence of the Universe is social. It has therefore made the inferior orders for the sake of the superior; and has suited the superior beings for one another. You see how it hath subordinated, and co-ordinated, and distributed to each according to its merit, and engaged the nobler beings to a mutual agreement and unanimity.

31. How have you behaved towards the Gods, towards your parents, your brothers, your wife, your children, your teachers, those who reared you, your friends, your intimates, your slaves? Can it be said that you have ever acted towards all of them in the spirit of the line:—

He wrought no harshness, spoke no unkind word?

Recollect all you have passed through, all that you have had strength to bear. Your life is now a tale that is told, and your service is all discharged. Recall the fair sights you have seen, the pleasures and the pains you have despised, the so-called glory that you have foregone, the unkindly men to whom you have shown kindness.

32. How is it that unskilled and ignorant souls disturb the skilful and intelligent? What, I ask, is the skilful and intelligent soul? It is that which knows the beginning and the end, and the reason which pervades all being, and by determined cycles rules the Universe for all time.

33. In a little space you will be only ashes and dry bones and a name, perhaps not even that. A name is but so much empty sound and echo, and the things which are so much prized in life are empty, mean, and rotten. We are as puppies that snap at one another, as children that quarrel, laugh, and presently weep again. But integrity, modesty, justice, and truth,

Up from the wide-wayed earth have soared to heaven.

What then should detain you here? Things sensible are ever changing and unstable. The senses are dull and easily deceived. The poor soul itself is a mere exhalation from blood. Fame in such a world is a thing of naught. What then? You await calmly extinction or transformation, whichever it may be. And till the fulness of the time be come what is to suffice you? What else than a life spent in fearing and praising the Gods, and in the practice of benevolence, toleration and forbearance towards men? And whatsoever lies beyond the bounds of flesh and breath, remember that it is neither yours nor in your power.

34. A prosperous life may be yours if only you can take the right path, and keep to it in all you think or do. Two advantages are common to Gods, to men, and to every rational soul. In the first place, nothing external to themselves has power to hinder them. In the second, their happiness lies in having mind and conduct disposed to justice, and in the power to make that the end of all desire.

35. If the fault be not my sin, nor a consequence of it, if there be no damage to the common good, why am I perturbed about it? Wherein is the harm to the common good?

36. Be not incautiously carried away by sentiment, but aid him that needs it according to your power and his desert. If his need be of the things which are indifferent, think not that he is harmed thereby, for so to think is an evil habit. But as, in the Comedy, the old man begs to have his fosterchild's top for a keepsake, though he knows well that it is a top and nothing more, so should you act also in the affairs of life.

You mount the rostra and cry aloud, "O man, have you forgotten what is the real value of what you seek?" "No, but the many are keen in their pursuit of it." "Are you then to be a fool because they are?"

In whatever case I had been left I could have made my fortune: for what is it to make a fortune but to confer good things upon one's self; and true good things are a worthy frame of mind, worthy impulses, worthy actions.

END OF THE FIFTH BOOK.

BOOK VI

1. The substance of the Universe is docile and pliable. The mind which governs it has in itself no source of evil-doing. It has no malice: it does no ill, and nothing is hurt by it. By its guidance all things come to be, and fulfil their being.

2. Act the part which is worthy of you, regarding not whether you be stiff with cold or comfortably warm; whether you be drowsy or refreshed with sleep; whether you be in good report or bad; whether you be dying or upon some other business. For death also is one piece of the business of life, and, here as elsewhere, it is enough to do well what comes to our hand.

3. Look within. Let not the proper quality or value of anything escape you.

4. All that exists will very speedily change; by rarefaction, if all substance be one; otherwise by dispersion.

5. The guiding mind knows what its own condition is, how, and upon what matter its work is done.

6. The best revenge is not to copy him that wronged you.

7. Find your sole delight and recreation in proceeding from one unselfish action to another, with God ever in mind.

8. The ruling part of you is that which rouses and steers itself, making itself what it wishes to be, and making all that happens take such appearance as it will.

9. All things are accomplished according to the will of universal nature. There is no other nature to influence them which either comprehends the former from without, or is contained within it, or exists externally, and independent of it.

10. The Universe is either a confusion ravelled and unravelled again, or else a unity compact of order and forethought. If it be the former, why should I wish to linger amid this aimless chaos and confusion, or have any further care than "how to become earth again"? Nay, why am I disturbed at all? Dissolution will overtake me, do what I please. But, if the latter be the case, I adore the Ruler of all things, I stand firm, and put my trust in him.

11. Whenever your situation forces trouble upon you, return quickly to yourself, and interrupt the rhythm of life no longer than you are compelled. Your grasp of the harmony will grow surer by continual recurrence to it.

12. Had you at one time both a step-mother and a mother, you would respect the former, yet you would be more constantly in your mother's company. Your court and your philosophy are step-mother and mother to you. Return then frequently to your true mother, and recreate yourself with her. Her consolation can make the court seem bearable to you, and you to it.

13. Keep these thoughts for meats and eatables: This that is before me is the dead carcase of a fish, a fowl, a hog. This Falernian is but a little grape juice. Think of your purple robes as sheep's wool stained in the blood of a shell-fish. Such conceptions, which touch reality so near, and set forth the sum and substance of these objects, are powerful indeed to display to us their despicable value. In this spirit we should act throughout life; and when things of great apparent worth present themselves, we should strip them naked, view their meanness, and cast aside the glowing description which makes them seem so glorious. Vanity is a great sophist, and most imposes on us when we believe ourselves to be busy about the noblest ends. Remember the saying of Crates about Xenocrates himself.

14. Most objects of vulgar admiration may be referred to certain general classes. There are, first, those which hold together by cohesion or by some organic unity, such as stone, timber, figs, vines or olives. The things which men, a shade more reasonable, admire are referred to the class which possesses animal life such as is seen in flocks and herds. When man's taste is still more cultured his admiration turns to things which can show a rational intelligence. But he admires this intelligence not as a universal principle, but only so far as he finds it expressed in art or industry, or, indeed, sometimes merely so far as it is exhibited by his retinue of artist slaves. But he who values rational intelligence as a universal thing, and as a social force, will care nothing for these other objects of admiration. He will, above all things, strive to preserve his own mind in all its rational and social instincts and activities; and to this end he will co-operate with any of his kind.

15. Some things hasten into being. Some hasten to be no more. Even as a thing is born some part of it is already dead. Flux and change are constantly renewing the world, just as the unbroken flow of time ever presents to us some new portion of eternity. In this vast river, on whose bosom there is no tarrying, what is there among the things that sweep by us that is worth the prizing? It is as if a man grew fond of one among a passing flight of sparrows, when already it had vanished from his sight. Our life itself is much like a vapour of the blood or a drawing in of air. Our momentary actions of inhalation and exhalation are one in kind with that whole power of breathing which, yesterday or the day before, we received at birth, and which we must restore again to the source from whence we drew it.

16. It is a small privilege to transpire like plants, or even to breathe as cattle or wild beasts do. To feel the impressions of sense, to be swayed like puppets by passion, to herd together and to live by bread; all this is no great thing. There is nothing here superior to our power of discharging our superfluous food. What, then, is of value? To be received with clapping of hands? No. Neither, therefore, is the applause of tongues more valuable, for the praises of the multitude are naught but the idle clapping of tongues. Dismiss the vanity called fame, and what remains to be prized? This, I think: in all things to act, or to restrain yourself from action, as best suits the particular structure of your nature. This is the end of all arts and studies, for every art aims at making what it produces well adapted to the work for which it was designed. The gardener, the vine-dresser, the horse-breaker, the dog-trainer all try for this; and what else is the aim of all education and teaching? Here, then, is what you may truly value: this well won, you will seek for nothing more. Will you, then, cease valuing the multitude of other things? If you do not, you will never attain to freedom, self-sufficiency, or tranquillity. You cannot escape envying, suspecting, and striving against those who have the power to deprive you of your cherished objects, nor plotting against men who are in possession of that on which you set your heart. The man who lacks any of these things must, of necessity, be distracted, and be for ever complaining against the Gods. But reverence and respect for your own intelligence will bring you to agreement with yourself, into concord with mankind, and into harmony with the Gods, whom you will praise for all their good gifts and guidance.

17. Upward, downward, round and round run the courses of the elements. But the course of virtue is like none of these; it follows a diviner path, well-directed in a way that is hard for us to understand.

18. Strange are the ways of men! They can speak no good word of the contemporaries with whom they live; yet they count it a great thing to gain the praises of a posterity whom they never saw nor shall see. As well might we grieve because we cannot hear the praises of our ancestors.

19. If a thing seems to you very difficult to accomplish, conclude not that it is beyond human power. But, if you see that anything is within man's power, and part of his proper work, conclude that you also may attain to it.

20. In the gymnasium, if some one scratches us with his nails, or in a sudden onset bruises our head, we express no resentment; we are not offended; nor do we suspect him for the future as one who is plotting against us. We are on our guard against him, it is true, but not as against an enemy or a suspected person. In all good humour we simply keep out of his way. Let us thus behave in other affairs of life, and overlook the many injuries which are done to us, as it were, by our antagonists in the gymnasium of the world. As I said, we may keep out of their way, but without suspicion or hatred.

21. If any one can convince or shew me that I am wrong in thought or deed, I will gladly change. It is truth that I seek; and truth never yet hurt any man. What does hurt is persistence in error or in ignorance.

22. I do my duty, and for the rest am not distracted by anything which is inanimate or irrational, or which has lost or ignores the proper way.

23. Use the brute creation, and also all material things, in the spirit of magnanimity and freedom which becomes him who has reason in using that which has it not. Towards men, who have reason, act in a social spirit. In every business call the Gods to aid thee, nor trouble how long this business shall endure; three hours spent therein may suffice you.

24. Alexander of Macedon and his muleteer, when they died, were in a like condition. They were either alike resumed into the seminal source of all things, or alike dispersed among the atoms.

25. Consider all the many things, both physical and spiritual, that are adoing within each of us at the very same instant of time; and you will wonder the less at the far greater multitudes of things, even all that is, which exist together in the one-and-all which we call the Universe.

26. Should some one ask you how the name Antoninus is written, would you not carefully pronounce to him each one of the letters? Should he then begin an angry dispute about it, would you also grow angry, and not rather mildly count over the several letters to him? Thus in life remember that each duty is made up of a number of elements. We should observe all these calmly; and, without anger at those who are angry with us, we should set about accomplishing the task which lies before us.

27. Is it not cruel to restrain men from pursuing what appears to be their own advantage? And yet, in a manner, you deny them this liberty when you shew anger at their errors. Men are assuredly attracted to what seems to be their own advantage. "Yes," you say, "but it is not their advantage." Instruct them, then, and make this evident to them, but without anger.

28. Death is the cessation of the sensual impressions, of the impulses of the passions, of the questionings of reason, and of the servitude to the flesh.

29. It is shame and dishonour that, in any man's life, the soul should faint from its duty while the body still holds out.

30. See to it that you fall not into Caesarism: avoid that stain, for it may come to you. Guard your simplicity, your goodness, your sincerity, your dignity, your reticence, your love of justice, your piety, your kindliness, your affection for your kin, and your constancy to your duty. Endeavour earnestly to continue such as philosophy would make you. Reverence the Gods, and help mankind. Life is short, and the one fruit of it in this world is a pure mind and unselfish conduct. Be in all things the disciple of Antonine. Imitate his resolute constancy to rational action, his level equability, his godliness, his serenity of countenance, his sweetness of temper, his contempt of vainglory, his keen attempts to comprehend things. Remember how he never quitted any subject till he had thoroughly examined it and understood it, and how he bore with those who blamed him unjustly, without making any angry retort: how he was never in a hurry; how he discouraged calumny; how closely he scanned the manners and actions of men; how cautious he was in reproaching any man; how free from fear, suspicion, or sophistry; how little contented him in the matter of house, furniture, dress, food, servants; how patient he was of labour, and how slow to anger. So abstemious was his life that he could hold out until evening without relieving himself, except at the usual hour. What a firm and loyal friend he was; how patient of frank opposition to his opinions; how glad if any one could set him right! How religious he was, and yet how free from superstition! Follow in his steps that your last hour may find you with a conscience as easy as his.

31. Sober yourself, recall your senses. Shake sleep from you, and know that it was a dream that troubled you; and, now that you are broad awake again, regard the waking world as you did the dream.

32. I am made up of a frail body and a soul. To the body all things are indifferent, because it cannot distinguish them; and to the mind all things are indifferent also which arise not from its own activities. All these are indeed in its own power, but it is concerned with only such of them as are present. Its past and future activities are indifferent to it now.

33. No toil for hand or foot is against Nature, so long as it is proper for hand or foot to do. No more, then, is toil contrary to the nature of man, as man, so long as he is doing work appointed for man to do; and if it be not contrary to his nature it cannot be evil for him.

34. How many are the pleasures that have been enjoyed by robbers, rakes, parricides, and tyrants!

35. Do you not see how common artificers, though they may humour the public to a certain extent, cling to the rules of their art, and cannot endure to depart from them? Is it not grievous, then, that the architect and the physician should shew greater respect for the rules of their several professions, than man shews for his own reason, which he possesses in common with the Gods?

36. Asia and Europe are mere corners of the Universe: the whole sea is but a drop, Athos a clod. All the present is but an instant in eternity. All things are small, changeable, and fleeting. Everything proceeds from the universal intelligence, either directly or as a consequence. Thus, the jaws of lions, poisons, all evil things such as thorns or mire, are the consequences of the grand and the beautiful. Do not, then, imagine that they are foreign to that which you revere, but consider well the source of all things.

37. He who has seen the present has seen all that either has been from all eternity, or will be to all eternity, for all things are alike in kind and form.

38. Consider frequently the connexion of all things in the Universe, and their relation to each other. All things are in a manner intermingled with one another, and are, therefore, mutually friendly. For one thing comes in due order after another, by virtue of local movements, and of the harmony and unity of the whole.

39. Adapt yourself to the things which your destiny has given you: love those with whom it is your lot to live, and love them with sincere affection.

40. A tool, an instrument, a utensil, is in good case when it is fit for its proper work: yet its maker remains not by it. But within the organisms of Nature there remains and resides the power which made them. You ought, therefore, to reverence this power the more, believing that if you act in deference to its will, all will happen to you in reason; for so in reason the Universe ranges all.

41. Whenever we imagine that anything which lies not in our power is good or evil for us, if the evil befall us or if we miss the good, we inevitably blame the Gods, and hate the men who are, or whom we suspect to be, the cause of our disaster or our loss. Our solicitude about such things leads to much injustice; but if we judge only the things that are in our power to be good or evil, there is no reason left for accusing the Gods or for hating men.

42. We are all co-operating in one great work, some with knowledge and understanding, others ignorantly and without design. It is in this sense, I think, that Heraclitus says that men are working even while they sleep, working together in all that is being done in the Universe. Each works in a different way; and even those contribute abundantly who murmur and try to oppose and to frustrate the course of nature. The world has need even of such as these. It remains then for you to make sure which is the class in which you rank yourself. The presiding mind will assuredly use you to good purpose one way or other; and will enlist you among its labourers and fellow-workers. But see to it that the part that falls to you lie not in the vulgar comic passage of the play, of which Chrysippus has spoken.

43. Does the sun pretend to perform the work of the rain, or Aesculapius that of Ceres? What of the several stars? Are they not different, yet all jointly working for the same end?

44. If the Gods took counsel about me and what should befall me, doubtless then-counsel was good. It is difficult to imagine Gods wanting in forethought, and what could move them to do me wilful harm? What advantage would thence accrue, either to themselves or to the Universe which is their special care? If they have not taken counsel about me in particular, they certainly have done so about the common interest of the Universe, and I therefore should accept cheerfully and contentedly the fate which is the outcome of their ordinance. If, indeed, they take no counsel about anything (which it were impious to believe), then let us quit our sacrifices, our prayers, and our oaths, and all acts of devotion which we now perform as if they lived and moved amongst us. But, granting that the

Gods take no thought for my affairs, I may still deliberate about myself. It is my business to consider my own interest. Now, each man's interest is that which agrees with the structure of his nature, and my nature is rational and social. As Antoninus, my city and my country is Rome; as a human being it is the world. That alone, then, which profits these two cities can profit me.

45. All that happens to the individual is of profit to the whole. This would suffice. But if you consider closely you will see that it is also a general truth that all that happens to one man is of profit to the rest of mankind. "Profit" here should be taken in a somewhat general sense, as referring to things indifferent.

46. In the amphitheatre and other such resorts the same or similar spectacles, continually presented, cloy at last. It is even so in all our experience of life. All things, first and last, are alike, and like derived. When shall the end be?

47. Think continually of all the men that are dead and gone, men of every sort and condition, of all manner of pursuits, and of every nation. Return back to Philistion, Phoebus, and Origanion. Pass down to other generations of the dead. We must all change our habitation and go to that place whither so many great orators, so many venerable philosophers, Heraclitus, Pythagoras, Socrates, and so many heroes have gone before, and so many generals and princes have followed. Add to these Eudoxus, Hipparchus, Archimedes, and other keen, great, laborious, cunning and arrogant spirits; yea, such as have wittily derided this fading mortal life which is but for a day, as did Menippus and his brethren. Consider that all these are long since in their graves. And wherein here is the harm for them; or even for men whose names are not remembered? The one precious thing in life is to spend it in a steady course of truth and justice, with kindliness even for the false and the unjust.

48. When you would cheer your heart, consider the several excellencies of those that live around you. Consider the activity of one, the modesty of another, the generosity of a third, and the other virtues of the rest. Nothing rejoices the heart so much as instances, the more the better, of goodness manifested in the characters of those around us. Let us, therefore, have such instances ever present for reflection.

49. Are you grieved that you weigh only these few pounds, and not three hundred? If not, is there greater reason to sorrow if you live only so many years and no longer? You are satisfied with your allotted quantity of matter; content yourself then likewise with the span of time appointed you.

50. Try to persuade men to agree with you; but whether they agree or not, pursue the course you have marked out when the principles of justice point that way. Should one oppose you by force, act with resignation, and shew not that you are hurt, use the obstruction for the exercise of some other virtue, and remember that your purpose involved the reservation that you were not to aim at impossibilities. What, after all, was your aim? To make some good effort such as this. Well, then, you have succeeded, even though your first purpose be not accomplished.

51. The vain-glorious man places his happiness in the action of others. The sensualist finds it in his own sensations. The wise man realizes it in his own work.

52. You have it in your power to form no opinion about this or that, and so to have peace of mind. Things material have no power to form our opinions for us.

53. Accustom yourself to attend closely to what is said by others, and as far as possible to penetrate into the mind of the speaker.

54. What profits not the swarm profits not the bee.

55. If the sailors revile their pilot, or the sick their physician, whom will they follow or obey? And how will the one secure safety to the crew, or the other health to the patients?

56. How many who entered the world with me are already departed!

57. To the jaundiced, honey seems bitter; and water is a thing of dread to those bitten by mad dogs. To boys a ball is a glorious thing. Why, then, am

I angry? Has error in the mind less power than a little bile in the jaundiced, or a little poison in him who is bitten?

58. No man can prevent you from living according to the plan of your nature; and nothing can befall you which is contrary to the plan of the nature of the Universe.

59. Consider what men are; whom they seek to please; what they expect to gain, and how they go about to compass their ends. Think how soon eternity will shroud all things, and how much is already shrouded.

END OF THE SIXTH BOOK.

BOOK VII.

1. What is vice? It is what you have often seen. In every instance of it keep in mind that you have often seen the like before. Search up and down; you will find sameness everywhere. Among the events which fill the history of ancient, middle, and present ages; among the things of which our cities and our households are full to-day, nothing is new, all is familiar and fleeting.

2. How can the great principles of life become dead if the impressions which correspond to them be not extinguished? These impressions you may still rekindle. I can always form the proper opinion of this or that; and, if so, why am I disturbed? What is external to my mind is of no consequence to it. Learn this, and you stand upright; you can always renew your life. See things again as once you saw them, and your life is made new again.

3. Your vain concern for shows, for stage plays, for flocks and herds, your little combats, are as bones cast for the contention of puppies, as baits dropped into a fishpond, as the toil of ants and the burdens that they bear, as the scampering of frightened mice, or the antics of puppets jerked by wires. It is then your duty amid all this to stand firm, kindly and not proud, yet to understand that a man's worth is just the worth of that which he pursues.

4. In conversation we should give good heed to what is said, and in every enterprise we should attend to what is done. In the latter case, at once look to the end in view, and, in the former, note the meaning intended.

5. Is my understanding sufficient for this business or not? If it be sufficient, I use it for the work in hand as an instrument given to me by nature. If it be not sufficient, I either give place to one better fitted for the achievement, or, if for some reason this be not a proper course, I do it as best I can, taking the aid of those who, by directing my mind, can accomplish something fit and serviceable for the common good. For all that I do, whether by myself or with the help of others, should be directed solely towards what is fit and useful for the public service.

6. How many of those who were once so mightily acclaimed are delivered up to oblivion! And how many of those who acclaimed them are dead and gone this many a day!

7. Be not ashamed of taking assistance. It is laid upon you to do your part, as on a soldier when the wall is stormed. What, then, if you are lame, and cannot scale the battlements alone, but can with another's help?

8. Be not troubled about the future. You will come to it, if need be, with the same power to reason, as you use upon your present business.

9. All things are twined together, in one sacred bond. Scarce is there one thing quite foreign to another. They are all ranged together, and leagued to form the same ordered whole. The Universe, compact of all things, is one; through all things runs one divinity; being is one; and law, which is the reason common to all intelligent creatures; and truth is one as well, that is if there be but one sort of perfection possible to all beings which are of the same nature and partake of the same rational power.

10. Everything material is soon engulfed in the matter of the whole, and every active cause is swiftly resumed into the Universal reason. The memory of all things is quickly buried in eternity.

11. In the reasoning being to act according to nature is to act according to reason.

12. Be upright either by nature or by correction.

13. In an organic unity bodily members play the same part as reasoning beings among separate existences, since both are fitted for one joint operation. This thought will come home to you the more vividly if you say often to yourself: "I am a member of the mighty organism which is made up of reasoning beings." If, instead of a member, you say that you are merely a part, you have not as yet attained to a heartfelt love of mankind. As yet you love not well-doing for its own sake alone, and you still perform your bare duty, with no thought that you are your own benefactor by the deed.

14. From the world without let what will affect whatever parts are subject to such affection. Let the part which suffers complain, if it will, of the suffering. But I, if I admit not that the hap is evil, remain uninjured. Not to admit it is surely in my power.

15. Let any one say or do what he pleases, I must be a good man. It is just as gold, or emeralds, or purple might say continually: "Let men do or say what they please, I must be an emerald, and retain my lustre."

16. The soul which rules you vexes not itself. It does not, for example, awake its own fears or arouse its own desires. If another can raise grief or terror in it, let him do so. By its own impressions it will not be led into such emotions.

Let the body take thought, if it can, for itself, lest it suffer anything, and complain when it suffers. The soul, by means of which we experience fear and sorrow, and by means of which, indeed, we receive any impression of these, will admit no suffering. You cannot force it to any such opinion.

The ruling part is, in itself, free from all dependence, unless it makes itself dependent. Similarly, it may be free from all disturbance and obstruction, if it does not disturb and obstruct itself.

17. To have good fortune is to have a good spirit, or a good mind. What do you here, Imagination? Be gone, I say, even as you came. I have no need for you. You came, you say, after your ancient fashion: I am not angry with you, only, be gone!

18. Do you dread change? What can come without it? What can be pleasanter or more proper to universal nature? Can you heat your bath unless wood undergoes a change? Can you be fed unless a change is wrought upon your food? Can any useful thing be done without changes? Do you not see, then, that this change also which is working in you is even such as these, and alike necessary to the nature of the Universe?

19. Through the substance of the Universe, as through a torrent, all bodies are borne. They are all of the same nature, and fellow-workers with the whole, even as our several members are fellow-workers with one another. How many a Chrysippus, how many a Socrates, how many an Epictetus hath the course of ages swallowed up! Let this thought be with you about every man, and upon all occasions.

20. For this alone I am concerned; that I do nothing that suits not the nature of man, nothing as man's nature would not have it, nothing that it wishes not yet.

21. The time is at hand when you shall forget all things, and when all shall forget you.

22. It is man's special business to love even those who err; and to this love you attain, if it is borne in upon you that even these sinners are your kin, and that they offend through ignorance and against their will. Remember also that in a little while both you and they must die: remember before all things that they have not harmed you, for they have not made your soul worse than it was before.

23. Presiding nature from the universal substance, as from wax, now forms a horse, now breaks it up again, making of its matter a tree, afterwards a man, and again something different. Each of these shapes subsists but for a little. Yet there is nothing dreadful for the chest in being taken to pieces, any more than there formerly was in being put together.

24. A wrathful look is completely against nature. When the countenance is often thus deformed, its beauty dies, in the end is quenched for ever, and cannot be revived again. Seek to comprehend from this very fact that it is against reason. And if the sense of moral evil be gone as well, why should a man wish to remain alive?

25. In a little space Nature, the supreme and universal ruler, will change all things that you behold; out of their substance she will make other things, and others again out of the substance of these, so that the Universe may be ever new.

26. Whenever someone offends you, consider straightway how he has erred in his conceptions of good or evil. When you see where his error lies you will pity him, and be neither surprised nor angry. Indeed you yourself perhaps still wrongly count good the same things as he does, or things just like them. Your duty then is to forgive. And, if you cease from these false ideas of good and bad, you will find it the easier to grant indulgence to him who is still mistaken.

27. Dwell not on what you lack so much as on what you have already. Select the best of what you have, and consider how passionately you would have longed for it had it not been yours. Yet be watchful, lest by this joy in what you have you accustom yourself to value it too highly; so that, if it should fail, you would be distressed.

28. Retire within yourself. The reasoning power that rules you naturally finds contentment with itself in just dealing, and in the calm which such dealing brings.

29. Blot out imagination. Check the brutal impulses of the passions. Confine your energies to the present time. Observe clearly all that happens either to yourself or to another. Divide and analyse all objects into cause and matter. Take thought for your last hour. Let another's sin remain where the guilt lies.

30. Apply your mind to what is said. Penetrate all happenings and the causes thereof.

31. Rejoice yourself with simplicity, modesty, and indifference to all things that lie between good and bad. Love mankind, and obey God. "All things," says someone, "go by law and order." But what if there be naught beyond the atoms? Even if that be so, suffice it to remember that all things, save very few, are swayed by law.

32. Concerning death: If the Universe be a concourse of atoms, death is a scattering of these; if it be an ordered unity, death is an extinction or a translation to another state.

33. Concerning pain: Pain which cannot be borne brings us deliverance. Pain that lasts musts needs be bearable. The mind can abstract itself from the body, and the soul takes no hurt. As to the parts which suffer by pain, let them, if they can, make their own protest.

34. Concerning glory: Consider the understanding of men, what they shun, and what they pursue. And reflect that, as heaps of sand are driven one upon another, and the later drifts bury and hide those that went before, so, too, in life the former ages are soon buried by the next.

35. This from Plato: "'To the man who has true grandeur of mind, and who contemplates all time and all being, can human life appear a great matter?' 'Impossible,' says the other. 'Can then such a one count death a thing of dread?' 'No, indeed.'"

36. It is a saying of Antisthenes, that it is the part of a king to do good and reap reproach.

37. It is a shameful thing that the countenance should obey the mind, should compose and order itself as the mind bids it, while the mind cannot compose and order itself as it wills.

38. *Vain is all anger at external things*

For they regard it nothing—

39. *Give joy to us and to the immortal Gods.*

40. *For life is, like the laden ear, cut down;*

And some must fall and some unreaped remain.

41. *Me and my children, if the Gods neglect,*

It is for some good reason.

42. *For I keep right and justice on my side.*

43. *Weep not with them, and still these throbs of woe.*

44. From Plato:—"I would make him this just answer, 'You are mistaken, my friend, to think that a man of any worth should count the chances of living and dying. Should he not rather, in all he does, consider simply whether he is acting justly or unjustly, whether he is playing the part of a good man or a bad?'"

45. He says again:—"In truth, Athenians, the matter stands thus: Wheresoever a man has chosen his stand, judging it the fittest for him, or wheresoever he is stationed by his commander, there, I think, he should stay at all hazards, making no account of death, or any other evil but dishonour."

46. Again:—"Consider, my friend, whether the truly noble and the truly good be not something quite apart from saving and being saved. The man who is a man indeed should not set his heart on living through a few more years of life, nor should he make that the end of his desire. Rather he should commit the matter to the will of God; assenting to the maxim which even women use, that 'no man can elude his destiny,' and studying in addition how he may spend the life that remains to him for the best."

47. Contemplate the courses of the stars, as one should do that revolves along with them. Consider also without ceasing the changes of elements, one into another. Speculations upon such things cleanse away the filth of this earthly life.

48. It is a good thought of Plato's, that when we discourse of men we should "look down, as from a high place," on all things earthly; on herds and armies; on husbandry and marriage; on partings, births, and deaths; on the tumults of the courts of justice; on the desert places of the earth; on the varied spectacle of savage nations; on feasting and lamentation; on traffic; on the medley of all things, and the order which emerges from their contrariety.

49. Consider the past, and the revolutions of so many Empires; and thence you may foresee what shall happen hereafter. It will be ever the same in all things; nor can events leave the rhythm in which they are now moving. Wherefore it is much the same to view human life for forty, as for a myriad of years. What more is there to see?

50. *To earth returns whatever sprang from earth,*

But what's of heavenly seed remounts to heaven.

This imports either the loosing of a knot of atoms, or a similar dispersion of immutable elements.

51. *By meats and drinks, and charms and magic arts*

Death's course they would divert, and thus escape.

. . . .

The gale that blows from God we must endure,

Toiling, but not repining....

52. He is a better wrestler than you, but not more public-spirited, more modest, or better prepared for the accidents of fate; not more gentle toward the short-comings of his neighbours.

53. Wherever we can act conformably to the reason which is common to Gods and men, there we have nothing to dread. Where we can profit by prosperous activity which proceeds in agreement with the constitution of our nature, we need suspect no harm.

54. In all places, and at all times you may devoutly accept your present fortune, and deal in justice with your present company. You may take pains to understand all arising imaginations, that none may steal upon you before you comprehend them.

55. Pry not into the souls of others; but rather look straight to the goal whither nature is leading you; whither the nature of the Universe by external events, and whither your own nature by the tendency of your own action. Each being must perform the part for which it was created. Now all other beings are created for the sake of those among them which have reason; as all lower things exist for the sake of things superior to them; and reasoning beings were created for one another. The leading principle in man's nature, then, is the social spirit; and the second is victory over the solicitations of the body. For it is proper to the workings of reason to set bounds to themselves, and never to be overpowered by the calls of sense or by the stirrings of passion, both of which are animal in their nature. The intellect claims to reign over these, and never to be subjected to them; and rightly, because it is equipped to command and use all the lower powers. The third element in the constitution of a reasoning being is caution against rashness and error. Let the soul go forth straight upon her way in the possession of these principles, and she stands seized of her full estate.

56. Consider yourself as dead, your life as finished and past. Live what yet remains according to Nature's laws, as an overplus granted to you beyond your hope.

57. Love that only which is your hap, which comes upon you as your part in Fate's great spinning. What, indeed, can fit you better?

58. Upon every accident keep in view those to whom the like has happened. They stormed at the event, wondered and complained. But now where are they? They are gone for ever. Why should you act the like part? Leave these unnatural commotions to fickle men who change and are changed. Yourself take thought how you may make good use of such events. Good use for them there is; they will make matter for good actions. Let it be your sole effort and desire to gain your own approval in every action; and remember that the material objects of both that effort and of that desire are things indifferent.

59. Look inward. Within is the fountain of Good. Dig constantly and it will ever well forth.

60. Keep the body steady, without irregularity, whether in its motions or in its postures. For, as the soul shews itself in the countenance by a wise and graceful air, it should require the same expressive power of the whole body. But all this must be practised without affectation.

61. The art of Life is more like that of the wrestler than of the dancer; for the wrestler must always be ready on his guard, and stand firm against the sudden, unforeseen efforts of his adversary.

62. Consider constantly what manner of men they are whose approbation you desire, and what may be the character of their souls. Then you will neither accuse such as err unwillingly, nor need their commendation when you look into the springs of their opinions and their desires.

63. "Every soul," says Plato, "parts unwillingly with truth." You may say the same of justice, temperance, good-nature, and every virtue. It is most necessary to keep this ever in mind; for, if you do, you will be more kindly towards all men.

64. In all pain keep in mind that there is no baseness in it, that it cannot harm the soul which guides you, nor destroy that soul as a reasoning or as a social force. In most pain you may find help in the saying of Epicurus, that "pain is neither unbearable nor everlasting, if you bear in mind its narrow limits, and allow no additions from your imagination." Remember also that we are fretted, though we see it not, by many things which are of the same nature as pain, things such as drowsiness, excessive heat, want of appetite. When any of these things annoy you, say to yourself that you are giving in to pain.

65. Look to it that you feel not towards the most inhuman of mankind, as they feel towards their fellows.

66. Whence do we conclude that Telauges had not a brighter genius than Socrates? 'Tis not enough that Socrates died more gloriously or argued more acutely with the sophists; or that he kept watch more patiently through a frosty night; or because, when ordered to arrest the innocent Salaminian, he judged it more noble to disobey; or because of any stately airs and graces he assumed in public, in which we may very justly refuse to believe. But, assuming all this true, when we consider Socrates, we must ask what manner of soul he had. Could he find contentment in acting with justice towards men, and with piety towards the Gods, neither vainly provoked by the vices of others, nor servilely flattering them in their ignorance; counting nothing strange that the Ruler of the Universe appointed, not sinking under anything as intolerable, and never yielding up his soul in surrender to the passions of the flesh.

67. Nature has not so blended the soul with the body that it cannot fix its own bounds, and execute its own office by itself. It is very possible to be a God among men, and yet be recognised by none. Remember that always, and this as well, that the happiness of life lies in very few things. And though you despair of becoming great in Logic or in Science, you need not despair of becoming a free man, full of modesty and unselfishness, and of obedience unto God.

68. It is in your power to live superior to all violence, and in the greatest calm of mind, were all men to rail against you as they pleased; and though wild beasts were to tear asunder the wretched members of this fleshly mass which has grown with your growth. What is to hinder the soul amid all this from preserving itself in all tranquillity, in just judgments about surrounding things, and in ready use of whatever is cast in its way? Judgment may say to accident:—"Your real nature is this or that, though you appear otherwise in the eyes of men." Use may say to circumstance:—"I was looking for you. To me all that is present is ever matter for rational and social virtue, in sum, for that art which is proper both to man and God. All that befalls is fit and familiar for the purposes of God or man. Nothing is either new or intractable, but everything is well known and fit to work upon."

69. It is the perfection of morals to spend each day as if it were the last of life, without excitement, without sloth, and without hypocrisy.

70. The Gods, who are immortal, are not vexed that in a long eternity they must ever bear with the wickedness and the multitude of sinners. Nay, they even lavish on them all manner of loving care. But you, who are presently to cease from being, can, forsooth, endure no more, though you are one of the sinners yourself!

71. It is ridiculous that you flee not from the vice that is in yourself, as you have it in your power to do; but are still striving to flee from the vice in others, which you can never do.

72. Whatever the rational and social faculty finds fit neither for rational nor for social ends, it justly ranks as inferior to itself.

73. When you have done a kind action, another has benefited. Why do you, like the fools, require some third thing in addition—a reputation for benevolence or a return for it.

74. No man wearies of what brings him gain, and your gain lies in acting according to nature. Be not weary, therefore, of gaining by the act which gives others gain.

75. Nature set about making an ordered universe; and now, either all that is follows a law of necessary consequence and connexion, or we must admit that there is least rationality in the things which are most excellent, and which appear to be most special objects for the impulses of the universal mind. Remembrance of this will give you calmness on many an occasion.

END OF THE SEVENTH BOOK.

BOOK VIII

1. For repressing vain glory, it serves to remember that it is no longer in your power to make your whole life, even from your youth onwards, a life worthy of a philosopher. It is known to many, and you yourself know also, how far you are from wisdom. Confusion is upon you, and it now can be no easy matter for you to gain the reputation of a philosopher. The conditions of your life are against it. Now therefore, as you see how the matter truly lies, put from you all thoughts of reputation among men; and let it suffice you to live so long as your nature wills, though that be but the scanty remnant of a life. Study, therefore, the will of your nature, and be solicitous about nothing else. You have made many efforts and wandered much, but you have nowhere found happiness; not in syllogisms, not in riches, not in fame or pleasure, not in anything. Where, then, is it? In acting that part which human nature requires. How can you act that part? By holding principles as the source of your desires and actions. What principles? The principles of good and evil: That nothing is good for a man which does not make him just, temperate, courageous, and free; and that nothing can be evil which tends not to make him the contrary of all these.

2. Upon every action ask yourself, what is the effect of this for me? Shall I never repent of it? I shall presently be dead, and all these things gone. What more should I desire if my present action is becoming to an intelligent and a social being, subject to the same law with Gods?

3. Alexander, Caesar, Pompey, what were they compared with Diogenes, Heraclitus, Socrates? These knew the nature of things, their causes and their matter, and the minds within them were at one. As to the former, how many things they schemed for, and to how many were they enslaved!

4. Men will go their ways none the less, though you burst in protest.

5. Before all things, be not perturbed. Everything comes to pass as directed by universal Nature, and in a little time you will be departed and gone, like Hadrianus and Augustus. Then, scan closely the nature of what has befallen, remembering that it is your duty to be a good man. Do unflinchingly whatever man's nature requires, and speak as seems most just, yet in kindliness, modesty, and sincerity.

6. It is Nature's work to transfer what is now here into another place, to change things, to carry them hence, and set them elsewhere. All is change, yet is there no need to fear innovation, for all obey the laws of custom, and in equal measure all things are apportioned.

7. For every nature it is sufficient that it goes on its way, and prospers. The rational nature prospers while it assents to no false or uncertain opinion, while it directs its impulses to unselfish ends alone, while it aims its desires and aversions only at the things within its power, and while it welcomes with contentment all that universal Nature ordains. The nature of each of us is part of universal Nature, as the leaf is part of the tree; the leaf, indeed, is part of an insensible and unreasoning system which can be obstructed in its workings; but human nature is part of that universal system which cannot be impeded, and which is intelligent and just. Hence is meted out, suitably to all, our proper portions of time, of matter, of active principle, of powers, and of events. Yet look not to find that each several thing corresponds exactly with any other. Consider rather the whole nature and circumstances of the one, and compare them with the whole of the other.

8. You lack leisure for reading; but leisure to repress all insolence you do not lack. You have leisure to keep yourself superior to pleasure and pain and vain glory, to restrain all anger against the ungrateful, nay, even to lavish loving care upon them.

9. Let no man any more hear you railing on the life of the court; nay, revile it not to your own hearing.

10. Repentance is a self-reproving, because we have neglected something useful. Whatever is good must be useful in some sort, and worthy of the care of a good and honourable man. Now, such a man could never repent of neglecting some opportunity of pleasure. Pleasure, then, is neither useful nor good.

11. Of each thing ask: What is this in itself and by its constitution? What is its substance or matter? What is its cause? What is its business in the Universe? How long shall it endure?

12. When you are reluctant to be roused from sleep, remember that it accords with your constitution and with human nature to perform social actions. Sleep is common to us with the brutes. Now, whatever accords with the nature of each species must be most proper, most fitting, and most delightful to it.

13. Constantly, and, if possible, on every occasion, apply to your imaginations the methods of Physics, Ethics, and Dialectic.

14. Whomsoever you meet, say straightway to yourself:—What are this man's principles of good and evil? For if he holds this or that doctrine concerning pleasure and pain, and the causes thereof, concerning glory and infamy, death and life, it will seem to me neither strange nor wondrous that this or that should be his conduct. I shall bear in mind that he has no choice but to act so.

15. Remember that, as 'tis folly to be surprised that a fig-tree bears figs, so is it equal folly to be surprised that the Universe produces those things of which it was ever fruitful. It is folly in a physician to be surprised that a man has fallen into a fever; or in a pilot that the wind has turned against him.

16. Remember that to change your course, and to follow any man who can set you right is no compromise of your freedom. The act is your own, performed on your own impulse and judgment, and according to your own understanding.

17. If the doing of this be in your own power, why do it thus? If it be in another's, whom do you accuse? The atoms or the Gods? To accuse either is a piece of madness. Therefore accuse no one. Set right, if you can, the cause of error; if you cannot, correct the result at least. If even that be impossible, what purpose can your accusations serve? Nothing should be done without a purpose.

18. That which dies falls not out of the Universe. If then it stays here, here too it suffers a change, and is resolved into those elements of which the world, and you too, consist. These also are changed, and murmur not.

19. The horse, the vine—all things are formed for some purpose. Where is the wonder? Even the sun saith, "I was formed for a certain work;" and similarly the other Gods. For what end are you formed? For pleasure? Look if your soul can endure this thought.

20. Nature has an aim in all things, in the end and surcease of them no less than in their beginning and continuance. It is even as a man casting a ball. Where, then, is the good for the ball in its rising; where the harm in dropping; where even is the harm when it has fallen down? Where is the bubble's good while it holds together, where is the evil when it is broken? So it is with the lamp which now burns and anon goes out.

21. Turn out the inner side of this body, and view it as it is. What shall it become when it grows old, or sickly, or decayed? The praiser and the praised, the rememberer and the remembered are of short continuance, and that in a mere corner of this narrow region, where, narrow though it be, men cannot live in concord, no, not even with themselves. And yet the whole world is but a point.

22. Attend well to what is before you, whether it be a principle, an act, or a word. This your suffering is well merited, for you would rather become good to-morrow than be good to-day.

23. Am I doing aught? Let me do it in a spirit of service to mankind. Does aught befall me? I accept it and refer it to the Gods, the universal source from which come all things in the chain of consequence.

24. The accompaniments of bathing: oil, sweat, filth, foul water—how nauseous are they all! Even so is every part of life, and everything that meets us.

25. Lucilla buried Verus, and soon followed him to the grave. Secunda saw the death of Maximus, and soon herself died. Epitynchanus buried Diotimus, and then Epitynchanus was buried. Antoninus mourned Faustina, and thereafter Antoninus was mourned. Celer buried Hadrian, and then Celer was buried. All go the same way. The cunning men who foretold the fates of others, or who swelled with pride—where are they now? Where are these keen wits, Charax, and Demetrius the Platonist, and Eudaemon, and their like? All were for a day, and are long dead and gone; some scarce remembered even for a little after death; some turned to fables; some faded even from the memory of tales. Wherefore remember this: either the poor mixture which is you, must be dispersed, or the faint breath of life must be quenched, or removed and brought into another place.

26. The joy of man is to do his proper business. And his proper business is to be kindly to his fellows, to rise above the stirrings of sense, to be critical of every plausible imagination, and to contemplate universal Nature and all her consequences.

27. We have all of us three relations: the first to the manifold occasions of our state; the second to the supreme divine cause from which proceed all things unto all men; the third to those with whom we live.

28. Pain is either an evil to the body; and then let the body so declare it; or an evil to the soul. But the soul can maintain her own serenity and calm; and refuse to conceive pain as an evil. All judgment, intention, desire and aversion are within the soul, to which no evil can ascend.

29. Blot out false imaginations, and say often to yourself:—It is now in my power to preserve my soul free from all wickedness, all lust, all confusion or disturbance. And then, as I truly discern the nature of things, I can use them all in due proportion. Be ever mindful of this power which Nature has given you.

30. Speak, whether in the Senate or elsewhere, with dignity rather than elegance; and let your words ever be sound and virtuous.

31. The court of Augustus, his wife, his daughter, his descendants and his ancestors; his sister, and Agrippa; his kinsmen, familiars and friends;

Areius and Maecenas; his physicians and his flamens—death has them all. Think next of the death of a whole house, such as Pompey's, and of what we meet sometimes inscribed on tombs: *He was the last of his race.* Last of all, consider the solicitude of the ancestors of such men to leave a succession of their own posterity. Yet, at the end, one must come the last, and with him dies all that house.

32. Order your life in its single acts, so that if each, as far as may be, attains its end, it will suffice. In this no one can hinder you. But, you say, may not something external withstand me?—Nothing can keep you from justice, temperance, and wisdom.—Yet, perhaps some other activity of mine may be obstructed.—True, but by yielding to this impediment, and by turning with calmness to that which is in your power, you may happen on another course of action equally suited to the ordered life of which we are speaking.

33. Receive the gifts of fortune without pride; and part with them without reluctance.

34. You have seen a hand, a foot, or a head, cut off from the rest of the body, and lying dead at a distance from it. Even such as these does he make himself, so far as he can, who repines at what befalls, who severs himself from his fellow-men, or who does any selfish deed. Are you cast forth from the natural unity? Nature made you to be a part of the whole, but you have cut yourself off from it. Yet here there is the glorious provision that you may re-unite yourself if you will. In no other case has God granted the privilege of re-union to a separated or severed part. Yet behold the goodness and bounty with which God hath honoured mankind. He first puts it in their power not to be severed from this unity; and then, even when they are thus severed, he suffers them to return once more, to take their places as parts of the whole, and to grow one with it again.

35. Universal Nature, as she has imparted to each rational being almost all its faculties and powers, has given to us this one in particular among them. As Nature converts to her use, ranges in destined order, and makes part of herself all that withstands or opposes her; so each rational being can make every impediment in his way a proper matter for himself to act upon, and can use it for his guiding purpose, whatever it may be.

36. Do not confound yourself by considering the whole of life, and by dwelling upon the multitude and greatness of the pains and troubles to which you may probably be exposed. As each presents itself ask yourself: Is there anything intolerable and insufferable in this? You will be ashamed to own it. And then recollect that it is neither the past nor the future that can oppress you, but always the present only. And the ills of the present will be much diminished if you restrict it within its own proper bounds, and take your soul to task if it cannot bear up even against this one thing.

37. Does Panthea or Pergamus now sit mourning at the tomb of Verus, or Chabrias or Diotimus at the tomb of Hadrian? Absurd! And if they were still mourning could their masters be sensible of it? Or if they were sensible of it, would it give them any pleasure? Or if they were pleased with it, could the mourners live for ever? Was it not fate that they should grow old men and women, and then die? What, then, would become of the illustrious dead when these faithful souls were gone? And all this toil for a vile body, naught but blood and corruption!

38. If you have keen sight, says the philosopher, use it in discretion and in wisdom.

39. In the constitution of the rational being I discern no virtue made to restrain justice; but I see continence made to restrain sensual pleasure.

40. Take away your opinion about the things that seem to give you pain, and you stand yourself upon the surest ground. What is that self?—It is reason.—I am not reason, you say.—So be it; then let not reason pain itself, but leave any part of you which suffers to its own opinions of the pain.

41. Obstruction of any sense is an evil for the animal nature; so is the obstruction of any of its impulses. There are other kinds of obstruction which are evil for the nature of plants. For the rational nature in like manner, therefore, obstruction of the understanding is evil. Apply all this to yourself. Do pain and pleasure affect you? Let the senses look to it. Does anything hinder your designs? If you have designed without the proper reservations, that in itself is an evil for you as a reasoning being. If you designed under the general reservation, you are neither hurt nor hindered. No man can hinder the proper work of the mind. Nor fire, nor sword, nor tyrant, nor calumny can reach it, nor any other thing, when it is become even as a sphere, complete and perfect within itself.

42. I have no right to vex myself who never yet willingly vexed any one.

43. Each man has his own pleasure. Mine lies in having my ruling part sound; without aversion to any man, or to any hap that may befall mankind. Yet let me look on all things with kindly eyes. Let me accept and use them all according to their worth.

44. See that you secure the benefit of the present time. They who pursue a fame which is to live after them reflect not that posterity will be men even as are those who vex them now, and that they too will be mortal. And afterwards, what shall signify to you the clatter of their voices, or the opinions they shall entertain about you?

45. Take me up and cast me where you will; I shall have my own divinity within me serene, that is, satisfied while its every state and action is according to the law of its proper constitution.

Is any event of such account that my soul should suffer for it or be the worse; that my soul should become abject and prostrate as a mean suppliant, or should be affrighted? Shall you find anything that is worth all this?

46. Nothing can befall a man which is not human fortune. Nothing can happen to an ox, to a vine, or to a stone which is not the natural destiny of their species. If, then, that alone can befall anything which is usual and natural, what cause is there for indignation? Universal Nature hath brought nothing upon you which you cannot bear.

47. When you are grieved about anything external it is not the thing itself which afflicts you, but your judgment about it. This judgment it is in your power to efface. If you are grieved about anything in your own disposition, who can prevent you from correcting your principles of life? If you are grieved because you do not set about some work which seems to you sound and virtuous, go about it effectually rather than grieve that it is undone.— But some superior force withstands.—Then grieve not, for the fault of the omission lies not in you.—But life is not worth living with this undone.—

Quit life then, in the same kindly spirit as though you had done it, and with goodwill even to those who withstand you.

48. Remember that the governing part becomes invincible when, collected into itself, it is satisfied in refusing to do what it would not, even when its resistance is unreasonable. What then will it be when, after due deliberation it has fixed its judgment according to reason? The soul, thus free from passions, is a strong fort; nor can a man find any stronger to which he can fly and become henceforth invincible. The man who has not discerned this is ignorant. He who has discerned and flies not thither is miserable.

49. Pronounce no more to yourself than what appearances directly declare. It is told you that so-and-so has spoken ill of you. This alone is told you, and not that you are hurt by it. I see my child is sick; this only I see. I do not see that he is in danger. Dwell thus upon first appearances; add nothing to them from within, and no harm befalls you: or rather add the recognition that all is part of the world's lot.

50. Is the gourd bitter? Put it from you. Are there thorns in the way? Walk aside. That is enough. Do not add, "Why were such things brought into the world?" The naturalist would laugh at you, just as would a carpenter or a shoemaker, if you began fault-finding because you saw shavings and parings from their work strewn about the workshop. These craftsmen have places where they can throw away this rubbish, but universal Nature has no such place outside her sphere. Yet the wonder of her art is that, having confined herself within certain bounds, she transforms into herself all things within her scope which seem to be corrupting, or waxing old and useless; and out of them she makes other new forms; so that she neither needs matter from without nor a place where to cast out her refuse. She is satisfied with her own space, her own material, and her own art.

51. Be not languid in action, nor confused in conversation, nor vague in your opinions. Let there be no sudden contractions or forth-sallyings of your soul. In your life be not over-hurried.

Men slay you, cut you to pieces, pursue you with curses. What has this to do with your soul remaining pure, prudent, temperate, and just? What if some one, standing by a clear sweet fountain, should reproach it? It would not cease to send forth its refreshing waters. Should he throw into it mud or dung, it will speedily scatter them and wash them away, and be in nowise stained thereby. How then shall you get this perpetual living fount within you? If you reserve yourself unto liberty every hour you live, in a spirit of calmness, simplicity, and modesty.

52. He who knows not what the Universe is knows not what is his place therein. He who knows not for what end it was created, knows not himself and knows not the world. He who is deficient in either of these parts of knowledge cannot even say for what end he himself was created. What sort of man then does he appear to you who pursues the applause or dreads the anger of those who know neither where nor what they are?

53. Do you wish to be praised by a man who curses himself thrice within an hour? Can you desire to please one who is not pleased with himself? Can he be pleased with himself who repents of almost everything he does?

54. No longer be content to breathe in harmony with the air which surrounds you; but set about feeling in sympathy with the intelligence which embraces all things. For the power of that intelligence is no less diffused, and no less pervasive for all who can draw it in, than is the virtue of the air for him who can breathe it.

55. There is no universal wickedness to hurt the world; and the particular wickedness of any individual hurts not another. It hurts himself alone, and even he has this gracious privilege that, as soon as he desires it, he may be free from it altogether.

56. To my will the will of another is as indifferent as his poor breath and flesh. And how much soever we were formed for the sake of each other, yet the governing part of each of us has its own proper power; otherwise the vice of another might become my own misery. God thought fit that this should not be; lest it should be in another's power to make me unhappy.

57. The sun seems to us diffused everywhere, pervasive of all things, yet never exhausted. This diffusion is a sort of extension, and hence the Greek word for rays is thought to be derived. You may observe the nature of a ray if you see it entering through some small hole into a darkened chamber. Its direction is straight; and it is reflected around when it falls upon any solid body, which shuts it off from the air beyond. There it stands and does not slip or fall. Now, such should be the flow and diffusion of the understanding; never exhausted, always extending; not violently or furiously dashing against the obstacles that meet it, nor falling aside, but resting there and illuminating whatever will receive it. That which will not transmit the light does but deprive itself of radiance.

58. He who dreads death dreads either the extinction of all sense or the experience of a new one. If all sense be extinguished, there can be no sense of evil. If a different sort of sense be acquired you become a different creature, and do not cease to live.

59. Men were created the one for the other. Teach them better then, or bear with them.

60. Mind moves in one way, and an arrow in another. The mind, when cautiously proceeding, or when casting round in deliberation about what to pursue, is nevertheless carried onward straight toward its proper mark.

61. Penetrate into the governing part of others; and also allow others to enter into your own.

END OF THE EIGHTH BOOK.

BOOK IX

1. He who does injustice commits impiety. For since universal Nature has formed the rational animals for one another; each to be useful to the other according to his merit, and never hurtful; he who transgresses this her will is clearly guilty of impiety against the most ancient and venerable of the Gods.

He who lies sins against the same divinity. For the nature of the whole is the nature of all things which exist; and things which exist are akin to all that has come to be. Nature, indeed, is called truth, and is the first cause of all truths. He, then, that lies willingly is guilty of impiety, in so far as by deceiving he works injury: and he also who lies unwillingly, in so far as he is out of tune with universal Nature, and in so far as he works disorder in the Universe by fighting against its design. He is at war with Nature who sets himself against the truth. He has neglected the means with which Nature furnished him, and cannot now distinguish false from true.

He, too, who pursues pleasure as good, and shuns pain as evil, is guilty of impiety. Such a one must needs frequently blame the common nature for unseemly awards of fortune to bad and to good men. For the bad often enjoy pleasures and possess the means to attain them, and the good often meet with pain and with what causes pain. Again, he who dreads pain must sometimes dread a thing which will make part of the world order, and this is impious. And he who pursues pleasure will not abstain from injustice, and this is clear impiety. In those things to which the common nature is indifferent (for she had not made both, were she not indifferent to either), he who would follow Nature ought, in this also, to be of like mind with her, and shew the like indifference. And whoever is not indifferent to pain and pleasure, life and death, glory and ignominy, all of which universal Nature uses indifferently, is clearly impious. By Nature using them indifferently, I mean that they befall indifferently all beings which exist, and ensue upon others in the great chain of consequence which began in the primal impulse of Providence. Providence, in pursuance of this impulse, and starting from a definite beginning, set about this fair structure of the universe when she had conceived the plan of all that was to be, and appointed the distinct powers which were to produce the several substances, changes, and successions.

2. It were the more desirable lot to depart from among men, unacquainted with falsehood, hypocrisy, luxury, or vanity. The next choice were to expire when cloyed with these vices. Have you then chosen rather to abide in evil; or has experience not yet persuaded you to fly from amidst the plague? For a corruption of the mind is far more a plague than any pestilential distemper or change in the surrounding air we breathe. The one is pestilence to animals as animals: but the other to men as men.

3. Despise not death; but receive it well content, as one of the things which Nature wills. For even as it is to be young, to be old, to grow up, to be full grown; even as it is to breed teeth, and beard, and to grow grey, to beget, to go with child, to be delivered; and to undergo all the effects of nature which life's seasons bring; such is it also to be dissolved in death. It becomes not therefore a man of wisdom to be careless, or impatient, or ostentatiously contemptuous about death; he should rather await its coming as one of the operations of nature. Even as now you await the season when the child of your wife's body shall issue into the light, await the hour when your soul shall fall out of these its teguments. If you wish for the common sort of comfort, here is a thought which goes to the heart. You will be completely resigned to death if you consider the things you are about to leave, and the morals of that confused crowd from which your soul is to be disengaged. It is far from right to be offended with them. It is even your duty to have a tender care for them, and to bear with them mildly. Yet remember that the parting, when it comes, will not be with men who think as you think. For the only thing which, if it might be, could hold you back and detain you in life, would be to live with those who had reached the same principles of life as you. But, as it is, you, seeing how great is the fatigue and toil arising from the jarring courses of those who live together, may cry: "Haste, death! lest I, too, should forget myself."

4. The sinner sins against himself. The wrong-doer wrongs himself by making himself evil.

5. Men are often unjust by omissions as well as by actions.

6. Be satisfied with your present opinion, if certain; with your present course of action, if social; with your present mood, if well pleased with all that comes upon you from without.

7. Wipe out impression; stay impulse; quench desire; and keep the governing part master of itself.

8. The soul distributed among the irrational animals is one. Rational beings, on the other hand, partake of one reasoning intelligence. Even so, there is one earth to all things earthy; and, for all of us who are endowed with sight and breath, there is one light by which to see, one air to breathe.

9. All things that share a common quality are strongly drawn to that which is of their own kind. The earthy tends towards the earth; fluids flow together, aerial bodies likewise; and naught but force prevents their confluence. Fire rises upward on account of the elemental fire; and it is so ready to join in kindling with all the fire that is here that any matter pretty dry is easily set on fire, because that which hinders its kindling is the weaker element in its composition. Thus also, then, whatever partakes of the common intellectual nature hastens in like manner, or even more markedly, towards that which is akin to it. For the more it excels other natures, the stronger is its tendency to mix with and adhere to its kind. Accordingly, among irrational creatures we find swarms of bees, herds of cattle, nurture of the young, and love, of a sort. For even in animals there is a soul; and in the more noble natures a mutual attraction is found to be at work, such as does not exist in plants, or stones, or wood. Among the rational animals, again, there are societies and friendships, families and assemblies; and, in war, treaties and truces. Among beings still more excellent, there subsists, though they be placed far asunder, a certain kind of union, as among the stars. Thus ascent in the scale can produce a sympathy even in things that are widely distant. But mark what happens among us. It is only intellectual beings who forget the social concern for one another, and the mutual tendency to union. Here alone the social confluence is not seen. Yet are they environed and held by it, though they strive to escape; and nature always prevails. Observe and you will see my meaning: for sooner may one find some earthy thing which joins with nothing earthy, than a man severed and separate from all men.

10. Man, God, and the Universe, all bear fruit; and each in their own season. Custom indeed has appropriated the expression to vines and the like; but that is nothing. Reason has its fruit both for all men and for itself, and produces just such other things as reason itself is.

11. If you can, teach men better. If not, remember that the virtue of charity was given you to be used in such a case. Nay, the Gods are patient with them, and even aid them in their pursuit of some things such as health, wealth, and glory, so gracious are they! You may be so too. Who hinders you?

12. Bear toil and pain, not as if wretched under it, nor as courting pity or admiration. Wish for one thing only; always to act or to refrain as social wisdom requires.

13. To-day I have escaped from all trouble; or rather I have cast out all trouble from me. For it was not without but within, in my own opinions.

14. All things are, in our experience, common; in their continuance but for a day; and in their matter sordid. All things now are as they were in the times of those we have buried.

15. Things stand without, by themselves, neither knowing or declaring aught to us concerning themselves. What is it then that pronounces upon them? The ruling part.

16. It is not in passive feeling, but in action, that the good and evil of the rational animal formed for society consists. Similarly his virtue or his vice lies not in feeling but in action.

17. To the stone thrown up it is no evil to fall; no good to rise.

18. Penetrate the souls of men, and you will see what judges you fear, and how they sit in judgment on themselves.

19. All things are in change. You yourself are under continual transmutation, and, in some sort, corruption. So is the whole universe.

20. Another's sin you must leave with himself.

21. The ceasing of any action, the extinction of any keen desire, or of any opinion, is as it were a death to them. This is no evil. Think again of the ages of your life; childhood, youth, manhood, old age. Each change of these was a death. Is there anything to dread here? Think now of your life as it was, first under your grandfather, then under your mother, then under your father; and, as you find there many other alterations, changes, and endings, ask yourself: Is there anything to dread here? Thus neither is there anything to dread in the cessation, ending, and change of your whole life.

22. Make swift appeal to your own ruling part, to that of the Universe, and to his who has offended you. To your own, that you may make it a mind disposed to justice; to that of the Universe, that you may remember of what you are a part; and to his, that you may know whether he has acted in ignorance or by design, and that you may also reflect that he is your kinsman.

23. You yourself are a part of a social system necessary to complete the whole. Accordingly, let your every action be a similar part of the social life. And if any action has not its reference, either immediate or distant, to the common good as its end, this action disorders your life and frustrates its unity. It is sedition like that of the man who, in a commonwealth, does all in his power to sever himself from the general harmony and concord.

24. Children's quarrels! Child's play! Poor spirits carrying about dead corpses! Such is our life. The 'Masque of the Dead' is intelligible by comparison.

25. Go to the quality of the cause; abstract it from the material, and contemplate it by itself. Determine then the time: how long, at furthest, this thing, of this peculiar quality, can naturally subsist.

26. You have endured innumerable sufferings by not being satisfied with your own ruling part when it does the things which it was formed to do. Enough then of that.

27. When another reproaches or hates you, or utters anything to that purpose; go to his soul; enter in there; and look what manner of man he is. You will see that you need not trouble yourself to make him think well or ill of you. Yet you should be kindly towards such men, for they are by nature your friends: and the Gods, too, aid them in all ways; by dreams, by oracles, and even in the things about which they are most eager.

28. The course of things in the world is ever the same; a continual rotation; up and down, from age to age. Either the Universal Mind exerts itself in every particular event, in which case you must accept what comes immediately from it: or it has exerted itself once and for all, and, as a result, all things go on for ever, in a necessary chain of consequence: or again atoms and indivisible particles are the origin of all things. In fine, if there be a God, all is well; and if there be only chance, you at least need not act by chance.

The earth will presently cover us all; and then this earth will itself be changed into other forms, and these again into others, and so on without end. And, if any one considers how swiftly those changes and transmutations roll on, like one wave upon another, he will despise all things mortal.

29. The universal cause is like a winter torrent. It sweeps all along with it. How very little worth are those poor creatures who pretend to understand affairs of state, and imagine they unite in themselves the statesman and the philosopher! The frothy fools! Do you, O man! that which Nature now requires of you. Set about it if you have the means; and look not around you to see if any be taking notice, neither hope to realize Plato's Republic. Be satisfied if the smallest thing go well. Consider even such an event as no small matter. For who can change the opinions of men? And without change of opinion what is their state but a slavery, under which they groan, while they pretend to obey? Come now; speak of Alexander, Philip, and Demetrius of Phalerum. They know best whether they understood what the common nature required of them, and whether they trained themselves accordingly. But, if they designed only to play the tragic hero, no one has condemned me to do the like. The work of philosophy is simple and modest. Lead me not astray in pursuit of a vainglorious stateliness.

30. Look down, as from some eminence, upon the innumerable herds, the countless solemn festivals, the voyaging of every sort, in tempests and in calms; the different states of those who come into life, enter upon life's associations, and leave it in the end. Consider, too, the life which others have lived formerly, the life they will live after you, and the life that barbarous peoples are now living. How many of these know not even your name; how many will quickly forget it; how many are there who perhaps praise you now, but will shortly blame you. Reflect, then, that neither is surviving fame a thing of value; nor present glory; nor anything at all.

31. Let nothing due to a cause outside yourself disturb your calm. In the workings of the active principle within you let there be justice: that is a bent of will and a course of action which have social good as their one end, and so are suited to your nature.

32. You can suppress many of the superfluous troubles which beset you, for they lie wholly in your own opinion. By this you will give ample room and ease to your life. You may compass this end by comprehending the whole Universe in your judgment; by contemplating eternity; and by reflecting on the swift changes of individual things, thinking how short is the time from their birth to their dissolution, how immense the space of ages before that birth, how equally infinite the eternity which shall succeed that dissolution.

33. All things that you see will quickly perish; and those who behold them perishing are very soon themselves to die. And he who dies oldest will be in like case with him who dies before his time.

34. What manner of souls have these men? What is the end of their striving; and on what accounts do they love and honour? Imagine their souls naked before you. When they fancy that their censures hurt, or their praises profit us, how great is their self-conceit!

35. Loss is naught but change; in change is the joy of universal Nature, and by her all things are ordered well. From the beginning of ages they have been shaped alike, and to all eternity they will be the same. How then can you say that all things have been, and ever will be evil; that among so many Gods there has been found no power to rectify; but that the Universe is condemned to endure the burden of never-ending ill?

36. How corrupt is the material substance of every thing, water, dust, bones, and foulness! Again; marble is but the concrete humour of the earth, gold and silver its heavy dregs. Our garments are but hair, the purple dye blood. All else is of a like nature. Breath, too, is just the same, ever changing from this to that.

37. Enough of this wretched life: enough of repining and apish trifling. Why are you disturbed? Are any of these troubles new? What excites you so? Is it the cause?

Then view it well. Is it the matter? View it also well. Besides these there is nothing. Wherefore at last act with more simplicity and goodness towards the Gods. Whether you look on this spectacle for a hundred years or for three it is the same.

38. If he has done wrong, the evil is with him: and perhaps, too, he has not done wrong.

39. Either all things proceed from one source of intelligence and come together in one body, in which case the part must not complain of what comes about for the benefit of the whole; or all is atoms, and there is nothing else but confused mixture and dissipation. Why then are you disturbed? Say to your soul: "Thou art dead: thou art rotten: thou hast turned beast, joined the herd, and dost feed along with them."

40. Either the Gods have power or they have none. If they have no power, why do you pray? If they have power, why do you not choose to pray to them for power neither to fear, nor to desire, nor to be grieved over any of these external things, rather than for their presence or their absence?

Surely, if the Gods can aid man at all, they can aid him in this. But perhaps you will say "the Gods have put this in my own power." Then is it not better to use that which is in your own power and preserve your liberty, than to set your heart on what is beyond your power and become an abject slave? And who has told you that the Gods aid us not in these things also which are in our power? Begin to pray about them and you will see. One man prays: "May I possess that woman!" Do you pray: "May I have no wish to possess her!" Another prays: "May I be delivered from so and so!" Pray you: "May I not need to be delivered from him!" A third cries: "May I not lose my child!" Let your prayer be: "May I not fear to lose him!" In fine, turn your prayers this way, and observe what comes of it.

41. Epicurus says: "In my sickness my conversations were not about the diseases of this poor body; nor did I speak of any such things to those who came to me. I continued to discourse as before on the principles of natural Philosophy, and was chiefly intent on the problem of how the mind, though it partakes in the violent commotions of the flesh, might remain undisturbed and keep guard on its own proper excellence. I permitted not the physicians," he continues, "to magnify their office, and vaunt themselves as if they were doing-something of great moment, but my life continued pleasant and happy." What he did then, in sickness, do you also if ye fall ill, or suffer any other misfortune. Never to depart from your philosophy whatever befalls you, never to join in the folly of the vulgar and the ignorant, is a maxim common to all the schools. Give your mind only to the business now in hand and to the means whereby it is to be accomplished.

42. When you are offended by the shamelessness of any man, straightway ask yourself: Can the world exist without shameless men? It cannot. Therefore do not demand what is impossible. Your enemy also is one of these shameless people who must needs be in the universe. Have the same question also at hand when you are shocked at craft, or perfidy, or any other sin. For while you remember that it is impossible that the class should not exist, you will be more charitable to each particular individual. It is useful also to have this reflection ready: What virtue has nature given to man wherewith to combat this fault? Against unreason she has given meekness as an antidote; against another weakness another power. You are also at full liberty to set right one who has wandered; now every wrong-doer is missing his proper aim and has gone astray. And then, in what are you injured? You will find that none of those at whom you are exasperated have done anything whereby your intellectual part was like to be the worse. Now anything which can really harm or hurt you has its subsistence there, and there alone. And wherein is it strange or evil that the man untaught acts after his kind? Look if you ought not rather to blame yourself for not having laid your account with his being guilty of such faults. Your reason gave you the means to conclude that it was probable that he would do this wrong; you forgot, and yet wonder that he has done it. But above all, when you are blaming any one for faithlessness or ingratitude, turn to yourself. The fault lies manifestly with you, if you trusted that a man of such a disposition could keep faith; or if, when you granted the favour, you did not grant it without ulterior views, and on the principle that the complete and immediate reward of your action lay in the doing of it. What would you more, when you have done a man a kindness? Is it not enough for you that you have acted in this according to your nature? Do you ask a reward for it? It is as if the eye were to ask a reward for seeing, or the feet for walking. For just as these parts are formed for a certain purpose, which when they fulfil according to their proper structure, they attain their proper end; so man, formed by nature to do kindness to his fellows, whenever he acts kindly, or in any other way works for the common good, has fulfilled the purpose of his creation, and has possession of what is his own.

END OF THE NINTH BOOK.

BOOK X

1. Wilt thou ever, O my soul, be good and single, and one, and naked, more open to view than the body which surrounds thee? Wilt thou ever taste of the loving and satisfied temper? Wilt thou ever be full and without wants, setting thy heart on nothing, animate or inanimate, for the enjoyment of pleasure; not desiring time for longer enjoyment; nor place, nor country, nor fine climate, nor congenial company? Wilt thou be satisfied with thy present state, and well pleased with every present circumstance? Wilt thou persuade thyself that all things are thine; that all is well with thee; that all comes to thee from the Gods; and that what is best for thee is what they are pleased to give, now and henceforth, for the preservation of that perfected being, which is good, just, and beautiful; which generates, combines, embraces, and includes all fleeting things that dissolve to bring forth others like themselves? Wilt thou never be able to live a fellow citizen with Gods and men, approving them and by them approved?

2. In so far as you are governed by nature only, observe carefully what nature demands; then do that freely, if thereby your nature as a living being be not made worse. Next you must consider what the nature of a living being demands, and allow yourself everything of this kind by which your nature as a rational being is not made worse. Now it is plain that what is rational is also social. Therefore follow these rules and trouble no further.

3. Whatever happens, Nature has either formed you able to bear it or unable. If able, then bear it as Nature has made you able, and fret not. If unable, yet do not fret, for when the trial has consumed you it too will pass away. Remember, however, that Nature has made you able to bear whatever it is in the power of your own opinion to make endurable or tolerable, if only you conceive it profitable or fit to be borne.

4. If a man is going wrong, instruct him kindly, and shew him his mistake. If you are unable to do this, blame yourself or none.

5. Whatever happens to you was prearranged for you from all eternity; and the concatenation of causes had from eternity interwoven your existence with this contingency.

6. Whether all be atoms, or there be a universal Law of Nature, let it be laid down first that I am a part of the whole which is governed by Nature; secondly, that I am associated with other parts like myself. Mindful of this, since I am a part, I shall not be dissatisfied with anything appointed me by the whole. For nothing is hurtful to the part which is profitable to the whole, since the whole contains nothing unprofitable to itself. All natural systems have this law in common, and the system of the Universe has another law besides; namely that it cannot be forced by any external cause to produce anything hurtful to itself. If therefore I remember that I am part of such a whole, I shall be satisfied with all that flows therefrom. And, inasmuch as I am associated with parts like myself, I will do nothing unsocial; but rather draw to my kind, turn my every endeavour to the public good, and shun the contrary. In such a course my life must needs run well, just as you would hold that the life of a citizen runs well when he passes on from one public-spirited action to another, and throws himself heartily into every task appointed him by the State.

7. The parts of the whole, I mean the parts which are contained in the Universe, must necessarily perish; "perish," let us say, meaning change. Now, if it be a necessary evil for the parts to perish, it could not be well for the whole that its parts should tend to change and be constructed to perish in various ways. Did Nature then set out to injure her own constituent parts, making them so that they are liable to evil and of necessity fall into it; or did it escape her notice that this comes to pass? Both suppositions are incredible. And if, dropping the notion of Nature, one were merely to put it that things are constituted so, then how ridiculous at the same time to say that the parts of the Universe are constituted so as to change, and also to wonder and fret at change or dissolution, as if it were something against the course of Nature; especially as everything is dissolved into the elements out of which it arose. For there is either a scattering of the elements of which a thing was constructed, or a conversion of these, of the solid into earth, of the spiritual into air. So that these constituents are resumed into the system of the Universe, which either undergoes periodical conflagration, or is renewed by never-ending changes. And do not imagine that you had all your earthy and aerial matter from your birth. For the whole of this was an accession of yesterday or the day before, from your food and from the air you breathed. It is this accession which changes, and not what your mother bore. And granting that this recent accession may incline you more to what is individual in your constitution; yet, I think, it alters nothing of what has just been said.

8. Having taken to yourself these titles: good, modest, true, prudent, even-tempered and magnanimous, look to it that you change them not; and, if you should come to lose them, seek them straightway again. And remember that prudence means for you reasoned observation of all things, and careful attention; even temper, cheerful acceptance of the lot appointed by universal Nature; magnanimity, the exaltation of the thinking part above any pleasant or painful commotions of the flesh, above vain-glory, above death and all such things. If you steadfastly maintain yourself in these titles, with no hankering after hearing them given to you by others, you will be a new man, and a new life will open for you. For to continue as you have been till now, in the same life of distraction and defilement, would mark you as a man devoid of sense, who clings to life like the half-eaten beast-fighters, who, though covered with wounds and gore, do yet appeal to be reserved until tomorrow, to be cast again in their wretchedness to the claws and fangs that lacerated them before. Take your stand then on these few titles; and if you are able to abide in them, abide, as one removed to the Islands of the Blest. But if you perceive that you are falling away, and cannot prevail; have the courage to retire into some corner where you may hope to prevail, or else depart from life altogether, not in anger but in all simplicity, freedom, and modesty, having done at least one thing in life well, by so leaving it. Now it will greatly help you to be mindful of your titles, if you recollect that the Gods desire not adulation, but that reasoning beings should grow in likeness to themselves; and further that a fig tree is set to bear figs, a dog to hunt, a bee to gather honey, and a man to do a man's work.

9. Mimes, war, panic, sloth, servility, will wipe out the sacred maxims which you have gathered by observing Nature and stored in your mind. You ought to look and act in every case so that not only shall the task before you be accomplished, but also your theoretic faculty exercised, and the self-confidence which springs from special knowledge preserved without ostentation or affected concealment. Will you ever attain to simplicity; to dignity; to a perfect discrimination in every case as to what a thing really is, what its true place in the Universe, what the time it may endure, what its composition, to whom it may belong, and who can give and take it away?

10. The spider exults when he has captured a fly; one man because he has taken a little hare, another because he has netted an anchovy, another because he has hunted down a wild boar or a bear; and another because he has conquered the Sarmatians. But are they not brigands all, if you look to their principles.

11. Acquire a method of perceiving how all things change into one another. Pursue this branch of Philosophy and continually exercise yourself therein. There is nothing so proper as this for cultivating greatness of mind. He who does so has already put off the body; and, having realized how soon he must depart from among men and leave all earthly things behind him, he resigns himself entirely to justice in all his own actions, and to the law of the Universe in everything else which happens. As for what any one may say or think of him or do against him, he gives it not a thought, but contents himself with these two things: to do justly what he has in hand, and to love the lot appointed for him. Such a man has thrown off all hurry and bustle; and has no other will but this, to keep the straight path according to the law, and to follow God whose path is ever straight.

12. What need for suspicion when it is open for you to consider what ought to be done? If you see your way, proceed in it calmly, inflexibly. If you do not see it, pause and consult the best advisers. If any other obstacle arise, proceed with prudent caution, according to the means you have;

keeping always close to what appears just. That is the best to which you can attain: and failure in that is the only proper miscarriage. He who in everything follows reason is always at leisure, yet ever ready for action, always cheerful, yet composed.

13. As soon as you awake ask yourself: Will it be of consequence to you if what is just and good be done by some other man? It will not. Have you forgotten what manner of men in bed and at table are those who make such display in praise and blame of others; what they do, what they shun and what they pursue; how they steal and how they rob, not with hands and feet but with their most precious part, whereby, if a man will, he may gain faith, modesty, truth, law, a good directing spirit?

14. To Nature, which gives and again resumes all things, the well-instructed, modest man will say: "Give what thou wilt; take again what thou wilt." And this he says, not with ostentation, but out of pure obedience and good will to Nature.

15. What remains to you of this life is little. Live as on a mountain. For it makes no difference whether we live here or there, provided we live like citizens everywhere in the world. Let men see and know you as a man indeed, living according to Nature. If they cannot endure you, let them slay you. It is better so than to live as they live.

16. Discourse no more of what a good man should be; but be one.

17. Constantly imagine all time and all existence; and think that every individual thing is in substance a fig seed, and in time the turn of an auger.

18. Consider each of the things around you as already dissolving, in a state of change, and as it were corrupting and being dissipated, or as, one and all, formed by Nature to die.

19. What sort of men are they when they are eating, sleeping, procreating, easing nature, and the like? Then see them lording it over their fellows, puffed up with pride, angry, or issuing judgments from on high! To how many were they slaves but lately, and why! And in what case will they shortly be?

20. That is for the advantage of every man which is brought by universal Nature; and for his advantage at the very time at which she brings it.

21. "Earth loves the rain;" "and the majestic Ether loves." The Universe loves to bring about whatever is coming to be. I then will say to the Universe: "What thou lovest I love." Is it not a common saying that, "so-and-so loves to happen?"

22. Either you are living here your accustomed life; or you are going abroad, and that at your own will: or you are dying, and your public office is discharged. Now, besides these there is nothing. Be therefore of good courage.

23. Keep this ever clear before you: that a country retreat is just like any other place. All things here go the same as on a mountain top, or on the sea beach, or where you will. You may always find that life of the wise man who, in Platonic phrase, "makes the city wall serve him for a shepherd's fold on the mountains."

24. What is my soul to me? What am I making of it, and to what purpose am I now using it? Is it void of understanding? Is it loosened and rent from the great community? Is it glued to, and mingled with, the flesh so as to follow each fleshly motion?

25. Whoever flies from his master is a runaway. Our master is the law, and the law-breaker is a runaway; and so is he also who through grief, or anger, or fear will not acquiesce in something that has happened, is happening, or will happen, in the course of things predestined by the all-ruling power which is the law, laying down for every man what is proper for him. He then who is afraid or grieved or angry, is a runaway.

26. He who has cast seed into the womb departs; another cause takes and works upon it and completes the child. How wonderful the result from such a beginning! The child, again, takes food down its throat; another cause takes and transforms it into sensation, motion, in a word into life and strength and other things, how many and surprising! Consider then these things happening in such hidden ways, and view the power which produces them just as we perceive the gravitation and levitation of bodies; not indeed with our eyes, yet none the less clearly.

27. Continually reflect that all that is happening now happened exactly in the same way before; and reflect that the like will happen again. Place before your eyes all that you have ever known from your own experience or from ancient history; dramas and scenes, all similar; such as the whole court of Hadrianus, the whole court of Antoninus, the whole court of Philip, of Alexander, of Croesus. All these were similar, only the actors different.

28. Imagine every one who is grieved or storms about anything whatever, to be like the pig in a sacrifice, which kicks and screams under the knife. Such, too, is he who, on his couch, deplores in silence, by himself, that we are all tied to our fate. Reflect also that only to a rational being is it given to submit to what happens willingly; the bare submission is a necessity upon all.

29. Look attentively on each particular thing you do, and ask yourself if death be a terror because it deprives you of this.

30. When you are offended at any one's fault, turn at once to yourself and consider of what similar fault you yourself are guilty; such as esteeming for good things, money, pleasure, a little glory, or the like. By fixing your attention on this you will speedily forget your anger, especially if it occur to you that he acts under compulsion and cannot do otherwise; else, if it be in your power, relieve him from the compulsion.

31. When you have seen Satyrio the Socratic, think of Eutyches or Hymen; when you have seen Euphrates, think of Eutychio or Silvanus. When Alciphron comes before you, think of Tropaeophorus; and when Xenophon think of Crito or Severus. When you look upon yourself think of any of the Caesars, and with every man likewise. Then let this occur to you: Where, now, are these? Nowhere; or who can tell? For thus you will see all human things to be smoke and nothingness; especially if you call to mind that what has once been changed will never exist again through all the infinity of time. Why then this concern? And why does it not suffice you to live out your short span in well ordered wise? What material, what a subject for Philosophy you are shunning! For what are all earthly things but exercises for the rational power, when it has viewed all things that occur in life accurately and in their natural order? Abide then until you have assimilated all these things, as a strong stomach assimilates every variety of food, as a bright fire turns whatever you throw upon it into flame and radiance.

32. Let no man have it in his power to say with truth of you that you are not a man of simplicity, candour, and goodness. But let him prove to be mistaken who holds any such opinion of you. This is quite in your power; for who shall hinder you from being good and single-hearted? Only do you determine to live no longer if you cannot be such a man; for neither does reason require, in that case, that you should.

33. In the present matter what is the soundest that can be done or said? For, whatever that may be, you are at liberty to do or say it. Make no excuses as if hindered. You will never cease from groaning until your disposition is such that what luxury is to men of pleasure, that to you is doing what is suitable to the constitution of man on every occasion that is thrown or falls in your way. You should regard as enjoyment everything which you are at liberty to do in accordance with your own proper nature; and this liberty you have everywhere. Now to the cylinder it is not given to move everywhere with its proper motion; nor to water, nor to fire, nor to any other thing that is governed by a natural law only, or by a soul irrational; for there are many circumstances which constrain and stop them. But intelligent reason can pursue through every obstacle the course for which it was created, and which it wills to follow. Set before your eyes this ease with which reason makes its way through all obstacles, as fire goes upwards, a stone downwards, or a cylinder down a slope, and seek for nothing further. The rest of man's difficulties are merely of the body, the lifeless part of him; or else they are such as cannot crush, or in any way injure him save through opinion, or the surrender of reason itself: otherwise he who suffered by them would himself straightway become evil. In the case of all other organisms, when mishap befalls, the sufferer is thereby rendered worse. But in this respect it may be said that a man becomes better and more praiseworthy by rightly using his circumstances. In fine, remember that nothing which hurts not the city hurts the man who is by nature a citizen; nor does that hurt the city which hurts not the law. Now, none of the things called misfortunes can hurt the law. Accordingly, what hurts not the law can hurt neither city nor citizen.

34. To the man who is penetrated with true principles, the shortest, the most common hint is a sufficient memorial to keep him free of sorrow and fear. Such as:—

> *Some leaves the winds blow down: the fruitful wood*
> *Breeds more meanwhile, which in springtide appear.*
> *Of men thus ends one race, while one is born.*

Your children are leaves; leaves, too, the creatures who confidently cry aloud and deal out eulogy, or, it may be, curses; or who carp and jeer in secret. Leaves, likewise, are they who transmit our fame to posterity. All these "in springtide appear;" then the wind shakes them down, and the forest grows more to take their places. Shortness of life is common to all things, yet you shun and pursue them, as though they were to have no ending. But a little and you will fall asleep; and anon others shall mourn for him who carried your bier.

35. The healthy eye ought to look on everything visible, and not to say, "I want green," like an eye that is diseased. Sound hearing or sense of smell ought to be ready for all that can be heard or smelt; and the healthy stomach should be equally disposed for all sorts of food, as a mill for all that it was built to grind. So also the healthy mind should be ready for all things that happen. That mind which says, "Let my children be spared, and let men applaud my every action," is as an eye which begs for green, or as teeth which require soft food.

36. There is no man so happily fated but that when he is dying some bystander will rejoice at the doom which is coming upon him. Were he a virtuous and wise man; will not some one at the last say within himself: "At last I shall breathe freely, unoppressed by this pedagogue. He was not indeed hard on any of us; but I always felt that he tacitly condemned us"? This they would say of a good man. But, in my own case, how many more reasons are there why a multitude would rejoice to be rid of me? You will reflect on this when dying, and depart with the less regret when you consider: "I am leaving a life from which my very partners, for whom I toiled, and prayed, and planned, are wishing me to begone; hoping, it may be, to gain some additional advantage from my departure." Why then should one strive for a longer sojourn here? Yet let not your parting with them be less pleasant on this account. Preserve your own character, remain to them friendly, benevolent, gracious. On the other hand, depart from your fellow-men, not as if torn away; but let your going be like that of one who dies an easy death, whose soul is gently released from the body. Nature knit and cemented you to your fellows, but now she parts you from them. I part, then, as from relations, not reluctant, but unconstrained. For death, too, is a thing accordant with nature.

37. Accustom yourself as much as possible, when any one takes any action, to consider only: To what end is he working? But begin at home; and examine yourself first of all.

38. Remember that the mover of the puppet strings is the hidden principle within. It is that which is eloquence; that which is life; that, if I may say so, which is the man. Never, in your imagination, confound that principle with the surrounding earthen vessel and the little organs that are kneaded on to it. Excepting that they grow upon us, they are like the carpenter's axe; since, without the moving and restraining principle, none of these parts in itself is of any greater service than the shuttle to the weaver, the pen to the writer, or the whip to the charioteer.

END OF THE TENTH BOOK.

BOOK XI

1. These are the characteristics of the rational soul: It beholds itself; it regulates itself in every part; it fashions itself as it wills; the fruit it bears itself enjoys, whereas the products of plants and of the lower animals are enjoyed by others. It reaches its individual end, wheresoever the close of life may overtake it. In a dance or an actor's part any interruption spoils the completeness of the whole action. Not so with the rational soul. At whatever point in its action, or wheresoever it is overtaken by death, it makes its part complete and all-sufficient; so that it can say, "I have received what is mine." Also it ranges through the whole universe, and the void around it, and discerns its plan. It stretches forth into limitless eternity, and grasps the periodical regeneration of all things, seeing and comprehending that those who come after us will see nothing new, and that those that went before saw no more than we have seen. Nay, a man of forty, of any tolerable understanding, has, because of the uniformity of things, seen, in a manner, all that has been or will be. Characteristic of the rational soul also are:—Love to all around us, truth, modesty; and respect for itself above all other things, which is characteristic also of the general law. Thus there is no discordance between right reason and the reason of justice.

2. You will think little of a pleasing song, a dance, or a gymnastic display, if you analyse the melody into its separate notes, and ask yourself regarding each, "Does this impress me?" You will blush to own it; and so also if you analyse the dance into its single motions and postures, and if you similarly treat the gymnastic display. In general then, except as regards virtue and virtuous action, remember to recur to the constituent parts of things, and by dissecting to despise them; and transfer this practice to life as a whole.

3. How happy is the soul that stands ready to part from the body when it must, and either to be extinguished or to be scattered, or to survive! But let this readiness arise from individual judgment, not from mere obstinacy, as with the Christians, but deliberately, with dignity, and with no affected air of tragedy; so that others may be led to a like disposition.

4. Have I done anything for the common good? Is not this itself my advantage? Let this thought be ever with you, and desist not.

5. What is your art? Well doing. And how else can this come than from sound general principles regarding Nature as a whole, and the constitution of man in particular?

6. First of all, tragedy was introduced to remind us that certain events happen, and are fated to happen as they do; and to teach us that what entertains us on the stage should not grieve us on the greater stage of the world. You see that such things must be accomplished; and that even they bore them who cried aloud, O Cithaeron! Our dramatic poets have said some excellent things; especially the following:—

> *Me and my children, if the Gods neglect,*
> *It is for some good reason*—and again,
> *Vain is all anger at external things;* and, *To reap our life like ears of ripened corn*—

and the like.

And after tragedy came the Old Comedy, using a schoolmaster's freedom of speech, and employing plain language with great profit to inculcate the duty of humility. To this end Diogenes used a method much the same. Next consider the nature of the Middle Comedy; and lastly for what purpose the New was introduced, which gradually degenerated into the mere ingenuity of artificial mimicry. It is well known that some useful things were said by the New Comic Writers; but what useful end had they in view in all their accumulated poetry and playmaking?

7. How manifest it is that no other course of life was more adapted to the practice of philosophy than that which now is yours.

8. A branch cut off from its adjacent branch must necessarily be severed from the whole tree. Even so a man, parted from any fellow-man, has fallen away from the whole social community. Now a branch is cut off by some external agency; but a man by his own action separates himself from his neighbour—by hatred and aversion, unaware that he has thus torn himself away from the universal polity. Yet there is always given us the good gift of Zeus, who founded the great community, whereby it is in our power to be reingrafted on our kind, and to become once more, natural parts completing the whole. Yet the frequent happening of such separations, makes the reunion and restoration of the separated member more and more difficult. And in general a branch which has grown from the first upon a tree, and remained a living part of it, is not like one which has been cut and reingrafted; as the gardeners would say, they are of the same growth but of different persuasion.

9. As those who oppose you in the path of right reason have no power to divert you from sane action, so let them not turn you away from amenity towards themselves. Be watchful alike to persist in stable judgment and action, and in meekness towards those who would hinder or otherwise molest you. It is equally weak to grow angry with them or to desist from action and submit to defeat. Both are equally deserters— he who runs away, and he who refuses to stand by friend and kinsman.

10. Nature cannot be inferior to Art. The Arts are but imitations of Nature. If this be so, that Nature which is the most perfect and comprehensive of all cannot be inferior to the best artistic skill. Now all Arts use inferior material for higher purposes; so also then does universal Nature. Hence the origin of justice, from which again the other virtues spring. Justice cannot be preserved if we are solicitous about things indifferent, if we are easily deceived, rash, and changeable.

11. If those things, the pursuit and avoidance of which trouble you, come not to you; but, as it happens, you go to them; then let your judgment be at peace concerning them, they will remain motionless, and you will no more be seen pursuing or avoiding them.

12. The sphere of the soul attains to perfect shape when it neither expands to what is without, nor contracts upon what is within; neither wrinkles nor collapses, but shines with a radiance whereby it discerns the truth of all things, both without itself and within.

13. Does any man contemn me? Let him look to that. And let me look to it that I be found doing or saying nothing worthy of his contempt. Does any one hate me? That is his affair. I shall be kind and good-natured to every one, and ready to shew his mistake to him that hates me; not in order to upbraid him, or to make a show of my patience, but from genuine goodness, like Phocion, if he indeed was sincere. Your inward character should be such that the Gods may see you neither angry nor repining at anything. What evil is it for you now to act according to your nature, and to accept now what is seasonable to the nature of the Universe; you, a man appointed to do some service for the common good?

14. Although they despise, yet they flatter one another. Although they desire to overtop, yet they cringe to one another.

15. How rotten and insincere is his profession who says, "I mean to deal straightforwardly with you." What are you doing, man? There is no need for such a preface. It will appear of itself. Such a profession should be written clearly on your forehead. A man's character should shine forth clearly from his eyes; as the beloved sees that he is so in the glances of those that love him. The straightforward, good man should be like one of rank odour who can be recognised by the passer by as soon as he approaches, whether he will or no. The ostentation of straightforwardness is the knife under the cloak. Nothing is baser than wolf-friendship. Shun it above all things. The good, straightforward, kindly man bears all these qualities in his eyes, and is not to be mistaken.

16. To live the best life is within the power of the soul, if it be indifferent to indifferent things. And it will be indifferent if it looks on all such things, severally and wholly, with discrimination; mindful that not one of them can impose upon us an opinion concerning itself, or can come of itself to us. Things stand motionless without; and it is we that form opinions about them within, and, as it were, write these opinions upon our hearts. We may avoid so writing them; or, if one has crept in unawares, we may instantly blot it out. 'Tis but for a short time that we shall need this vigilance, and then life will cease. For the rest, why should we hold this to be difficult? If it be according to Nature, rejoice in it, and it will become easy for you. If it be contrary to Nature, search out what suits your nature, and follow it diligently, even though it be attended with no glory; for every man will be forgiven for seeking his own proper good.

17. Consider whence each thing came, of what it was compounded, into what it will be changed, how it will be with it when changed, and that it will suffer no evil.

18. As to those who offend me, let me consider:— *First*, how I am related to mankind; that we are formed, the one for the other; and that, in another respect, I was set over them as the ram over the flock, and the bull over the herd. Consider yet more deeply, thus:—There is either an empire of atoms, or an intelligent Nature governing the whole. If the latter, the inferior beings are created for the superior, and the superior for each other.

Secondly: Consider what manner of men they are at table, in bed, or elsewhere; and especially by what principles they hold themselves bound, and with what arrogance they entertain them.

Thirdly: If they act rightly, we ought not to take it amiss; and, if not rightly, manifestly they do so without intention and in ignorance. For no soul is willingly deprived of truth, or of the faculty of treating every man as he deserves. Accordingly men are grieved to be called unjust, ungrateful, greedy, and, in short, sinners against their neighbours.

Fourthly: You yourself do often sin, and are no better than another. And, if you abstain from certain sins, still you have the disposition to commit them, even if through cowardice, fear for your character, or other meanness, you hold back.

Fifthly: You cannot even be perfectly sure that wrong has been done, for many things admit of justification. And, generally speaking, a man must have learned much before he can pronounce surely upon the conduct of others.

Sixthly: When you are vexed or worried overmuch, remember that man's life is but for a moment, and that in a little we shall all be laid to rest.

Seventhly: It is not the acts of others that disturb us. Their actions reside in their own souls. Our own opinions alone disturb us. Away with them then; will that you entertain no thought of calamity befallen you, and the anger is gone. But how remove them? By reasoning that there is no dishonour; for, if you hold not that dishonour alone is evil, verily you must fall into many crimes, you may become a robber, or any sort of villain.

Eighthly: How much worse evils we suffer from anger and grief about certain things than from the things themselves about which these passions arise.

Ninthly: Meekness is invincible if it be genuine, without simper or hypocrisy. For what can the most insolent of men do to you, if you persist in civility towards him; and, if occasion offers, admonish him gently and deliberately, shew him the better way at the very moment that he is endeavouring to harm you? "Nay, my son; we were born for something better. No hurt can come to me; it is yourself you hurt, my son." And point out to him delicately, and as a general principle, how the matter stands; that bees and other gregarious animals do not act like him. But this must be done without irony or reproach, rather with loving-kindness and no bitterness of spirit; not as though you were reading him a lesson, or seeking admiration from any bystander, but as if you designed your remarks for him alone, though others may be present.

Remember these nine precepts as gifts received from the Muses; and begin now to be human for the rest of your life. Beware equally of being angry with men and of flattering them. Both are unsocial and lead to mischief. In all anger recollect that wrath is not becoming to a man; but that meekness and gentleness, as they are more human, are also more manly. Strength and nerves and courage are the portion of the meek and gentle man; and not of the irascible and impatient. For the nearer a man attains to freedom from passion, the nearer he comes to strength. A weak man in grief is like a weak man in anger. Both are hurt, and both give way.

If you want a tenth gift, from the Leader of the Muses, take this:— To expect the wicked not to sin is madness. It is to expect an impossibility. But to allow them to injure others, and to forbid them to injure you, is foolish and tyrannical.

19. There are four states of the soul against which you must continually and especially be upon your guard; and which, when detected, should be effaced, by remarking thus of each. "This thought is unnecessary. This tends to social dissolution. You could not say this from your heart; and to speak otherwise than from the heart you must regard as the most absurd conduct." And, fourthly, whatever causes self-reproach is an overpowering or subjection of the diviner part within you to the less honourable and mortal part, the body, and to its grosser tendencies.

20. The serial and igneous parts of which you are compounded, although they naturally tend upwards, nevertheless obey the general law of the Universe, and are retained here in composition. The earthy and humid parts of you, though they naturally tend downwards, are nevertheless supported and remain where they are, although not in their natural situation. Thus the elements, wheresoever placed by the superior power, obey the whole; waiting till the signal shall sound again for their dissolution. Is it not grievous that the intellectual part alone should be disobedient, and fret at its function? Yet is no violence done to it, nothing imposed contrary to its nature. Still it is impatient, and tends to opposition. For all its tendencies towards injustice, debauchery, wrath, sorrows, and fears are so many departures from Nature. And, when the soul frets at any particular event, it is deserting its appointed station. It is formed for holiness and piety toward God, no less than for justice. These last are branches of social goodness even more venerable than the practice of justice.

21. He whose aim in life is not always one and the same cannot himself be one and the same through his whole life. But singleness of aim is not sufficient, unless you consider also what that aim ought to be. For, as there is not agreement of opinion regarding all those things which are reckoned good by the majority, but only as regards some of them such as are of public utility; so your aim should be social and political. For he alone who directs all his personal aims to such an end can reach a uniform course of conduct, and thus be ever the same man.

22. Remember the country mouse and the town mouse; and how the latter feared and trembled.

23. Socrates called the maxims of the vulgar hobgoblins, bogies to frighten children.

24. The Spartans at their public shows set seats for strangers in the shade, but sat themselves where they found room.

25. Socrates made this excuse for not going to Perdiccas upon his invitation: "Lest I should come to the worst of all ends, by receiving favours which I could not return."

26. In the writings of the Ephesians there is a precept, frequently to call to remembrance some of those who cultivated virtue of old.

27. The Pythagoreans recommended that we should look at the heavens in the morning, to put us in mind of beings that go on doing their proper work uniformly and continuously; and of their order, purity and naked simplicity; for there is no veil upon a star.

28. Think of Socrates clad in a skin, when Xanthippe had taken his cloak and gone out; and what he said to his friends, who were ashamed, and would have left him when they saw him dressed in such an extraordinary fashion.

29. In writing and reading you must be led before you can lead. Much more is this so in life.

30. *Yourself a slave, your speech cannot be free.*

31. *And my heart laughed within me.*

32. *Virtue herself they blame with harshest words.*

33. To look for figs in winter is madness; and so it is to long for a child that may no longer be yours.

34. Epictetus said that, when you kiss your child, you should whisper within yourself: "To-morrow perhaps he may die." "Ill-omened words!"

say you. "The words have no evil omen," says he, "but simply indicate an act of Nature. Is it of evil omen to say the corn is reaped?"

35. The green grape, the ripe cluster, the dried grape are all changes, not into nothing, but into that which is not at present.

36. No man can rob you of your liberty of action; as has been said by Epictetus.

37. He tells us also that we must find out the true art of assenting; and in treating of our impulses he says that we must be vigilant in restraining them, that they may act with proper reservation, with public spirit, with due sense of proportion; also that we should refrain utterly from sensual passion; and not be restive in matters where we have no control.

38. The contention is not about any chance matter, said he, but as to whether we are insane or sane.

39. What do you desire? says Socrates. To have the souls of rational beings or of irrational? Rational. Rational of what kind, virtuous or vicious? Virtuous. Why then do you not seek after such souls? Because we have them already. Why then do you fight and stand at variance?

END OF THE ELEVENTH BOOK.

BOOK XII

1. All that you desire to compass by devious means is yours already, if you will but freely take it. That is to say, if you will leave behind you all that is past, commit the future to Providence, and regulate the present in piety and justice. In piety that you may love your appointed lot; for Nature gave it to you and you to it. In justice, that you may speak the truth with-out constraint or guile; that you may do what is lawful and proper; that you may not be hindered by the wickedness of others, or by their opinion, or their talk, or by any sensation of this poor surrounding body, for the part concerned may look to that. If then, now that you are near your exit, setting behind you all other things, you will hold alone in reverence your ruling part, the spirit divine within you; if you will cease to dread the end of life, but rather fear to miss the beginning of life according to Nature, you will be a man, worthy of the ordered Universe that produced you; you will cease to be a stranger in your own country, gaping in wonder at every daily happening, caught up by this trifle or by that.

2. God beholds all souls bare and stripped of these corporeal vessels, husk, and refuse. By his intelligence alone he touches that only which has been instilled by him and has emanated from himself. If you would but inure yourself to do the like, you would be eased of many a torment. For he who regards not the surrounding flesh will not waste his leisure in thinking about vesture, house, or fame, or other mere external furniture or accoutrement.

3. Three parts there are of which you are compact; body, soul, intelligence. Of these the two first are yours in so far as they must have your care; the third only is properly your own. And if you will cast away from yourself, that is from your mind, all that others do or say, all that you yourself have done or said, all your fears for the future, all the uncontrollable accompaniments of the body that envelops you and of its congenital soul, and all that is whirled in the besieging vortex that races without, so that your intellectual power, made pure, and set above the accidents of fate, may live its own life in freedom, just, resigned, veracious; if, I repeat, you cast out from your soul all comes of excessive attachment either to the past or to the future, then you will become in the words of Empedocles,

A faultless sphere rejoiced in endless rest.

You will study to live the only life there is to live, to wit the present; and you will be able, till death shall come, to spend what remains of life in noble tranquillity, at peace with the spirit within.

4. I have wondered often how it comes that, while every man loves himself beyond all others, yet he holds his own opinion of himself in less esteem than the opinion of others. Yet, if a God or some wise teacher came and ordered a man to conceive and design nothing which he would not utter the moment it occurred to him, he would not abide the ordeal for a single day. Thus we stand in greater awe of our neighbours' opinion of us than we do of our own.

5. How can it be that the Gods, who have ordered all things well for man's advantage, overlooked one thing only, to wit that some of the best of mankind, who have held the closest relations with things divine, and by pious works and holy ministry become intimate with the Divinity, once dead, should arise no more, but be altogether extinguished? If this be truly so, be well assured that, if it ought to have been otherwise they would have made it otherwise. Had it been right it would have been practicable; and had it been according to Nature, Nature would have effected it. From its not being so, if it really be not so, be persuaded that it ought not to have been. You see that, in debating this matter, you are pleading a point of justice with the Gods. Now we would not thus plead with the Gods were they not perfectly good and just. And, if they are so, they have left nothing unjustly and unreasonably neglected in their administration.

6. Essay even tasks that you despair of executing. The left hand, which in other things is of little value for want of use, yet holds the bridle more firmly than the right, for in this it has practice.

7. Consider how death ought to find you, both as to body and as to soul. Think of the shortness of life, of the eternities before and after, and of the infirmity of all material things.

8. Contemplate the fundamental causes stripped of disguises. Think what pain is, what pleasure is, what death, and what fame. Consider how many are themselves the causes of all the disquiet that they suffer; how no man may be hindered by another; how all is matter of opinion.

9. In the use of principles we should be like the pugilist rather than the swordsman. For when the latter drops the sword which he uses he is undone. But the former has his hand always by him and needs but to wield it.

10. Consider well the nature of things, distinguishing between matter, cause, and purpose.

11. What a glorious power is given to man, never to do any action of which God will not approve, and to welcome whatever God appoints for him!

12. As to what happens in the course of nature, the Gods are not to be blamed. They never do wrong, willingly or unwillingly. Neither are men to be blamed, for they do no wrong willingly. There is therefore none to blame.

13. How ridiculous, and how like a foreigner, is he who is surprised at anything which happens in life!

14. There is either a fatal necessity, an unalterable order, or a placable Providence, or a blind confusion without a governor. If there be an unalterable necessity, why strive against it? If there be a Providence admitting of propitiation, make yourself worthy of the divine aid. If there be an ungoverned confusion, be comforted; seeing that in this tempest you have within yourself a guiding intelligence. And, if the wave should carry you away, let it carry away the carcase and the animal life, for the intellectual part of you it will not carry away.

15. If the light of a lamp shine and lose not its radiance until it be extinguished, shall truth, justice, and temperance be extinguished in you before your own extinction.

16. When you have the impression that a man has sinned, say to yourself: "How do I know that this is sin?" And, if he has sinned, consider that he stands self-condemned: and thus, as it were, has torn his own face.

He that would wish the wicked not to sin is like one who would have the fig tree not have juice in its figs, would have infants not cry, horses not neigh, and other inevitable things not happen. What shall the wicked man do, having a wicked disposition? If you are so keen, cure it.

17. If a thing be not becoming, do it not; if not true, say it not.

18. Endeavour always to see in everything what it is that causes your impression; and unfold it by distinguishing the cause, the matter, the relation to other things, and the period within which it must cease to exist.

19. Perceive at last that there is within you something better and more divine than the immediate cause of your sensations of pleasure and pain; something, in short, beyond the strings which move the puppet. What is now my thought? Is it fear? Suspicion? Lust? Or any such passion?

20. In the first place, let nothing be done at random or without an object. In the second let your object never be other than the common good.

21. Yet a little, and you shall be no more; nor shall any of these things remain which you now behold, nor any of those who are now living. It is the nature of all things to change, to turn, and to corrupt; in order that other things may, in their course, spring out of them.

22. Reflect that everything is matter of opinion; and opinion rests with yourself, suppress then your opinion, what time you will, and like one who has doubled the cape and reached the bay, you will have calm and stillness everywhere, never a wave.

23. Any one natural operation, ending at its proper time, suffers no ill by ceasing, nor does the agent therein suffer any ill by its thus ceasing. In like manner, as to the whole series of actions which is life, if it ends in its season it suffers no ill by ceasing, nor is he who thus completes his series, in any evil case. The season and the term are assigned by Nature; sometimes even by your own nature, as in old age; but always by the nature of the whole, by the interchange of whose parts the Universe still remains fresh and in its bloom. Now, that is always good and seasonable which is advantageous to the nature of the whole. Wherefore the ceasing of life cannot be evil to the individual. There is no turpitude in it, since it is beyond our power, and contains nothing contrary to the common advantage. Nay, it is good, since it is seasonable and advantageous to the whole, and, congruent with the order of the Universe. Thus, too, he is led by God who goes the same way with God, and that by like inclination.

24. Have these three thoughts always at hand: First, as to your action, do nothing inconsiderately, or otherwise than justice herself would have acted. As for external events, they either happen by chance or by providence; now, no man should quarrel with chance or censure providence. Second, examine what each thing is, from its seed to its quickening; and from its quickening to its death; of what materials it is composed, and into what it will be resolved. Third, reflect that could you be raised on high, and from thence behold all human affairs, you would discern their great variety, conscious at the same time of the crowds of serial and etherial inhabitants around us; but were you so raised ever so often, you would always see the same things, all uniform and of brief duration. Can we set our pride on such matters?

25. "Cast away opinion, and you are saved." Who then hinders you from casting it away?

26. When you fret at anything, you have forgotten that all happens in accordance with the nature of the Universe, and that the wrong done was another's. This, too, that whatever happens has happened, and will happen, and is now happening everywhere. You have also forgotten how great is the bond between any man and all the human race, a bond not of blood and seed, but of common intelligence. You have forgotten that the intelligence of every man is divine, and an efflux from God; also that no man is proprietor of anything: his children, his body, his very life are given of God. You have forgotten, too, that everything is matter of opinion; and that it is the present moment only that one can live or lose.

27. Bring to frequent recollection those who have grieved about anything overmuch, those who have been pre-eminent in the extreme of glory or misfortune, in feuds or other circumstances of fate. Then stop and ask, Where are they all now? Smoke and ashes, and an old tale; or perhaps not even a tale. Pass them all in review: Fabius Catullinus in the country, Lucius Lupus in his gardens, Stertinius at Baiae, Tiberius at Capreae, Velius Rufus, and, in fine, all eminence attended with the high regard of men. How cheap is all that is so eagerly pursued? And how much better does it become a philosopher to show himself, in the part of the material world allotted to him, just, temperate, and obedient to the Gods; and this with simplicity; for most intolerable of all is the pride of false humility.

28. To those who ask, "Where have you seen the Gods, and how assured yourself of their existence, that you worship them?" make this reply: First, they are visible, even to the eye. Again, my own soul I cannot see, and yet I reverence it. Thus, too, as regards the Gods, I continually feel their power; and so I know that they exist, and I worship them.

29. The safety of life is to see the whole nature of everything, and to discern the matter and the form of its constitution; also to do justice with all your heart, and to speak the truth. What remains but to enjoy life, adding one good to an another, so as not to lose the smallest interval?

30. There is but one light of the sun, although it be scattered upon walls and hills, and a myriad other objects. There is but one common substance, although it be divided among ten thousand bodies having as many different qualities. There is but one soul, though it be distributed among countless different natures and individual forms. There is but one intelligent spirit, though it may seem to be divided. The other parts of these individuals of which we have spoken, such as breath and matter, are void of perception and of mutual affection; yet even they are held together by the intelligent spirit and gravitate together. But intelligence has a special tendency to its kind, and unites therewith, and the community of feeling is not broken.

31. What do you desire? To live on? Or is it to feel or to desire? To grow and to decay again? To speak or think? Which of all these seems worthy to be desired? And, if each and all of them is despicable, proceed to the last that remains, to follow reason and God. Now, it is repugnant to reverence for reason and for God to grieve at the loss by death of these other despicable things.

32. How small a part of the boundless immensity of the ages is allotted to each of us, and presently that will vanish in eternity! How little is ours of the universal substance; how little of the universal spirit! On what a little clod of the whole earth do we creep! Considering all this, reckon nothing great except to act as your nature leads you, and to endure what universal Nature brings to pass.

33. How is it with your ruling part? On this all depends. All other things, within or without our control, are but corpses, dust, and smoke.

34. This most of all must rouse you to despise death: That even those who held pleasure to be good and pain to be evil nevertheless despised it.

35. To him who holds that alone to be good which comes in proper season, who cares not whether he has acted oftener or less often according to right reason; to whom it makes no difference whether he behold the universe for a longer time or a shorter—for this man death also has no terror.

36. You have lived, O man, as a citizen of this great city; of what consequence to you whether for five years or for three? What comes by law is fair to all. Where then is the calamity, if you are sent out of the city, by no tyrant or unjust judge, but Nature herself who at first introduced you, just as the praetor who engaged the actor again dismisses him from the stage? "But," say you, "I have not spoken my five acts, but only three." True, but in life three acts make up the play. For he sets the end who was responsible for its composition at the first, and for its present dissolution. You are responsible for neither. Depart then graciously; for he who dismisses you is gracious.

THE END.

HISTORICAL EMPORIUM

Est. 2003

Buy at... HISTORICAL EMPORIUM

Whose **REPUTATION** is *celebrated* world-wide as the pre-eminent clothing source for the **ADVENTUROUS** and *Fashionable*.

We are...

REVERED
by our customers

REVILED
by our competitors

RESPECTED
by all who know us

NO LOCAL DEALER CAN COMPETE WITH OUR QUALITY, VARIETY AND INCOMPARIBLE CUSTOMER SERVICE!

ACCEPT NO SUBSTITUTE!
If you require **clothing and supplies** as stylish and **stout-hearted** as you, contact us immediately to be outfitted.

800-997-4311

HistoricalEmporium.com

THE LIFE AND ADVENTURES OF SANTA CLAUS

BY L. FRANK BAUM

YOUTH

1. Burzee

Have you heard of the great Forest of Burzee? Nurse used to sing of it when I was a child. She sang of the big tree-trunks, standing close together, with their roots intertwining below the earth and their branches intertwining above it; of their rough coating of bark and queer, gnarled limbs; of the bushy foliage that roofed the entire forest, save where the sunbeams found a path through which to touch the ground in little spots and to cast weird and curious shadows over the mosses, the lichens and the drifts of dried leaves.

The Forest of Burzee is mighty and grand and awesome to those who steal beneath its shade. Coming from the sunlit meadows into its mazes it seems at first gloomy, then pleasant, and afterward filled with never-ending delights.

For hundreds of years it has flourished in all its magnificence, the silence of its inclosure unbroken save by the chirp of busy chipmunks, the growl of wild beasts and the songs of birds.

Yet Burzee has its inhabitants—for all this. Nature peopled it in the beginning with Fairies, Knooks, Ryls and Nymphs. As long as the Forest stands it will be a home, a refuge and a playground to these sweet immortals, who revel undisturbed in its depths.

Civilization has never yet reached Burzee. Will it ever, I wonder?

2. The Child of the Forest

Once, so long ago our great-grandfathers could scarcely have heard it mentioned, there lived within the great Forest of Burzee a wood-nymph named Necile. She was closely related to the mighty Queen Zurline, and her home was beneath the shade of a widespreading oak. Once every year, on Budding Day, when the trees put forth their new buds, Necile held the Golden Chalice of Ak to the lips of the Queen, who drank therefrom to the prosperity of the Forest. So you see she was a nymph of some importance, and, moreover, it is said she was highly regarded because of her beauty and grace.

When she was created she could not have told; Queen Zurline could not have told; the great Ak himself could not have told. It was long ago when the world was new and nymphs were needed to guard the forests and to minister to the wants of the young trees. Then, on some day not remembered, Necile sprang into being; radiant, lovely, straight and slim as the sapling she was created to guard.

Her hair was the color that lines a chestnut-bur; her eyes were blue in the sunlight and purple in the shade; her cheeks bloomed with the faint pink that edges the clouds at sunset; her lips were full red, pouting and sweet. For costume she adopted oak-leaf green; all the wood-nymphs dress in that color and know no other so desirable. Her dainty feet were sandal-clad, while her head remained bare of covering other than her silken tresses.

Necile's duties were few and simple. She kept hurtful weeds from growing beneath her trees and sapping the earth-food required by her charges. She frightened away the Gadgols, who took evil delight in flying against the tree-trunks and wounding them so that they drooped and died from the poisonous contact. In dry seasons she carried water from the brooks and pools and moistened the roots of her thirsty dependents.

That was in the beginning. The weeds had now learned to avoid the forests where wood-nymphs dwelt; the loathsome Gadgols no longer dared come nigh; the trees had become old and sturdy and could bear the drought better than when fresh-sprouted. So Necile's duties were lessened, and time grew laggard, while succeeding years became more tiresome and uneventful than the nymph's joyous spirit loved.

Truly the forest-dwellers did not lack amusement. Each full moon they danced in the Royal Circle of the Queen. There were also the Feast of Nuts, the Jubilee of Autumn Tintings, the solemn ceremony of Leaf Shedding and the revelry of Budding Day. But these periods of enjoyment were far apart, and left many weary hours between.

That a wood-nymph should grow discontented was not thought of by Necile's sisters. It came upon her only after many years of brooding. But when once she had settled in her mind that life was irksome she had no patience with her condition, and longed to do something of real interest and to pass her days in ways hitherto undreamed of by forest nymphs. The Law of the Forest alone restrained her from going forth in search of adventure.

While this mood lay heavy upon pretty Necile it chanced that the great Ak visited the Forest of Burzee and allowed the wood-nymphs as was their wont—to lie at his feet and listen to the words of wisdom that fell from his lips. Ak is the Master Woodsman of the world; he sees everything, and knows more than the sons of men.

That night he held the Queen's hand, for he loved the nymphs as a father loves his children; and Necile lay at his feet with many of her sisters and earnestly harkened as he spoke.

"We live so happily, my fair ones, in our forest glades," said Ak, stroking his grizzled beard thoughtfully, "that we know nothing of the sorrow and misery that fall to the lot of those poor mortals who inhabit the open spaces of the earth. They are not of our race, it is true, yet compassion well befits beings so fairly favored as ourselves. Often as I pass by the dwelling of some suffering mortal I am tempted to stop and banish the poor thing's misery. Yet suffering, in moderation, is the natural lot of mortals, and it is not our place to interfere with the laws of Nature."

"Nevertheless," said the fair Queen, nodding her golden head at the Master Woodsman, "it would not be a vain guess that Ak has often assisted these hapless mortals."

Ak smiled.

"Sometimes," he replied, "when they are very young—'children,' the mortals call them—I have stopped to rescue them from misery. The men and women I dare not interfere with; they must bear the burdens Nature has imposed upon them. But the helpless infants, the innocent children of men, have a right to be happy until they become full-grown and able to bear the trials of humanity. So I feel I am justified in assisting them. Not long ago—a year, maybe—I found four poor children huddled in a wooden hut, slowly freezing to death. Their parents had gone to a neighboring village for food, and had left a fire to warm their little ones while they were absent. But a storm arose and drifted the snow in their path, so they were long on the road. Meantime the fire went out and the frost crept into the bones of the waiting children."

"Poor things!" murmured the Queen softly. "What did you do?"

"I called Nelko, bidding him fetch wood from my forests and breathe upon it until the fire blazed again and warmed the little room where the children lay. Then they ceased shivering and fell asleep until their parents came."

"I am glad you did thus," said the good Queen, beaming upon the Master; and Necile, who had eagerly listened to every word, echoed in a whisper: "I, too, am glad!"

"And this very night," continued Ak, "as I came to the edge of Burzee I heard a feeble cry, which I judged came from a human infant. I looked about me and found, close to the forest, a helpless babe, lying quite naked upon the grasses and wailing piteously. Not far away, screened by the forest, crouched Shiegra, the lioness, intent upon devouring the infant for her evening meal."

"And what did you do, Ak?" asked the Queen, breathlessly.

"Not much, being in a hurry to greet my nymphs. But I commanded Shiegra to lie close to the babe, and to give it her milk to quiet its hunger. And I told her to send word throughout the forest, to all beasts and reptiles, that the child should not be harmed."

"I am glad you did thus," said the good Queen again, in a tone of relief; but this time Necile did not echo her words, for the nymph, filled with a strange resolve, had suddenly stolen away from the group.

Swiftly her lithe form darted through the forest paths until she reached the edge of mighty Burzee, when she paused to gaze curiously about her. Never until now had she ventured so far, for the Law of the Forest had placed the nymphs in its inmost depths.

Necile knew she was breaking the Law, but the thought did not give pause to her dainty feet. She had decided to see with her own eyes this infant Ak had told of, for she had never yet beheld a child of man. All the immortals are full-grown; there are no children among them. Peering through the trees Necile saw the child lying on the grass. But now it was sweetly sleeping, having been comforted by the milk drawn from Shiegra.

It was not old enough to know what peril means; if it did not feel hunger it was content.

Softly the nymph stole to the side of the babe and knelt upon the sward, her long robe of rose leaf color spreading about her like a gossamer cloud. Her lovely countenance expressed curiosity and surprise, but, most of all, a tender, womanly pity. The babe was newborn, chubby and pink. It was entirely helpless. While the nymph gazed the infant opened its eyes, smiled upon her, and stretched out two dimpled arms. In another instant Necile had caught it to her breast and was hurrying with it through the forest paths.

3. The Adoption

The Master Woodsman suddenly rose, with knitted brows. "There is a strange presence in the Forest," he declared. Then the Queen and her nymphs turned and saw standing before them Necile, with the sleeping infant clasped tightly in her arms and a defiant look in her deep blue eyes.

And thus for a moment they remained, the nymphs filled with surprise and consternation, but the brow of the Master Woodsman gradually clearing as he gazed intently upon the beautiful immortal who had wilfully broken the Law. Then the great Ak, to the wonder of all, laid his hand softly on Necile's flowing locks and kissed her on her fair forehead.

"For the first time within my knowledge," said he, gently, "a nymph has defied me and my laws; yet in my heart can I find no word of chiding. What is your desire, Necile?"

"Let me keep the child!" she answered, beginning to tremble and falling on her knees in supplication.

"Here, in the Forest of Burzee, where the human race has never yet penetrated?" questioned Ak.

"Here, in the Forest of Burzee," replied the nymph, boldly. "It is my home, and I am weary for lack of occupation. Let me care for the babe! See how weak and helpless it is. Surely it can not harm Burzee nor the Master Woodsman of the World!"

"But the Law, child, the Law!" cried Ak, sternly.

"The Law is made by the Master Woodsman," returned Necile; "if he bids me care for the babe he himself has saved from death, who in all the world dare oppose me?" Queen Zurline, who had listened intently to this conversation, clapped her pretty hands gleefully at the nymph's answer.

"You are fairly trapped, O Ak!" she exclaimed, laughing. "Now, I pray you, give heed to Necile's petition."

The Woodsman, as was his habit when in thought, stroked his grizzled beard slowly. Then he said:

"She shall keep the babe, and I will give it my protection. But I warn you all that as this is the first time I have relaxed the Law, so shall it be the last time. Never more, to the end of the World, shall a mortal be adopted by an immortal. Otherwise would we abandon our happy existence for one of trouble and anxiety. Good night, my nymphs!"

Then Ak was gone from their midst, and Necile hurried away to her bower to rejoice over her new-found treasure.

4. Claus

ANOTHER DAY FOUND NECILE'S BOWER THE MOST POPULAR PLACE IN THE FOR-est. The nymphs clustered around her and the child that lay asleep in her lap, with expressions of curiosity and delight. Nor were they wanting in praises for the great Ak's kindness in allowing Necile to keep the babe and to care for it. Even the Queen came to peer into the innocent childish face and to hold a helpless, chubby fist in her own fair hand.

"What shall we call him, Necile?" she asked, smiling. "He must have a name, you know."

"Let him be called Claus," answered Necile, "for that means 'a little one.'"

"Rather let him be called Neclaus,"** returned the Queen, "for that will mean 'Necile's little one.'"

The nymphs clapped their hands in delight, and Neclaus became the infant's name, although Necile loved best to call him Claus, and in afterdays many of her sisters followed her example.

Necile gathered the softest moss in all the forest for Claus to lie upon, and she made his bed in her own bower. Of food the infant had no lack. The nymphs searched the forest for bell-udders, which grow upon the goa-tree and when opened are found to be filled with sweet milk. And the soft-eyed does willingly gave a share of their milk to support the little stranger, while Shiegra, the lioness, often crept stealthily into Necile's bower and purred softly as she lay beside the babe and fed it.

So the little one flourished and grew big and sturdy day by day, while Necile taught him to speak and to walk and to play.

His thoughts and words were sweet and gentle, for the nymphs knew no evil and their hearts were pure and loving. He became the pet of the forest, for Ak's decree had forbidden beast or reptile to molest him, and he walked fearlessly wherever his will guided him.

Presently the news reached the other immortals that the nymphs of Burzee had adopted a human infant, and that the act had been sanctioned by the great Ak. Therefore many of them came to visit the little stranger, looking upon him with much interest. First the Ryls, who are first cousins to the wood-nymphs, although so differently formed. For the Ryls are required to watch over the flowers and plants, as the nymphs watch over the forest trees. They search the wide world for the food required by the roots of the flowering plants, while the brilliant colors possessed by the full-blown flowers are due to the dyes placed in the soil by the Ryls, which are drawn through the little veins in the roots and the body of the plants, as they reach maturity. The Ryls are a busy people, for their flowers bloom and fade continually, but they are merry and light-hearted and are very popular with the other immortals.

Next came the Knooks, whose duty it is to watch over the beasts of the world, both gentle and wild. The Knooks have a hard time of it, since many of the beasts are ungovernable and rebel against restraint. But they know how to manage them, after all, and you will find that certain laws of the Knooks are obeyed by even the most ferocious animals. Their anxieties make the Knooks look old and worn and crooked, and their natures are a bit rough from associating with wild creatures continually; yet they are most useful to humanity and to the world in general, as their laws are the only laws the forest beasts recognize except those of the Master Woodsman.

Then there were the Fairies, the guardians of mankind, who were much interested in the adoption of Claus because their own laws forbade them to become familiar with their human charges. There are instances on record where the Fairies have shown themselves to human beings, and have even conversed with them; but they are supposed to guard the lives of mankind unseen and unknown, and if they favor some people more than others it is because these have won such distinction fairly, as the Fairies are very just and impartial. But the idea of adopting a child of men had never occurred to them because it was in every way opposed to their laws; so their curiosity was intense to behold the little stranger adopted by Necile and her sister nymphs.

Claus looked upon the immortals who thronged around him with fearless eyes and smiling lips. He rode laughingly upon the shoulders of the merry Ryls; he mischievously pulled the gray beards of the low-browed Knooks; he rested his curly head confidently upon the dainty bosom of the Fairy Queen herself. And the Ryls loved the sound of his laughter; the Knooks loved his courage; the Fairies loved his innocence.

The boy made friends of them all, and learned to know their laws intimately. No forest flower was trampled beneath his feet, lest the friendly Ryls should be grieved. He never interfered with the beasts of the forest, lest his friends the Knooks should become angry. The Fairies he loved dearly, but, knowing nothing of mankind, he could not understand that he was the only one of his race admitted to friendly intercourse with them.

Indeed, Claus came to consider that he alone, of all the forest people, had no like nor fellow. To him the forest was the world. He had no idea that millions of toiling, striving human creatures existed.

And he was happy and content.

** Some people have spelled this name Nicklaus and others Nicolas, which is the reason that Santa Claus is still known in some lands as St. Nicolas. But, of course, Neclaus is his right name, and Claus the nickname given him by his adopted mother, the fair nymph Necile.

5. The Master Woodsman

YEARS PASS SWIFTLY IN BURZEE, FOR THE NYMPHS HAVE NO NEED TO REGARD time in any way. Even centuries make no change in the dainty creatures; ever and ever they remain the same, immortal and unchanging.

Claus, however, being mortal, grew to manhood day by day. Necile was disturbed, presently, to find him too big to lie in her lap, and he had a desire for other food than milk. His stout legs carried him far into Burzee's heart, where he gathered supplies of nuts and berries, as well as several sweet and wholesome roots, which suited his stomach better than the belludders. He sought Necile's bower less frequently, till finally it became his custom to return thither only to sleep.

The nymph, who had come to love him dearly, was puzzled to comprehend the changed nature of her charge, and unconsciously altered her own mode of life to conform to his whims. She followed him readily through the forest paths, as did many of her sister nymphs, explaining as they walked all the mysteries of the gigantic wood and the habits and nature of the living things which dwelt beneath its shade.

The language of the beasts became clear to little Claus; but he never could understand their sulky and morose tempers. Only the squirrels, the mice and the rabbits seemed to possess cheerful and merry natures; yet would the boy laugh when the panther growled, and stroke the bear's glossy coat while the creature snarled and bared its teeth menacingly. The growls and snarls were not for Claus, he well knew, so what did they matter?

He could sing the songs of the bees, recite the poetry of the wood-flowers and relate the history of every blinking owl in Burzee. He helped the Ryls to feed their plants and the Knooks to keep order among the animals. The little immortals regarded him as a privileged person, being especially protected by Queen Zurline and her nymphs and favored by the great Ak himself.

One day the Master Woodsman came back to the forest of Burzee. He had visited, in turn, all his forests throughout the world, and they were many and broad.

Not until he entered the glade where the Queen and her nymphs were assembled to greet him did Ak remember the child he had permitted Necile to adopt. Then he found, sitting familiarly in the circle of lovely immortals, a broad-shouldered, stalwart youth, who, when erect, stood fully as high as the shoulder of the Master himself.

Ak paused, silent and frowning, to bend his piercing gaze upon Claus. The clear eyes met his own steadfastly, and the Woodsman gave a sigh of relief as he marked their placid depths and read the youth's brave and innocent heart. Nevertheless, as Ak sat beside the fair Queen, and the golden chalice, filled with rare nectar, passed from lip to lip, the Master Woodsman was strangely silent and reserved, and stroked his beard many times with a thoughtful motion.

With morning he called Claus aside, in kindly fashion, saying:

"Bid good by, for a time, to Necile and her sisters; for you shall accompany me on my journey through the world."

The venture pleased Claus, who knew well the honor of being companion of the Master Woodsman of the world. But Necile wept for the first time in her life, and clung to the boy's neck as if she could not bear to let him go. The nymph who had mothered this sturdy youth was still as dainty, as charming and beautiful as when she had dared to face Ak with the babe clasped to her breast; nor was her love less great. Ak beheld the two clinging together, seemingly as brother and sister to one another, and again he wore his thoughtful look.

6. Claus Discovers Humanity

TAKING CLAUS TO A SMALL CLEARING IN THE FOREST, THE MASTER SAID: "Place your hand upon my girdle and hold fast while we journey through the air; for now shall we encircle the world and look upon many of the haunts of those men from whom you are descended."

These words caused Claus to marvel, for until now he had thought himself the only one of his kind upon the earth; yet in silence he grasped firmly the girdle of the great Ak, his astonishment forbidding speech.

Then the vast forest of Burzee seemed to fall away from their feet, and the youth found himself passing swiftly through the air at a great height.

Ere long there were spires beneath them, while buildings of many shapes and colors met their downward view. It was a city of men, and Ak, pausing to descend, led Claus to its inclosure. Said the Master:

"So long as you hold fast to my girdle you will remain unseen by all mankind, though seeing clearly yourself. To release your grasp will be to separate yourself forever from me and your home in Burzee."

One of the first laws of the Forest is obedience, and Claus had no thought of disobeying the Master's wish. He clung fast to the girdle and remained invisible.

Thereafter with each moment passed in the city the youth's wonder grew. He, who had supposed himself created differently from all others, now found the earth swarming with creatures of his own kind.

"Indeed," said Ak, "the immortals are few; but the mortals are many."

Claus looked earnestly upon his fellows. There were sad faces, gay and reckless faces, pleasant faces, anxious faces and kindly faces, all mingled in puzzling disorder. Some worked at tedious tasks; some strutted in impudent conceit; some were thoughtful and grave while others seemed happy and content. Men of many natures were there, as everywhere, and Claus found much to please him and much to make him sad.

But especially he noted the children—first curiously, then eagerly, then lovingly. Ragged little ones rolled in the dust of the streets, playing with scraps and pebbles. Other children, gaily dressed, were propped upon cushions and fed with sugar-plums. Yet the children of the rich were not happier than those playing with the dust and pebbles, it seemed to Claus.

"Childhood is the time of man's greatest content," said Ak, following the youth's thoughts. "'Tis during these years of innocent pleasure that the little ones are most free from care."

"Tell me," said Claus, "why do not all these babies fare alike?"

"Because they are born in both cottage and palace," returned the Master. "The difference in the wealth of the parents determines the lot of the child. Some are carefully tended and clothed in silks and dainty linen; others are neglected and covered with rags."

"Yet all seem equally fair and sweet," said Claus, thoughtfully.

"While they are babes—yes;" agreed Ak. "Their joy is in being alive, and they do not stop to think. In after years the doom of mankind overtakes them, and they find they must struggle and worry, work and fret, to gain the wealth that is so dear to the hearts of men. Such things are unknown in the Forest where you were reared." Claus was silent a moment. Then he asked:

"Why was I reared in the forest, among those who are not of my race?"

Then Ak, in gentle voice, told him the story of his babyhood: how he had been abandoned at the forest's edge and left a prey to wild beasts, and how the loving nymph Necile had rescued him and brought him to manhood under the protection of the immortals.

"Yet I am not of them," said Claus, musingly.

"You are not of them," returned the Woodsman. "The nymph who cared for you as a mother seems now like a sister to you; by and by, when you grow old and gray, she will seem like a daughter. Yet another brief span and you will be but a memory, while she remains Necile."

"Then why, if man must perish, is he born?" demanded the boy.

"Everything perishes except the world itself and its keepers," answered Ak. "But while life lasts everything on earth has its use. The wise seek ways to be helpful to the world, for the helpful ones are sure to live again."

Much of this Claus failed to understand fully, but a longing seized him to become helpful to his fellows, and he remained grave and thoughtful while they resumed their journey.

They visited many dwellings of men in many parts of the world, watching farmers toil in the fields, warriors dash into cruel fray, and merchants exchange their goods for bits of white and yellow metal. And everywhere the eyes of Claus sought out the children in love and pity, for the thought of his own helpless babyhood was strong within him and he yearned to give help to the innocent little ones of his race even as he had been succored by the kindly nymph.

Day by day the Master Woodsman and his pupil traversed the earth, Ak speaking but seldom to the youth who clung steadfastly to his girdle, but guiding him into all places where he might become familiar with the lives of human beings.

And at last they returned to the grand old Forest of Burzee, where the Master set Claus down within the circle of nymphs, among whom the pretty Necile anxiously awaited him.

The brow of the great Ak was now calm and peaceful; but the brow of Claus had become lined with deep thought. Necile sighed at the change in her foster-son, who until now had been ever joyous and smiling, and the thought came to her that never again would the life of the boy be the same as before this eventful journey with the Master.

7. Claus Leaves the Forest

WHEN GOOD QUEEN ZURLINE HAD TOUCHED THE GOLDEN CHALICE WITH HER fair lips and it had passed around the circle in honor of the travelers' return, the Master Woodsman of the World, who had not yet spoken, turned his gaze frankly upon Claus and said:

"Well?"

The boy understood, and rose slowly to his feet beside Necile. Once only his eyes passed around the familiar circle of nymphs, every one of whom he remembered as a loving comrade; but tears came unbidden to dim his sight, so he gazed thereafter steadfastly at the Master.

"I have been ignorant," said he, simply, "until the great Ak in his kindness taught me who and what I am. You, who live so sweetly in your forest bowers, ever fair and youthful and innocent, are no fit comrades for a son of humanity. For I have looked upon man, finding him doomed to live for a brief space upon earth, to toil for the things he needs, to fade into old age, and then to pass away as the leaves in autumn. Yet every man has his mission, which is to leave the world better, in some way, than he found it. I am of the race of men, and man's lot is my lot. For your tender care of the poor, forsaken babe you adopted, as well as for your loving comradeship during my boyhood, my heart will ever overflow with gratitude. My foster-mother," here he stopped and kissed Necile's white forehead, "I shall love and cherish while life lasts. But I must leave you, to take my part in the endless struggle to which humanity is doomed, and to live my life in my own way."

"What will you do?" asked the Queen, gravely.

"I must devote myself to the care of the children of mankind, and try to make them happy," he answered. "Since your own tender care of a babe brought to me happiness and strength, it is just and right that I devote my life to the pleasure of other babes. Thus will the memory of the loving nymph Necile be planted within the hearts of thousands of my race for many years to come, and her kindly act be recounted in song and in story while the world shall last. Have I spoken well, O Master?"

"You have spoken well," returned Ak, and rising to his feet he continued: "Yet one thing must not be forgotten. Having been adopted as the child of the Forest, and the playfellow of the nymphs, you have gained a distinction which forever separates you from your kind. Therefore, when you go forth into the world of men you shall retain the protection of the Forest, and the powers you now enjoy will remain with you to assist you in your labors. In any need you may call upon the Nymphs, the Ryls, the Knooks and the Fairies, and they will serve you gladly. I, the Master Woodsman of the World, have said it, and my Word is the Law!"

Claus looked upon Ak with grateful eyes.

"This will make me mighty among men," he replied. "Protected by these kind friends I may be able to make thousands of little children happy. I will try very hard to do my duty, and I know the Forest people will give me their sympathy and help."

"We will!" said the Fairy Queen, earnestly.

"We will!" cried the merry Ryls, laughing.

"We will!" shouted the crooked Knooks, scowling.

"We will!" exclaimed the sweet nymphs, proudly. But Necile said nothing. She only folded Claus in her arms and kissed him tenderly.

"The world is big," continued the boy, turning again to his loyal friends, "but men are everywhere. I shall begin my work near my friends, so that if I meet with misfortune I can come to the Forest for counsel or help."

With that he gave them all a loving look and turned away. There was no need to say good by, by for him the sweet, wild life of the Forest was over. He went forth bravely to meet his doom—the doom of the race of man—the necessity to worry and work.

But Ak, who knew the boy's heart, was merciful and guided his steps.

Coming through Burzee to its eastern edge Claus reached the Laughing Valley of Hohaho. On each side were rolling green hills, and a brook wandered midway between them to wind afar off beyond the valley. At his back was the grim Forest; at the far end of the valley a broad plain. The eyes of the young man, which had until now reflected his grave thoughts, became brighter as he stood silent, looking out upon the Laughing Valley. Then on a sudden his eyes twinkled, as stars do on a still night, and grew merry and wide.

For at his feet the cowslips and daisies smiled on him in friendly regard; the breeze whistled gaily as it passed by and fluttered the locks on his forehead; the brook laughed joyously as it leaped over the pebbles and swept around the green curves of its banks; the bees sang sweet songs as they flew from dandelion to daffodil; the beetles chirruped happily in the long grass, and the sunbeams glinted pleasantly over all the scene.

"Here," cried Claus, stretching out his arms as if to embrace the Valley, "will I make my home!"

That was many, many years ago. It has been his home ever since. It is his home now.

MANHOOD

1. The Laughing Valley

WHEN CLAUS CAME THE VALLEY WAS EMPTY SAVE FOR THE GRASS, THE BROOK, the wildflowers, the bees and the butterflies. If he would make his home here and live after the fashion of men he must have a house. This puzzled him at first, but while he stood smiling in the sunshine he suddenly found beside him old Nelko, the servant of the Master Woodsman. Nelko bore an ax, strong and broad, with blade that gleamed like burnished silver. This he placed in the young man's hand, then disappeared without a word.

Claus understood, and turning to the Forest's edge he selected a number of fallen tree-trunks, which he began to clear of their dead branches. He would not cut into a living tree. His life among the nymphs who guarded the Forest had taught him that a live tree is sacred, being a created thing endowed with feeling. But with the dead and fallen trees it was different. They had fulfilled their destiny, as active members of the Forest community, and now it was fitting that their remains should minister to the needs of man.

The ax bit deep into the logs at every stroke. It seemed to have a force of its own, and Claus had but to swing and guide it.

When shadows began creeping over the green hills to lie in the Valley overnight, the young man had chopped many logs into equal lengths and proper shapes for building a house such as he had seen the poorer classes of men inhabit. Then, resolving to await another day before he tried to fit the logs together, Claus ate some of the sweet roots he well knew how to find, drank deeply from the laughing brook, and lay down to sleep on the grass, first seeking a spot where no flowers grew, lest the weight of his body should crush them.

And while he slumbered and breathed in the perfume of the wondrous Valley the Spirit of Happiness crept into his heart and drove out all terror and care and misgivings. Never more would the face of Claus be clouded with anxieties; never more would the trials of life weigh him down as with a burden. The Laughing Valley had claimed him for its own.

Would that we all might live in that delightful place!—but then, maybe, it would become overcrowded. For ages it had awaited a tenant. Was it chance that led young Claus to make his home in this happy vale? Or may we guess that his thoughtful friends, the immortals, had directed his steps when he wandered away from Burzee to seek a home in the great world?

Certain it is that while the moon peered over the hilltop and flooded with its soft beams the body of the sleeping stranger, the Laughing Valley was filled with the queer, crooked shapes of the friendly Knooks. These people spoke no words, but worked with skill and swiftness. The logs Claus had trimmed with his bright ax were carried to a spot beside the brook and fitted one upon another, and during the night a strong and roomy dwelling was built.

The birds came sweeping into the Valley at daybreak, and their songs, so seldom heard in the deep wood, aroused the stranger. He rubbed the web of sleep from his eyelids and looked around. The house met his gaze.

"I must thank the Knooks for this," said he, gratefully. Then he walked to his dwelling and entered at the doorway. A large room faced him, having a fireplace at the end and a table and bench in the middle. Beside the fireplace was a cupboard. Another doorway was beyond. Claus entered here, also, and saw a smaller room with a bed against the wall and a stool set near a small stand. On the bed were many layers of dried moss brought from the Forest.

"Indeed, it is a palace!" exclaimed the smiling Claus. "I must thank the good Knooks again, for their knowledge of man's needs as well as for their labors in my behalf."

He left his new home with a glad feeling that he was not quite alone in the world, although he had chosen to abandon his Forest life. Friendships are not easily broken, and the immortals are everywhere.

Upon reaching the brook he drank of the pure water, and then sat down on the bank to laugh at the mischievous gambols of the ripples as they pushed one another against rocks or crowded desperately to see which should first reach the turn beyond. And as they raced away he listened to the song they sang:

> "Rushing, pushing, on we go!
> Not a wave may gently flow-
> All are too excited.
> Ev'ry drop, delighted,
> Turns to spray in merry play
> As we tumble on our way!"

Next Claus searched for roots to eat, while the daffodils turned their little eyes up to him laughingly and lisped their dainty song:

> "Blooming fairly, growing rarely,
> Never flowerets were so gay!
> Perfume breathing, joy bequeathing,
> As our colors we display."

It made Claus laugh to hear the little things voice their happiness as they nodded gracefully on their stems. But another strain caught his ear as the sunbeams fell gently across his face and whispered:

> "Here is gladness, that our rays
> Warm the valley through the days;
> Here is happiness, to give
> Comfort unto all who live!"

"Yes!" cried Claus in answer, "there is happiness and joy in all things here. The Laughing Valley is a valley of peace and good-will."

He passed the day talking with the ants and beetles and exchanging jokes with the light-hearted butterflies. And at night he lay on his bed of soft moss and slept soundly.

Then came the Fairies, merry but noiseless, bringing skillets and pots and dishes and pans and all the tools necessary to prepare food and to comfort a mortal. With these they filled cupboard and fireplace, finally placing a stout suit of wool clothing on the stool by the bedside.

When Claus awoke he rubbed his eyes again, and laughed, and spoke aloud his thanks to the Fairies and the Master Woodsman who had sent them. With eager joy he examined all his new possessions, wondering what some might be used for. But, in the days when he had clung to the girdle of the great Ak and visited the cities of men, his eyes had been quick to note all the manners and customs of the race to which he belonged; so he guessed from the gifts brought by the Fairies that the Master expected him hereafter to live in the fashion of his fellow-creatures.

"Which means that I must plow the earth and plant corn," he reflected; "so that when winter comes I shall have garnered food in plenty."

But, as he stood in the grassy Valley, he saw that to turn up the earth in furrows would be to destroy hundreds of pretty, helpless flowers, as well as thousands of the tender blades of grass. And this he could not bear to do.

Therefore he stretched out his arms and uttered a peculiar whistle he had learned in the Forest, afterward crying:

"Ryls of the Field Flowers—come to me!"

Instantly a dozen of the queer little Ryls were squatting upon the ground before him, and they nodded to him in cheerful greeting.

Claus gazed upon them earnestly.

"Your brothers of the Forest," he said, "I have known and loved many years. I shall love you, also, when we have become friends. To me the laws of the Ryls, whether those of the Forest or of the field, are sacred. I have never wilfully destroyed one of the flowers you tend so carefully; but I must plant grain to use for food during the cold winter, and how am I to do this without killing the little creatures that sing to me so prettily of their fragrant blossoms?"

The Yellow Ryl, he who tends the buttercups, made answer:

"Fret not, friend Claus. The great Ak has spoken to us of you. There is better work for you in life than to labor for food, and though, not being of the Forest, Ak has no command over us, nevertheless are we glad to favor one he loves. Live, therefore, to do the good work you are resolved to undertake. We, the Field Ryls, will attend to your food supplies."

After this speech the Ryls were no longer to be seen, and Claus drove from his mind the thought of tilling the earth.

When next he wandered back to his dwelling a bowl of fresh milk stood upon the table; bread was in the cupboard and sweet honey filled a dish beside it. A pretty basket of rosy apples and new-plucked grapes was also awaiting him. He called out "Thanks, my friends!" to the invisible Ryls, and straightway began to eat of the food.

Thereafter, when hungry, he had but to look into the cupboard to find goodly supplies brought by the kindly Ryls. And the Knooks cut and stacked much wood for his fireplace. And the Fairies brought him warm blankets and clothing.

So began his life in the Laughing Valley, with the favor and friendship of the immortals to minister to his every want.

2. How Claus Made the First Toy

TRULY OUR CLAUS HAD WISDOM, FOR HIS GOOD FORTUNE BUT STRENGTHENED his resolve to befriend the little ones of his own race. He knew his plan was approved by the immortals, else they would not have favored him so greatly.

So he began at once to make acquaintance with mankind. He walked through the Valley to the plain beyond, and crossed the plain in many directions to reach the abodes of men. These stood singly or in groups of dwellings called villages, and in nearly all the houses, whether big or little, Claus found children.

The youngsters soon came to know his merry, laughing face and the kind glance of his bright eyes; and the parents, while they regarded the young man with some scorn for loving children more than their elders, were content that the girls and boys had found a playfellow who seemed willing to amuse them.

So the children romped and played games with Claus, and the boys rode upon his shoulders, and the girls nestled in his strong arms, and the babies clung fondly to his knees. Wherever the young man chanced to be, the sound of childish laughter followed him; and to understand this better you must know that children were much neglected in those days and received little attention from their parents, so that it became to them a marvel that so goodly a man as Claus devoted his time to making them happy. And those who knew him were, you may be sure, very happy indeed. The sad faces of the poor and abused grew bright for once; the cripple smiled despite his misfortune; the ailing ones hushed their moans and the grieved ones their cries when their merry friend came nigh to comfort them.

Only at the beautiful palace of the Lord of Lerd and at the frowning castle of the Baron Braun was Claus refused admittance. There were children at both places; but the servants at the palace shut the door in the young stranger's face, and the fierce Baron threatened to hang him from an iron hook on the castle walls. Whereupon Claus sighed and went back to the poorer dwellings where he was welcome.

After a time the winter drew near.

The flowers lived out their lives and faded and disappeared; the beetles burrowed far into the warm earth; the butterflies deserted the meadows; and the voice of the brook grew hoarse, as if it had taken cold.

One day snowflakes filled all the air in the Laughing Valley, dancing boisterously toward the earth and clothing in pure white raiment the roof of Claus's dwelling.

At night Jack Frost rapped at the door.

"Come in!" cried Claus.

"Come out!" answered Jack, "for you have a fire inside."

So Claus came out. He had known Jack Frost in the Forest, and liked the jolly rogue, even while he mistrusted him.

"There will be rare sport for me to-night, Claus!" shouted the sprite. "Isn't this glorious weather? I shall nip scores of noses and ears and toes before daybreak."

"If you love me, Jack, spare the children," begged Claus.

"And why?" asked the other, in surprise.

"They are tender and helpless," answered Claus.

"But I love to nip the tender ones!" declared Jack. "The older ones are tough, and tire my fingers."

"The young ones are weak, and can not fight you," said Claus.

"True," agreed Jack, thoughtfully. "Well, I will not pinch a child this night—if I can resist the temptation," he promised. "Good night, Claus!"

"Good night."

The young man went in and closed the door, and Jack Frost ran on to the nearest village.

Claus threw a log on the fire, which burned up brightly. Beside the hearth sat Blinkie, a big cat given him by Peter the Knook. Her fur was soft and glossy, and she purred never-ending songs of contentment.

"I shall not see the children again soon," said Claus to the cat, who kindly paused in her song to listen. "The winter is upon us, the snow will be deep for many days, and I shall be unable to play with my little friends."

The cat raised a paw and stroked her nose thoughtfully, but made no reply. So long as the fire burned and Claus sat in his easy chair by the hearth she did not mind the weather.

So passed many days and many long evenings. The cupboard was always full, but Claus became weary with having nothing to do more than to feed the fire from the big wood-pile the Knooks had brought him.

One evening he picked up a stick of wood and began to cut it with his sharp knife. He had no thought, at first, except to occupy his time, and he whistled and sang to the cat as he carved away portions of the stick. Puss sat up on her haunches and watched him, listening at the same time to her master's merry whistle, which she loved to hear even more than her own purring songs.

Claus glanced at puss and then at the stick he was whittling, until presently the wood began to have a shape, and the shape was like the head of a cat, with two ears sticking upward.

Claus stopped whistling to laugh, and then both he and the cat looked at the wooden image in some surprise. Then he carved out the eyes and the nose, and rounded the lower part of the head so that it rested upon a neck.

Puss hardly knew what to make of it now, and sat up stiffly, as if watching with some suspicion what would come next.

Claus knew. The head gave him an idea. He plied his knife carefully and with skill, forming slowly the body of the cat, which he made to sit upon its haunches as the real cat did, with her tail wound around her two front legs.

The work cost him much time, but the evening was long and he had nothing better to do. Finally he gave a loud and delighted laugh at the result of his labors and placed the wooden cat, now completed, upon the hearth opposite the real one.

Puss thereupon glared at her image, raised her hair in anger, and uttered a defiant mew. The wooden cat paid no attention, and Claus, much amused, laughed again.

Then Blinkie advanced toward the wooden image to eye it closely and smell of it intelligently: Eyes and nose told her the creature was wood, in spite of its natural appearance; so puss resumed her seat and her purring, but as she neatly washed her face with her padded paw she cast more than one admiring glance at her clever master. Perhaps she felt the same satisfaction we feel when we look upon good photographs of ourselves.

The cat's master was himself pleased with his handiwork, without knowing exactly why. Indeed, he had great cause to congratulate himself that night, and all the children throughout the world should have joined him rejoicing. For Claus had made his first toy.

3. How the Ryls Colored the Toys

A HUSH LAY ON THE LAUGHING VALLEY NOW. SNOW COVERED IT LIKE A WHITE spread and pillows of downy flakes drifted before the dwelling where Claus sat feeding the blaze of the fire. The brook gurgled on beneath a heavy sheet of ice and all living plants and insects nestled close to Mother Earth to keep warm. The face of the moon was hid by dark clouds, and the wind, delighting in the wintry sport, pushed and whirled the snowflakes in so many directions that they could get no chance to fall to the ground.

Claus heard the wind whistling and shrieking in its play and thanked the good Knooks again for his comfortable shelter. Blinkie washed her face lazily and stared at the coals with a look of perfect content. The toy cat sat opposite the real one and gazed straight ahead, as toy cats should.

Suddenly Claus heard a noise that sounded different from the voice of the wind. It was more like a wail of suffering and despair.

He stood up and listened, but the wind, growing boisterous, shook the door and rattled the windows to distract his attention. He waited until the wind was tired and then, still listening, he heard once more the shrill cry of distress.

Quickly he drew on his coat, pulled his cap over his eyes and opened the door. The wind dashed in and scattered the embers over the hearth, at the same time blowing Blinkie's fur so furiously that she crept under the table to escape. Then the door was closed and Claus was outside, peering anxiously into the darkness.

The wind laughed and scolded and tried to push him over, but he stood firm. The helpless flakes stumbled against his eyes and dimmed his sight, but he rubbed them away and looked again. Snow was everywhere, white and glittering. It covered the earth and filled the air.

The cry was not repeated.

Claus turned to go back into the house, but the wind caught him unawares and he stumbled and fell across a snowdrift. His hand plunged into the drift and touched something that was not snow. This he seized and, pulling it gently toward him, found it to be a child. The next moment he had lifted it in his arms and carried it into the house.

The wind followed him through the door, but Claus shut it out quickly. He laid the rescued child on the hearth, and brushing away the snow he discovered it to be Weekum, a little boy who lived in a house beyond the Valley.

Claus wrapped a warm blanket around the little one and rubbed the frost from its limbs. Before long the child opened his eyes and, seeing where he was, smiled happily. Then Claus warmed milk and fed it to the boy slowly, while the cat looked on with sober curiosity. Finally the little one curled up in his friend's arms and sighed and fell asleep, and Claus, filled with gladness that he had found the wanderer, held him closely while he slumbered.

The wind, finding no more mischief to do, climbed the hill and swept on toward the north. This gave the weary snowflakes time to settle down to earth, and the Valley became still again.

The boy, having slept well in the arms of his friend, opened his eyes and sat up. Then, as a child will, he looked around the room and saw all that it contained.

"Your cat is a nice cat, Claus," he said, at last. "Let me hold it."

But puss objected and ran away.

"The other cat won't run, Claus," continued the boy. "Let me hold that one." Claus placed the toy in his arms, and the boy held it lovingly and kissed the tip of its wooden ear.

"How did you get lost in the storm, Weekum?" asked Claus.

"I started to walk to my auntie's house and lost my way," answered Weekum.

"Were you frightened?"

"It was cold," said Weekum, "and the snow got in my eyes, so I could not see. Then I kept on till I fell in the snow, without knowing where I was, and the wind blew the flakes over me and covered me up."

Claus gently stroked his head, and the boy looked up at him and smiled.

"I'm all right now," said Weekum.

"Yes," replied Claus, happily. "Now I will put you in my warm bed, and you must sleep until morning, when I will carry you back to your mother."

"May the cat sleep with me?" asked the boy.

"Yes, if you wish it to," answered Claus.

"It's a nice cat!" Weekum said, smiling, as Claus tucked the blankets around him; and presently the little one fell asleep with the wooden toy in his arms.

When morning came the sun claimed the Laughing Valley and flooded it with his rays; so Claus prepared to take the lost child back to its mother.

"May I keep the cat, Claus?" asked Weekum. "It's nicer than real cats. It doesn't run away, or scratch or bite. May I keep it?"

"Yes, indeed," answered Claus, pleased that the toy he had made could give pleasure to the child. So he wrapped the boy and the wooden cat in a warm cloak, perching the bundle upon his own broad shoulders, and then he tramped through the snow and the drifts of the Valley and across the plain beyond to the poor cottage where Weekum's mother lived.

"See, mama!" cried the boy, as soon as they entered, "I've got a cat!"

The good woman wept tears of joy over the rescue of her darling and thanked Claus many times for his kind act. So he carried a warm and happy heart back to his home in the Valley.

That night he said to puss: "I believe the children will love the wooden cats almost as well as the real ones, and they can't hurt them by pulling their tails and ears. I'll make another."

So this was the beginning of his great work.

The next cat was better made than the first. While Claus sat whittling it out the Yellow Ryl came in to make him a visit, and so pleased was he with the man's skill that he ran away and brought several of his fellows.

There sat the Red Ryl, the Black Ryl, the Green Ryl, the Blue Ryl and the Yellow Ryl in a circle on the floor, while Claus whittled and whistled and the wooden cat grew into shape.

"If it could be made the same color as the real cat, no one would know the difference," said the Yellow Ryl, thoughtfully.

"The little ones, maybe, would not know the difference," replied Claus, pleased with the idea.

"I will bring you some of the red that I color my roses and tulips with," cried the Red Ryl; "and then you can make the cat's lips and tongue red."

"I will bring some of the green that I color my grasses and leaves with," said the Green Ryl; "and then you can color the cat's eyes green."

"They will need a bit of yellow, also," remarked the Yellow Ryl; "I must fetch some of the yellow that I use to color my buttercups and goldenrods with."

"The real cat is black," said the Black Ryl; "I will bring some of the black that I use to color the eyes of my pansies with, and then you can paint your wooden cat black."

"I see you have a blue ribbon around Blinkie's neck," added the Blue Ryl. "I will get some of the color that I use to paint the bluebells and forget-me-nots with, and then you can carve a wooden ribbon on the toy cat's neck and paint it blue."

So the Ryls disappeared, and by the time Claus had finished carving out the form of the cat they were all back with the paints and brushes.

They made Blinkie sit upon the table, that Claus might paint the toy cat just the right color, and when the work was done the Ryls declared it was exactly as good as a live cat.

"That is, to all appearances," added the Red Ryl.

Blinkie seemed a little offended by the attention bestowed upon the toy, and that she might not seem to approve the imitation cat she walked to the corner of the hearth and sat down with a dignified air.

But Claus was delighted, and as soon as morning came he started out and tramped through the snow, across the Valley and the plain, until he came to a village. There, in a poor hut near the walls of the beautiful palace of the Lord of Lerd, a little girl lay upon a wretched cot, moaning with pain.

Claus approached the child and kissed her and comforted her, and then he drew the toy cat from beneath his coat, where he had hidden it, and placed it in her arms.

Ah, how well he felt himself repaid for his labor and his long walk when he saw the little one's eyes grow bright with pleasure! She hugged the kitty tight to her breast, as if it had been a precious gem, and would not let it go for a single moment. The fever was quieted, the pain grew less, and she fell into a sweet and refreshing sleep.

Claus laughed and whistled and sang all the way home. Never had he been so happy as on that day.

When he entered his house he found Shiegra, the lioness, awaiting him. Since his babyhood Shiegra had loved Claus, and while he dwelt in the Forest she had often come to visit him at Necile's bower. After Claus had gone to live in the Laughing Valley Shiegra became lonely and ill at ease, and now she had braved the snow-drifts, which all lions abhor, to see him once more. Shiegra was getting old and her teeth were beginning to fall out, while the hairs that tipped her ears and tail had changed from tawny-yellow to white.

Claus found her lying on his hearth, and he put his arms around the neck of the lioness and hugged her lovingly. The cat had retired into a far corner. She did not care to associate with Shiegra.

Claus told his old friend about the cats he had made, and how much pleasure they had given Weekum and the sick girl. Shiegra did not know much about children; indeed, if she met a child she could scarcely be trusted not to devour it. But she was interested in Claus' new labors, and said:

"These images seem to me very attractive. Yet I can not see why you should make cats, which are very unimportant animals. Suppose, now that I am here, you make the image of a lioness, the Queen of all beasts. Then, indeed, your children will be happy—and safe at the same time!"

Claus thought this was a good suggestion. So he got a piece of wood and sharpened his knife, while Shiegra crouched upon the hearth at his feet. With much care he carved the head in the likeness of the lioness, even to the two fierce teeth that curved over her lower lip and the deep, frowning lines above her wide-open eyes.

When it was finished he said:

"You have a terrible look, Shiegra."

"Then the image is like me," she answered; "for I am indeed terrible to all who are not my friends."

Claus now carved out the body, with Shiegra's long tail trailing behind it. The image of the crouching lioness was very life-like.

"It pleases me," said Shiegra, yawning and stretching her body gracefully. "Now I will watch while you paint."

He brought the paints the Ryls had given him from the cupboard and colored the image to resemble the real Shiegra.

The lioness placed her big, padded paws upon the edge of the table and raised herself while she carefully examined the toy that was her likeness.

"You are indeed skillful!" she said, proudly. "The children will like that better than cats, I'm sure."

Then snarling at Blinkie, who arched her back in terror and whined fearfully, she walked away toward her forest home with stately strides.

4. How Little Mayrie Became Frightened

THE WINTER WAS OVER NOW, AND ALL THE LAUGHING VALLEY WAS FILLED with joyous excitement. The brook was so happy at being free once again that it gurgled more boisterously than ever and dashed so recklessly against the rocks that it sent showers of spray high in the air. The grass thrust its sharp little blades upward through the mat of dead stalks where it had hidden from the snow, but the flowers were yet too timid to show themselves, although the Ryls were busy feeding their roots. The sun was in remarkably good humor, and sent his rays dancing merrily throughout the Valley.

Claus was eating his dinner one day when he heard a timid knock on his door.

"Come in!" he called.

No one entered, but after a pause came another rapping.

Claus jumped up and threw open the door. Before him stood a small girl holding a smaller brother fast by the hand.

"Is you Tlaus?" she asked, shyly.

"Indeed I am, my dear!" he answered, with a laugh, as he caught both children in his arms and kissed them. "You are very welcome, and you have come just in time to share my dinner."

He took them to the table and fed them with fresh milk and nut-cakes. When they had eaten enough he asked:

"Why have you made this long journey to see me?"

"I wants a tat!" replied little Mayrie; and her brother, who had not yet learned to speak many words, nodded his head and exclaimed like an echo: "Tat!"

"Oh, you want my toy cats, do you?" returned Claus, greatly pleased to discover that his creations were so popular with children.

The little visitors nodded eagerly.

"Unfortunately," he continued, "I have but one cat now ready, for I carried two to children in the town yesterday. And the one I have shall be given to your brother, Mayrie, because he is the smaller; and the next one I make shall be for you."

The boy's face was bright with smiles as he took the precious toy Claus held out to him; but little Mayrie covered her face with her arm and began to sob grievously.

"I—I—I wants a t—t—tat now!" she wailed.

Her disappointment made Claus feel miserable for a moment. Then he suddenly remembered Shiegra.

"Don't cry, darling!" he said, soothingly; "I have a toy much nicer than a cat, and you shall have that."

He went to the cupboard and drew out the image of the lioness, which he placed on the table before Mayrie.

The girl raised her arm and gave one glance at the fierce teeth and glaring eyes of the beast, and then, uttering a terrified scream, she rushed from the house. The boy followed her, also screaming lustily, and even dropping his precious cat in his fear.

For a moment Claus stood motionless, being puzzled and astonished. Then he threw Shiegra's image into the cupboard and ran after the children, calling to them not to be frightened.

Little Mayrie stopped in her flight and her brother clung to her skirt; but they both cast fearful glances at the house until Claus had assured them many times that the beast had been locked in the cupboard.

"Yet why were you frightened at seeing it?" he asked. "It is only a toy to play with!"

"It's bad!" said Mayrie, decidedly, "an'—an'—just horrid, an' not a bit nice, like tats!"

"Perhaps you are right," returned Claus, thoughtfully. "But if you will return with me to the house I will soon make you a pretty cat."

So they timidly entered the house again, having faith in their friend's words; and afterward they had the joy of watching Claus carve out a cat from a bit of wood and paint it in natural colors. It did not take him long to do this, for he had become skillful with his knife by this time, and Mayrie loved her toy the more dearly because she had seen it made.

After his little visitors had trotted away on their journey homeward Claus sat long in deep thought. And he then decided that such fierce creatures as his friend the lioness would never do as models from which to fashion his toys.

"There must be nothing to frighten the dear babies," he reflected; "and while I know Shiegra well, and am not afraid of her, it is but natural that children should look upon her image with terror. Hereafter I will choose such mild-mannered animals as squirrels and rabbits and deer and lambkins from which to carve my toys, for then the little ones will love rather than fear them."

He began his work that very day, and before bedtime had made a wooden rabbit and a lamb. They were not quite so lifelike as the cats had been, because they were formed from memory, while Blinkie had sat very still for Claus to look at while he worked.

But the new toys pleased the children nevertheless, and the fame of Claus' playthings quickly spread to every cottage on plain and in village. He always carried his gifts to the sick or crippled children, but those who were strong enough walked to the house in the Valley to ask for them, so a little path was soon worn from the plain to the door of the toy-maker's cottage.

First came the children who had been playmates of Claus, before he began to make toys. These, you may be sure, were well supplied. Then children who lived farther away heard of the wonderful images and made journeys to the Valley to secure them. All little ones were welcome, and never a one went away empty-handed.

This demand for his handiwork kept Claus busily occupied, but he was quite happy in knowing the pleasure he gave to so many of the dear children. His friends the immortals were pleased with his success and supported him bravely.

The Knooks selected for him clear pieces of soft wood, that his knife might not be blunted in cutting them; the Ryls kept him supplied with paints of all colors and brushes fashioned from the tips of timothy grasses; the Fairies discovered that the workman needed saws and chisels and hammers and nails, as well as knives, and brought him a goodly array of such tools.

Claus soon turned his living room into a most wonderful workshop. He built a bench before the window, and arranged his tools and paints so that he could reach everything as he sat on his stool. And as he finished toy after toy to delight the hearts of little children he found himself growing so gay and happy that he could not refrain from singing and laughing and whistling all the day long.

"It's because I live in the Laughing Valley, where everything else laughs!" said Claus.

But that was not the reason.

5. How Bessie Blithesome Came to the Laughing Valley

ONE DAY, AS CLAUS SAT BEFORE HIS DOOR TO ENJOY THE SUNSHINE WHILE HE busily carved the head and horns of a toy deer, he looked up and discovered a glittering cavalcade of horsemen approaching through the Valley.

When they drew nearer he saw that the band consisted of a score of men-at-arms, clad in bright armor and bearing in their hands spears and battle-axes. In front of these rode little Bessie Blithesome, the pretty daughter of that proud Lord of Lerd who had once driven Claus from his palace. Her palfrey was pure white, its bridle was covered with glittering gems, and its saddle draped with cloth of gold, richly broidered. The soldiers were sent to protect her from harm while she journeyed.

Claus was surprised, but he continued to whittle and to sing until the cavalcade drew up before him. Then the little girl leaned over the neck of her palfrey and said:

"Please, Mr. Claus, I want a toy!"

Her voice was so pleading that Claus jumped up at once and stood beside her. But he was puzzled how to answer her request.

"You are a rich lord's daughter," said he, "and have all that you desire."

"Except toys," added Bessie. "There are no toys in all the world but yours."

"And I make them for the poor children, who have nothing else to amuse them," continued Claus.

"Do poor children love to play with toys more than rich ones?" asked Bessie.

"I suppose not," said Claus, thoughtfully.

"Am I to blame because my father is a lord? Must I be denied the pretty toys I long for because other children are poorer than I?" she inquired earnestly.

"I'm afraid you must, dear," he answered; "for the poor have nothing else with which to amuse themselves. You have your pony to ride, your servants to wait on you, and every comfort that money can procure."

"But I want toys!" cried Bessie, wiping away the tears that forced themselves into her eyes. "If I can not have them, I shall be very unhappy."

Claus was troubled, for her grief recalled to him the thought that his desire was to make all children happy, without regard to their condition in life. Yet, while so many poor children were clamoring for his toys he could not bear to give one to them to Bessie Blithesome, who had so much already to make her happy.

"Listen, my child," said he, gently; "all the toys I am now making are promised to others. But the next shall be yours, since your heart so longs for it. Come to me again in two days and it shall be ready for you."

Bessie gave a cry of delight, and leaning over her pony's neck she kissed Claus prettily upon his forehead. Then, calling to her men-at-arms, she rode gaily away, leaving Claus to resume his work.

"If I am to supply the rich children as well as the poor ones," he thought, "I shall not have a spare moment in the whole year! But is it right I should give to the rich? Surely I must go to Necile and talk with her about this matter."

So when he had finished the toy deer, which was very like a deer he had known in the Forest glades, he walked into Burzee and made his way to the bower of the beautiful Nymph Necile, who had been his foster mother.

She greeted him tenderly and lovingly, listening with interest to his story of the visit of Bessie Blithesome.

"And now tell me," said he, "shall I give toys to rich children?"

"We of the Forest know nothing of riches," she replied. "It seems to me that one child is like another child, since they are all made of the same clay, and that riches are like a gown, which may be put on or taken away, leaving the child unchanged. But the Fairies are guardians of mankind, and know mortal children better than I. Let us call the Fairy Queen."

This was done, and the Queen of the Fairies sat beside them and heard Claus relate his reasons for thinking the rich children could get along without his toys, and also what the Nymph had said.

"Necile is right," declared the Queen; "for, whether it be rich or poor, a child's longings for pretty playthings are but natural. Rich Bessie's heart may suffer as much grief as poor Mayrie's; she can be just as lonely and discontented, and just as gay and happy. I think, friend Claus, it is your duty to make all little ones glad, whether they chance to live in palaces or in cottages."

"Your words are wise, fair Queen," replied Claus, "and my heart tells me they are as just as they are wise. Hereafter all children may claim my services."

Then he bowed before the gracious Fairy and, kissing Necile's red lips, went back into his Valley.

At the brook he stopped to drink, and afterward he sat on the bank and took a piece of moist clay in his hands while he thought what sort of toy he should make for Bessie Blithesome. He did not notice that his fingers were working the clay into shape until, glancing downward, he found he had unconsciously formed a head that bore a slight resemblance to the Nymph Necile!

At once he became interested. Gathering more of the clay from the bank he carried it to his house. Then, with the aid of his knife and a bit of wood he succeeded in working the clay into the image of a toy nymph. With skillful strokes he formed long, waving hair on the head and covered the body with a gown of oakleaves, while the two feet sticking out at the bottom of the gown were clad in sandals.

But the clay was soft, and Claus found he must handle it gently to avoid ruining his pretty work.

"Perhaps the rays of the sun will draw out the moisture and cause the clay to become hard," he thought. So he laid the image on a flat board and placed it in the glare of the sun.

This done, he went to his bench and began painting the toy deer, and soon he became so interested in the work that he forgot all about the clay nymph. But next morning, happening to notice it as it lay on the board, he found the sun had baked it to the hardness of stone, and it was strong enough to be safely handled.

Claus now painted the nymph with great care in the likeness of Necile, giving it deep-blue eyes, white teeth, rosy lips and ruddy-brown hair. The gown he colored oak-leaf green, and when the paint was dry Claus himself was charmed with the new toy. Of course it was not nearly so lovely as the real Necile; but, considering the material of which it was made, Claus thought it was very beautiful.

When Bessie, riding upon her white palfrey, came to his dwelling next day, Claus presented her with the new toy. The little girl's eyes were brighter than ever as she examined the pretty image, and she loved it at once, and held it close to her breast, as a mother does to her child.

"What is it called, Claus?" she asked.

Now Claus knew that Nymphs do not like to be spoken of by mortals, so he could not tell Bessie it was an image of Necile he had given her. But as it was a new toy he searched his mind for a new name to call it by, and the first word he thought of he decided would do very well.

"It is called a dolly, my dear," he said to Bessie.

"I shall call the dolly my baby," returned Bessie, kissing it fondly; "and I shall tend it and care for it just as Nurse cares for me. Thank you very much, Claus; your gift has made me happier than I have ever been before!"

Then she rode away, hugging the toy in her arms, and Claus, seeing her delight, thought he would make another dolly, better and more natural than the first.

He brought more clay from the brook, and remembering that Bessie had called the dolly her baby he resolved to form this one into a baby's image. That was no difficult task to the clever workman, and soon the baby dolly was lying on the board and placed in the sun to dry. Then, with the clay that was left, he began to make an image of Bessie Blithesome herself.

This was not so easy, for he found he could not make the silken robe of the lord's daughter out of the common clay. So he called the Fairies to his aid, and asked them to bring him colored silks with which to make a real dress for the clay image. The Fairies set off at once on their errand, and before nightfall they returned with a generous supply of silks and laces and golden threads.

Claus now became impatient to complete his new dolly, and instead of waiting for the next day's sun he placed the clay image upon his hearth and covered it over with glowing coals. By morning, when he drew the dolly from the ashes, it had baked as hard as if it had lain a full day in the hot sun.

Now our Claus became a dressmaker as well as a toymaker. He cut the lavender silk, and neaty sewed it into a beautiful gown that just fitted the new dolly. And he put a lace collar around its neck and pink silk shoes on its feet. The natural color of baked clay is a light gray, but Claus painted the face to resemble the color of flesh, and he gave the dolly Bessie's brown eyes and golden hair and rosy cheeks.

It was really a beautiful thing to look upon, and sure to bring joy to some childish heart. While Claus was admiring it he heard a knock at his door, and little Mayrie entered. Her face was sad and her eyes red with continued weeping.

"Why, what has grieved you, my dear?" asked Claus, taking the child in his arms.

"I've—I've—bwoke my tat!" sobbed Mayrie.

"How?" he inquired, his eyes twinkling.

"I—I dwopped him, an' bwoke off him's tail; an'—an'—then I dwopped him an' bwoke off him's ear! An'—an' now him's all spoilt!"

Claus laughed.

"Never mind, Mayrie dear," he said. "How would you like this new dolly, instead of a cat?"

Mayrie looked at the silk-robed dolly and her eyes grew big with astonishment.

"Oh, Tlaus!" she cried, clapping her small hands together with rapture; "tan I have 'at boo'ful lady?"

"Do you like it?" he asked.

"I love it!" said she. "It's better 'an tats!"

"Then take it, dear, and be careful not to break it."

Mayrie took the dolly with a joy that was almost reverent, and her face dimpled with smiles as she started along the path toward home.

6. The Wickedness of the Awgwas

I MUST NOW TELL YOU SOMETHING ABOUT THE AWGWAS, THAT TERRIBLE RACE of creatures which caused our good Claus so much trouble and nearly succeeded in robbing the children of the world of their earliest and best friend.

I do not like to mention the Awgwas, but they are a part of this history, and can not be ignored. They were neither mortals nor immortals, but stood midway between those classes of beings. The Awgwas were invisible to ordinary people, but not to immortals. They could pass swiftly through the air from one part of the world to another, and had the power of influencing the minds of human beings to do their wicked will.

They were of gigantic stature and had coarse, scowling countenances which showed plainly their hatred of all mankind. They possessed no consciences whatever and delighted only in evil deeds.

Their homes were in rocky, mountainous places, from whence they sallied forth to accomplish their wicked purposes.

The one of their number that could think of the most horrible deed for them to do was always elected the King Awgwa, and all the race obeyed his orders. Sometimes these creatures lived to become a hundred years old, but usually they fought so fiercely among themselves that many were destroyed in combat, and when they died that was the end of them. Mortals were powerless to harm them and the immortals shuddered when the Awgwas were mentioned, and always avoided them. So they flourished for many years unopposed and accomplished much evil.

I am glad to assure you that these vile creatures have long since perished and passed from earth; but in the days when Claus was making his first toys they were a numerous and powerful tribe.

One of the principal sports of the Awgwas was to inspire angry passions in the hearts of little children, so that they quarreled and fought with one another. They would tempt boys to eat of unripe fruit, and then delight in the pain they suffered; they urged little girls to disobey their parents, and then would laugh when the children were punished. I do not know what causes a child to be naughty in these days, but when the Awgwas were on earth naughty children were usually under their influence.

Now, when Claus began to make children happy he kept them out of the power of the Awgwas; for children possessing such lovely playthings as he gave them had no wish to obey the evil thoughts the Awgwas tried to thrust into their minds.

Therefore, one year when the wicked tribe was to elect a new King, they chose an Awgwa who proposed to destroy Claus and take him away from the children.

"There are, as you know, fewer naughty children in the world since Claus came to the Laughing Valley and began to make his toys," said the new King, as he squatted upon a rock and looked around at the scowling faces of his people. "Why, Bessie Blithesome has not stamped her foot once this month, nor has Mayrie's brother slapped his sister's face or thrown the puppy into the rain-barrel. Little Weekum took his bath last night without screaming or struggling, because his mother had promised he should take his toy cat to bed with him! Such a condition of affairs is awful for any Awgwa to think of, and the only way we can direct the naughty actions of children is to take this person Claus away from them."

"Good! good!" cried the big Awgwas, in a chorus, and they clapped their hands to applaud the speech of the King.

"But what shall we do with him?" asked one of the creatures.

"I have a plan," replied the wicked King; and what his plan was you will soon discover.

That night Claus went to bed feeling very happy, for he had completed no less than four pretty toys during the day, and they were sure, he thought, to make four little children happy. But while he slept the band of invisible Awgwas surrounded his bed, bound him with stout cords, and then flew away with him to the middle of a dark forest in far off Ethop, where they laid him down and left him.

When morning came Claus found himself thousands of miles from any human being, a prisoner in the wild jungle of an unknown land.

From the limb of a tree above his head swayed a huge python, one of those reptiles that are able to crush a man's bones in their coils. A few yards away crouched a savage panther, its glaring red eyes fixed full on the helpless Claus. One of those monstrous spotted spiders whose sting is death crept stealthily toward him over the matted leaves, which shriveled and turned black at its very touch.

But Claus had been reared in Burzee, and was not afraid.

"Come to me, ye Knooks of the Forest!" he cried, and gave the low, peculiar whistle that the Knooks know.

The panther, which was about to spring upon its victim, turned and slunk away. The python swung itself into the tree and disappeared among the leaves. The spider stopped short in its advance and hid beneath a rotting log.

Claus had no time to notice them, for he was surrounded by a band of harsh-featured Knooks, more crooked and deformed in appearance than any he had ever seen.

"Who are you that call on us?" demanded one, in a gruff voice.

"The friend of your brothers in Burzee," answered Claus. "I have been brought here by my enemies, the Awgwas, and left to perish miserably. Yet now I implore your help to release me and to send me home again."

"Have you the sign?" asked another.

"Yes," said Claus.

They cut his bonds, and with his free arms he made the secret sign of the Knooks.

Instantly they assisted him to stand upon his feet, and they brought him food and drink to strengthen him.

"Our brothers of Burzee make queer friends," grumbled an ancient Knook whose flowing beard was pure white. "But he who knows our secret sign and signal is entitled to our help, whoever he may be. Close your eyes, stranger, and we will conduct you to your home. Where shall we seek it?"

"'Tis in the Laughing Valley," answered Claus, shutting his eyes.

"There is but one Laughing Valley in the known world, so we can not go astray," remarked the Knook.

As he spoke the sound of his voice seemed to die away, so Claus opened his eyes to see what caused the change. To his astonishment he found himself seated on the bench by his own door, with the Laughing Valley spread out before him. That day he visited the Wood-Nymphs and related his adventure to Queen Zurline and Necile.

"The Awgwas have become your enemies," said the lovely Queen, thoughtfully; "so we must do all we can to protect you from their power."

"It was cowardly to bind him while he slept," remarked Necile, with indignation.

"The evil ones are ever cowardly," answered Zurline, "but our friend's slumber shall not be disturbed again."

The Queen herself came to the dwelling of Claus that evening and placed her Seal on every door and window, to keep out the Awgwas. And under the Seal of Queen Zurline was placed the Seal of the Fairies and the Seal of the Ryls and the Seals of the Knooks, that the charm might become more powerful.

And Claus carried his toys to the children again, and made many more of the little ones happy.

You may guess how angry the King Awgwa and his fierce band were when it was known to them that Claus had escaped from the Forest of Ethop.

They raged madly for a whole week, and then held another meeting among the rocks.

"It is useless to carry him where the Knooks reign," said the King, "for he has their protection. So let us cast him into a cave of our own mountains, where he will surely perish."

This was promptly agreed to, and the wicked band set out that night to seize Claus. But they found his dwelling guarded by the Seals of the Immortals and were obliged to go away baffled and disappointed.

"Never mind," said the King; "he does not sleep always!"

Next day, as Claus traveled to the village across the plain, where he intended to present a toy squirrel to a lame boy, he was suddenly set upon by the Awgwas, who seized him and carried him away to the mountains.

There they thrust him within a deep cavern and rolled many huge rocks against the entrance to prevent his escape.

Deprived thus of light and food, and with little air to breathe, our Claus was, indeed, in a pitiful plight. But he spoke the mystic words of the Fairies, which always command their friendly aid, and they came to his rescue and transported him to the Laughing Valley in the twinkling of an eye.

Thus the Awgwas discovered they might not destroy one who had earned the friendship of the immortals; so the evil band sought other means of keeping Claus from bringing happiness to children and so making them obedient.

Whenever Claus set out to carry his toys to the little ones an Awgwa, who had been set to watch his movements, sprang upon him and snatched the toys from his grasp. And the children were no more disappointed than was Claus when he was obliged to return home disconsolate. Still he persevered, and made many toys for his little friends and started with them for the villages. And always the Awgwas robbed him as soon as he had left the Valley.

They threw the stolen playthings into one of their lonely caverns, and quite a heap of toys accumulated before Claus became discouraged and gave up all attempts to leave the Valley. Then children began coming to him, since they found he did not go to them; but the wicked Awgwas flew around them and caused their steps to stray and the paths to become crooked, so never a little one could find a way into the Laughing Valley.

Lonely days now fell upon Claus, for he was denied the pleasure of bringing happiness to the children whom he had learned to love. Yet he bore up bravely, for he thought surely the time would come when the Awgwas would abandon their evil designs to injure him.

He devoted all his hours to toy-making, and when one plaything had been completed he stood it on a shelf he had built for that purpose. When the shelf became filled with rows of toys he made another one, and filled that also. So that in time he had many shelves filled with gay and beautiful toys representing horses, dogs, cats, elephants, lambs, rabbits and deer, as well as pretty dolls of all sizes and balls and marbles of baked clay painted in gay colors.

Often, as he glanced at this array of childish treasures, the heart of good old Claus became sad, so greatly did he long to carry the toys to his children. And at last, because he could bear it no longer, he ventured to go to the great Ak, to whom he told the story of his persecution by the Awgwas, and begged the Master Woodsman to assist him.

7. The Great Battle Between Good and Evil

AK LISTENED GRAVELY TO THE RECITAL OF CLAUS, STROKING HIS BEARD THE while with the slow, graceful motion that betokened deep thought. He nodded approvingly when Claus told how the Knooks and Fairies had saved him from death, and frowned when he heard how the Awgwas had stolen the children's toys. At last he said:

"From the beginning I have approved the work you are doing among the children of men, and it annoys me that your good deeds should be thwarted by the Awgwas. We immortals have no connection whatever with the evil creatures who have attacked you. Always have we avoided them, and they, in turn, have hitherto taken care not to cross our pathway. But in this matter I find they have interfered with one of our friends, and I will ask them to abandon their persecutions, as you are under our protection."

Claus thanked the Master Woodsman most gratefully and returned to his Valley, while Ak, who never delayed carrying out his promises, at once traveled to the mountains of the Awgwas.

There, standing on the bare rocks, he called on the King and his people to appear.

Instantly the place was filled with throngs of the scowling Awgwas, and their King, perching himself on a point of rock, demanded fiercely:

"Who dares call on us?"

"It is I, the Master Woodsman of the World," responded Ak.

"Here are no forests for you to claim," cried the King, angrily. "We owe no allegiance to you, nor to any immortal!"

"That is true," replied Ak, calmly. "Yet you have ventured to interfere with the actions of Claus, who dwells in the Laughing Valley, and is under our protection."

Many of the Awgwas began muttering at this speech, and their King turned threateningly on the Master Woodsman.

"You are set to rule the forests, but the plains and the valleys are ours!" he shouted. "Keep to your own dark woods! We will do as we please with Claus."

"You shall not harm our friend in any way!" replied Ak.

"Shall we not?" asked the King, impudently. "You will see! Our powers are vastly superior to those of mortals, and fully as great as those of immortals."

"It is your conceit that misleads you!" said Ak, sternly. "You are a transient race, passing from life into nothingness. We, who live forever, pity but despise you. On earth you are scorned by all, and in Heaven you have no place! Even the mortals, after their earth life, enter another existence for all time, and so are your superiors. How then dare you, who are neither mortal nor immortal, refuse to obey my wish?"

The Awgwas sprang to their feet with menacing gestures, but their King motioned them back.

"Never before," he cried to Ak, while his voice trembled with rage, "has an immortal declared himself the master of the Awgwas! Never shall an immortal venture to interfere with our actions again! For we will avenge your scornful words by killing your friend Claus within three days. Nor you, nor all the immortals can save him from our wrath. We defy your powers! Begone, Master Woodsman of the World! In the country of the Awgwas you have no place."

"It is war!" declared Ak, with flashing eyes.

"It is war!" returned the King, savagely. "In three days your friend will be dead."

The Master turned away and came to his Forest of Burzee, where he called a meeting of the immortals and told them of the defiance of the Awgwas and their purpose to kill Claus within three days.

The little folk listened to him quietly.

"What shall we do?" asked Ak.

"These creatures are of no benefit to the world," said the Prince of the Knooks; "we must destroy them."

"Their lives are devoted only to evil deeds," said the Prince of the Ryls. "We must destroy them."

"They have no conscience, and endeavor to make all mortals as bad as themselves," said the Queen of the Fairies. "We must destroy them."

"They have defied the great Ak, and threaten the life of our adopted son," said beautiful Queen Zurline. "We must destroy them."

The Master Woodsman smiled.

"You speak well," said he. "These Awgwas we know to be a powerful race, and they will fight desperately; yet the outcome is certain. For we who live can never die, even though conquered by our enemies, while every Awgwa who is struck down is one foe the less to oppose us. Prepare, then, for battle, and let us resolve to show no mercy to the wicked!"

Thus arose that terrible war between the immortals and the spirits of evil which is sung of in Fairyland to this very day.

The King Awgwa and his band determined to carry out the threat to destroy Claus. They now hated him for two reasons: he made children happy and was a friend of the Master Woodsman. But since Ak's visit they had reason to fear the opposition of the immortals, and they dreaded defeat. So the King sent swift messengers to all parts of the world to summon every evil creature to his aid.

And on the third day after the declaration of war a mighty army was at the command of the King Awgwa. There were three hundred Asiatic Dragons, breathing fire that consumed everything it touched. These hated mankind and all good spirits. And there were the three-eyed Giants of

Tatary, a host in themselves, who liked nothing better than to fight. And next came the Black Demons from Patalonia, with great spreading wings like those of a bat, which swept terror and misery through the world as they beat upon the air. And joined to these were the Goozzle-Goblins, with long talons as sharp as swords, with which they clawed the flesh from their foes. Finally, every mountain Awgwa in the world had come to participate in the great battle with the immortals.

The King Awgwa looked around upon this vast army and his heart beat high with wicked pride, for he believed he would surely triumph over his gentle enemies, who had never before been known to fight. But the Master Woodsman had not been idle. None of his people was used to warfare, yet now that they were called upon to face the hosts of evil they willingly prepared for the fray.

Ak had commanded them to assemble in the Laughing Valley, where Claus, ignorant of the terrible battle that was to be waged on his account, was quietly making his toys.

Soon the entire Valley, from hill to hill, was filled with the little immortals. The Master Woodsman stood first, bearing a gleaming ax that shone like burnished silver. Next came the Ryls, armed with sharp thorns from bramblebushes. Then the Knooks, bearing the spears they used when they were forced to prod their savage beasts into submission. The Fairies, dressed in white gauze with rainbow-hued wings, bore golden wands, and the Wood-nymphs, in their uniforms of oak-leaf green, carried switches from ash trees as weapons.

Loud laughed the Awgwa King when he beheld the size and the arms of his foes. To be sure the mighty ax of the Woodsman was to be dreaded, but the sweet-faced Nymphs and pretty Fairies, the gentle Ryls and crooked Knooks were such harmless folk that he almost felt shame at having called such a terrible host to oppose them.

"Since these fools dare fight," he said to the leader of the Tatary Giants, "I will overwhelm them with our evil powers!"

To begin the battle he poised a great stone in his left hand and cast it full against the sturdy form of the Master Woodsman, who turned it aside with his ax. Then rushed the three-eyed Giants of Tatary upon the Knooks, and the Goozzle-Goblins upon the Ryls, and the firebreathing Dragons upon the sweet Fairies. Because the Nymphs were Ak's own people the band of Awgwas sought them out, thinking to overcome them with ease.

But it is the Law that while Evil, unopposed, may accomplish terrible deeds, the powers of Good can never be overthrown when opposed to Evil. Well had it been for the King Awgwa had he known the Law!

His ignorance cost him his existence, for one flash of the ax borne by the Master Woodsman of the World cleft the wicked King in twain and rid the earth of the vilest creature it contained.

Greatly marveled the Tatary Giants when the spears of the little Knooks pierced their thick walls of flesh and sent them reeling to the ground with howls of agony.

Woe came upon the sharp-taloned Goblins when the thorns of the Ryls reached their savage hearts and let their life-blood sprinkle all the plain. And afterward from every drop a thistle grew.

The Dragons paused astonished before the Fairy wands, from whence rushed a power that caused their fiery breaths to flow back on themselves so that they shriveled away and died.

As for the Awgwas, they had scant time to realize how they were destroyed, for the ash switches of the Nymphs bore a charm unknown to any Awgwa, and turned their foes into clods of earth at the slightest touch!

When Ak leaned upon his gleaming ax and turned to look over the field of battle he saw the few Giants who were able to run disappearing over the distant hills on their return to Tatary. The Goblins had perished every one, as had the terrible Dragons, while all that remained of the wicked Awgwas was a great number of earthen hillocks dotting the plain.

And now the immortals melted from the Valley like dew at sunrise, to resume their duties in the Forest, while Ak walked slowly and thoughtfully to the house of Claus and entered.

"You have many toys ready for the children," said the Woodsman, "and now you may carry them across the plain to the dwellings and the villages without fear."

"Will not the Awgwas harm me?" asked Claus, eagerly.

"The Awgwas," said Ak, "have perished!"

Now I will gladly have done with wicked spirits and with fighting and bloodshed. It was not from choice that I told of the Awgwas and their allies, and of their great battle with the immortals. They were part of this history, and could not be avoided.

8. The First Journey with the Reindeer

THOSE WERE HAPPY DAYS FOR CLAUS WHEN HE CARRIED HIS ACCUMULATION OF toys to the children who had awaited them so long. During his imprisonment in the Valley he had been so industrious that all his shelves were filled with playthings, and after quickly supplying the little ones living near by he saw he must now extend his travels to wider fields.

Remembering the time when he had journeyed with Ak through all the world, he knew children were everywhere, and he longed to make as many as possible happy with his gifts.

So he loaded a great sack with all kinds of toys, slung it upon his back that he might carry it more easily, and started off on a longer trip than he had yet undertaken.

Wherever he showed his merry face, in hamlet or in farmhouse, he received a cordial welcome, for his fame had spread into far lands. At each village the children swarmed about him, following his footsteps wherever he went; and the women thanked him gratefully for the joy he brought their little ones; and the men looked upon him curiously that he should devote his time to such a queer occupation as toy-making. But every one smiled on him and gave him kindly words, and Claus felt amply repaid for his long journey.

When the sack was empty he went back again to the Laughing Valley and once more filled it to the brim. This time he followed another road, into a different part of the country, and carried happiness to many children who never before had owned a toy or guessed that such a delightful plaything existed.

After a third journey, so far away that Claus was many days walking the distance, the store of toys became exhausted and without delay he set about making a fresh supply.

From seeing so many children and studying their tastes he had acquired several new ideas about toys.

The dollies were, he had found, the most delightful of all playthings for babies and little girls, and often those who could not say "dolly" would call for a "doll" in their sweet baby talk. So Claus resolved to make many dolls, of all sizes, and to dress them in bright-colored clothing. The older boys—and even some of the girls—loved the images of animals, so he still made cats and elephants and horses. And many of the little fellows had musical natures, and longed for drums and cymbals and whistles and horns. So he made a number of toy drums, with tiny sticks to beat them with; and he made whistles from the willow trees, and horns from the bog-reeds, and cymbals from bits of beaten metal.

All this kept him busily at work, and before he realized it the winter season came, with deeper snows than usual, and he knew he could not leave the Valley with his heavy pack. Moreover, the next trip would take him farther from home than every before, and Jack Frost was mischievous enough to nip his nose and ears if he undertook the long journey while the Frost King reigned. The Frost King was Jack's father and never reproved him for his pranks.

So Claus remained at his work-bench; but he whistled and sang as merrily as ever, for he would allow no disappointment to sour his temper or make him unhappy.

One bright morning he looked from his window and saw two of the deer he had known in the Forest walking toward his house.

Claus was surprised; not that the friendly deer should visit him, but that they walked on the surface of the snow as easily as if it were solid ground, notwithstanding the fact that throughout the Valley the snow lay many feet deep. He had walked out of his house a day or two before and had sunk to his armpits in a drift.

So when the deer came near he opened the door and called to them:

"Good morning, Flossie! Tell me how you are able to walk on the snow so easily."

"It is frozen hard," answered Flossie.

"The Frost King has breathed on it," said Glossie, coming up, "and the surface is now as solid as ice."

"Perhaps," remarked Claus, thoughtfully, "I might now carry my pack of toys to the children."

"Is it a long journey?" asked Flossie.

"Yes; it will take me many days, for the pack is heavy," answered Claus.

"Then the snow would melt before you could get back," said the deer. "You must wait until spring, Claus."

Claus sighed. "Had I your fleet feet," said he, "I could make the journey in a day."

"But you have not," returned Glossie, looking at his own slender legs with pride.

"Perhaps I could ride upon your back," Claus ventured to remark, after a pause.

"Oh no; our backs are not strong enough to bear your weight," said Flossie, decidedly. "But if you had a sledge, and could harness us to it, we might draw you easily, and your pack as well."

"I'll make a sledge!" exclaimed Claus. "Will you agree to draw me if I do?"

"Well," replied Flossie, "we must first go and ask the Knooks, who are our guardians, for permission; but if they consent, and you can make a sledge and harness, we will gladly assist you."

"Then go at once!" cried Claus, eagerly. "I am sure the friendly Knooks will give their consent, and by the time you are back I shall be ready to harness you to my sledge."

Flossie and Glossie, being deer of much intelligence, had long wished to see the great world, so they gladly ran over the frozen snow to ask the Knooks if they might carry Claus on his journey.

Meantime the toy-maker hurriedly began the construction of a sledge, using material from his wood-pile. He made two long runners that turned upward at the front ends, and across these nailed short boards, to make a platform. It was soon completed, but was as rude in appearance as it is possible for a sledge to be.

The harness was more difficult to prepare, but Claus twisted strong cords together and knotted them so they would fit around the necks of the deer, in the shape of a collar. From these ran other cords to fasten the deer to the front of the sledge.

Before the work was completed Glossie and Flossie were back from the Forest, having been granted permission by Will Knook to make the journey with Claus provided they would to Burzee by daybreak the next morning.

"That is not a very long time," said Flossie; "but we are swift and strong, and if we get started by this evening we can travel many miles during the night."

Claus decided to make the attempt, so he hurried on his preparations as fast as possible. After a time he fastened the collars around the necks of his steeds and harnessed them to his rude sledge. Then he placed a stool on the little platform, to serve as a seat, and filled a sack with his prettiest toys.

"How do you intend to guide us?" asked Glossie. "We have never been out of the Forest before, except to visit your house, so we shall not know the way."

Claus thought about that for a moment. Then he brought more cords and fastened two of them to the spreading antlers of each deer, one on the right and the other on the left.

"Those will be my reins," said Claus, "and when I pull them to the right or to the left you must go in that direction. If I do not pull the reins at all you may go straight ahead."

"Very well," answered Glossie and Flossie; and then they asked: "Are you ready?"

Claus seated himself upon the stool, placed the sack of toys at his feet, and then gathered up the reins.

"All ready!" he shouted; "away we go!"

The deer leaned forward, lifted their slender limbs, and the next moment away flew the sledge over the frozen snow. The swiftness of the motion surprised Claus, for in a few strides they were across the Valley and gliding over the broad plain beyond.

The day had melted into evening by the time they started; for, swiftly as Claus had worked, many hours had been consumed in making his preparations. But the moon shone brightly to light their way, and Claus soon decided it was just as pleasant to travel by night as by day.

The deer liked it better; for, although they wished to see something of the world, they were timid about meeting men, and now all the dwellers in the towns and farmhouses were sound asleep and could not see them.

Away and away they sped, on and on over the hills and through the valleys and across the plains until they reached a village where Claus had never been before.

Here he called on them to stop, and they immediately obeyed. But a new difficulty now presented itself, for the people had locked their doors when they went to bed, and Claus found he could not enter the houses to leave his toys.

"I am afraid, my friends, we have made our journey for nothing," said he, "for I shall be obliged to carry my playthings back home again without giving them to the children of this village."

"What's the matter?" asked Flossie.

"The doors are locked," answered Claus, "and I can not get in."

Glossie looked around at the houses. The snow was quite deep in that village, and just before them was a roof only a few feet above the sledge. A broad chimney, which seemed to Glossie big enough to admit Claus, was at the peak of the roof.

"Why don't you climb down that chimney?" asked Glossie.

Claus looked at it.

"That would be easy enough if I were on top of the roof," he answered.

"Then hold fast and we will take you there," said the deer, and they gave one bound to the roof and landed beside the big chimney.

"Good!" cried Claus, well pleased, and he slung the pack of toys over his shoulder and got into the chimney.

There was plenty of soot on the bricks, but he did not mind that, and by placing his hands and knees against the sides he crept downward until he had reached the fireplace. Leaping lightly over the smoldering coals he found himself in a large sitting-room, where a dim light was burning.

From this room two doorways led into smaller chambers. In one a woman lay asleep, with a baby beside her in a crib.

Claus laughed, but he did not laugh aloud for fear of waking the baby. Then he slipped a big doll from his pack and laid it in the crib. The little one smiled, as if it dreamed of the pretty plaything it was to find on the morrow, and Claus crept softly from the room and entered at the other doorway.

Here were two boys, fast asleep with their arms around each other's neck. Claus gazed at them lovingly a moment and then placed upon the bed a drum, two horns and a wooden elephant.

He did not linger, now that his work in this house was done, but climbed the chimney again and seated himself on his sledge.

"Can you find another chimney?" he asked the reindeer.

"Easily enough," replied Glossie and Flossie.

Down to the edge of the roof they raced, and then, without pausing, leaped through the air to the top of the next building, where a huge, old-fashioned chimney stood.

"Don't be so long, this time," called Flossie, "or we shall never get back to the Forest by daybreak."

Claus made a trip down this chimney also and found five children sleeping in the house, all of whom were quickly supplied with toys.

When he returned the deer sprang to the next roof, but on descending the chimney Claus found no children there at all. That was not often the case in this village, however, so he lost less time than you might suppose in visiting the dreary homes where there were no little ones.

When he had climbed down the chimneys of all the houses in that village, and had left a toy for every sleeping child, Claus found that his great sack was not yet half emptied.

"Onward, friends!" he called to the deer; "we must seek another village."

So away they dashed, although it was long past midnight, and in a surprisingly short time they came to a large city, the largest Claus had ever visited since he began to make toys. But, nothing daunted by the throng of houses, he set to work at once and his beautiful steeds carried him rapidly from one roof to another, only the highest being beyond the leaps of the agile deer.

At last the supply of toys was exhausted and Claus seated himself in the sledge, with the empty sack at his feet, and turned the heads of Glossie and Flossie toward home.

Presently Flossie asked:

"What is that gray streak in the sky?"

"It is the coming dawn of day," answered Claus, surprised to find that it was so late.

"Good gracious!" exclaimed Glossie; "then we shall not be home by daybreak, and the Knooks will punish us and never let us come again."

"We must race for the Laughing Valley and make our best speed," returned Flossie; "so hold fast, friend Claus!"

Claus held fast and the next moment was flying so swiftly over the snow that he could not see the trees as they whirled past. Up hill and down dale, swift as an arrow shot from a bow they dashed, and Claus shut his eyes to keep the wind out of them and left the deer to find their own way.

It seemed to him they were plunging through space, but he was not at all afraid. The Knooks were severe masters, and must be obeyed at all hazards, and the gray streak in the sky was growing brighter every moment.

Finally the sledge came to a sudden stop and Claus, who was taken unawares, tumbled from his seat into a snowdrift. As he picked himself up he heard the deer crying:

"Quick, friend, quick! Cut away our harness!"

He drew his knife and rapidly severed the cords, and then he wiped the moisture from his eyes and looked around him.

The sledge had come to a stop in the Laughing Valley, only a few feet, he found, from his own door. In the East the day was breaking, and turning to the edge of Burzee he saw Glossie and Flossie just disappearing in the Forest.

9. "Santa Claus!"

Claus thought that none of the children would ever know where the toys came from which they found by their bedsides when they wakened the following morning. But kindly deeds are sure to bring fame, and fame has many wings to carry its tidings into far lands; so for miles and miles in every direction people were talking of Claus and his wonderful gifts to children. The sweet generousness of his work caused a few selfish folk to sneer, but even these were forced to admit their respect for a man so gentle-natured that he loved to devote his life to pleasing the helpless little ones of his race.

Therefore the inhabitants of every city and village had been eagerly watching the coming of Claus, and remarkable stories of his beautiful playthings were told the children to keep them patient and contented.

When, on the morning following the first trip of Claus with his deer, the little ones came running to their parents with the pretty toys they had found, and asked from whence they came, there was but one reply to the question.

"The good Claus must have been here, my darlings; for his are the only toys in all the world!"

"But how did he get in?" asked the children.

At this the fathers shook their heads, being themselves unable to understand how Claus had gained admittance to their homes; but the mothers, watching the glad faces of their dear ones, whispered that the good Claus was no mortal man but assuredly a Saint, and they piously blessed his name for the happiness he had bestowed upon their children.

"A Saint," said one, with bowed head, "has no need to unlock doors if it pleases him to enter our homes."

And, afterward, when a child was naughty or disobedient, its mother would say:

"You must pray to the good Santa Claus for forgiveness. He does not like naughty children, and, unless you repent, he will bring you no more pretty toys."

But Santa Claus himself would not have approved this speech. He brought toys to the children because they were little and helpless, and because he loved them. He knew that the best of children were sometimes naughty, and that the naughty ones were often good. It is the way with children, the world over, and he would not have changed their natures had he possessed the power to do so.

And that is how our Claus became Santa Claus. It is possible for any man, by good deeds, to enshrine himself as a Saint in the hearts of the people.

10. Christmas Eve

THE DAY THAT BROKE AS CLAUS RETURNED FROM HIS NIGHT RIDE WITH GLOSSie and Flossie brought to him a new trouble. Will Knook, the chief guardian of the deer, came to him, surly and ill-tempered, to complain that he had kept Glossie and Flossie beyond daybreak, in opposition to his orders.

"Yet it could not have been very long after daybreak," said Claus.

"It was one minute after," answered Will Knook, "and that is as bad as one hour. I shall set the stinging gnats on Glossie and Flossie, and they will thus suffer terribly for their disobedience."

"Don't do that!" begged Claus. "It was my fault."

But Will Knook would listen to no excuses, and went away grumbling and growling in his ill-natured way.

For this reason Claus entered the Forest to consult Necile about rescuing the good deer from punishment. To his delight he found his old friend, the Master Woodsman, seated in the circle of Nymphs.

Ak listened to the story of the night journey to the children and of the great assistance the deer had been to Claus by drawing his sledge over the frozen snow.

"I do not wish my friends to be punished if I can save them," said the toy-maker, when he had finished the relation. "They were only one minute late, and they ran swifter than a bird flies to get home before daybreak."

Ak stroked his beard thoughtfully a moment, and then sent for the Prince of the Knooks, who rules all his people in Burzee, and also for the Queen of the Fairies and the Prince of the Ryls.

When all had assembled Claus told his story again, at Ak's command, and then the Master addressed the Prince of the Knooks, saying:

"The good work that Claus is doing among mankind deserves the support of every honest immortal. Already he is called a Saint in some of the towns, and before long the name of Santa Claus will be lovingly known in every home that is blessed with children. Moreover, he is a son of our Forest, so we owe him our encouragement. You, Ruler of the Knooks, have known him these many years; am I not right in saying he deserves our friendship?"

The Prince, crooked and sour of visage as all Knooks are, looked only upon the dead leaves at his feet and muttered: "You are the Master Woodsman of the World!"

Ak smiled, but continued, in soft tones: "It seems that the deer which are guarded by your people can be of great assistance to Claus, and as they seem willing to draw his sledge I beg that you will permit him to use their services whenever he pleases."

The Prince did not reply, but tapped the curled point of his sandal with the tip of his spear, as if in thought.

Then the Fairy Queen spoke to him in this way: "If you consent to Ak's request I will see that no harm comes to your deer while they are away from the Forest."

And the Prince of the Ryls added: "For my part I will allow to every deer that assists Claus the privilege of eating my casa plants, which give strength, and my grawle plants, which give fleetness of foot, and my marbon plants, which give long life."

And the Queen of the Nymphs said: "The deer which draw the sledge of Claus will be permitted to bathe in the Forest pool of Nares, which will give them sleek coats and wonderful beauty."

The Prince of the Knooks, hearing these promises, shifted uneasily on his seat, for in his heart he hated to refuse a request of his fellow immortals, although they were asking an unusual favor at his hands, and the Knooks are unaccustomed to granting favors of any kind. Finally he turned to his servants and said:

"Call Will Knook."

When surly Will came and heard the demands of the immortals he protested loudly against granting them.

"Deer are deer," said he, "and nothing but deer. Were they horses it would be right to harness them like horses. But no one harnesses deer because they are free, wild creatures, owing no service of any sort to mankind. It would degrade my deer to labor for Claus, who is only a man in spite of the friendship lavished on him by the immortals."

"You have heard," said the Prince to Ak. "There is truth in what Will says."

"Call Glossie and Flossie," returned the Master.

The deer were brought to the conference and Ak asked them if they objected to drawing the sledge for Claus.

"No, indeed!" replied Glossie; "we enjoyed the trip very much."

"And we tried to get home by daybreak," added Flossie, "but were unfortunately a minute too late."

"A minute lost at daybreak doesn't matter," said Ak. "You are forgiven for that delay."

"Provided it does not happen again," said the Prince of the Knooks, sternly.

"And will you permit them to make another journey with me?" asked Claus, eagerly.

The Prince reflected while he gazed at Will, who was scowling, and at the Master Woodsman, who was smiling.

Then he stood up and addressed the company as follows:

"Since you all urge me to grant the favor I will permit the deer to go with Claus once every year, on Christmas Eve, provided they always return to the Forest by daybreak. He may select any number he pleases, up to ten, to draw his sledge, and those shall be known among us as Reindeer, to distinguish them from the others. And they shall bathe in the Pool of Nares, and eat the casa and grawle and marbon plants and shall be under the especial protection of the Fairy Queen. And now cease scowling, Will Knook, for my words shall be obeyed!"

He hobbled quickly away through the trees, to avoid the thanks of Claus and the approval of the other immortals, and Will, looking as cross as ever, followed him.

But Ak was satisfied, knowing that he could rely on the promise of the Prince, however grudgingly given; and Glossie and Flossie ran home, kicking up their heels delightedly at every step.

"When is Christmas Eve?" Claus asked the Master.

"In about ten days," he replied.

"Then I can not use the deer this year," said Claus, thoughtfully, "for I shall not have time enough to make my sackful of toys."

"The shrewd Prince foresaw that," responded Ak, "and therefore named Christmas Eve as the day you might use the deer, knowing it would cause you to lose an entire year."

"If I only had the toys the Awgwas stole from me," said Claus, sadly, "I could easily fill my sack for the children."

"Where are they?" asked the Master.

"I do not know," replied Claus, "but the wicked Awgwas probably hid them in the mountains."

Ak turned to the Fairy Queen.

"Can you find them?" he asked.

"I will try," she replied, brightly.

Then Claus went back to the Laughing Valley, to work as hard as he could, and a band of Fairies immediately flew to the mountain that had been haunted by the Awgwas and began a search for the stolen toys.

The Fairies, as we well know, possess wonderful powers; but the cunning Awgwas had hidden the toys in a deep cave and covered the opening with rocks, so no one could look in. Therefore all search for the missing playthings proved in vain for several days, and Claus, who sat at home waiting for news from the Fairies, almost despaired of getting the toys before Christmas Eve.

He worked hard every moment, but it took considerable time to carve out and to shape each toy and to paint it properly, so that on the morning before Christmas Eve only half of one small shelf above the window was filled with playthings ready for the children.

But on this morning the Fairies who were searching in the mountains had a new thought. They joined hands and moved in a straight line through the rocks that formed the mountain, beginning at the topmost peak and working downward, so that no spot could be missed by their bright eyes. And at last they discovered the cave where the toys had been heaped up by the wicked Awgwas.

It did not take them long to burst open the mouth of the cave, and then each one seized as many toys as he could carry and they all flew to Claus and laid the treasure before him.

The good man was rejoiced to receive, just in the nick of time, such a store of playthings with which to load his sledge, and he sent word to Glossie and Flossie to be ready for the journey at nightfall.

With all his other labors he had managed to find time, since the last trip, to repair the harness and to strengthen his sledge, so that when the deer came to him at twilight he had no difficulty in harnessing them.

"We must go in another direction to-night," he told them, "where we shall find children I have never yet visited. And we must travel fast and work quickly, for my sack is full of toys and running over the brim!"

So, just as the moon arose, they dashed out of the Laughing Valley and across the plain and over the hills to the south. The air was sharp and frosty and the starlight touched the snowflakes and made them glitter like countless diamonds. The reindeer leaped onward with strong, steady bounds, and Claus' heart was so light and merry that he laughed and sang while the wind whistled past his ears:

> "With a ho, ho, ho!
> And a ha, ha, ha!
> And a ho, ho! ha, ha, hee!
> Now away we go
> O'er the frozen snow,
> As merry as we can be!"

Jack Frost heard him and came racing up with his nippers, but when he saw it was Claus he laughed and turned away again.

The mother owls heard him as he passed near a wood and stuck their heads out of the hollow places in the tree-trunks; but when they saw who it was they whispered to the owlets nestling near them that it was only Santa Claus carrying toys to the children. It is strange how much those mother owls know.

Claus stopped at some of the scattered farmhouses and climbed down the chimneys to leave presents for the babies. Soon after he reached a village and worked merrily for an hour distributing playthings among the sleeping little ones. Then away again he went, signing his joyous carol:

> "Now away we go
> O'er the gleaming snow,
> While the deer run swift and free!
> For to girls and boys
> We carry the toys
> That will fill their hearts with glee!"

The deer liked the sound of his deep bass voice and kept time to the song with their hoofbeats on the hard snow; but soon they stopped at another chimney and Santa Claus, with sparkling eyes and face brushed red by the wind, climbed down its smoky sides and left a present for every child the house contained.

It was a merry, happy night. Swiftly the deer ran, and busily their driver worked to scatter his gifts among the sleeping children.

But the sack was empty at last, and the sledge headed homeward; and now again the race with daybreak began. Glossie and Flossie had no mind to be rebuked a second time for tardiness, so they fled with a swiftness that enabled them to pass the gale on which the Frost King rode, and soon brought them to the Laughing Valley.

It is true when Claus released his steeds from their harness the eastern sky was streaked with gray, but Glossie and Flossie were deep in the Forest before day fairly broke.

Claus was so wearied with his night's work that he threw himself upon his bed and fell into a deep slumber, and while he slept the Christmas sun appeared in the sky and shone upon hundreds of happy homes where the sound of childish laughter proclaimed that Santa Claus had made them a visit.

God bless him! It was his first Christmas Eve, and for hundreds of years since then he has nobly fulfilled his mission to bring happiness to the hearts of little children.

11. How the First Stockings Were Hung by the Chimneys

WHEN YOU REMEMBER THAT NO CHILD, UNTIL SANTA CLAUS BEGAN HIS TRAVELS, had ever known the pleasure of possessing a toy, you will understand how joy crept into the homes of those who had been favored with a visit from the good man, and how they talked of him day by day in loving tones and were honestly grateful for his kindly deeds. It is true that great warriors and mighty kings and clever scholars of that day were often spoken of by the people; but no one of them was so greatly beloved as Santa Claus, because none other was so unselfish as to devote himself to making others happy. For a generous deed lives longer than a great battle or a king's decree or a scholar's essay, because it spreads and leaves its mark on all nature and endures through many generations.

The bargain made with the Knook Prince changed the plans of Claus for all future time; for, being able to use the reindeer on but one night of each year, he decided to devote all the other days to the manufacture of playthings, and on Christmas Eve to carry them to the children of the world.

But a year's work would, he knew, result in a vast accumulation of toys, so he resolved to build a new sledge that would be larger and stronger and better-fitted for swift travel than the old and clumsy one.

His first act was to visit the Gnome King, with whom he made a bargain to exchange three drums, a trumpet and two dolls for a pair of fine steel runners, curled beautifully at the ends. For the Gnome King had children of his own, who, living in the hollows under the earth, in mines and caverns, needed something to amuse them.

In three days the steel runners were ready, and when Claus brought the playthings to the Gnome King, his Majesty was so greatly pleased with them that he presented Claus with a string of sweet-toned sleigh-bells, in addition to the runners.

"These will please Glossie and Flossie," said Claus, as he jingled the bells and listened to their merry sound. "But I should have two strings of bells, one for each deer."

"Bring me another trumpet and a toy cat," replied the King, "and you shall have a second string of bells like the first."

"It is a bargain!" cried Claus, and he went home again for the toys.

The new sledge was carefully built, the Knooks bringing plenty of strong but thin boards to use in its construction. Claus made a high, rounding dash-board to keep off the snow cast behind by the fleet hoofs of the deer; and he made high sides to the platform so that many toys could be carried, and finally he mounted the sledge upon the slender steel runners made by the Gnome King.

It was certainly a handsome sledge, and big and roomy. Claus painted it in bright colors, although no one was likely to see it during his midnight journeys, and when all was finished he sent for Glossie and Flossie to come and look at it.

The deer admired the sledge, but gravely declared it was too big and heavy for them to draw.

"We might pull it over the snow, to be sure," said Glossie; "but we would not pull it fast enough to enable us to visit the far-away cities and villages and return to the Forest by daybreak."

"Then I must add two more deer to my team," declared Claus, after a moment's thought.

"The Knook Prince allowed you as many as ten. Why not use them all?" asked Flossie. "Then we could speed like the lightning and leap to the highest roofs with ease."

"A team of ten reindeer!" cried Claus, delightedly. "That will be splendid. Please return to the Forest at once and select eight other deer as like yourselves as possible. And you must all eat of the casa plant, to become strong, and of the grawle plant, to become fleet of foot, and of the marbon plant, that you may live long to accompany me on my journeys. Likewise it will be well for you to bathe in the Pool of Nares, which the lovely Queen Zurline declares will render you rarely beautiful. Should you perform these duties faithfully there is no doubt that on next Christmas Eve my ten reindeer will be the most powerful and beautiful steeds the world has ever seen!"

So Glossie and Flossie went to the Forest to choose their mates, and Claus began to consider the question of a harness for them all.

In the end he called upon Peter Knook for assistance, for Peter's heart is as kind as his body is crooked, and he is remarkably shrewd, as well. And Peter agreed to furnish strips of tough leather for the harness.

This leather was cut from the skins of lions that had reached such an advanced age that they died naturally, and on one side was tawny hair while the other side was cured to the softness of velvet by the deft Knooks. When Claus received these strips of leather he sewed them neatly into a harness for the ten reindeer, and it proved strong and serviceable and lasted him for many years.

The harness and sledge were prepared at odd times, for Claus devoted most of his days to the making of toys. These were now much better than the first ones had been, for the immortals often came to his house to watch him work and to offer suggestions. It was Necile's idea to make some of the dolls say "papa" and "mama." It was a thought of the Knooks to put a squeak inside the lambs, so that when a child squeezed them they would say "baa-a-a-a!" And the Fairy Queen advised Claus to put whistles in the birds, so they could be made to sing, and wheels on the horses, so children could draw them around. Many animals perished in the Forest, from one cause or another, and their fur was brought to Claus that he might cover with it the small images of beasts he made for playthings. A merry Ryl suggested that Claus make a donkey with a nodding head, which he did, and afterward found that it amused the little ones immensely. And so the toys grew in beauty and attractiveness every day, until they were the wonder of even the immortals.

When another Christmas Eve drew near there was a monster load of beautiful gifts for the children ready to be loaded upon the big sledge. Claus filled three sacks to the brim, and tucked every corner of the sledge-box full of toys besides.

Then, at twilight, the ten reindeer appeared and Flossie introduced them all to Claus. They were Racer and Pacer, Reckless and Speckless, Fearless and Peerless, and Ready and Steady, who, with Glossie and Flossie, made up the ten who have traversed the world these hundreds of years with their generous master. They were all exceedingly beautiful, with slender limbs, spreading antlers, velvety dark eyes and smooth coats of fawn color spotted with white.

Claus loved them at once, and has loved them ever since, for they are loyal friends and have rendered him priceless service.

The new harness fitted them nicely and soon they were all fastened to the sledge by twos, with Glossie and Flossie in the lead. These wore the strings of sleigh-bells, and were so delighted with the music they made that they kept prancing up and down to make the bells ring.

Claus now seated himself in the sledge, drew a warm robe over his knees and his fur cap over his ears, and cracked his long whip as a signal to start.

Instantly the ten leaped forward and were away like the wind, while jolly Claus laughed gleefully to see them run and shouted a song in his big, hearty voice:

> "With a ho, ho, ho!
> And a ha, ha, ha!
> And a ho, ho, ha, ha, hee!
> Now away we go
> O'er the frozen snow,
> As merry as we can be!
>
> There are many joys
> In our load of toys,
> As many a child will know;
> We'll scatter them wide
> On our wild night ride
> O'er the crisp and sparkling snow!"

Now it was on this same Christmas Eve that little Margot and her brother Dick and her cousins Ned and Sara, who were visiting at Margot's house, came in from making a snow man, with their clothes damp, their mittens dripping and their shoes and stockings wet through and through. They were not scolded, for Margot's mother knew the snow was melting, but they were sent early to bed that their clothes might be hung over chairs to dry. The shoes were placed on the red tiles of the hearth, where the heat from the hot embers would strike them, and the stockings were carefully hung in a row by the chimney, directly over the fireplace. That was the reason Santa Claus noticed them when he came down the chimney that night and all the household were fast asleep. He was in a tremendous hurry and seeing the stockings all belonged to children he quickly stuffed his toys into them and dashed up the chimney again, appearing on the roof so suddenly that the reindeer were astonished at his agility.

"I wish they would all hang up their stockings," he thought, as he drove to the next chimney. "It would save me a lot of time and I could then visit more children before daybreak."

When Margot and Dick and Ned and Sara jumped out of bed next morning and ran downstairs to get their stockings from the fireplace they were filled with delight to find the toys from Santa Claus inside them. In fact, I think they found more presents in their stockings than any other children of that city had received, for Santa Claus was in a hurry and did not stop to count the toys.

Of course they told all their little friends about it, and of course every one of them decided to hang his own stockings by the fireplace the next Christmas Eve. Even Bessie Blithesome, who made a visit to that city with her father, the great Lord of Lerd, heard the story from the children and hung her own pretty stockings by the chimney when she returned home at Christmas time.

On his next trip Santa Claus found so many stockings hung up in anticipation of his visit that he could fill them in a jiffy and be away again in half the time required to hunt the children up and place the toys by their bedsides.

The custom grew year after year, and has always been a great help to Santa Claus. And, with so many children to visit, he surely needs all the help we are able to give him.

12. The First Christmas Tree

CLAUS HAD ALWAYS KEPT HIS PROMISE TO THE KNOOKS BY RETURNING TO THE Laughing Valley by daybreak, but only the swiftness of his reindeer has enabled him to do this, for he travels over all the world.

He loved his work and he loved the brisk night ride on his sledge and the gay tinkle of the sleigh-bells. On that first trip with the ten reindeer only Glossie and Flossie wore bells; but each year thereafter for eight years Claus carried presents to the children of the Gnome King, and that good-natured monarch gave him in return a string of bells at each visit, so that finally every one of the ten deer was supplied, and you may imagine what a merry tune the bells played as the sledge sped over the snow.

The children's stockings were so long that it required a great many toys to fill them, and soon Claus found there were other things besides toys that children love. So he sent some of the Fairies, who were always his good friends, into the Tropics, from whence they returned with great bags full of oranges and bananas which they had plucked from the trees. And other Fairies flew to the wonderful Valley of Phunnyland, where delicious candies and bonbons grow thickly on the bushes, and returned laden with many boxes of sweetmeats for the little ones. These things Santa Claus, on each Christmas Eve, placed in the long stockings, together with his toys, and the children were glad to get them, you may be sure.

There are also warm countries where there is no snow in winter, but Claus and his reindeer visited them as well as the colder climes, for there were little wheels inside the runners of his sledge which permitted it to run as smoothly over bare ground as on the snow. And the children who lived in the warm countries learned to know the name of Santa Claus as well as those who lived nearer to the Laughing Valley.

Once, just as the reindeer were ready to start on their yearly trip, a Fairy came to Claus and told him of three little children who lived beneath a rude tent of skins on a broad plain where there were no trees whatever. These poor babies were miserable and unhappy, for their parents were ignorant people who neglected them sadly. Claus resolved to visit these children before he returned home, and during his ride he picked up the bushy top of a pine tree which the wind had broken off and placed it in his sledge.

It was nearly morning when the deer stopped before the lonely tent of skins where the poor children lay asleep. Claus at once planted the bit of pine tree in the sand and stuck many candles on the branches. Then he hung some of his prettiest toys on the tree, as well as several bags of candies. It did not take long to do all this, for Santa Claus works quickly, and when all was ready he lighted the candles and, thrusting his head in at the opening of the tent, he shouted:

"Merry Christmas, little ones!"

With that he leaped into his sledge and was out of sight before the children, rubbing the sleep from their eyes, could come out to see who had called them.

You can imagine the wonder and joy of those little ones, who had never in their lives known a real pleasure before, when they saw the tree, sparkling with lights that shone brilliant in the gray dawn and hung with toys enough to make them happy for years to come! They joined hands and danced around the tree, shouting and laughing, until they were obliged to pause for breath. And their parents, also, came out to look and wonder, and thereafter had more respect and consideration for their children, since Santa Claus had honored them with such beautiful gifts.

The idea of the Christmas tree pleased Claus, and so the following year he carried many of them in his sledge and set them up in the homes of poor people who seldom saw trees, and placed candles and toys on the branches. Of course he could not carry enough trees in one load of all who wanted them, but in some homes the fathers were able to get trees and have them all ready for Santa Claus when he arrived; and these the good Claus always decorated as prettily as possible and hung with toys enough for all the children who came to see the tree lighted.

These novel ideas and the generous manner in which they were carried out made the children long for that one night in the year when their friend Santa Claus should visit them, and as such anticipation is very pleasant and comforting the little ones gleaned much happiness by wondering what would happen when Santa Claus next arrived.

Perhaps you remember that stern Baron Braun who once drove Claus from his castle and forbade him to visit his children? Well, many years afterward, when the old Baron was dead and his son ruled in his place, the new Baron Braun came to the house of Claus with his train of knights and pages and henchmen and, dismounting from his charger, bared his head humbly before the friend of children.

"My father did not know your goodness and worth," he said, "and therefore threatened to hang you from the castle walls. But I have children of my own, who long for a visit from Santa Claus, and I have come to beg that you will favor them hereafter as you do other children."

Claus was pleased with this speech, for Castle Braun was the only place he had never visited, and he gladly promised to bring presents to the Baron's children the next Christmas Eve.

The Baron went away contented, and Claus kept his promise faithfully.

Thus did this man, through very goodness, conquer the hearts of all; and it is no wonder he was ever merry and gay, for there was no home in the wide world where he was not welcomed more royally than any king.

OLD AGE

1. The Mantle of Immortality

AND NOW WE COME TO A TURNING-POINT IN THE CAREER OF SANTA CLAUS, and it is my duty to relate the most remarkable that has happened since the world began or mankind was created.

We have followed the life of Claus from the time he was found a helpless infant by the Wood-Nymph Necile and reared to manhood in the great Forest of Burzee. And we know how he began to make toys for children and how, with the assistance and goodwill of the immortals, he was able to distribute them to the little ones throughout the world.

For many years he carried on this noble work; for the simple, hard-working life he led gave him perfect health and strength. And doubtless a man can live longer in the beautiful Laughing Valley, where there are no cares and everything is peaceful and merry, than in any other part of the world.

But when many years had rolled away Santa Claus grew old. The long beard of golden brown that once covered his cheeks and chin gradually became gray, and finally turned to pure white. His hair was white, too, and there were wrinkles at the corners of his eyes, which showed plainly when he laughed. He had never been a very tall man, and now he became fat, and waddled very much like a duck when he walked. But in spite of these things he remained as lively as ever, and was just as jolly and gay, and his kind eyes sparkled as brightly as they did that first day when he came to the Laughing Valley.

Yet a time is sure to come when every mortal who has grown old and lived his life is required to leave this world for another; so it is no wonder that, after Santa Claus had driven his reindeer on many and many a

Christmas Eve, those stanch friends finally whispered among themselves that they had probably drawn his sledge for the last time.

Then all the Forest of Burzee became sad and all the Laughing Valley was hushed; for every living thing that had known Claus had used to love him and to brighten at the sound of his footsteps or the notes of his merry whistle.

No doubt the old man's strength was at last exhausted, for he made no more toys, but lay on his bed as in a dream.

The Nymph Necile, she who had reared him and been his foster-mother, was still youthful and strong and beautiful, and it seemed to her but a short time since this aged, gray-bearded man had lain in her arms and smiled on her with his innocent, baby lips.

In this is shown the difference between mortals and immortals.

It was fortunate that the great Ak came to the Forest at this time. Necile sought him with troubled eyes and told him of the fate that threatened their friend Claus.

At once the Master became grave, and he leaned upon his ax and stroked his grizzled beard thoughtfully for many minutes. Then suddenly he stood up straight, and poised his powerful head with firm resolve, and stretched out his great right arm as if determined on doing some mighty deed. For a thought had come to him so grand in its conception that all the world might well bow before the Master Woodsman and honor his name forever!

It is well known that when the great Ak once undertakes to do a thing he never hesitates an instant. Now he summoned his fleetest messengers, and sent them in a flash to many parts of the earth. And when they were gone he turned to the anxious Necile and comforted her, saying:

"Be of good heart, my child; our friend still lives. And now run to your Queen and tell her that I have summoned a council of all the immortals of the world to meet with me here in Burzee this night. If they obey, and harken unto my words, Claus will drive his reindeer for countless ages yet to come."

At midnight there was a wondrous scene in the ancient Forest of Burzee, where for the first time in many centuries the rulers of the immortals who inhabit the earth were gathered together.

There was the Queen of the Water Sprites, whose beautiful form was as clear as crystal but continually dripped water on the bank of moss where she sat. And beside her was the King of the Sleep Fays, who carried a wand from the end of which a fine dust fell all around, so that no mortal could keep awake long enough to see him, as mortal eyes were sure to close in sleep as soon as the dust filled them. And next to him sat the Gnome King, whose people inhabit all that region under the earth's surface, where they guard the precious metals and the jewel stones that lie buried in rock and ore. At his right hand stood the King of the Sound Imps, who had wings on his feet, for his people are swift to carry all sounds that are made. When they are busy they carry the sounds but short distances, for there are many of them; but sometimes they speed with the sounds to places miles and miles away from where they are made. The King of the Sound Imps had an anxious and careworn face, for most people have no consideration for his Imps and, especially the boys and girls, make a great many unnecessary sounds which the Imps are obliged to carry when they might be better employed.

The next in the circle of immortals was the King of the Wind Demons, slender of frame, restless and uneasy at being confined to one place for even an hour. Once in a while he would leave his place and circle around the glade, and each time he did this the Fairy Queen was obliged to untangle the flowing locks of her golden hair and tuck them back of her pink ears. But she did not complain, for it was not often that the King of the Wind Demons came into the heart of the Forest. After the Fairy Queen, whose home you know was in old Burzee, came the King of the Light Elves, with his two Princes, Flash and Twilight, at his back. He never went anywhere without his Princes, for they were so mischievous that he dared not let them wander alone.

Prince Flash bore a lightning-bolt in his right hand and a horn of gunpowder in his left, and his bright eyes roved constantly around, as if he longed to use his blinding flashes. Prince Twilight held a great snuffer in one hand and a big black cloak in the other, and it is well known that unless Twilight is carefully watched the snuffers or the cloak will throw everything into darkness, and Darkness is the greatest enemy the King of the Light Elves has.

In addition to the immortals I have named were the King of the Knooks, who had come from his home in the jungles of India; and the King of the Ryls, who lived among the gay flowers and luscious fruits of Valencia. Sweet Queen Zurline of the Wood-Nymphs completed the circle of immortals.

But in the center of the circle sat three others who possessed powers so great that all the Kings and Queens showed them reverence.

These were Ak, the Master Woodsman of the World, who rules the forests and the orchards and the groves; and Kern, the Master Husbandman of the World, who rules the grain fields and the meadows and the gardens; and Bo, the Master Mariner of the World, who rules the seas and all the craft that float thereon. And all other immortals are more or less subject to these three.

When all had assembled the Master Woodsman of the World stood up to address them, since he himself had summoned them to the council.

Very clearly he told them the story of Claus, beginning at the time when as a babe he had been adopted a child of the Forest, and telling of his noble and generous nature and his life-long labors to make children happy.

"And now," said Ak, "when he had won the love of all the world, the Spirit of Death is hovering over him. Of all men who have inhabited the earth none other so well deserves immortality, for such a life can not be spared so long as there are children of mankind to miss him and to grieve over his loss. We immortals are the servants of the world, and to serve the world we were permitted in the Beginning to exist. But what one of us is more worthy of immortality than this man Claus, who so sweetly ministers to the little children?"

He paused and glanced around the circle, to find every immortal listening to him eagerly and nodding approval. Finally the King of the Wind Demons, who had been whistling softly to himself, cried out:

"What is your desire, O Ak?"

"To bestow upon Claus the Mantle of Immortality!" said Ak, boldly.

That this demand was wholly unexpected was proved by the immortals springing to their feet and looking into each other's face with dismay and then upon Ak with wonder. For it was a grave matter, this parting with the Mantle of Immortality.

The Queen of the Water Sprites spoke in her low, clear voice, and the words sounded like raindrops splashing upon a window-pane.

"In all the world there is but one Mantle of Immortality," she said.

The King of the Sound Fays added:

"It has existed since the Beginning, and no mortal has ever dared to claim it."

And the Master Mariner of the World arose and stretched his limbs, saying:

"Only by the vote of every immortal can it be bestowed upon a mortal."

"I know all this," answered Ak, quietly. "But the Mantle exists, and if it was created, as you say, in the Beginning, it was because the Supreme Master knew that some day it would be required. Until now no mortal has deserved it, but who among you dares deny that the good Claus deserves it? Will you not all vote to bestow it upon him?"

They were silent, still looking upon one another questioningly.

"Of what use is the Mantle of Immortality unless it is worn?" demanded Ak. "What will it profit any one of us to allow it to remain in its lonely shrine for all time to come?"

"Enough!" cried the Gnome King, abruptly. "We will vote on the matter, yes or no. For my part, I say yes!"

"And I!" said the Fairy Queen, promptly, and Ak rewarded her with a smile.

"My people in Burzee tell me they have learned to love him; therefore I vote to give Claus the Mantle," said the King of the Ryls.

"He is already a comrade of the Knooks," announced the ancient King of that band. "Let him have immortality!"

"Let him have it—let him have it!" sighed the King of the Wind Demons.

"Why not?" asked the King of the Sleep Fays. "He never disturbs the slumbers my people allow humanity. Let the good Claus be immortal!"

"I do not object," said the King of the Sound Imps.

"Nor I," murmured the Queen of the Water Sprites.

"If Claus does not receive the Mantle it is clear none other can ever claim it," remarked the King of the Light Elves, "so let us have done with the thing for all time."

"The Wood-Nymphs were first to adopt him," said Queen Zurline. "Of course I shall vote to make him immortal."

Ak now turned to the Master Husbandman of the World, who held up his right arm and said "Yes!"

And the Master Mariner of the World did likewise, after which Ak, with sparkling eyes and smiling face, cried out:

"I thank you, fellow immortals! For all have voted 'yes,' and so to our dear Claus shall fall the one Mantle of Immortality that it is in our power to bestow!"

"Let us fetch it at once," said the Fay King; "I'm in a hurry."

They bowed assent, and instantly the Forest glade was deserted. But in a place midway between the earth and the sky was suspended a gleaming crypt of gold and platinum, aglow with soft lights shed from the facets of countless gems. Within a high dome hung the precious Mantle of Immortality, and each immortal placed a hand on the hem of the splendid Robe and said, as with one voice:

"We bestow this Mantle upon Claus, who is called the Patron Saint of Children!"

At this the Mantle came away from its lofty crypt, and they carried it to the house in the Laughing Valley.

The Spirit of Death was crouching very near to the bedside of Claus, and as the immortals approached she sprang up and motioned them back with an angry gesture. But when her eyes fell upon the Mantle they bore she shrank away with a low moan of disappointment and quitted that house forever.

Softly and silently the immortal Band dropped upon Claus the precious Mantle, and it closed about him and sank into the outlines of his body and disappeared from view. It became a part of his being, and neither mortal nor immortal might ever take it from him.

Then the Kings and Queens who had wrought this great deed dispersed to their various homes, and all were well contented that they had added another immortal to their Band.

And Claus slept on, the red blood of everlasting life coursing swiftly through his veins; and on his brow was a tiny drop of water that had fallen from the ever-melting gown of the Queen of the Water Sprites, and over his lips hovered a tender kiss that had been left by the sweet Nymph Necile.

For she had stolen in when the others were gone to gaze with rapture upon the immortal form of her foster son.

2. When the World Grew Old

THE NEXT MORNING, WHEN SANTA CLAUS OPENED HIS EYES AND GAZED AROUND the familiar room, which he had feared he might never see again, he was astonished to find his old strength renewed and to feel the red blood of perfect health coursing through his veins. He sprang from his bed and stood where the bright sunshine came in through his window and flooded him with its merry, dancing rays. He did not then understand what had happened to restore to him the vigor of youth, but in spite of the fact that his beard remained the color of snow and that wrinkles still lingered in the corners of his bright eyes, old Santa Claus felt as brisk and merry as a boy of sixteen, and was soon whistling contentedly as he busied himself fashioning new toys.

Then Ak came to him and told of the Mantle of Immortality and how Claus had won it through his love for little children.

It made old Santa look grave for a moment to think he had been so favored; but it also made him glad to realize that now he need never fear being parted from his dear ones. At once he began preparations for making a remarkable assortment of pretty and amusing playthings, and in larger quantities than ever before; for now that he might always devote himself to this work he decided that no child in the world, poor or rich, should hereafter go without a Christmas gift if he could manage to supply it.

The world was new in the days when dear old Santa Claus first began toy-making and won, by his loving deeds, the Mantle of Immortality. And the task of supplying cheering words, sympathy and pretty playthings to all the young of his race did not seem a difficult undertaking at all. But every year more and more children were born into the world, and these, when they grew up, began spreading slowly over all the face of the earth, seeking new homes; so that Santa Claus found each year that his journeys must extend farther and farther from the Laughing Valley, and that the packs of toys must be made larger and ever larger.

So at length he took counsel with his fellow immortals how his work might keep pace with the increasing number of children that none might be neglected. And the immortals were so greatly interested in his labors that they gladly rendered him their assistance. Ak gave him his man Kilter, "the silent and swift." And the Knook Prince gave him Peter, who was more crooked and less surly than any of his brothers. And the Ryl Prince gave him Nuter, the sweetest tempered Ryl ever known. And the Fairy Queen gave him Wisk, that tiny, mischievous but lovable Fairy who knows today almost as many children as does Santa Claus himself.

With these people to help make the toys and to keep his house in order and to look after the sledge and the harness, Santa Claus found it much easier to prepare his yearly load of gifts, and his days began to follow one another smoothly and pleasantly.

Yet after a few generations his worries were renewed, for it was remarkable how the number of people continued to grow, and how many more children there were every year to be served. When the people filled all the cities and lands of one country they wandered into another part of the world; and the men cut down the trees in many of the great forests that had been ruled by Ak, and with the wood they built new cities, and where the forests had been were fields of grain and herds of browsing cattle.

You might think the Master Woodsman would rebel at the loss of his forests; but not so. The wisdom of Ak was mighty and farseeing.

"The world was made for men," said he to Santa Claus, "and I have but guarded the forests until men needed them for their use. I am glad my strong trees can furnish shelter for men's weak bodies, and warm them through the cold winters. But I hope they will not cut down all the trees, for mankind needs the shelter of the woods in summer as much as the warmth of blazing logs in winter. And, however crowded the world may grow, I do not think men will ever come to Burzee, nor to the Great Black Forest, nor to the wooded wilderness of Braz; unless they seek their shades for pleasure and not to destroy their giant trees."

By and by people made ships from the tree-trunks and crossed over oceans and built cities in far lands; but the oceans made little difference to the journeys of Santa Claus. His reindeer sped over the waters as swiftly as over land, and his sledge headed from east to west and followed in the wake of the sun. So that as the earth rolled slowly over Santa Claus had all of twenty-four hours to encircle it each Christmas Eve, and the speedy reindeer enjoyed these wonderful journeys more and more.

So year after year, and generation after generation, and century after century, the world grew older and the people became more numerous and the labors of Santa Claus steadily increased. The fame of his good deeds spread to every household where children dwelt. And all the little ones loved him dearly; and the fathers and mothers honored him for the happiness he had given them when they too were young; and the aged grandsires and granddames remembered him with tender gratitude and blessed his name.

3. The Deputies of Santa Claus

HOWEVER, THERE WAS ONE EVIL FOLLOWING IN THE PATH OF CIVILIZATION that caused Santa Claus a vast amount of trouble before he discovered a way to overcome it. But, fortunately, it was the last trial he was forced to undergo.

One Christmas Eve, when his reindeer had leaped to the top of a new building, Santa Claus was surprised to find that the chimney had been built much smaller than usual. But he had no time to think about it just then, so he drew in his breath and made himself as small as possible and slid down the chimney.

"I ought to be at the bottom by this time," he thought, as he continued to slip downward; but no fireplace of any sort met his view, and by and by he reached the very end of the chimney, which was in the cellar.

"This is odd!" he reflected, much puzzled by this experience. "If there is no fireplace, what on earth is the chimney good for?"

Then he began to climb out again, and found it hard work—the space being so small. And on his way up he noticed a thin, round pipe sticking through the side of the chimney, but could not guess what it was for.

Finally he reached the roof and said to the reindeer:

"There was no need of my going down that chimney, for I could find no fireplace through which to enter the house. I fear the children who live there must go without playthings this Christmas."

Then he drove on, but soon came to another new house with a small chimney. This caused Santa Claus to shake his head doubtfully, but he tried the chimney, nevertheless, and found it exactly like the other. Moreover, he nearly stuck fast in the narrow flue and tore his jacket trying to get out again; so, although he came to several such chimneys that night, he did not venture to descend any more of them.

"What in the world are people thinking of, to build such useless chimneys?" he exclaimed. "In all the years I have traveled with my reindeer I have never seen the like before."

True enough; but Santa Claus had not then discovered that stoves had been invented and were fast coming into use. When he did find it out he wondered how the builders of those houses could have so little consideration for him, when they knew very well it was his custom to climb down chimneys and enter houses by way of the fireplaces. Perhaps the men who built those houses had outgrown their own love for toys, and were indifferent whether Santa Claus called on their children or not. Whatever the explanation might be, the poor children were forced to bear the burden of grief and disappointment.

The following year Santa Claus found more and more of the new-fashioned chimneys that had no fireplaces, and the next year still more. The third year, so numerous had the narrow chimneys become, he even had a few toys left in his sledge that he was unable to give away, because he could not get to the children.

The matter had now become so serious that it worried the good man greatly, and he decided to talk it over with Kilter and Peter and Nuter and Wisk.

Kilter already knew something about it, for it had been his duty to run around to all the houses, just before Christmas, and gather up the notes and letters to Santa Claus that the children had written, telling what they wished put in their stockings or hung on their Christmas trees. But Kilter was a silent fellow, and seldom spoke of what he saw in the cities and villages. The others were very indignant.

"Those people act as if they do not wish their children to be made happy!" said sensible Peter, in a vexed tone. "The idea of shutting out such a generous friend to their little ones!"

"But it is my intention to make children happy whether their parents wish it or not," returned Santa Claus. "Years ago, when I first began making toys, children were even more neglected by their parents than they are now; so I have learned to pay no attention to thoughtless or selfish parents, but to consider only the longings of childhood."

"You are right, my master," said Nuter, the Ryl; "many children would lack a friend if you did not consider them, and try to make them happy."

"Then," declared the laughing Wisk, "we must abandon any thought of using these new-fashioned chimneys, but become burglars, and break into the houses some other way."

"What way?" asked Santa Claus.

"Why, walls of brick and wood and plaster are nothing to Fairies. I can easily pass through them whenever I wish, and so can Peter and Nuter and Kilter. Is it not so, comrades?"

"I often pass through the walls when I gather up the letters," said Kilter, and that was a long speech for him, and so surprised Peter and Nuter that their big round eyes nearly popped out of their heads.

"Therefore," continued the Fairy, "you may as well take us with you on your next journey, and when we come to one of those houses with stoves instead of fireplaces we will distribute the toys to the children without the need of using a chimney."

"That seems to me a good plan," replied Santa Claus, well pleased at having solved the problem. "We will try it next year."

That was how the Fairy, the Pixie, the Knook and the Ryl all rode in the sledge with their master the following Christmas Eve; and they had no trouble at all in entering the new-fashioned houses and leaving toys for the children that lived in them.

And their deft services not only relieved Santa Claus of much labor, but enabled him to complete his own work more quickly than usual, so that the merry party found themselves at home with an empty sledge a full hour before daybreak.

The only drawback to the journey was that the mischievous Wisk persisted in tickling the reindeer with a long feather, to see them jump; and Santa Claus found it necessary to watch him every minute and to tweak his long ears once or twice to make him behave himself.

But, taken all together, the trip was a great success, and to this day the four little folk always accompany Santa Claus on his yearly ride and help him in the distribution of his gifts.

But the indifference of parents, which had so annoyed the good Saint, did not continue very long, and Santa Claus soon found they were really anxious he should visit their homes on Christmas Eve and leave presents for their children.

So, to lighten his task, which was fast becoming very difficult indeed, old Santa decided to ask the parents to assist him.

"Get your Christmas trees all ready for my coming," he said to them; "and then I shall be able to leave the presents without loss of time, and you can put them on the trees when I am gone."

And to others he said: "See that the children's stockings are hung up in readiness for my coming, and then I can fill them as quick as a wink."

And often, when parents were kind and good-natured, Santa Claus would simply fling down his package of gifts and leave the fathers and mothers to fill the stockings after he had darted away in his sledge.

"I will make all loving parents my deputies!" cried the jolly old fellow, "and they shall help me do my work. For in this way I shall save many precious minutes and few children need be neglected for lack of time to visit them."

Besides carrying around the big packs in his swift-flying sledge old Santa began to send great heaps of toys to the toy-shops, so that if parents wanted larger supplies for their children they could easily get them; and if any children were, by chance, missed by Santa Claus on his yearly rounds, they could go to the toy-shops and get enough to make them happy and contented. For the loving friend of the little ones decided that no child, if he could help it, should long for toys in vain. And the toy-shops also proved convenient whenever a child fell ill, and needed a new toy to amuse it; and sometimes, on birthdays, the fathers and mothers go to the toy-shops and get pretty gifts for their children in honor of the happy event.

Perhaps you will now understand how, in spite of the bigness of the world, Santa Claus is able to supply all the children with beautiful gifts. To be sure, the old gentleman is rarely seen in these days; but it is not because he tries to keep out of sight, I assure you. Santa Claus is the same loving friend of children that in the old days used to play and romp with them by the hour; and I know he would love to do the same now, if he had the time. But, you see, he is so busy all the year making toys, and so hurried on that one night when he visits our homes with his packs, that he comes and goes among us like a flash; and it is almost impossible to catch a glimpse of him.

And, although there are millions and millions more children in the world than there used to be, Santa Claus has never been known to complain of their increasing numbers.

"The more the merrier!" he cries, with his jolly laugh; and the only difference to him is the fact that his little workmen have to make their busy fingers fly faster every year to satisfy the demands of so many little ones.

"In all this world there is nothing so beautiful as a happy child," says good old Santa Claus; and if he had his way the children would all be beautiful, for all would be happy.

The End.

SNAPSHOT IN TIME

NEW YORK IN 1900: SAILORS HEADED TO SHORE FOR CHRISTMAS LEAVE.

EXTRA HOLIDAY SNAPSHOT!

A STEREOGRAPH CARD, POSSIBLY FROM 1897; SANTA IS TELEPHONING FOR SUPPLIES.

THE CASTLE OF OTRANTO

BY HORACE WALPOLE

The following introduction and preface are from the first
edition, published in 1901 by:

CASSELL AND COMPANY, Limited
LONDON, PARIS, NEW YORK & MELBOURNE

INTRODUCTION

Horace Walpole was the youngest son of Sir Robert Walpole, the great statesman, who died Earl of Orford. He was born in 1717, the year in which his father resigned office, remaining in opposition for almost three years before his return to a long tenure of power. Horace Walpole was educated at Eton, where he formed a school friendship with Thomas Gray, who was but a few months older. In 1739 Gray was traveling companion with Walpole in France and Italy until they differed and parted; but the friendship was afterwards renewed, and remained firm to the end. Horace Walpole went from Eton to King's College, Cambridge, and entered Parliament in 1741, the year before his father's final resignation and acceptance of an earldom. His way of life was made easy to him. As Usher of the Exchequer, Comptroller of the Pipe, and Clerk of the Estreats in the Exchequer, he received nearly two thousand a year for doing nothing, lived with his father, and amused himself.

Horace Walpole idled, and amused himself with the small life of the fashionable world to which he was proud of belonging, though he had a quick eye for its vanities. He had social wit, and liked to put it to small uses. But he was not an empty idler, and there were seasons when he could become a sharp judge of himself. "I am sensible," he wrote to his most intimate friend, "I am sensible of having more follies and weaknesses and fewer real good qualities than most men. I sometimes reflect on this, though, I own, too seldom. I always want to begin acting like a man, and a sensible one, which I think I might be if I would." He had deep home affections, and, under many polite affectations, plenty of good sense.

Horace Walpole's father died in 1745. The eldest son, who succeeded to the earldom, died in 1751, and left a son, George, who was for a time insane, and lived until 1791. As George left no child, the title and estates passed to Horace Walpole, then seventy-four years old, and the only uncle who survived. Horace Walpole thus became Earl of Orford, during the last six years of his life. As to the title, he said that he felt himself being called names in his old age. He died unmarried, in the year 1797, at the age of eighty.

He had turned his house at Strawberry Hill, by the Thames, near Twickenham, into a Gothic villa—eighteenth-century Gothic—and amused himself by spending freely upon its adornment with such things as were then fashionable as objects of taste. But he delighted also in his flowers and his trellises of roses, and the quiet Thames. When confined by gout to his London house in Arlington Street, flowers from Strawberry Hill and a bird were necessary consolations. He set up also at Strawberry Hill a private printing press, at which he printed his friend Gray's poems, also in 1758 his own "Catalogue of the Royal and Noble Authors of England," and five volumes of "Anecdotes of Painting in England," between 1762 and 1771.

Horace Walpole produced *The Castle of Otranto* in 1765, at the mature age of forty-eight. It was suggested by a dream from which he said he waked one morning, and of which "all I could recover was, that I had thought myself in an ancient castle (a very natural dream for a head like mine, filled with Gothic story), and that on the uppermost banister of a great staircase I saw a gigantic hand in armour. In the evening I sat down and began to write, without knowing in the least what I intended to say or relate." So began the tale which professed to be translated by "William Marshal, gentleman, from the Italian of Onuphro Muralto, canon of the Church of St. Nicholas, at Otranto." It was written in two months. Walpole's friend Gray reported to him that at Cambridge the book made "some of them cry a little, and all in general afraid to go to bed o' nights." *The Castle of Otranto* was, in its own way, an early sign of the reaction towards romance in the latter part of the last century. This gives it interest. But it has had many followers, and the hardy modern reader, when he reads Gray's note from Cambridge, needs to be reminded of its date.

H. M.

PREFACE TO THE FIRST EDITION

The following work was found in the library of an ancient Catholic family in the north of England. It was printed at Naples, in the black letter, in the year 1529. How much sooner it was written does not appear. The principal incidents are such as were believed in the darkest ages of Christianity; but the language and conduct have nothing that savours of barbarism. The style is the purest Italian.

If the story was written near the time when it is supposed to have happened, it must have been between 1095, the era of the first Crusade, and 1243, the date of the last, or not long afterwards. There is no other circumstance in the work that can lead us to guess at the period in which the scene is laid: the names of the actors are evidently fictitious, and probably disguised on purpose: yet the Spanish names of the domestics seem to indicate that this work was not composed until the establishment of the Arragonian Kings in Naples had made Spanish appellations familiar in that country. The beauty of the diction, and the zeal of the author (moderated, however, by singular judgment) concur to make me think that the date of the composition was little antecedent to that of the impression. Letters were then in their most flourishing state in Italy, and contributed to dispel the empire of superstition, at that time so forcibly attacked by the reformers. It is not unlikely that an artful priest might endeavour to turn their own arms on the innovators, and might avail himself of his abilities as an author to confirm the populace in their ancient errors and superstitions. If this was his view, he has certainly acted with signal address. Such a work as the following would enslave a hundred vulgar minds beyond half the books of controversy that have been written from the days of Luther to the present hour.

This solution of the author's motives is, however, offered as a mere conjecture. Whatever his views were, or whatever effects the execution of them might have, his work can only be laid before the public at present as a matter of entertainment. Even as such, some apology for it is necessary. Miracles, visions, necromancy, dreams, and other preternatural events, are exploded now even from romances. That was not the case when our author wrote; much less when the story itself is supposed to have happened. Belief in every kind of prodigy was so established in those dark ages, that an author would not be faithful to the manners of the times, who should omit all mention of them. He is not bound to believe them himself, but he must represent his actors as believing them.

If this air of the miraculous is excused, the reader will find nothing else unworthy of his perusal. Allow the possibility of the facts, and all the actors comport themselves as persons would do in their situation. There is no bombast, no similes, flowers, digressions, or unnecessary descriptions. Everything tends directly to the catastrophe. Never is the reader's attention relaxed. The rules of the drama are almost observed throughout the conduct of the piece. The characters are well drawn, and still better maintained. Terror, the author's principal engine, prevents the story from ever languishing; and it is so often contrasted by pity, that the mind is kept up in a constant vicissitude of interesting passions.

Some persons may perhaps think the characters of the domestics too little serious for the general cast of the story; but besides their opposition to the principal personages, the art of the author is very observable in his conduct of the subalterns. They discover many passages essential to the story, which could not be well brought to light but by their *naïveté* and simplicity. In particular, the womanish terror and foibles of Bianca, in the last chapter, conduce essentially towards advancing the catastrophe.

It is natural for a translator to be prejudiced in favour of his adopted work. More impartial readers may not be so much struck with the beauties of this piece as I was. Yet I am not blind to my author's defects. I could wish he had grounded his plan on a more useful moral than this: that "the sins of fathers are visited on their children to the third and fourth generation." I doubt whether, in his time, any more than at present, ambition curbed its appetite of dominion from the dread of so remote a punishment. And yet this moral is weakened by that less direct insinuation, that even such anathema may be diverted by devotion to St. Nicholas. Here the interest of the Monk plainly gets the better of the judgment of the author. However, with all its faults, I have no doubt but the English reader will be pleased with a sight of this performance. The piety that reigns throughout, the lessons of virtue that are inculcated, and the rigid purity of the sentiments, exempt this work from the censure to which romances are but too liable. Should it meet with the success I hope for, I may be encouraged to reprint the original Italian, though it will tend to depreciate my own labour. Our language falls far short of the charms of the Italian, both for variety and harmony. The latter is peculiarly excellent for simple narrative. It is difficult in English to relate without falling too low or rising too high; a fault obviously occasioned by the little care taken to speak pure language in common conversation. Every Italian or Frenchman of any rank piques himself on speaking his own tongue correctly and with choice. I cannot flatter myself with having done justice to my author in this respect: his style is as elegant as his conduct of the passions is masterly. It is a pity that he did not apply his talents to what they were evidently proper for—the theatre.

I will detain the reader no longer, but to make one short remark. Though the machinery is invention, and the names of the actors imaginary, I cannot but believe that the groundwork of the story is founded on truth. The scene is undoubtedly laid in some real castle. The author seems frequently, without design, to describe particular parts. "The chamber," says he, "on the right hand;" "the door on the left hand;" "the distance from the chapel to Conrad's apartment:" these and other passages are strong presumptions that the author had some certain building in his eye. Curious persons, who have leisure to employ in such researches, may possibly discover in the Italian writers the foundation on which our author has built. If a catastrophe, at all resembling that which he describes, is believed to have given rise to this work, it will contribute to interest the reader, and will make the "Castle of Otranto" a still more moving story.

SONNET TO THE RIGHT HONOURABLE
LADY MARY COKE

The gentle maid, whose hapless tale
These melancholy pages speak;
Say, gracious lady, shall she fail
To draw the tear adown thy cheek?
No; never was thy pitying breast
Insensible to human woes;
Tender, tho' firm, it melts distrest
For weaknesses it never knows.
Oh! guard the marvels I relate
Of fell ambition scourg'd by fate,
From reason's peevish blame.
Blest with thy smile, my dauntless sail
I dare expand to Fancy's gale,
For sure thy smiles are Fame.

CHAPTER I

Manfred, Prince of Otranto, had one son and one daughter: the latter, a most beautiful virgin, aged eighteen, was called Matilda. Conrad, the son, was three years younger, a homely youth, sickly, and of no promising disposition; yet he was the darling of his father, who never showed any symptoms of affection to Matilda. Manfred had contracted a marriage for his son with the Marquis of Vicenza's daughter, Isabella; and she had already been delivered by her guardians into the hands of Manfred, that he might celebrate the wedding as soon as Conrad's infirm state of health would permit.

Manfred's impatience for this ceremonial was remarked by his family and neighbours. The former, indeed, apprehending the severity of their Prince's disposition, did not dare to utter their surmises on this precipitation. Hippolita, his wife, an amiable lady, did sometimes venture to represent the danger of marrying their only son so early, considering his great youth, and greater infirmities; but she never received any other answer than reflections on her own sterility, who had given him but one heir. His tenants and subjects were less cautious in their discourses. They attributed this hasty wedding to the Prince's dread of seeing accomplished an ancient prophecy, which was said to have pronounced that the castle and lordship of Otranto "should pass from the present family, whenever the real owner should be grown too large to inhabit it." It was difficult to make any sense of this prophecy; and still less easy to conceive what it had to do with the marriage in question. Yet these mysteries, or contradictions, did not make the populace adhere the less to their opinion.

Young Conrad's birthday was fixed for his espousals. The company was assembled in the chapel of the Castle, and everything ready for beginning the divine office, when Conrad himself was missing. Manfred, impatient of the least delay, and who had not observed his son retire, despatched one of his attendants to summon the young Prince. The servant, who had not stayed long enough to have crossed the court to Conrad's apartment, came running back breathless, in a frantic manner, his eyes staring, and foaming at the mouth. He said nothing, but pointed to the court.

The company were struck with terror and amazement. The Princess Hippolita, without knowing what was the matter, but anxious for her son, swooned away. Manfred, less apprehensive than enraged at the procrastination of the nuptials, and at the folly of his domestic, asked imperiously what was the matter? The fellow made no answer, but continued pointing towards the courtyard; and at last, after repeated questions put to him, cried out, "Oh! the helmet! the helmet!"

In the meantime, some of the company had run into the court, from whence was heard a confused noise of shrieks, horror, and surprise. Manfred, who began to be alarmed at not seeing his son, went himself to get information of what occasioned this strange confusion. Matilda remained endeavouring to assist her mother, and Isabella stayed for the same purpose, and to avoid showing any impatience for the bridegroom, for whom, in truth, she had conceived little affection.

The first thing that struck Manfred's eyes was a group of his servants endeavouring to raise something that appeared to him a mountain of sable plumes. He gazed without believing his sight.

"What are ye doing?" cried Manfred, wrathfully; "where is my son?"

A volley of voices replied, "Oh! my Lord! the Prince! the Prince! the helmet! the helmet!"

Shocked with these lamentable sounds, and dreading he knew not what, he advanced hastily,—but what a sight for a father's eyes!—he beheld his child dashed to pieces, and almost buried under an enormous helmet, an hundred times more large than any casque ever made for human being, and shaded with a proportionable quantity of black feathers.

The horror of the spectacle, the ignorance of all around how this misfortune had happened, and above all, the tremendous phenomenon before him, took away the Prince's speech. Yet his silence lasted longer than even grief could occasion. He fixed his eyes on what he wished in vain to believe a vision; and seemed less attentive to his loss, than buried in meditation on the stupendous object that had occasioned it. He touched, he examined the fatal casque; nor could even the bleeding mangled remains of the young Prince divert the eyes of Manfred from the portent before him.

All who had known his partial fondness for young Conrad, were as much surprised at their Prince's insensibility, as thunderstruck themselves at the miracle of the helmet. They conveyed the disfigured corpse into the hall, without receiving the least direction from Manfred. As little was he attentive to the ladies who remained in the chapel. On the contrary, without mentioning the unhappy princesses, his wife and daughter, the first sounds that dropped from Manfred's lips were, "Take care of the Lady Isabella."

The domestics, without observing the singularity of this direction, were guided by their affection to their mistress, to consider it as peculiarly addressed to her situation, and flew to her assistance. They conveyed her to her chamber more dead than alive, and indifferent to all the strange circumstances she heard, except the death of her son.

Matilda, who doted on her mother, smothered her own grief and amazement, and thought of nothing but assisting and comforting her afflicted parent. Isabella, who had been treated by Hippolita like a daughter, and who returned that tenderness with equal duty and affection, was scarce less assiduous about the Princess; at the same time endeavouring to partake and lessen the weight of sorrow which she saw Matilda strove to suppress, for whom she had conceived the warmest sympathy of friendship. Yet her own situation could not help finding its place in her thoughts. She felt no concern for the death of young Conrad, except commiseration; and she was not sorry to be delivered from a marriage which had promised her little felicity, either from her destined bridegroom, or from the severe temper of Manfred, who, though he had distinguished her by great indulgence, had imprinted her mind with terror, from his causeless rigour to such amiable princesses as Hippolita and Matilda.

While the ladies were conveying the wretched mother to her bed, Manfred remained in the court, gazing on the ominous casque, and regardless of the crowd which the strangeness of the event had now assembled around him. The few words he articulated, tended solely to inquiries, whether any man knew from whence it could have come? Nobody could give him the least information. However, as it seemed to be the sole object of his curiosity, it soon became so to the rest of the spectators, whose conjectures were as absurd and improbable, as the catastrophe itself was unprecedented. In the midst of their senseless guesses, a young peasant, whom rumour had drawn thither from a neighbouring village, observed that the miraculous helmet was exactly like that on the figure in black marble of Alfonso the Good, one of their former princes, in the church of St. Nicholas.

"Villain! What sayest thou?" cried Manfred, starting from his trance in a tempest of rage, and seizing the young man by the collar; "how darest thou utter such treason? Thy life shall pay for it."

The spectators, who as little comprehended the cause of the Prince's fury as all the rest they had seen, were at a loss to unravel this new circumstance. The young peasant himself was still more astonished, not conceiving how he had offended the Prince. Yet recollecting himself, with a mixture of grace and humility, he disengaged himself from Manfred's grip, and then with an obeisance, which discovered more jealousy of innocence than dismay, he asked, with respect, of what he was guilty? Manfred, more enraged at the vigour, however decently exerted, with which the young man had shaken off his hold, than appeased by his submission, ordered his attendants to seize him, and, if he had not been withheld by his friends whom he had invited to the nuptials, would have poignarded the peasant in their arms.

During this altercation, some of the vulgar spectators had run to the great church, which stood near the castle, and came back open-mouthed, declaring that the helmet was missing from Alfonso's statue. Manfred, at this news, grew perfectly frantic; and, as if he sought a subject on which to vent the tempest within him, he rushed again on the young peasant, crying—

"Villain! Monster! Sorcerer! 'tis thou hast done this! 'tis thou hast slain my son!"

The mob, who wanted some object within the scope of their capacities, on whom they might discharge their bewildered reasoning, caught the words from the mouth of their lord, and re-echoed—

"Ay, ay; 'tis he, 'tis he: he has stolen the helmet from good Alfonso's tomb, and dashed out the brains of our young Prince with it," never reflecting how enormous the disproportion was between the marble helmet that had been in the church, and that of steel before their eyes; nor how impossible it was for a youth seemingly not twenty, to wield a piece of armour of so prodigious a weight.

The folly of these ejaculations brought Manfred to himself: yet whether provoked at the peasant having observed the resemblance between the two helmets, and thereby led to the farther discovery of the absence of that in the church, or wishing to bury any such rumour under so impertinent a supposition, he gravely pronounced that the young man was certainly a necromancer, and that till the Church could take cognisance of the affair, he would have the Magician, whom they had thus detected, kept prisoner under the helmet itself, which he ordered his attendants to raise, and place the young man under it; declaring he should be kept there without food, with which his own infernal art might furnish him.

It was in vain for the youth to represent against this preposterous sentence: in vain did Manfred's friends endeavour to divert him from this savage and ill-grounded resolution. The generality were charmed with their lord's decision, which, to their apprehensions, carried great appearance of justice, as the Magician was to be punished by the very instrument with which he had offended: nor were they struck with the least compunction at the probability of the youth being starved, for they firmly believed that, by his diabolic skill, he could easily supply himself with nutriment.

Manfred thus saw his commands even cheerfully obeyed; and appointing a guard with strict orders to prevent any food being conveyed to the prisoner, he dismissed his friends and attendants, and retired to his own chamber, after locking the gates of the castle, in which he suffered none but his domestics to remain.

In the meantime, the care and zeal of the young Ladies had brought the Princess Hippolita to herself, who amidst the transports of her own sorrow frequently demanded news of her lord, would have dismissed her attendants to watch over him, and at last enjoined Matilda to leave her, and visit and comfort her father. Matilda, who wanted no affectionate duty to Manfred, though she trembled at his austerity, obeyed the orders of Hippolita, whom she tenderly recommended to Isabella; and inquiring of the domestics for her father, was informed that he was retired to his chamber, and had commanded that nobody should have admittance to him. Concluding that he was immersed in sorrow for the death of her brother, and fearing to renew his tears by the sight of his sole remaining child, she hesitated whether she should break in upon his affliction; yet solicitude for him, backed by the commands of her mother, encouraged her to venture disobeying the orders he had given; a fault she had never been guilty of before.

The gentle timidity of her nature made her pause for some minutes at his door. She heard him traverse his chamber backwards, and forwards with disordered steps; a mood which increased her apprehensions. She was, however, just going to beg admittance, when Manfred suddenly opened the door; and as it was now twilight, concurring with the disorder of his mind, he did not distinguish the person, but asked angrily, who it was? Matilda replied, trembling—

"My dearest father, it is I, your daughter."

Manfred, stepping back hastily, cried, "Begone! I do not want a daughter;" and flinging back abruptly, clapped the door against the terrified Matilda.

She was too well acquainted with her father's impetuosity to venture a second intrusion. When she had a little recovered the shock of so bitter a reception, she wiped away her tears to prevent the additional stab that the knowledge of it would give to Hippolita, who questioned her in the most anxious terms on the health of Manfred, and how he bore his loss. Matilda assured her he was well, and supported his misfortune with manly fortitude.

"But will he not let me see him?" said Hippolita mournfully; "will he not permit me to blend my tears with his, and shed a mother's sorrows in the bosom of her Lord? Or do you deceive me, Matilda? I know how Manfred doted on his son: is not the stroke too heavy for him? has he not sunk under it? You do not answer me—alas! I dread the worst!—Raise me, my maidens; I will, I will see my Lord. Bear me to him instantly: he is dearer to me even than my children."

Matilda made signs to Isabella to prevent Hippolita's rising; and both those lovely young women were using their gentle violence to stop and calm the Princess, when a servant, on the part of Manfred, arrived and told Isabella that his Lord demanded to speak with her.

"With me!" cried Isabella.

"Go," said Hippolita, relieved by a message from her Lord: "Manfred cannot support the sight of his own family. He thinks you less disordered than we are, and dreads the shock of my grief. Console him, dear Isabella, and tell him I will smother my own anguish rather than add to his."

As it was now evening the servant who conducted Isabella bore a torch before her. When they came to Manfred, who was walking impatiently about the gallery, he started, and said hastily—

"Take away that light, and begone."

Then shutting the door impetuously, he flung himself upon a bench against the wall, and bade Isabella sit by him. She obeyed trembling.

"I sent for you, Lady," said he—and then stopped under great appearance of confusion.

"My Lord!"

"Yes, I sent for you on a matter of great moment," resumed he. "Dry your tears, young Lady—you have lost your bridegroom. Yes, cruel fate! and I have lost the hopes of my race! But Conrad was not worthy of your beauty."

"How, my Lord!" said Isabella; "sure you do not suspect me of not feeling the concern I ought: my duty and affection would have always—"

"Think no more of him," interrupted Manfred; "he was a sickly, puny child, and Heaven has perhaps taken him away, that I might not trust the honours of my house on so frail a foundation. The line of Manfred calls for numerous supports. My foolish fondness for that boy blinded the eyes of my prudence—but it is better as it is. I hope, in a few years, to have reason to rejoice at the death of Conrad."

Words cannot paint the astonishment of Isabella. At first she apprehended that grief had disordered Manfred's understanding. Her next thought suggested that this strange discourse was designed to ensnare her: she feared that Manfred had perceived her indifference for his son: and in consequence of that idea she replied—

"Good my Lord, do not doubt my tenderness: my heart would have accompanied my hand. Conrad would have engrossed all my care; and wherever fate shall dispose of me, I shall always cherish his memory, and regard your Highness and the virtuous Hippolita as my parents."

"Curse on Hippolita!" cried Manfred. "Forget her from this moment, as I do. In short, Lady, you have missed a husband undeserving of your charms: they shall now be better disposed of. Instead of a sickly boy, you shall have a husband in the prime of his age, who will know how to value your beauties, and who may expect a numerous offspring."

"Alas, my Lord!" said Isabella, "my mind is too sadly engrossed by the recent catastrophe in your family to think of another marriage. If ever my father returns, and it shall be his pleasure, I shall obey, as I did when I consented to give my hand to your son: but until his return, permit me to remain under your hospitable roof, and employ the melancholy hours in assuaging yours, Hippolita's, and the fair Matilda's affliction."

"I desired you once before," said Manfred angrily, "not to name that woman: from this hour she must be a stranger to you, as she must be to me. In short, Isabella, since I cannot give you my son, I offer you myself."

"Heavens!" cried Isabella, waking from her delusion, "what do I hear? You! my Lord! You! My father-in-law! the father of Conrad! the husband of the virtuous and tender Hippolita!"

"I tell you," said Manfred imperiously, "Hippolita is no longer my wife; I divorce her from this hour. Too long has she cursed me by her unfruitfulness. My fate depends on having sons, and this night I trust will give a new date to my hopes."

At those words he seized the cold hand of Isabella, who was half dead with fright and horror. She shrieked, and started from him, Manfred rose to pursue her, when the moon, which was now up, and gleamed in at the opposite casement, presented to his sight the plumes of the fatal helmet, which rose to the height of the windows, waving backwards and forwards in a tempestuous manner, and accompanied with a hollow and rustling sound. Isabella, who gathered courage from her situation, and who dreaded nothing so much as Manfred's pursuit of his declaration, cried—

"Look, my Lord! see, Heaven itself declares against your impious intentions!"

"Heaven nor Hell shall impede my designs," said Manfred, advancing again to seize the Princess.

At that instant the portrait of his grandfather, which hung over the bench where they had been sitting, uttered a deep sigh, and heaved its breast.

Isabella, whose back was turned to the picture, saw not the motion, nor knew whence the sound came, but started, and said—

"Hark, my Lord! What sound was that?" and at the same time made towards the door.

Manfred, distracted between the flight of Isabella, who had now reached the stairs, and yet unable to keep his eyes from the picture, which began to move, had, however, advanced some steps after her, still looking backwards on the portrait, when he saw it quit its panel, and descend on the floor with a grave and melancholy air.

"Do I dream?" cried Manfred, returning; "or are the devils themselves in league against me? Speak, infernal spectre! Or, if thou art my grandsire, why dost thou too conspire against thy wretched descendant, who too dearly pays for—" Ere he could finish the sentence, the vision sighed again, and made a sign to Manfred to follow him.

"Lead on!" cried Manfred; "I will follow thee to the gulf of perdition."

The spectre marched sedately, but dejected, to the end of the gallery, and turned into a chamber on the right hand. Manfred accompanied him at a little distance, full of anxiety and horror, but resolved. As he would have entered the chamber, the door was clapped to with violence by an invisible hand. The Prince, collecting courage from this delay, would have forcibly burst open the door with his foot, but found that it resisted his utmost efforts.

"Since Hell will not satisfy my curiosity," said Manfred, "I will use the human means in my power for preserving my race; Isabella shall not escape me."

The lady, whose resolution had given way to terror the moment she had quitted Manfred, continued her flight to the bottom of the principal staircase. There she stopped, not knowing whither to direct her steps, nor how to escape from the impetuosity of the Prince. The gates of the castle, she knew, were locked, and guards placed in the court. Should she, as her heart prompted her, go and prepare Hippolita for the cruel destiny that awaited her, she did not doubt but Manfred would seek her there, and that his violence would incite him to double the injury he meditated, without leaving room for them to avoid the impetuosity of his passions. Delay might give him time to reflect on the horrid measures he had conceived, or produce some circumstance in her favour, if she could—for that night, at least—avoid his odious purpose. Yet where conceal herself? How avoid the pursuit he would infallibly make throughout the castle?

As these thoughts passed rapidly through her mind, she recollected a subterraneous passage which led from the vaults of the castle to the church of St. Nicholas. Could she reach the altar before she was overtaken, she knew even Manfred's violence would not dare to profane the sacredness of the place; and she determined, if no other means of deliverance offered, to shut herself up for ever among the holy virgins whose convent was contiguous to the cathedral. In this resolution, she seized a lamp that burned at the foot of the staircase, and hurried towards the secret passage.

The lower part of the castle was hollowed into several intricate cloisters; and it was not easy for one under so much anxiety to find the door that opened into the cavern. An awful silence reigned throughout those subterraneous regions, except now and then some blasts of wind that shook the doors she had passed, and which, grating on the rusty hinges, were re-echoed through that long labyrinth of darkness. Every murmur struck her with new terror; yet more she dreaded to hear the wrathful voice of Manfred urging his domestics to pursue her.

She trod as softly as impatience would give her leave, yet frequently stopped and listened to hear if she was followed. In one of those moments she thought she heard a sigh. She shuddered, and recoiled a few paces. In a moment she thought she heard the step of some person. Her blood curdled; she concluded it was Manfred. Every suggestion that horror could inspire rushed into her mind. She condemned her rash flight, which had thus exposed her to his rage in a place where her cries were not likely to draw anybody to her assistance. Yet the sound seemed not to come from behind. If Manfred knew where she was, he must have followed her. She was still in one of the cloisters, and the steps she had heard were too distinct to proceed from the way she had come. Cheered with this reflection, and hoping to find a friend in whoever was not the Prince, she was going to advance, when a door that stood ajar, at some distance to the left, was opened gently: but ere her lamp, which she held up, could discover who opened it, the person retreated precipitately on seeing the light.

Isabella, whom every incident was sufficient to dismay, hesitated whether she should proceed. Her dread of Manfred soon outweighed every other terror. The very circumstance of the person avoiding her gave her a sort of courage. It could only be, she thought, some domestic belonging to the castle. Her gentleness had never raised her an enemy, and conscious innocence made her hope that, unless sent by the Prince's order to seek her, his servants would rather assist than prevent her flight. Fortifying herself with these reflections, and believing by what she could observe that she was near the mouth of the subterraneous cavern, she approached the door that had been opened; but a sudden gust of wind that met her at the door extinguished her lamp, and left her in total darkness.

Words cannot paint the horror of the Princess's situation. Alone in so dismal a place, her mind imprinted with all the terrible events of the day, hopeless of escaping, expecting every moment the arrival of Manfred, and far from tranquil on knowing she was within reach of somebody, she knew not whom, who for some cause seemed concealed thereabouts; all these thoughts crowded on her distracted mind, and she was ready to sink under her apprehensions. She addressed herself to every saint in heaven, and inwardly implored their assistance. For a considerable time she remained in an agony of despair.

At last, as softly as was possible, she felt for the door, and having found it, entered trembling into the vault from whence she had heard the sigh and steps. It gave her a kind of momentary joy to perceive an imperfect ray of clouded moonshine gleam from the roof of the vault, which seemed to be fallen in, and from whence hung a fragment of earth or building, she could not distinguish which, that appeared to have been crushed inwards. She advanced eagerly towards this chasm, when she discerned a human form standing close against the wall.

She shrieked, believing it the ghost of her betrothed Conrad. The figure, advancing, said, in a submissive voice—

"Be not alarmed, Lady; I will not injure you."

Isabella, a little encouraged by the words and tone of voice of the stranger, and recollecting that this must be the person who had opened the door, recovered her spirits enough to reply—

"Sir, whoever you are, take pity on a wretched Princess, standing on the brink of destruction. Assist me to escape from this fatal castle, or in a few moments I may be made miserable for ever."

"Alas!" said the stranger, "what can I do to assist you? I will die in your defence; but I am unacquainted with the castle, and want—"

"Oh!" said Isabella, hastily interrupting him; "help me but to find a trap-door that must be hereabout, and it is the greatest service you can do me, for I have not a minute to lose."

Saying these words, she felt about on the pavement, and directed the stranger to search likewise, for a smooth piece of brass enclosed in one of the stones.

"That," said she, "is the lock, which opens with a spring, of which I know the secret. If we can find that, I may escape—if not, alas! courteous stranger, I fear I shall have involved you in my misfortunes: Manfred will suspect you for the accomplice of my flight, and you will fall a victim to his resentment."

"I value not my life," said the stranger, "and it will be some comfort to lose it in trying to deliver you from his tyranny."

"Generous youth," said Isabella, "how shall I ever requite—"

As she uttered those words, a ray of moonshine, streaming through a cranny of the ruin above, shone directly on the lock they sought.

"Oh! transport!" said Isabella; "here is the trap-door!" and, taking out the key, she touched the spring, which, starting aside, discovered an iron ring. "Lift up the door," said the Princess.

The stranger obeyed, and beneath appeared some stone steps descending into a vault totally dark.

"We must go down here," said Isabella. "Follow me; dark and dismal as it is, we cannot miss our way; it leads directly to the church of St. Nicholas. But, perhaps," added the Princess modestly, "you have no reason to leave the castle, nor have I farther occasion for your service; in a few minutes I shall be safe from Manfred's rage—only let me know to whom I am so much obliged."

"I will never quit you," said the stranger eagerly, "until I have placed you in safety—nor think me, Princess, more generous than I am; though you are my principal care—"

The stranger was interrupted by a sudden noise of voices that seemed approaching, and they soon distinguished these words—

"Talk not to me of necromancers; I tell you she must be in the castle; I will find her in spite of enchantment."

"Oh, heavens!" cried Isabella; "it is the voice of Manfred! Make haste, or we are ruined! and shut the trap-door after you."

Saying this, she descended the steps precipitately; and as the stranger hastened to follow her, he let the door slip out of his hands: it fell, and the spring closed over it. He tried in vain to open it, not having observed Isabella's method of touching the spring; nor had he many moments to make an essay. The noise of the falling door had been heard by Manfred, who, directed by the sound, hastened thither, attended by his servants with torches.

"It must be Isabella," cried Manfred, before he entered the vault. "She is escaping by the subterraneous passage, but she cannot have got far."

What was the astonishment of the Prince when, instead of Isabella, the light of the torches discovered to him the young peasant whom he thought confined under the fatal helmet!

"Traitor!" said Manfred; "how camest thou here? I thought thee in durance above in the court."

"I am no traitor," replied the young man boldly, "nor am I answerable for your thoughts."

"Presumptuous villain!" cried Manfred; "dost thou provoke my wrath? Tell me, how hast thou escaped from above? Thou hast corrupted thy guards, and their lives shall answer it."

"My poverty," said the peasant calmly, "will disculpate them: though the ministers of a tyrant's wrath, to thee they are faithful, and but too willing to execute the orders which you unjustly imposed upon them."

"Art thou so hardy as to dare my vengeance?" said the Prince; "but tortures shall force the truth from thee. Tell me; I will know thy accomplices."

"There was my accomplice!" said the youth, smiling, and pointing to the roof.

Manfred ordered the torches to be held up, and perceived that one of the cheeks of the enchanted casque had forced its way through the pavement of the court, as his servants had let it fall over the peasant, and had broken through into the vault, leaving a gap, through which the peasant had pressed himself some minutes before he was found by Isabella.

"Was that the way by which thou didst descend?" said Manfred.

"It was," said the youth.

"But what noise was that," said Manfred, "which I heard as I entered the cloister?"

"A door clapped," said the peasant; "I heard it as well as you."

"What door?" said Manfred hastily.

"I am not acquainted with your castle," said the peasant; "this is the first time I ever entered it, and this vault the only part of it within which I ever was."

"But I tell thee," said Manfred (wishing to find out if the youth had discovered the trap-door), "it was this way I heard the noise. My servants heard it too."

"My Lord," interrupted one of them officiously, "to be sure it was the trap-door, and he was going to make his escape."

"Peace, blockhead!" said the Prince angrily; "if he was going to escape, how should he come on this side? I will know from his own mouth what noise it was I heard. Tell me truly; thy life depends on thy veracity."

"My veracity is dearer to me than my life," said the peasant; "nor would I purchase the one by forfeiting the other."

"Indeed, young philosopher!" said Manfred contemptuously; "tell me, then, what was the noise I heard?"

"Ask me what I can answer," said he, "and put me to death instantly if I tell you a lie."

Manfred, growing impatient at the steady valour and indifference of the youth, cried—

"Well, then, thou man of truth, answer! Was it the fall of the trap-door that I heard?"

"It was," said the youth.

"It was!" said the Prince; "and how didst thou come to know there was a trap-door here?"

"I saw the plate of brass by a gleam of moonshine," replied he.

"But what told thee it was a lock?" said Manfred. "How didst thou discover the secret of opening it?"

"Providence, that delivered me from the helmet, was able to direct me to the spring of a lock," said he.

"Providence should have gone a little farther, and have placed thee out of the reach of my resentment," said Manfred. "When Providence had taught thee to open the lock, it abandoned thee for a fool, who did not know how to make use of its favours. Why didst thou not pursue the path pointed out for thy escape? Why didst thou shut the trap-door before thou hadst descended the steps?"

"I might ask you, my Lord," said the peasant, "how I, totally unacquainted with your castle, was to know that those steps led to any outlet? but I scorn to evade your questions. Wherever those steps lead to, perhaps I should have explored the way—I could not be in a worse situation than I was. But the truth is, I let the trap-door fall: your immediate arrival followed. I had given the alarm—what imported it to me whether I was seized a minute sooner or a minute later?"

"Thou art a resolute villain for thy years," said Manfred; "yet on reflection I suspect thou dost but trifle with me. Thou hast not yet told me how thou didst open the lock."

"That I will show you, my Lord," said the peasant; and, taking up a fragment of stone that had fallen from above, he laid himself on the trap-door, and began to beat on the piece of brass that covered it, meaning to gain time for the escape of the Princess. This presence of mind, joined to the frankness of the youth, staggered Manfred. He even felt a disposition towards pardoning one who had been guilty of no crime. Manfred was not one of those savage tyrants who wanton in cruelty unprovoked. The circumstances of his fortune had given an asperity to his temper, which was naturally humane; and his virtues were always ready to operate, when his passions did not obscure his reason.

While the Prince was in this suspense, a confused noise of voices echoed through the distant vaults. As the sound approached, he distinguished the clamours of some of his domestics, whom he had dispersed through the castle in search of Isabella, calling out—

"Where is my Lord? where is the Prince?"

"Here I am," said Manfred, as they came nearer; "have you found the Princess?"

The first that arrived, replied, "Oh, my Lord! I am glad we have found you."

"Found me!" said Manfred; "have you found the Princess?"

"We thought we had, my Lord," said the fellow, looking terrified, "but—"

"But, what?" cried the Prince; "has she escaped?"

"Jaquez and I, my Lord—"

"Yes, I and Diego," interrupted the second, who came up in still greater consternation.

"Speak one of you at a time," said Manfred; "I ask you, where is the Princess?"

"We do not know," said they both together; "but we are frightened out of our wits."

"So I think, blockheads," said Manfred; "what is it has scared you thus?"

"Oh! my Lord," said Jaquez, "Diego has seen such a sight! your Highness would not believe our eyes."

"What new absurdity is this?" cried Manfred; "give me a direct answer, or, by Heaven—"

"Why, my Lord, if it please your Highness to hear me," said the poor fellow, "Diego and I—"

"Yes, I and Jaquez—" cried his comrade.

"Did not I forbid you to speak both at a time?" said the Prince: "you, Jaquez, answer; for the other fool seems more distracted than thou art; what is the matter?"

"My gracious Lord," said Jaquez, "if it please your Highness to hear me; Diego and I, according to your Highness's orders, went to search for the young Lady; but being comprehensive that we might meet the ghost of my young Lord, your Highness's son, God rest his soul, as he has not received Christian burial—"

"Sot!" cried Manfred in a rage; "is it only a ghost, then, that thou hast seen?"

"Oh! worse! worse! my Lord," cried Diego: "I had rather have seen ten whole ghosts."

"Grant me patience!" said Manfred; "these blockheads distract me. Out of my sight, Diego! and thou, Jaquez, tell me in one word, art thou sober? art thou raving? thou wast wont to have some sense: has the other sot frightened himself and thee too? Speak; what is it he fancies he has seen?"

"Why, my Lord," replied Jaquez, trembling, "I was going to tell your Highness, that since the calamitous misfortune of my young Lord, God rest his precious soul! not one of us your Highness's faithful servants—indeed we are, my Lord, though poor men—I say, not one of us has dared to set a foot about the castle, but two together: so Diego and I, thinking that my young Lady might be in the great gallery, went up there to look for her, and tell her your Highness wanted something to impart to her."

"O blundering fools!" cried Manfred; "and in the meantime, she has made her escape, because you were afraid of goblins!—Why, thou knave! she left me in the gallery; I came from thence myself."

"For all that, she may be there still for aught I know," said Jaquez; "but the devil shall have me before I seek her there again—poor Diego! I do not believe he will ever recover it."

"Recover what?" said Manfred; "am I never to learn what it is has terrified these rascals?—but I lose my time; follow me, slave; I will see if she is in the gallery."

"For Heaven's sake, my dear, good Lord," cried Jaquez, "do not go to the gallery. Satan himself I believe is in the chamber next to the gallery."

Manfred, who hitherto had treated the terror of his servants as an idle panic, was struck at this new circumstance. He recollected the apparition of the portrait, and the sudden closing of the door at the end of the gallery. His voice faltered, and he asked with disorder—

"What is in the great chamber?"

"My Lord," said Jaquez, "when Diego and I came into the gallery, he went first, for he said he had more courage than I. So when we came into the gallery we found nobody. We looked under every bench and stool; and still we found nobody."

"Were all the pictures in their places?" said Manfred.

"Yes, my Lord," answered Jaquez; "but we did not think of looking behind them."

"Well, well!" said Manfred; "proceed."

"When we came to the door of the great chamber," continued Jaquez, "we found it shut."

"And could not you open it?" said Manfred.

"Oh! yes, my Lord; would to Heaven we had not!" replied he—"nay, it was not I neither; it was Diego: he was grown foolhardy, and would go on, though I advised him not—if ever I open a door that is shut again—"

"Trifle not," said Manfred, shuddering, "but tell me what you saw in the great chamber on opening the door."

"I, my Lord!" said Jaquez; "I was behind Diego; but I heard the noise."

"Jaquez," said Manfred, in a solemn tone of voice; "tell me, I adjure thee by the souls of my ancestors, what was it thou sawest? what was it thou heardest?"

"It was Diego saw it, my Lord, it was not I," replied Jaquez; "I only heard the noise. Diego had no sooner opened the door, than he cried out, and ran back. I ran back too, and said, 'Is it the ghost?' 'The ghost! no, no,' said Diego, and his hair stood on end—'it is a giant, I believe; he is all clad in armour, for I saw his foot and part of his leg, and they are as large as the helmet below in the court.' As he said these words, my Lord, we heard a violent motion and the rattling of armour, as if the giant was rising, for Diego has told me since that he believes the giant was lying down, for the foot and leg were stretched at length on the floor. Before we could get to the end of the gallery, we heard the door of the great chamber clap behind us, but we did not dare turn back to see if the giant was following us—yet, now I think on it, we must have heard him if he had pursued us—but for Heaven's sake, good my Lord, send for the chaplain, and have the castle exorcised, for, for certain, it is enchanted."

"Ay, pray do, my Lord," cried all the servants at once, "or we must leave your Highness's service."

"Peace, dotards!" said Manfred, "and follow me; I will know what all this means."

"We! my Lord!" cried they with one voice; "we would not go up to the gallery for your Highness's revenue." The young peasant, who had stood silent, now spoke.

"Will your Highness," said he, "permit me to try this adventure? My life is of consequence to nobody; I fear no bad angel, and have offended no good one."

"Your behaviour is above your seeming," said Manfred, viewing him with surprise and admiration—"hereafter I will reward your bravery—but now," continued he with a sigh, "I am so circumstanced, that I dare trust no eyes but my own. However, I give you leave to accompany me."

Manfred, when he first followed Isabella from the gallery, had gone directly to the apartment of his wife, concluding the Princess had retired thither. Hippolita, who knew his step, rose with anxious fondness to meet her Lord, whom she had not seen since the death of their son. She would have flown in a transport mixed of joy and grief to his bosom, but he pushed her rudely off, and said—

"Where is Isabella?"

"Isabella! my Lord!" said the astonished Hippolita.

"Yes, Isabella," cried Manfred imperiously; "I want Isabella."

"My Lord," replied Matilda, who perceived how much his behaviour had shocked her mother, "she has not been with us since your Highness summoned her to your apartment."

"Tell me where she is," said the Prince; "I do not want to know where she has been."

"My good Lord," says Hippolita, "your daughter tells you the truth: Isabella left us by your command, and has not returned since;—but, my good Lord, compose yourself: retire to your rest: this dismal day has disordered you. Isabella shall wait your orders in the morning."

"What, then, you know where she is!" cried Manfred. "Tell me directly, for I will not lose an instant—and you, woman," speaking to his wife, "order your chaplain to attend me forthwith."

"Isabella," said Hippolita calmly, "is retired, I suppose, to her chamber: she is not accustomed to watch at this late hour. Gracious my Lord," continued she, "let me know what has disturbed you. Has Isabella offended you?"

"Trouble me not with questions," said Manfred, "but tell me where she is."

"Matilda shall call her," said the Princess. "Sit down, my Lord, and resume your wonted fortitude."

"What, art thou jealous of Isabella?" replied he, "that you wish to be present at our interview!"

"Good heavens! my Lord," said Hippolita, "what is it your Highness means?"

"Thou wilt know ere many minutes are passed," said the cruel Prince. "Send your chaplain to me, and wait my pleasure here."

At these words he flung out of the room in search of Isabella, leaving the amazed ladies thunderstruck with his words and frantic deportment, and lost in vain conjectures on what he was meditating.

Manfred was now returning from the vault, attended by the peasant and a few of his servants whom he had obliged to accompany him. He ascended the staircase without stopping till he arrived at the gallery, at the door of which he met Hippolita and her chaplain. When Diego had been dismissed by Manfred, he had gone directly to the Princess's apartment with the alarm of what he had seen. That excellent Lady, who no more than Manfred doubted of the reality of the vision, yet affected to treat it as a delirium of the servant. Willing, however, to save her Lord from any additional shock, and prepared by a series of griefs not to tremble at any accession to it, she determined to make herself the first sacrifice, if fate had marked the present hour for their destruction. Dismissing the reluctant Matilda to her rest, who in vain sued for leave to accompany her mother, and attended only by her chaplain, Hippolita had visited the gallery and great chamber; and now with more serenity of soul than she had felt for many hours, she met her Lord, and assured him that the vision of the gigantic leg and foot was all a fable; and no doubt an impression made by fear, and the dark and dismal hour of the night, on the minds of his servants. She and the chaplain had examined the chamber, and found everything in the usual order.

Manfred, though persuaded, like his wife, that the vision had been no work of fancy, recovered a little from the tempest of mind into which so many strange events had thrown him. Ashamed, too, of his inhuman treatment of a Princess who returned every injury with new marks of tenderness and duty, he felt returning love forcing itself into his eyes; but not less ashamed of feeling remorse towards one against whom he was inwardly meditating a yet more bitter outrage, he curbed the yearnings of his heart, and did not dare to lean even towards pity. The next transition of his soul was to exquisite villainy.

Presuming on the unshaken submission of Hippolita, he flattered himself that she would not only acquiesce with patience to a divorce, but would obey, if it was his pleasure, in endeavouring to persuade Isabella to give him her hand—but ere he could indulge his horrid hope, he reflected that Isabella was not to be found. Coming to himself, he gave orders that every avenue to the castle should be strictly guarded, and charged his domestics on pain of their lives to suffer nobody to pass out. The young peasant, to whom he spoke favourably, he ordered to remain in a small chamber on the stairs, in which there was a pallet-bed, and the key of which he took away himself, telling the youth he would talk with him in the morning. Then dismissing his attendants, and bestowing a sullen kind of half-nod on Hippolita, he retired to his own chamber.

CHAPTER II

Matilda, who by Hippolita's order had retired to her apartment, was ill-disposed to take any rest. The shocking fate of her brother had deeply affected her. She was surprised at not seeing Isabella; but the strange words which had fallen from her father, and his obscure menace to the Princess his wife, accompanied by the most furious behaviour, had filled her gentle mind with terror and alarm. She waited anxiously for the return of Bianca, a young damsel that attended her, whom she had sent to learn what was become of Isabella. Bianca soon appeared, and informed her mistress of what she had gathered from the servants, that Isabella was nowhere to be found. She related the adventure of the young peasant who had been discovered in the vault, though with many simple additions from the incoherent accounts of the domestics; and she dwelt principally on the gigantic leg and foot which had been seen in the gallery-chamber. This last circumstance had terrified Bianca so much, that she was rejoiced when Matilda told her that she would not go to rest, but would watch till the Princess should rise.

The young Princess wearied herself in conjectures on the flight of Isabella, and on the threats of Manfred to her mother. "But what business could he have so urgent with the chaplain?" said Matilda, "Does he intend to have my brother's body interred privately in the chapel?"

"Oh, Madam!" said Bianca, "now I guess. As you are become his heiress, he is impatient to have you married: he has always been raving for more sons; I warrant he is now impatient for grandsons. As sure as I live,

Madam, I shall see you a bride at last.—Good madam, you won't cast off your faithful Bianca: you won't put Donna Rosara over me now you are a great Princess."

"My poor Bianca," said Matilda, "how fast your thoughts amble! I a great princess! What hast thou seen in Manfred's behaviour since my brother's death that bespeaks any increase of tenderness to me? No, Bianca; his heart was ever a stranger to me—but he is my father, and I must not complain. Nay, if Heaven shuts my father's heart against me, it overpays my little merit in the tenderness of my mother—O that dear mother! yes, Bianca, 'tis there I feel the rugged temper of Manfred. I can support his harshness to me with patience; but it wounds my soul when I am witness to his causeless severity towards her."

"Oh! Madam," said Bianca, "all men use their wives so, when they are weary of them."

"And yet you congratulated me but now," said Matilda, "when you fancied my father intended to dispose of me!"

"I would have you a great Lady," replied Bianca, "come what will. I do not wish to see you moped in a convent, as you would be if you had your will, and if my Lady, your mother, who knows that a bad husband is better than no husband at all, did not hinder you.—Bless me! what noise is that! St. Nicholas forgive me! I was but in jest."

"It is the wind," said Matilda, "whistling through the battlements in the tower above: you have heard it a thousand times."

"Nay," said Bianca, "there was no harm neither in what I said: it is no sin to talk of matrimony—and so, Madam, as I was saying, if my Lord Manfred should offer you a handsome young Prince for a bridegroom, you would drop him a curtsey, and tell him you would rather take the veil?"

"Thank Heaven! I am in no such danger," said Matilda: "you know how many proposals for me he has rejected—"

"And you thank him, like a dutiful daughter, do you, Madam? But come, Madam; suppose, to-morrow morning, he was to send for you to the great council chamber, and there you should find at his elbow a lovely young Prince, with large black eyes, a smooth white forehead, and manly curling locks like jet; in short, Madam, a young hero resembling the picture of the good Alfonso in the gallery, which you sit and gaze at for hours together—"

"Do not speak lightly of that picture," interrupted Matilda sighing; "I know the adoration with which I look at that picture is uncommon—but I am not in love with a coloured panel. The character of that virtuous Prince, the veneration with which my mother has inspired me for his memory, the orisons which, I know not why, she has enjoined me to pour forth at his tomb, all have concurred to persuade me that somehow or other my destiny is linked with something relating to him."

"Lord, Madam! how should that be?" said Bianca; "I have always heard that your family was in no way related to his: and I am sure I cannot conceive why my Lady, the Princess, sends you in a cold morning or a damp evening to pray at his tomb: he is no saint by the almanack. If you must pray, why does she not bid you address yourself to our great St. Nicholas? I am sure he is the saint I pray to for a husband."

"Perhaps my mind would be less affected," said Matilda, "if my mother would explain her reasons to me: but it is the mystery she observes, that inspires me with this—I know not what to call it. As she never acts from caprice, I am sure there is some fatal secret at bottom—nay, I know there is: in her agony of grief for my brother's death she dropped some words that intimated as much."

"Oh! dear Madam," cried Bianca, "what were they?"

"No," said Matilda, "if a parent lets fall a word, and wishes it recalled, it is not for a child to utter it."

"What! was she sorry for what she had said?" asked Bianca; "I am sure, Madam, you may trust me—"

"With my own little secrets when I have any, I may," said Matilda; "but never with my mother's: a child ought to have no ears or eyes but as a parent directs."

"Well! to be sure, Madam, you were born to be a saint," said Bianca, "and there is no resisting one's vocation: you will end in a convent at last. But there is my Lady Isabella would not be so reserved to me: she will let me talk to her of young men: and when a handsome cavalier has come to the castle, she has owned to me that she wished your brother Conrad resembled him."

"Bianca," said the Princess, "I do not allow you to mention my friend disrespectfully. Isabella is of a cheerful disposition, but her soul is pure as virtue itself. She knows your idle babbling humour, and perhaps has now and then encouraged it, to divert melancholy, and enliven the solitude in which my father keeps us—"

"Blessed Mary!" said Bianca, starting, "there it is again! Dear Madam, do you hear nothing? this castle is certainly haunted!"

"Peace!" said Matilda, "and listen! I did think I heard a voice—but it must be fancy: your terrors, I suppose, have infected me."

"Indeed! indeed! Madam," said Bianca, half-weeping with agony, "I am sure I heard a voice."

"Does anybody lie in the chamber beneath?" said the Princess.

"Nobody has dared to lie there," answered Bianca, "since the great astrologer, that was your brother's tutor, drowned himself. For certain, Madam, his ghost and the young Prince's are now met in the chamber below—for Heaven's sake let us fly to your mother's apartment!"

"I charge you not to stir," said Matilda. "If they are spirits in pain, we may ease their sufferings by questioning them. They can mean no hurt to us, for we have not injured them—and if they should, shall we be more safe in one chamber than in another? Reach me my beads; we will say a prayer, and then speak to them."

"Oh! dear Lady, I would not speak to a ghost for the world!" cried Bianca. As she said those words they heard the casement of the little chamber below Matilda's open. They listened attentively, and in a few minutes thought they heard a person sing, but could not distinguish the words.

"This can be no evil spirit," said the Princess, in a low voice; "it is undoubtedly one of the family—open the window, and we shall know the voice."

"I dare not, indeed, Madam," said Bianca.

"Thou art a very fool," said Matilda, opening the window gently herself. The noise the Princess made was, however, heard by the person beneath, who stopped; and they concluded had heard the casement open.

"Is anybody below?" said the Princess; "if there is, speak."

"Yes," said an unknown voice.

"Who is it?" said Matilda.

"A stranger," replied the voice.

"What stranger?" said she; "and how didst thou come there at this unusual hour, when all the gates of the castle are locked?"

"I am not here willingly," answered the voice. "But pardon me, Lady, if I have disturbed your rest; I knew not that I was overheard. Sleep had forsaken me; I left a restless couch, and came to waste the irksome hours with gazing on the fair approach of morning, impatient to be dismissed from this castle."

"Thy words and accents," said Matilda, "are of melancholy cast; if thou art unhappy, I pity thee. If poverty afflicts thee, let me know it; I will mention thee to the Princess, whose beneficent soul ever melts for the distressed, and she will relieve thee."

"I am indeed unhappy," said the stranger; "and I know not what wealth is. But I do not complain of the lot which Heaven has cast for me; I am young and healthy, and am not ashamed of owing my support to myself—yet think me not proud, or that I disdain your generous offers. I will remember you in my orisons, and will pray for blessings on your gracious self and your noble mistress—if I sigh, Lady, it is for others, not for myself."

"Now I have it, Madam," said Bianca, whispering the Princess; "this is certainly the young peasant; and, by my conscience, he is in love—Well! this is a charming adventure!—do, Madam, let us sift him. He does not know you, but takes you for one of my Lady Hippolita's women."

"Art thou not ashamed, Bianca!" said the Princess. "What right have we to pry into the secrets of this young man's heart? He seems virtuous and frank, and tells us he is unhappy. Are those circumstances that authorise us to make a property of him? How are we entitled to his confidence?"

"Lord, Madam! how little you know of love!" replied Bianca; "why, lovers have no pleasure equal to talking of their mistress."

"And would you have *me* become a peasant's confidante?" said the Princess.

"Well, then, let me talk to him," said Bianca; "though I have the honour of being your Highness's maid of honour, I was not always so great. Besides, if love levels ranks, it raises them too; I have a respect for any young man in love."

"Peace, simpleton!" said the Princess. "Though he said he was unhappy, it does not follow that he must be in love. Think of all that has happened to-day, and tell me if there are no misfortunes but what love causes.—Stranger," resumed the Princess, "if thy misfortunes have not been occasioned by thy own fault, and are within the compass of the Princess Hippolita's power to redress, I will take upon me to answer that she will be thy protectress. When thou art dismissed from this castle, repair to holy father Jerome, at the convent adjoining to the church of St. Nicholas, and make thy story known to him, as far as thou thinkest meet. He will not fail to inform the Princess, who is the mother of all that want her assistance. Farewell; it is not seemly for me to hold farther converse with a man at this unwonted hour."

"May the saints guard thee, gracious Lady!" replied the peasant; "but oh! if a poor and worthless stranger might presume to beg a minute's audience farther; am I so happy? the casement is not shut; might I venture to ask—"

"Speak quickly," said Matilda; "the morning dawns apace: should the labourers come into the fields and perceive us—What wouldst thou ask?"

"I know not how, I know not if I dare," said the young stranger, faltering; "yet the humanity with which you have spoken to me emboldens—Lady! dare I trust you?"

"Heavens!" said Matilda, "what dost thou mean? With what wouldst thou trust me? Speak boldly, if thy secret is fit to be entrusted to a virtuous breast."

"I would ask," said the peasant, recollecting himself, "whether what I have heard from the domestics is true, that the Princess is missing from the castle?"

"What imports it to thee to know?" replied Matilda. "Thy first words bespoke a prudent and becoming gravity. Dost thou come hither to pry into the secrets of Manfred? Adieu. I have been mistaken in thee." Saying these words she shut the casement hastily, without giving the young man time to reply.

"I had acted more wisely," said the Princess to Bianca, with some sharpness, "if I had let thee converse with this peasant; his inquisitiveness seems of a piece with thy own."

"It is not fit for me to argue with your Highness," replied Bianca; "but perhaps the questions I should have put to him would have been more to the purpose than those you have been pleased to ask him."

"Oh! no doubt," said Matilda; "you are a very discreet personage! May I know what *you* would have asked him?"

"A bystander often sees more of the game than those that play," answered Bianca. "Does your Highness think, Madam, that this question about my Lady Isabella was the result of mere curiosity? No, no, Madam, there is more in it than you great folks are aware of. Lopez told me that all the servants believe this young fellow contrived my Lady Isabella's escape; now, pray, Madam, observe you and I both know that my Lady Isabella never much fancied the Prince your brother. Well! he is killed just in a critical minute—I accuse nobody. A helmet falls from the moon—so, my Lord, your father says; but Lopez and all the servants say that this young spark is a magician, and stole it from Alfonso's tomb—"

"Have done with this rhapsody of impertinence," said Matilda.

"Nay, Madam, as you please," cried Bianca; "yet it is very particular though, that my Lady Isabella should be missing the very same day, and that this young sorcerer should be found at the mouth of the trap-door. I accuse nobody; but if my young Lord came honestly by his death—"

"Dare not on thy duty," said Matilda, "to breathe a suspicion on the purity of my dear Isabella's fame."

"Purity, or not purity," said Bianca, "gone she is—a stranger is found that nobody knows; you question him yourself; he tells you he is in love, or unhappy, it is the same thing—nay, he owned he was unhappy about others; and is anybody unhappy about another, unless they are in love with them? and at the very next word, he asks innocently, pour soul! if my Lady Isabella is missing."

"To be sure," said Matilda, "thy observations are not totally without foundation—Isabella's flight amazes me. The curiosity of the stranger is very particular; yet Isabella never concealed a thought from me."

"So she told you," said Bianca, "to fish out your secrets; but who knows, Madam, but this stranger may be some Prince in disguise? Do, Madam, let me open the window, and ask him a few questions."

"No," replied Matilda, "I will ask him myself, if he knows aught of Isabella; he is not worthy I should converse farther with him." She was going to open the casement, when they heard the bell ring at the postern-gate of the castle, which is on the right hand of the tower, where Matilda lay. This prevented the Princess from renewing the conversation with the stranger.

After continuing silent for some time, "I am persuaded," said she to Bianca, "that whatever be the cause of Isabella's flight it had no unworthy motive. If this stranger was accessory to it, she must be satisfied with his fidelity and worth. I observed, did not you, Bianca? that his words were tinctured with an uncommon infusion of piety. It was no ruffian's speech; his phrases were becoming a man of gentle birth."

"I told you, Madam," said Bianca, "that I was sure he was some Prince in disguise."

"Yet," said Matilda, "if he was privy to her escape, how will you account for his not accompanying her in her flight? why expose himself unnecessarily and rashly to my father's resentment?"

"As for that, Madam," replied she, "if he could get from under the helmet, he will find ways of eluding your father's anger. I do not doubt but he has some talisman or other about him."

"You resolve everything into magic," said Matilda; "but a man who has any intercourse with infernal spirits, does not dare to make use of those tremendous and holy words which he uttered. Didst thou not observe with what fervour he vowed to remember *me* to heaven in his prayers? Yes; Isabella was undoubtedly convinced of his piety."

"Commend me to the piety of a young fellow and a damsel that consult to elope!" said Bianca. "No, no, Madam, my Lady Isabella is of another guess mould than you take her for. She used indeed to sigh and lift up her eyes in your company, because she knows you are a saint; but when your back was turned—"

"You wrong her," said Matilda; "Isabella is no hypocrite; she has a due sense of devotion, but never affected a call she has not. On the contrary, she always combated my inclination for the cloister; and though I own the mystery she has made to me of her flight confounds me; though it seems inconsistent with the friendship between us; I cannot forget the disinterested warmth with which she always opposed my taking the veil. She wished to see me married, though my dower would have been a loss to her and my brother's children. For her sake I will believe well of this young peasant."

"Then you do think there is some liking between them," said Bianca. While she was speaking, a servant came hastily into the chamber and told the Princess that the Lady Isabella was found.

"Where?" said Matilda.

"She has taken sanctuary in St. Nicholas's church," replied the servant; "Father Jerome has brought the news himself; he is below with his Highness."

"Where is my mother?" said Matilda.

"She is in her own chamber, Madam, and has asked for you."

Manfred had risen at the first dawn of light, and gone to Hippolita's apartment, to inquire if she knew aught of Isabella. While he was questioning her, word was brought that Jerome demanded to speak with him. Manfred, little suspecting the cause of the Friar's arrival, and knowing he was employed by Hippolita in her charities, ordered him to be admitted, intending to leave them together, while he pursued his search after Isabella.

"Is your business with me or the Princess?" said Manfred.

"With both," replied the holy man. "The Lady Isabella—"

"What of her?" interrupted Manfred, eagerly.

"Is at St. Nicholas's altar," replied Jerome.

"That is no business of Hippolita," said Manfred with confusion; "let us retire to my chamber, Father, and inform me how she came thither."

"No, my Lord," replied the good man, with an air of firmness and authority, that daunted even the resolute Manfred, who could not help revering the saint-like virtues of Jerome; "my commission is to both, and with your Highness's good-liking, in the presence of both I shall deliver it; but first, my Lord, I must interrogate the Princess, whether she is acquainted with the cause of the Lady Isabella's retirement from your castle."

"No, on my soul," said Hippolita; "does Isabella charge me with being privy to it?"

"Father," interrupted Manfred, "I pay due reverence to your holy profession; but I am sovereign here, and will allow no meddling priest to interfere in the affairs of my domestic. If you have aught to say attend me to my chamber; I do not use to let my wife be acquainted with the secret affairs of my state; they are not within a woman's province."

"My Lord," said the holy man, "I am no intruder into the secrets of families. My office is to promote peace, to heal divisions, to preach repentance, and teach mankind to curb their headstrong passions. I forgive your Highness's uncharitable apostrophe; I know my duty, and am the minister of a mightier prince than Manfred. Hearken to him who speaks through my organs."

Manfred trembled with rage and shame. Hippolita's countenance declared her astonishment and impatience to know where this would end. Her silence more strongly spoke her observance of Manfred.

"The Lady Isabella," resumed Jerome, "commends herself to both your Highnesses; she thanks both for the kindness with which she has been treated in your castle: she deplores the loss of your son, and her own misfortune in not becoming the daughter of such wise and noble Princes, whom she shall always respect as Parents; she prays for uninterrupted union and felicity between you" [Manfred's colour changed]: "but as it is no longer possible for her to be allied to you, she entreats your consent to remain in sanctuary, till she can learn news of her father, or, by the certainty of his death, be at liberty, with the approbation of her guardians, to dispose of herself in suitable marriage."

"I shall give no such consent," said the Prince, "but insist on her return to the castle without delay: I am answerable for her person to her guardians, and will not brook her being in any hands but my own."

"Your Highness will recollect whether that can any longer be proper," replied the Friar.

"I want no monitor," said Manfred, colouring; "Isabella's conduct leaves room for strange suspicions—and that young villain, who was at least the accomplice of her flight, if not the cause of it—"

"The cause!" interrupted Jerome; "was a *young* man the cause?"

"This is not to be borne!" cried Manfred. "Am I to be bearded in my own palace by an insolent Monk? Thou art privy, I guess, to their amours."

"I would pray to heaven to clear up your uncharitable surmises," said Jerome, "if your Highness were not satisfied in your conscience how unjustly you accuse me. I do pray to heaven to pardon that uncharitableness: and I implore your Highness to leave the Princess at peace in that holy place, where she is not liable to be disturbed by such vain and worldly fantasies as discourses of love from any man."

"Cant not to me," said Manfred, "but return and bring the Princess to her duty."

"It is my duty to prevent her return hither," said Jerome. "She is where orphans and virgins are safest from the snares and wiles of this world; and nothing but a parent's authority shall take her thence."

"I am her parent," cried Manfred, "and demand her."

"She wished to have you for her parent," said the Friar; "but Heaven that forbad that connection has for ever dissolved all ties betwixt you: and I announce to your Highness—"

"Stop! audacious man," said Manfred, "and dread my displeasure."

"Holy Father," said Hippolita, "it is your office to be no respecter of persons: you must speak as your duty prescribes: but it is my duty to hear nothing that it pleases not my Lord I should hear. Attend the Prince to his chamber. I will retire to my oratory, and pray to the blessed Virgin to inspire you with her holy counsels, and to restore the heart of my gracious Lord to its wonted peace and gentleness."

"Excellent woman!" said the Friar. "My Lord, I attend your pleasure."

Manfred, accompanied by the Friar, passed to his own apartment, where shutting the door, "I perceive, Father," said he, "that Isabella has acquainted you with my purpose. Now hear my resolve, and obey. Reasons of state, most urgent reasons, my own and the safety of my people, demand that I should have a son. It is in vain to expect an heir from Hippolita. I have made choice of Isabella. You must bring her back; and you must do more. I know the influence you have with Hippolita: her conscience is in your hands. She is, I allow, a faultless woman: her soul is set on heaven, and scorns the little grandeur of this world: you can withdraw her from it entirely. Persuade her to consent to the dissolution of our marriage, and to retire into a monastery—she shall endow one if she will; and she shall have the means of being as liberal to your order as she or you can wish. Thus you will divert the calamities that are hanging over our heads, and have the merit of saving the principality of Otranto from destruction. You are a prudent man, and though the warmth of my temper betrayed me into some unbecoming expressions, I honour your virtue, and wish to be indebted to you for the repose of my life and the preservation of my family."

"The will of heaven be done!" said the Friar. "I am but its worthless instrument. It makes use of my tongue to tell thee, Prince, of thy unwarrantable designs. The injuries of the virtuous Hippolita have mounted to the throne of pity. By me thou art reprimanded for thy adulterous intention of repudiating her: by me thou art warned not to pursue the incestuous design on thy contracted daughter. Heaven that delivered her from thy fury, when the judgments so recently fallen on thy house ought to have inspired thee with other thoughts, will continue to watch over her. Even I, a poor and despised Friar, am able to protect her from thy violence—I, sinner as I am, and uncharitably reviled by your Highness as an accomplice of I know not what amours, scorn the allurements with which it has pleased thee to tempt mine honesty. I love my order; I honour devout souls; I respect the piety of thy Princess—but I will not betray the confidence she reposes in me, nor serve even the cause of religion by foul and sinful compliances—but forsooth! the welfare of the state depends on your Highness having a son! Heaven mocks the short-sighted views of man. But yester-morn, whose house was so great, so flourishing as Manfred's?—where is young Conrad now?—My Lord, I respect your tears—but I mean not to check them—let them flow, Prince! They will weigh more with heaven toward the welfare of thy subjects, than a marriage, which, founded on lust or policy, could never prosper. The sceptre, which passed from the race of Alfonso to thine, cannot be preserved by a match which the church will never allow. If it is the will of the Most High that Manfred's name must perish, resign yourself, my Lord, to its decrees; and thus deserve a crown that can never pass away. Come, my Lord; I like this sorrow—let us return to the Princess: she is not apprised of your cruel intentions; nor did I mean more than to alarm you. You saw with what gentle patience, with what efforts of love, she heard, she rejected hearing, the extent of your guilt. I know she longs to fold you in her arms, and assure you of her unalterable affection."

"Father," said the Prince, "you mistake my compunction: true, I honour Hippolita's virtues; I think her a Saint; and wish it were for my soul's health to tie faster the knot that has united us—but alas! Father, you know not the bitterest of my pangs! it is some time that I have had scruples on the legality of our union: Hippolita is related to me in the fourth degree—it is true, we had a dispensation: but I have been informed that she had also been contracted to another. This it is that sits heavy at my heart: to this state of unlawful wedlock I impute the visitation that has fallen on me in the death of Conrad!—ease my conscience of this burden:

dissolve our marriage, and accomplish the work of godliness—which your divine exhortations have commenced in my soul."

How cutting was the anguish which the good man felt, when he perceived this turn in the wily Prince! He trembled for Hippolita, whose ruin he saw was determined; and he feared if Manfred had no hope of recovering Isabella, that his impatience for a son would direct him to some other object, who might not be equally proof against the temptation of Manfred's rank. For some time the holy man remained absorbed in thought. At length, conceiving some hopes from delay, he thought the wisest conduct would be to prevent the Prince from despairing of recovering Isabella. Her the Friar knew he could dispose, from her affection to Hippolita, and from the aversion she had expressed to him for Manfred's addresses, to second his views, till the censures of the church could be fulminated against a divorce. With this intention, as if struck with the Prince's scruples, he at length said:

"My Lord, I have been pondering on what your Highness has said; and if in truth it is delicacy of conscience that is the real motive of your repugnance to your virtuous Lady, far be it from me to endeavour to harden your heart. The church is an indulgent mother: unfold your griefs to her: she alone can administer comfort to your soul, either by satisfying your conscience, or upon examination of your scruples, by setting you at liberty, and indulging you in the lawful means of continuing your lineage. In the latter case, if the Lady Isabella can be brought to consent—"

Manfred, who concluded that he had either over-reached the good man, or that his first warmth had been but a tribute paid to appearance, was overjoyed at this sudden turn, and repeated the most magnificent promises, if he should succeed by the Friar's mediation. The well-meaning priest suffered him to deceive himself, fully determined to traverse his views, instead of seconding them.

"Since we now understand one another," resumed the Prince, "I expect, Father, that you satisfy me in one point. Who is the youth that I found in the vault? He must have been privy to Isabella's flight: tell me truly, is he her lover? or is he an agent for another's passion? I have often suspected Isabella's indifference to my son: a thousand circumstances crowd on my mind that confirm that suspicion. She herself was so conscious of it, that while I discoursed her in the gallery, she outran my suspicions, and endeavoured to justify herself from coolness to Conrad."

The Friar, who knew nothing of the youth, but what he had learnt occasionally from the Princess, ignorant what was become of him, and not sufficiently reflecting on the impetuosity of Manfred's temper, conceived that it might not be amiss to sow the seeds of jealousy in his mind: they might be turned to some use hereafter, either by prejudicing the Prince against Isabella, if he persisted in that union or by diverting his attention to a wrong scent, and employing his thoughts on a visionary intrigue, prevent his engaging in any new pursuit. With this unhappy policy, he answered in a manner to confirm Manfred in the belief of some connection between Isabella and the youth. The Prince, whose passions wanted little fuel to throw them into a blaze, fell into a rage at the idea of what the Friar suggested.

"I will fathom to the bottom of this intrigue," cried he; and quitting Jerome abruptly, with a command to remain there till his return, he hastened to the great hall of the castle, and ordered the peasant to be brought before him.

"Thou hardened young impostor!" said the Prince, as soon as he saw the youth; "what becomes of thy boasted veracity now? it was Providence, was it, and the light of the moon, that discovered the lock of the trap-door to thee? Tell me, audacious boy, who thou art, and how long thou hast been acquainted with the Princess—and take care to answer with less equivocation than thou didst last night, or tortures shall wring the truth from thee."

The young man, perceiving that his share in the flight of the Princess was discovered, and concluding that anything he should say could no longer be of any service or detriment to her, replied—

"I am no impostor, my Lord, nor have I deserved opprobrious language. I answered to every question your Highness put to me last night with the same veracity that I shall speak now: and that will not be from fear of your tortures, but because my soul abhors a falsehood. Please to repeat your questions, my Lord; I am ready to give you all the satisfaction in my power."

"You know my questions," replied the Prince, "and only want time to prepare an evasion. Speak directly; who art thou? and how long hast thou been known to the Princess?"

"I am a labourer at the next village," said the peasant; "my name is Theodore. The Princess found me in the vault last night: before that hour I never was in her presence."

"I may believe as much or as little as I please of this," said Manfred; "but I will hear thy own story before I examine into the truth of it. Tell me, what reason did the Princess give thee for making her escape? thy life depends on thy answer."

"She told me," replied Theodore, "that she was on the brink of destruction, and that if she could not escape from the castle, she was in danger in a few moments of being made miserable for ever."

"And on this slight foundation, on a silly girl's report," said Manfred, "thou didst hazard my displeasure?"

"I fear no man's displeasure," said Theodore, "when a woman in distress puts herself under my protection."

During this examination, Matilda was going to the apartment of Hippolita. At the upper end of the hall, where Manfred sat, was a boarded gallery with latticed windows, through which Matilda and Bianca were to pass. Hearing her father's voice, and seeing the servants assembled round him, she stopped to learn the occasion. The prisoner soon drew her attention: the steady and composed manner in which he answered, and the gallantry of his last reply, which were the first words she heard distinctly, interested her in his favour. His person was noble, handsome, and commanding, even in that situation: but his countenance soon engrossed her whole care.

"Heavens! Bianca," said the Princess softly, "do I dream? or is not that youth the exact resemblance of Alfonso's picture in the gallery?"

She could say no more, for her father's voice grew louder at every word.

"This bravado," said he, "surpasses all thy former insolence. Thou shalt experience the wrath with which thou darest to trifle. Seize him," continued Manfred, "and bind him—the first news the Princess hears of her champion shall be, that he has lost his head for her sake."

"The injustice of which thou art guilty towards me," said Theodore, "convinces me that I have done a good deed in delivering the Princess from thy tyranny. May she be happy, whatever becomes of me!"

"This is a lover!" cried Manfred in a rage: "a peasant within sight of death is not animated by such sentiments. Tell me, tell me, rash boy, who thou art, or the rack shall force thy secret from thee."

"Thou hast threatened me with death already," said the youth, "for the truth I have told thee: if that is all the encouragement I am to expect for sincerity, I am not tempted to indulge thy vain curiosity farther."

"Then thou wilt not speak?" said Manfred.

"I will not," replied he.

"Bear him away into the courtyard," said Manfred; "I will see his head this instant severed from his body."

Matilda fainted at hearing those words. Bianca shrieked, and cried—"Help! help! the Princess is dead!"

Manfred started at this ejaculation, and demanded what was the matter! The young peasant, who heard it too, was struck with horror, and asked eagerly the same question; but Manfred ordered him to be hurried into the court, and kept there for execution, till he had informed himself of the cause of Bianca's shrieks. When he learned the meaning, he treated it as a womanish panic, and ordering Matilda to be carried to her apartment, he rushed into the court, and calling for one of his guards, bade Theodore kneel down, and prepare to receive the fatal blow.

The undaunted youth received the bitter sentence with a resignation that touched every heart but Manfred's. He wished earnestly to know the meaning of the words he had heard relating to the Princess; but fearing to exasperate the tyrant more against her, he desisted. The only boon he deigned to ask was, that he might be permitted to have a confessor, and make his peace with heaven. Manfred, who hoped by the confessor's means to come at the youth's history, readily granted his request; and being convinced that Father Jerome was now in his interest, he ordered him to be called and shrive the prisoner. The holy man, who had little foreseen the catastrophe that his imprudence occasioned, fell on his knees to the Prince, and adjured him in the most solemn manner not to shed innocent blood. He accused himself in the bitterest terms for his indiscretion, endeavoured to disculpate the youth, and left no method untried to soften the tyrant's rage. Manfred, more incensed than appeased by Jerome's intercession, whose retraction now made him suspect he had been imposed upon by both, commanded the Friar to do his duty, telling him he would not allow the prisoner many minutes for confession.

"Nor do I ask many, my Lord," said the unhappy young man. "My sins, thank heaven, have not been numerous; nor exceed what might be expected at my years. Dry your tears, good Father, and let us despatch. This is a bad world; nor have I had cause to leave it with regret."

"Oh wretched youth!" said Jerome; "how canst thou bear the sight of me with patience? I am thy murderer! it is I have brought this dismal hour upon thee!"

"I forgive thee from my soul," said the youth, "as I hope heaven will pardon me. Hear my confession, Father; and give me thy blessing."

"How can I prepare thee for thy passage as I ought?" said Jerome. "Thou canst not be saved without pardoning thy foes—and canst thou forgive that impious man there?"

"I can," said Theodore; "I do."

"And does not this touch thee, cruel Prince?" said the Friar.

"I sent for thee to confess him," said Manfred, sternly; "not to plead for him. Thou didst first incense me against him—his blood be upon thy head!"

"It will! it will!" said the good man, in an agony of sorrow. "Thou and I must never hope to go where this blessed youth is going!"

"Despatch!" said Manfred; "I am no more to be moved by the whining of priests than by the shrieks of women."

"What!" said the youth; "is it possible that my fate could have occasioned what I heard! Is the Princess then again in thy power?"

"Thou dost but remember me of my wrath," said Manfred. "Prepare thee, for this moment is thy last."

The youth, who felt his indignation rise, and who was touched with the sorrow which he saw he had infused into all the spectators, as well as into the Friar, suppressed his emotions, and putting off his doublet, and unbuttoning his collar, knelt down to his prayers. As he stooped, his shirt slipped down below his shoulder, and discovered the mark of a bloody arrow.

"Gracious heaven!" cried the holy man, starting; "what do I see? It is my child! my Theodore!"

The passions that ensued must be conceived; they cannot be painted. The tears of the assistants were suspended by wonder, rather than stopped by joy. They seemed to inquire in the eyes of their Lord what they ought to feel. Surprise, doubt, tenderness, respect, succeeded each other in the countenance of the youth. He received with modest submission the effusion of the old man's tears and embraces. Yet afraid of giving a loose to hope, and suspecting from what had passed the inflexibility of Manfred's temper, he cast a glance towards the Prince, as if to say, canst thou be unmoved at such a scene as this?

Manfred's heart was capable of being touched. He forgot his anger in his astonishment; yet his pride forbad his owning himself affected. He even doubted whether this discovery was not a contrivance of the Friar to save the youth.

"What may this mean?" said he. "How can he be thy son? Is it consistent with thy profession or reputed sanctity to avow a peasant's offspring for the fruit of thy irregular amours!"

"Oh, God!" said the holy man, "dost thou question his being mine? Could I feel the anguish I do if I were not his father? Spare him! good Prince! spare him! and revile me as thou pleasest."

"Spare him! spare him!" cried the attendants; "for this good man's sake!"

"Peace!" said Manfred, sternly. "I must know more ere I am disposed to pardon. A Saint's bastard may be no saint himself."

"Injurious Lord!" said Theodore, "add not insult to cruelty. If I am this venerable man's son, though no Prince, as thou art, know the blood that flows in my veins—"

"Yes," said the Friar, interrupting him, "his blood is noble; nor is he that abject thing, my Lord, you speak him. He is my lawful son, and Sicily can boast of few houses more ancient than that of Falconara. But alas! my Lord, what is blood! what is nobility! We are all reptiles, miserable, sinful creatures. It is piety alone that can distinguish us from the dust whence we sprung, and whither we must return."

"Truce to your sermon," said Manfred; "you forget you are no longer Friar Jerome, but the Count of Falconara. Let me know your history; you will have time to moralise hereafter, if you should not happen to obtain the grace of that sturdy criminal there."

"Mother of God!" said the Friar, "is it possible my Lord can refuse a father the life of his only, his long-lost, child! Trample me, my Lord, scorn, afflict me, accept my life for his, but spare my son!"

"Thou canst feel, then," said Manfred, "what it is to lose an only son! A little hour ago thou didst preach up resignation to me: *my* house, if fate so pleased, must perish—but the Count of Falconara—"

"Alas! my Lord," said Jerome, "I confess I have offended; but aggravate not an old man's sufferings! I boast not of my family, nor think of such vanities—it is nature, that pleads for this boy; it is the memory of the dear woman that bore him. Is she, Theodore, is she dead?"

"Her soul has long been with the blessed," said Theodore.

"Oh! how?" cried Jerome, "tell me—no—she is happy! Thou art all my care now!—Most dread Lord! will you—will you grant me my poor boy's life?"

"Return to thy convent," answered Manfred; "conduct the Princess hither; obey me in what else thou knowest; and I promise thee the life of thy son."

"Oh! my Lord," said Jerome, "is my honesty the price I must pay for this dear youth's safety?"

"For me!" cried Theodore. "Let me die a thousand deaths, rather than stain thy conscience. What is it the tyrant would exact of thee? Is the Princess still safe from his power? Protect her, thou venerable old man; and let all the weight of his wrath fall on me."

Jerome endeavoured to check the impetuosity of the youth; and ere Manfred could reply, the trampling of horses was heard, and a brazen trumpet, which hung without the gate of the castle, was suddenly sounded. At the same instant the sable plumes on the enchanted helmet, which still remained at the other end of the court, were tempestuously agitated, and nodded thrice, as if bowed by some invisible wearer.

CHAPTER III

Manfred's heart misgave him when he beheld the plumage on the miraculous casque shaken in concert with the sounding of the brazen trumpet.

"Father!" said he to Jerome, whom he now ceased to treat as Count of Falconara, "what mean these portents? If I have offended—" the plumes were shaken with greater violence than before.

"Unhappy Prince that I am," cried Manfred. "Holy Father! will you not assist me with your prayers?"

"My Lord," replied Jerome, "heaven is no doubt displeased with your mockery of its servants. Submit yourself to the church; and cease to persecute her ministers. Dismiss this innocent youth; and learn to respect the holy character I wear. Heaven will not be trifled with: you see—" the trumpet sounded again.

"I acknowledge I have been too hasty," said Manfred. "Father, do you go to the wicket, and demand who is at the gate."

"Do you grant me the life of Theodore?" replied the Friar.

"I do," said Manfred; "but inquire who is without!"

Jerome, falling on the neck of his son, discharged a flood of tears, that spoke the fulness of his soul.

"You promised to go to the gate," said Manfred.

"I thought," replied the Friar, "your Highness would excuse my thanking you first in this tribute of my heart."

"Go, dearest Sir," said Theodore; "obey the Prince. I do not deserve that you should delay his satisfaction for me."

Jerome, inquiring who was without, was answered, "A Herald."

"From whom?" said he.

"From the Knight of the Gigantic Sabre," said the Herald; "and I must speak with the usurper of Otranto."

Jerome returned to the Prince, and did not fail to repeat the message in the very words it had been uttered. The first sounds struck Manfred with terror; but when he heard himself styled usurper, his rage rekindled, and all his courage revived.

"Usurper!—insolent villain!" cried he; "who dares to question my title? Retire, Father; this is no business for Monks: I will meet this presumptuous man myself. Go to your convent and prepare the Princess's return. Your son shall be a hostage for your fidelity: his life depends on your obedience."

"Good heaven! my Lord," cried Jerome, "your Highness did but this instant freely pardon my child—have you so soon forgot the interposition of heaven?"

"Heaven," replied Manfred, "does not send Heralds to question the title of a lawful Prince. I doubt whether it even notifies its will through Friars—but that is your affair, not mine. At present you know my pleasure; and it is not a saucy Herald that shall save your son, if you do not return with the Princess."

It was in vain for the holy man to reply. Manfred commanded him to be conducted to the postern-gate, and shut out from the castle. And he ordered some of his attendants to carry Theodore to the top of the black tower, and guard him strictly; scarce permitting the father and son to exchange a hasty embrace at parting. He then withdrew to the hall, and seating himself in princely state, ordered the Herald to be admitted to his presence.

"Well! thou insolent!" said the Prince, "what wouldst thou with me?"

"I come," replied he, "to thee, Manfred, usurper of the principality of Otranto, from the renowned and invincible Knight, the Knight of the Gigantic Sabre: in the name of his Lord, Frederic, Marquis of Vicenza, he demands the Lady Isabella, daughter of that Prince, whom thou hast basely and traitorously got into thy power, by bribing her false guardians during his absence; and he requires thee to resign the principality of

Otranto, which thou hast usurped from the said Lord Frederic, the nearest of blood to the last rightful Lord, Alfonso the Good. If thou dost not instantly comply with these just demands, he defies thee to single combat to the last extremity." And so saying the Herald cast down his warder.

"And where is this braggart who sends thee?" said Manfred.

"At the distance of a league," said the Herald: "he comes to make good his Lord's claim against thee, as he is a true knight, and thou an usurper and ravisher."

Injurious as this challenge was, Manfred reflected that it was not his interest to provoke the Marquis. He knew how well founded the claim of Frederic was; nor was this the first time he had heard of it. Frederic's ancestors had assumed the style of Princes of Otranto, from the death of Alfonso the Good without issue; but Manfred, his father, and grandfather, had been too powerful for the house of Vicenza to dispossess them. Frederic, a martial and amorous young Prince, had married a beautiful young lady, of whom he was enamoured, and who had died in childbed of Isabella. Her death affected him so much that he had taken the cross and gone to the Holy Land, where he was wounded in an engagement against the infidels, made prisoner, and reported to be dead. When the news reached Manfred's ears, he bribed the guardians of the Lady Isabella to deliver her up to him as a bride for his son Conrad, by which alliance he had proposed to unite the claims of the two houses. This motive, on Conrad's death, had co-operated to make him so suddenly resolve on espousing her himself; and the same reflection determined him now to endeavour at obtaining the consent of Frederic to this marriage. A like policy inspired him with the thought of inviting Frederic's champion into the castle, lest he should be informed of Isabella's flight, which he strictly enjoined his domestics not to disclose to any of the Knight's retinue.

"Herald," said Manfred, as soon as he had digested these reflections, "return to thy master, and tell him, ere we liquidate our differences by the sword, Manfred would hold some converse with him. Bid him welcome to my castle, where by my faith, as I am a true Knight, he shall have courteous reception, and full security for himself and followers. If we cannot adjust our quarrel by amicable means, I swear he shall depart in safety, and shall have full satisfaction according to the laws of arms: So help me God and His holy Trinity!"

The Herald made three obeisances and retired.

During this interview Jerome's mind was agitated by a thousand contrary passions. He trembled for the life of his son, and his first thought was to persuade Isabella to return to the castle. Yet he was scarce less alarmed at the thought of her union with Manfred. He dreaded Hippolita's unbounded submission to the will of her Lord; and though he did not doubt but he could alarm her piety not to consent to a divorce, if he could get access to her; yet should Manfred discover that the obstruction came from him, it might be equally fatal to Theodore. He was impatient to know whence came the Herald, who with so little management had questioned the title of Manfred: yet he did not dare absent himself from the convent, lest Isabella should leave it, and her flight be imputed to him. He returned disconsolately to the monastery, uncertain on what conduct to resolve. A Monk, who met him in the porch and observed his melancholy air, said—

"Alas! brother, is it then true that we have lost our excellent Princess Hippolita?"

The holy man started, and cried, "What meanest thou, brother? I come this instant from the castle, and left her in perfect health."

"Martelli," replied the other Friar, "passed by the convent but a quarter of an hour ago on his way from the castle, and reported that her Highness was dead. All our brethren are gone to the chapel to pray for her happy transit to a better life, and willed me to wait thy arrival. They know thy holy attachment to that good Lady, and are anxious for the affliction it will cause in thee—indeed we have all reason to weep; she was a mother to our house. But this life is but a pilgrimage; we must not murmur—we shall all follow her! May our end be like hers!"

"Good brother, thou dreamest," said Jerome. "I tell thee I come from the castle, and left the Princess well. Where is the Lady Isabella?"

"Poor Gentlewoman!" replied the Friar; "I told her the sad news, and offered her spiritual comfort. I reminded her of the transitory condition of mortality, and advised her to take the veil: I quoted the example of the holy Princess Sanchia of Arragon."

"Thy zeal was laudable," said Jerome, impatiently; "but at present it was unnecessary: Hippolita is well—at least I trust in the Lord she is; I heard nothing to the contrary—yet, methinks, the Prince's earnestness— Well, brother, but where is the Lady Isabella?"

"I know not," said the Friar; "she wept much, and said she would retire to her chamber."

Jerome left his comrade abruptly, and hastened to the Princess, but she was not in her chamber. He inquired of the domestics of the convent, but could learn no news of her. He searched in vain throughout the monastery and the church, and despatched messengers round the neighbourhood, to get intelligence if she had been seen; but to no purpose. Nothing could equal the good man's perplexity. He judged that Isabella, suspecting Manfred of having precipitated his wife's death, had taken the alarm, and withdrawn herself to some more secret place of concealment. This new flight would probably carry the Prince's fury to the height. The report of Hippolita's death, though it seemed almost incredible, increased his consternation; and though Isabella's escape bespoke her aversion of Manfred for a husband, Jerome could feel no comfort from it, while it endangered the life of his son. He determined to return to the castle, and made several of his brethren accompany him to attest his innocence to Manfred, and, if necessary, join their intercession with his for Theodore.

The Prince, in the meantime, had passed into the court, and ordered the gates of the castle to be flung open for the reception of the stranger Knight and his train. In a few minutes the cavalcade arrived. First came two harbingers with wands. Next a herald, followed by two pages and two trumpets. Then a hundred foot-guards. These were attended by as many horse. After them fifty footmen, clothed in scarlet and black, the colours of the Knight. Then a led horse. Two heralds on each side of a gentleman on horseback bearing a banner with the arms of Vicenza and Otranto quarterly—a circumstance that much offended Manfred—but he stifled his resentment. Two more pages. The Knight's confessor telling his beads. Fifty more footmen clad as before. Two Knights habited in complete armour, their beavers down, comrades to the principal Knight. The squires of the two Knights, carrying their shields and devices. The Knight's own squire. A hundred gentlemen bearing an enormous sword, and seeming to faint under the weight of it. The Knight himself on a chestnut steed, in complete armour, his lance in the rest, his face entirely concealed by his vizor, which was surmounted by a large plume of scarlet and black feathers. Fifty foot-guards with drums and trumpets closed the procession, which wheeled off to the right and left to make room for the principal Knight.

As soon as he approached the gate he stopped; and the herald advancing, read again the words of the challenge. Manfred's eyes were fixed on the gigantic sword, and he scarce seemed to attend to the cartel: but his attention was soon diverted by a tempest of wind that rose behind him. He turned and beheld the Plumes of the enchanted helmet agitated in the same extraordinary manner as before. It required intrepidity like Manfred's not to sink under a concurrence of circumstances that seemed to announce his fate. Yet scorning in the presence of strangers to betray the courage he had always manifested, he said boldly—

"Sir Knight, whoever thou art, I bid thee welcome. If thou art of mortal mould, thy valour shall meet its equal: and if thou art a true Knight, thou wilt scorn to employ sorcery to carry thy point. Be these omens from heaven or hell, Manfred trusts to the righteousness of his cause and to the aid of St. Nicholas, who has ever protected his house. Alight, Sir Knight, and repose thyself. To-morrow thou shalt have a fair field, and heaven befriend the juster side!"

The Knight made no reply, but dismounting, was conducted by Manfred to the great hall of the castle. As they traversed the court, the Knight stopped to gaze on the miraculous casque; and kneeling down, seemed to pray inwardly for some minutes. Rising, he made a sign to the Prince to lead on. As soon as they entered the hall, Manfred proposed to the stranger to disarm, but the Knight shook his head in token of refusal.

"Sir Knight," said Manfred, "this is not courteous, but by my good faith I will not cross thee, nor shalt thou have cause to complain of the Prince of Otranto. No treachery is designed on my part; I hope none is intended on thine; here take my gage" (giving him his ring): "your friends and you shall enjoy the laws of hospitality. Rest here until refreshments are brought. I will but give orders for the accommodation of your train, and return to you." The three Knights bowed as accepting his courtesy. Manfred directed the stranger's retinue to be conducted to an adjacent hospital, founded by the Princess Hippolita for the reception of pilgrims. As they made the circuit of the court to return towards the gate, the gigantic sword burst from the supporters, and falling to the ground opposite to the helmet, remained immovable. Manfred, almost hardened to preternatural appearances, surmounted the shock of this new prodigy; and returning to the hall, where by this time the feast was ready, he invited his silent guests to take their places. Manfred, however ill his heart was at ease, endeavoured to inspire the company with mirth. He put several questions to them, but was answered only by signs. They raised their vizors but sufficiently to feed themselves, and that sparingly.

"Sirs" said the Prince, "ye are the first guests I ever treated within these walls who scorned to hold any intercourse with me: nor has it oft been customary, I ween, for princes to hazard their state and dignity against strangers and mutes. You say you come in the name of Frederic of Vicenza; I have ever heard that he was a gallant and courteous Knight; nor would he, I am bold to say, think it beneath him to mix in social converse with a Prince that is his equal, and not unknown by deeds in arms. Still ye are silent—well! be it as it may—by the laws of hospitality and chivalry ye are masters under this roof: ye shall do your pleasure. But come, give me a goblet of wine; ye will not refuse to pledge me to the healths of your fair mistresses."

The principal Knight sighed and crossed himself, and was rising from the board.

"Sir Knight," said Manfred, "what I said was but in sport. I shall constrain you in nothing: use your good liking. Since mirth is not your mood, let us be sad. Business may hit your fancies better. Let us withdraw, and hear if what I have to unfold may be better relished than the vain efforts I have made for your pastime."

Manfred then conducting the three Knights into an inner chamber, shut the door, and inviting them to be seated, began thus, addressing himself to the chief personage:—

"You come, Sir Knight, as I understand, in the name of the Marquis of Vicenza, to re-demand the Lady Isabella, his daughter, who has been contracted in the face of Holy Church to my son, by the consent of her legal guardians; and to require me to resign my dominions to your Lord, who gives himself for the nearest of blood to Prince Alfonso, whose soul God rest! I shall speak to the latter article of your demands first. You must know, your Lord knows, that I enjoy the principality of Otranto from my father, Don Manuel, as he received it from his father, Don Ricardo. Alfonso, their predecessor, dying childless in the Holy Land, bequeathed his estates to my grandfather, Don Ricardo, in consideration of his faithful services." The stranger shook his head.

"Sir Knight," said Manfred, warmly, "Ricardo was a valiant and upright man; he was a pious man; witness his munificent foundation of the adjoining church and two convents. He was peculiarly patronised by St. Nicholas—my grandfather was incapable—I say, Sir, Don Ricardo was incapable—excuse me, your interruption has disordered me. I venerate the memory of my grandfather. Well, Sirs, he held this estate; he held it by his good sword and by the favour of St. Nicholas—so did my father; and so, Sirs, will I, come what come will. But Frederic, your Lord, is nearest in blood. I have consented to put my title to the issue of the sword. Does that imply a vicious title? I might have asked, where is Frederic your Lord? Report speaks him dead in captivity. You say, your actions say, he lives—I question it not—I might, Sirs, I might—but I do not. Other Princes would bid Frederic take his inheritance by force, if he can: they would not stake their dignity on a single combat: they would not submit it to the decision of unknown mutes!—pardon me, gentlemen, I am too warm: but suppose yourselves in my situation: as ye are stout Knights, would it not move your choler to have your own and the honour of your ancestors called in question?" "But to the point. Ye require me to deliver up the Lady Isabella. Sirs, I must ask if ye are authorised to receive her?"

The Knight nodded.

"Receive her," continued Manfred; "well, you are authorised to receive her, but, gentle Knight, may I ask if you have full powers?"

The Knight nodded.

"'Tis well," said Manfred; "then hear what I have to offer. Ye see, gentlemen, before you, the most unhappy of men!" (he began to weep); "afford me your compassion; I am entitled to it, indeed I am. Know, I have lost my only hope, my joy, the support of my house—Conrad died yester morning."

The Knights discovered signs of surprise.

"Yes, Sirs, fate has disposed of my son. Isabella is at liberty."

"Do you then restore her?" cried the chief Knight, breaking silence.

"Afford me your patience," said Manfred. "I rejoice to find, by this testimony of your goodwill, that this matter may be adjusted without blood. It is no interest of mine dictates what little I have farther to say. Ye behold in me a man disgusted with the world: the loss of my son has weaned me from earthly cares. Power and greatness have no longer any charms in my eyes. I wished to transmit the sceptre I had received from my ancestors with honour to my son—but that is over! Life itself is so indifferent to me, that I accepted your defiance with joy. A good Knight cannot go to the grave with more satisfaction than when falling in his vocation: whatever is the will of heaven, I submit; for alas! Sirs, I am a man of many sorrows. Manfred is no object of envy, but no doubt you are acquainted with my story."

The Knight made signs of ignorance, and seemed curious to have Manfred proceed.

"Is it possible, Sirs," continued the Prince, "that my story should be a secret to you? Have you heard nothing relating to me and the Princess Hippolita?"

They shook their heads.

"No! Thus, then, Sirs, it is. You think me ambitious: ambition, alas! is composed of more rugged materials. If I were ambitious, I should not for so many years have been a prey to all the hell of conscientious scruples. But I weary your patience: I will be brief. Know, then, that I have long been troubled in mind on my union with the Princess Hippolita. Oh! Sirs, if ye were acquainted with that excellent woman! if ye knew that I adore her like a mistress, and cherish her as a friend—but man was not born for perfect happiness! She shares my scruples, and with her consent I have brought this matter before the church, for we are related within the forbidden degrees. I expect every hour the definitive sentence that must separate us for ever—I am sure you feel for me—I see you do—pardon these tears!"

The Knights gazed on each other, wondering where this would end.

Manfred continued—

"The death of my son betiding while my soul was under this anxiety, I thought of nothing but resigning my dominions, and retiring for ever from the sight of mankind. My only difficulty was to fix on a successor, who would be tender of my people, and to dispose of the Lady Isabella, who is dear to me as my own blood. I was willing to restore the line of Alfonso, even in his most distant kindred. And though, pardon me, I am satisfied it was his will that Ricardo's lineage should take place of his own relations; yet where was I to search for those relations? I knew of none but Frederic, your Lord; he was a captive to the infidels, or dead; and were he living, and at home, would he quit the flourishing State of Vicenza for the inconsiderable principality of Otranto? If he would not, could I bear the thought of seeing a hard, unfeeling, Viceroy set over my poor faithful people? for, Sirs, I love my people, and thank heaven am beloved by them. But ye will ask whither tends this long discourse? Briefly, then, thus, Sirs. Heaven in your arrival seems to point out a remedy for these difficulties and my misfortunes. The Lady Isabella is at liberty; I shall soon be so. I would submit to anything for the good of my people. Were it not the best, the only way to extinguish the feuds between our families, if I was to take the Lady Isabella to wife? You start. But though Hippolita's virtues will ever be dear to me, a Prince must not consider himself; he is born for his people." A servant at that instant entering the chamber apprised Manfred that Jerome and several of his brethren demanded immediate access to him.

The Prince, provoked at this interruption, and fearing that the Friar would discover to the strangers that Isabella had taken sanctuary, was going to forbid Jerome's entrance. But recollecting that he was certainly arrived to notify the Princess's return, Manfred began to excuse himself to the Knights for leaving them for a few moments, but was prevented by the arrival of the Friars. Manfred angrily reprimanded them for their intrusion, and would have forced them back from the chamber; but Jerome was too much agitated to be repulsed. He declared aloud the flight of Isabella, with protestations of his own innocence.

Manfred, distracted at the news, and not less at its coming to the knowledge of the strangers, uttered nothing but incoherent sentences, now upbraiding the Friar, now apologising to the Knights, earnest to know what was become of Isabella, yet equally afraid of their knowing; impatient to pursue her, yet dreading to have them join in the pursuit. He offered to despatch messengers in quest of her, but the chief Knight, no longer keeping silence, reproached Manfred in bitter terms for his dark and ambiguous dealing, and demanded the cause of Isabella's first absence from the castle. Manfred, casting a stern look at Jerome, implying a command of silence, pretended that on Conrad's death he had placed her in sanctuary until he could determine how to dispose of her. Jerome, who trembled for his son's life, did not dare contradict this falsehood, but one of his brethren, not under the same anxiety, declared frankly that she had fled to their church in the preceding night. The Prince in vain endeavoured to stop this discovery, which overwhelmed him with shame and confusion. The principal stranger, amazed at the contradictions he heard, and more than half persuaded that Manfred had secreted the Princess, notwithstanding the concern he expressed at her flight, rushing to the door, said—

"Thou traitor Prince! Isabella shall be found."

Manfred endeavoured to hold him, but the other Knights assisting their comrade, he broke from the Prince, and hastened into the court, demanding his attendants. Manfred, finding it vain to divert him from the pursuit, offered to accompany him and summoning his attendants, and taking Jerome and some of the Friars to guide them, they issued from the castle; Manfred privately giving orders to have the Knight's company secured, while to the knight he affected to despatch a messenger to require their assistance.

The company had no sooner quitted the castle than Matilda, who felt herself deeply interested for the young peasant, since she had seen him condemned to death in the hall, and whose thoughts had been taken up with concerting measures to save him, was informed by some of the female attendants that Manfred had despatched all his men various ways in pursuit of Isabella. He had in his hurry given this order in general terms, not meaning to extend it to the guard he had set upon Theodore, but forgetting it. The domestics, officious to obey so peremptory a Prince, and urged by their own curiosity and love of novelty to join in any precipitate chase, had to a man left the castle. Matilda disengaged herself from her women, stole up to the black tower, and unbolting the door, presented herself to the astonished Theodore.

"Young man," said she, "though filial duty and womanly modesty condemn the step I am taking, yet holy charity, surmounting all other ties, justifies this act. Fly; the doors of thy prison are open: my father and his domestics are absent; but they may soon return. Be gone in safety; and may the angels of heaven direct thy course!"

"Thou art surely one of those angels!" said the enraptured Theodore: "none but a blessed saint could speak, could act—could look—like thee. May I not know the name of my divine protectress? Methought thou namedst thy father. Is it possible? Can Manfred's blood feel holy pity! Lovely Lady, thou answerest not. But how art thou here thyself? Why dost thou neglect thy own safety, and waste a thought on a wretch like Theodore? Let us fly together: the life thou bestowest shall be dedicated to thy defence."

"Alas! thou mistakest," said Matilda, sighing: "I am Manfred's daughter, but no dangers await me."

"Amazement!" said Theodore; "but last night I blessed myself for yielding thee the service thy gracious compassion so charitably returns me now."

"Still thou art in an error," said the Princess; "but this is no time for explanation. Fly, virtuous youth, while it is in my power to save thee: should my father return, thou and I both should indeed have cause to tremble."

"How!" said Theodore; "thinkest thou, charming maid, that I will accept of life at the hazard of aught calamitous to thee? Better I endured a thousand deaths."

"I run no risk," said Matilda, "but by thy delay. Depart; it cannot be known that I have assisted thy flight."

"Swear by the saints above," said Theodore, "that thou canst not be suspected; else here I vow to await whatever can befall me."

"Oh! thou art too generous," said Matilda; "but rest assured that no suspicion can alight on me."

"Give me thy beauteous hand in token that thou dost not deceive me," said Theodore; "and let me bathe it with the warm tears of gratitude."

"Forbear!" said the Princess; "this must not be."

"Alas!" said Theodore, "I have never known but calamity until this hour—perhaps shall never know other fortune again: suffer the chaste raptures of holy gratitude: 'tis my soul would print its effusions on thy hand."

"Forbear, and be gone," said Matilda. "How would Isabella approve of seeing thee at my feet?"

"Who is Isabella?" said the young man with surprise.

"Ah, me! I fear," said the Princess, "I am serving a deceitful one. Hast thou forgot thy curiosity this morning?"

"Thy looks, thy actions, all thy beauteous self seem an emanation of divinity," said Theodore; "but thy words are dark and mysterious. Speak, Lady; speak to thy servant's comprehension."

"Thou understandest but too well!" said Matilda; "but once more I command thee to be gone: thy blood, which I may preserve, will be on my head, if I waste the time in vain discourse."

"I go, Lady," said Theodore, "because it is thy will, and because I would not bring the grey hairs of my father with sorrow to the grave. Say but, adored Lady, that I have thy gentle pity."

"Stay," said Matilda; "I will conduct thee to the subterraneous vault by which Isabella escaped; it will lead thee to the church of St. Nicholas, where thou mayst take sanctuary."

"What!" said Theodore, "was it another, and not thy lovely self that I assisted to find the subterraneous passage?"

"It was," said Matilda; "but ask no more; I tremble to see thee still abide here; fly to the sanctuary."

"To sanctuary," said Theodore; "no, Princess; sanctuaries are for helpless damsels, or for criminals. Theodore's soul is free from guilt, nor will wear the appearance of it. Give me a sword, Lady, and thy father shall learn that Theodore scorns an ignominious flight."

"Rash youth!" said Matilda; "thou wouldst not dare to lift thy presumptuous arm against the Prince of Otranto?"

"Not against thy father; indeed, I dare not," said Theodore. "Excuse me, Lady; I had forgotten. But could I gaze on thee, and remember thou art sprung from the tyrant Manfred! But he is thy father, and from this moment my injuries are buried in oblivion."

A deep and hollow groan, which seemed to come from above, startled the Princess and Theodore.

"Good heaven! we are overheard!" said the Princess. They listened; but perceiving no further noise, they both concluded it the effect of pent-up vapours. And the Princess, preceding Theodore softly, carried him to her father's armoury, where, equipping him with a complete suit, he was conducted by Matilda to the postern-gate.

"Avoid the town," said the Princess, "and all the western side of the castle. 'Tis there the search must be making by Manfred and the strangers; but hie thee to the opposite quarter. Yonder behind that forest to the east is a chain of rocks, hollowed into a labyrinth of caverns that reach to the sea coast. There thou mayst lie concealed, till thou canst make signs to some vessel to put on shore, and take thee off. Go! heaven be thy guide!—and sometimes in thy prayers remember—Matilda!"

Theodore flung himself at her feet, and seizing her lily hand, which with struggles she suffered him to kiss, he vowed on the earliest opportunity to get himself knighted, and fervently entreated her permission to swear himself eternally her knight. Ere the Princess could reply, a clap of thunder was suddenly heard that shook the battlements. Theodore, regardless of the tempest, would have urged his suit: but the Princess, dismayed, retreated hastily into the castle, and commanded the youth to be gone with an air that would not be disobeyed. He sighed, and retired, but with eyes fixed on the gate, until Matilda, closing it, put an end to an interview, in which the hearts of both had drunk so deeply of a passion, which both now tasted for the first time.

Theodore went pensively to the convent, to acquaint his father with his deliverance. There he learned the absence of Jerome, and the pursuit that was making after the Lady Isabella, with some particulars of whose story he now first became acquainted. The generous gallantry of his nature prompted him to wish to assist her; but the Monks could lend him no lights to guess at the route she had taken. He was not tempted to wander far in search of her, for the idea of Matilda had imprinted itself so strongly on his heart, that he could not bear to absent himself at much distance from her abode. The tenderness Jerome had expressed for him concurred to confirm this reluctance; and he even persuaded himself that filial affection was the chief cause of his hovering between the castle and monastery.

Until Jerome should return at night, Theodore at length determined to repair to the forest that Matilda had pointed out to him. Arriving there, he sought the gloomiest shades, as best suited to the pleasing melancholy that reigned in his mind. In this mood he roved insensibly to the caves which had formerly served as a retreat to hermits, and were now reported round the country to be haunted by evil spirits. He recollected to have heard this tradition; and being of a brave and adventurous disposition, he willingly indulged his curiosity in exploring the secret recesses of this labyrinth. He had not penetrated far before he thought he heard the steps of some person who seemed to retreat before him.

Theodore, though firmly grounded in all our holy faith enjoins to be believed, had no apprehension that good men were abandoned without cause to the malice of the powers of darkness. He thought the place more likely to be infested by robbers than by those infernal agents who are reported to molest and bewilder travellers. He had long burned with impatience to approve his valour. Drawing his sabre, he marched sedately onwards, still directing his steps as the imperfect rustling sound before him led the way. The armour he wore was a like indication to the person who avoided him. Theodore, now convinced that he was not mistaken, redoubled his pace, and evidently gained on the person that fled, whose haste increasing, Theodore came up just as a woman fell breathless before him. He hasted to raise her, but her terror was so great that he apprehended she would faint in his arms. He used every gentle word to dispel her alarms, and assured her that far from injuring, he would defend her at the peril of his life. The Lady recovering her spirits from his courteous demeanour, and gazing on her protector, said—

"Sure, I have heard that voice before!"

"Not to my knowledge," replied Theodore; "unless, as I conjecture, thou art the Lady Isabella."

"Merciful heaven!" cried she. "Thou art not sent in quest of me, art thou?" And saying those words, she threw herself at his feet, and besought him not to deliver her up to Manfred.

"To Manfred!" cried Theodore—"no, Lady; I have once already delivered thee from his tyranny, and it shall fare hard with me now, but I will place thee out of the reach of his daring."

"Is it possible," said she, "that thou shouldst be the generous unknown whom I met last night in the vault of the castle? Sure thou art not a mortal, but my guardian angel. On my knees, let me thank—"

"Hold! gentle Princess," said Theodore, "nor demean thyself before a poor and friendless young man. If heaven has selected me for thy deliverer, it will accomplish its work, and strengthen my arm in thy cause. But come, Lady, we are too near the mouth of the cavern; let us seek its inmost recesses. I can have no tranquillity till I have placed thee beyond the reach of danger."

"Alas! what mean you, sir?" said she. "Though all your actions are noble, though your sentiments speak the purity of your soul, is it fitting that

I should accompany you alone into these perplexed retreats? Should we be found together, what would a censorious world think of my conduct?"

"I respect your virtuous delicacy," said Theodore; "nor do you harbour a suspicion that wounds my honour. I meant to conduct you into the most private cavity of these rocks, and then at the hazard of my life to guard their entrance against every living thing. Besides, Lady," continued he, drawing a deep sigh, "beauteous and all perfect as your form is, and though my wishes are not guiltless of aspiring, know, my soul is dedicated to another; and although—" A sudden noise prevented Theodore from proceeding. They soon distinguished these sounds—

"Isabella! what, ho! Isabella!" The trembling Princess relapsed into her former agony of fear. Theodore endeavoured to encourage her, but in vain. He assured her he would die rather than suffer her to return under Manfred's power; and begging her to remain concealed, he went forth to prevent the person in search of her from approaching.

At the mouth of the cavern he found an armed Knight, discoursing with a peasant, who assured him he had seen a lady enter the passes of the rock. The Knight was preparing to seek her, when Theodore, placing himself in his way, with his sword drawn, sternly forbad him at his peril to advance.

"And who art thou, who darest to cross my way?" said the Knight, haughtily.

"One who does not dare more than he will perform," said Theodore.

"I seek the Lady Isabella," said the Knight, "and understand she has taken refuge among these rocks. Impede me not, or thou wilt repent having provoked my resentment."

"Thy purpose is as odious as thy resentment is contemptible," said Theodore. "Return whence thou camest, or we shall soon know whose resentment is most terrible."

The stranger, who was the principal Knight that had arrived from the Marquis of Vicenza, had galloped from Manfred as he was busied in getting information of the Princess, and giving various orders to prevent her falling into the power of the three Knights. Their chief had suspected Manfred of being privy to the Princess's absconding, and this insult from a man, who he concluded was stationed by that Prince to secrete her, confirming his suspicions, he made no reply, but discharging a blow with his sabre at Theodore, would soon have removed all obstruction, if Theodore, who took him for one of Manfred's captains, and who had no sooner given the provocation than prepared to support it, had not received the stroke on his shield. The valour that had so long been smothered in his breast broke forth at once; he rushed impetuously on the Knight, whose pride and wrath were not less powerful incentives to hardy deeds. The combat was furious, but not long. Theodore wounded the Knight in three several places, and at last disarmed him as he fainted by the loss of blood.

The peasant, who had fled on the first onset, had given the alarm to some of Manfred's domestics, who, by his orders, were dispersed through the forest in pursuit of Isabella. They came up as the Knight fell, whom they soon discovered to be the noble stranger. Theodore, notwithstanding his hatred to Manfred, could not behold the victory he had gained without emotions of pity and generosity. But he was more touched when he learned the quality of his adversary, and was informed that he was no retainer, but an enemy, of Manfred. He assisted the servants of the latter in disarming the Knight, and in endeavouring to stanch the blood that flowed from his wounds. The Knight recovering his speech, said, in a faint and faltering voice—

"Generous foe, we have both been in an error. I took thee for an instrument of the tyrant; I perceive thou hast made the like mistake. It is too late for excuses. I faint. If Isabella is at hand—call her—I have important secrets to—"

"He is dying!" said one of the attendants; "has nobody a crucifix about them? Andrea, do thou pray over him."

"Fetch some water," said Theodore, "and pour it down his throat, while I hasten to the Princess."

Saying this, he flew to Isabella, and in few words told her modestly that he had been so unfortunate by mistake as to wound a gentleman from her father's court, who wished, ere he died, to impart something of consequence to her.

The Princess, who had been transported at hearing the voice of Theodore, as he called to her to come forth, was astonished at what she heard. Suffering herself to be conducted by Theodore, the new proof of whose valour recalled her dispersed spirits, she came where the bleeding Knight lay speechless on the ground. But her fears returned when she beheld the domestics of Manfred. She would again have fled if Theodore had not made her observe that they were unarmed, and had not threatened them with instant death if they should dare to seize the Princess.

The stranger, opening his eyes, and beholding a woman, said, "Art thou—pray tell me truly—art thou Isabella of Vicenza?"

"I am," said she: "good heaven restore thee!"

"Then thou—then thou"—said the Knight, struggling for utterance—"seest—thy father. Give me one—"

"Oh! amazement! horror! what do I hear! what do I see!" cried Isabella. "My father! You my father! How came you here, Sir? For heaven's sake, speak! Oh! run for help, or he will expire!"

"'Tis most true," said the wounded Knight, exerting all his force; "I am Frederic thy father. Yes, I came to deliver thee. It will not be. Give me a parting kiss, and take—"

"Sir," said Theodore, "do not exhaust yourself; suffer us to convey you to the castle."

"To the castle!" said Isabella. "Is there no help nearer than the castle? Would you expose my father to the tyrant? If he goes thither, I dare not accompany him; and yet, can I leave him!"

"My child," said Frederic, "it matters not for me whither I am carried. A few minutes will place me beyond danger; but while I have eyes to dote on thee, forsake me not, dear Isabella! This brave Knight—I know not who he is—will protect thy innocence. Sir, you will not abandon my child, will you?"

Theodore, shedding tears over his victim, and vowing to guard the Princess at the expense of his life, persuaded Frederic to suffer himself to be conducted to the castle. They placed him on a horse belonging to one of the domestics, after binding up his wounds as well as they were able. Theodore marched by his side; and the afflicted Isabella, who could not bear to quit him, followed mournfully behind.

CHAPTER IV

The sorrowful troop no sooner arrived at the castle, than they were met by Hippolita and Matilda, whom Isabella had sent one of the domestics before to advertise of their approach. The ladies causing Frederic to be conveyed into the nearest chamber, retired, while the surgeons examined his wounds. Matilda blushed at seeing Theodore and Isabella together; but endeavoured to conceal it by embracing the latter, and condoling with her on her father's mischance. The surgeons soon came to acquaint Hippolita that none of the Marquis's wounds were dangerous; and that he was desirous of seeing his daughter and the Princesses.

Theodore, under pretence of expressing his joy at being freed from his apprehensions of the combat being fatal to Frederic, could not resist the impulse of following Matilda. Her eyes were so often cast down on meeting his, that Isabella, who regarded Theodore as attentively as he gazed on Matilda, soon divined who the object was that he had told her in the cave engaged his affections. While this mute scene passed, Hippolita demanded of Frederic the cause of his having taken that mysterious course for reclaiming his daughter; and threw in various apologies to excuse her Lord for the match contracted between their children.

Frederic, however incensed against Manfred, was not insensible to the courtesy and benevolence of Hippolita: but he was still more struck with the lovely form of Matilda. Wishing to detain them by his bedside, he informed Hippolita of his story. He told her that, while prisoner to the infidels, he had dreamed that his daughter, of whom he had learned no news since his captivity, was detained in a castle, where she was in danger of the most dreadful misfortunes: and that if he obtained his liberty, and repaired to a wood near Joppa, he would learn more. Alarmed at this dream, and incapable of obeying the direction given by it, his chains became more grievous than ever. But while his thoughts were occupied on the means of obtaining his liberty, he received the agreeable news that the confederate Princes who were warring in Palestine had paid his ransom. He instantly set out for the wood that had been marked in his dream.

For three days he and his attendants had wandered in the forest without seeing a human form: but on the evening of the third they came to a cell, in which they found a venerable hermit in the agonies of death. Applying rich cordials, they brought the fainting man to his speech.

"My sons," said he, "I am bounden to your charity—but it is in vain—I am going to my eternal rest—yet I die with the satisfaction of performing the will of heaven. When first I repaired to this solitude, after seeing my country become a prey to unbelievers—it is alas! above fifty years since I was witness to that dreadful scene! St. Nicholas appeared to me, and revealed a secret, which he bade me never disclose to mortal man, but on my death-bed. This is that tremendous hour, and ye are no doubt the chosen warriors to whom I was ordered to reveal my trust. As soon as ye have done the last offices to this wretched corse, dig under the seventh tree on the left hand of this poor cave, and your pains will—Oh! good heaven receive my soul!" With those words the devout man breathed his last.

"By break of day," continued Frederic, "when we had committed the holy relics to earth, we dug according to direction. But what was our astonishment when about the depth of six feet we discovered an enormous sabre—the very weapon yonder in the court. On the blade, which was then partly out of the scabbard, though since closed by our efforts in removing it, were written the following lines—no; excuse me, Madam," added the Marquis, turning to Hippolita; "if I forbear to repeat them: I respect your sex and rank, and would not be guilty of offending your ear with sounds injurious to aught that is dear to you."

He paused. Hippolita trembled. She did not doubt but Frederic was destined by heaven to accomplish the fate that seemed to threaten her house. Looking with anxious fondness at Matilda, a silent tear stole down her cheek: but recollecting herself, she said—

"Proceed, my Lord; heaven does nothing in vain; mortals must receive its divine behests with lowliness and submission. It is our part to deprecate its wrath, or bow to its decrees. Repeat the sentence, my Lord; we listen resigned."

Frederic was grieved that he had proceeded so far. The dignity and patient firmness of Hippolita penetrated him with respect, and the tender silent affection with which the Princess and her daughter regarded each other, melted him almost to tears. Yet apprehensive that his forbearance to obey would be more alarming, he repeated in a faltering and low voice the following lines:

"Where'er a casque that suits this sword is found, With perils is thy daughter compass'd round; Alfonso's blood alone can save the maid, And quiet a long restless Prince's shade."

"What is there in these lines," said Theodore impatiently, "that affects these Princesses? Why were they to be shocked by a mysterious delicacy, that has so little foundation?"

"Your words are rude, young man," said the Marquis; "and though fortune has favoured you once—"

"My honoured Lord," said Isabella, who resented Theodore's warmth, which she perceived was dictated by his sentiments for Matilda, "discompose not yourself for the glosing of a peasant's son: he forgets the reverence he owes you; but he is not accustomed—"

Hippolita, concerned at the heat that had arisen, checked Theodore for his boldness, but with an air acknowledging his zeal; and changing the conversation, demanded of Frederic where he had left her Lord? As the Marquis was going to reply, they heard a noise without, and rising to inquire the cause, Manfred, Jerome, and part of the troop, who had met an imperfect rumour of what had happened, entered the chamber. Manfred advanced hastily towards Frederic's bed to condole with him on his misfortune, and to learn the circumstances of the combat, when starting in an agony of terror and amazement, he cried—

"Ha! what art thou? thou dreadful spectre! is my hour come?"

"My dearest, gracious Lord," cried Hippolita, clasping him in her arms, "what is it you see! Why do you fix your eye-balls thus?"

"What!" cried Manfred breathless; "dost thou see nothing, Hippolita? Is this ghastly phantom sent to me alone—to me, who did not—"

"For mercy's sweetest self, my Lord," said Hippolita, "resume your soul, command your reason. There is none here, but us, your friends."

"What, is not that Alfonso?" cried Manfred. "Dost thou not see him? can it be my brain's delirium?"

"This! my Lord," said Hippolita; "this is Theodore, the youth who has been so unfortunate."

"Theodore!" said Manfred mournfully, and striking his forehead; "Theodore or a phantom, he has unhinged the soul of Manfred. But how comes he here? and how comes he in armour?"

"I believe he went in search of Isabella," said Hippolita.

"Of Isabella!" said Manfred, relapsing into rage; "yes, yes, that is not doubtful—. But how did he escape from durance in which I left him? Was it Isabella, or this hypocritical old Friar, that procured his enlargement?"

"And would a parent be criminal, my Lord," said Theodore, "if he meditated the deliverance of his child?"

Jerome, amazed to hear himself in a manner accused by his son, and without foundation, knew not what to think. He could not comprehend how Theodore had escaped, how he came to be armed, and to encounter Frederic. Still he would not venture to ask any questions that might tend to inflame Manfred's wrath against his son. Jerome's silence convinced Manfred that he had contrived Theodore's release.

"And is it thus, thou ungrateful old man," said the Prince, addressing himself to the Friar, "that thou repayest mine and Hippolita's bounties? And not content with traversing my heart's nearest wishes, thou armest thy bastard, and bringest him into my own castle to insult me!"

"My Lord," said Theodore, "you wrong my father: neither he nor I are capable of harbouring a thought against your peace. Is it insolence thus to surrender myself to your Highness's pleasure?" added he, laying his sword respectfully at Manfred's feet. "Behold my bosom; strike, my Lord, if you suspect that a disloyal thought is lodged there. There is not a sentiment engraven on my heart that does not venerate you and yours."

The grace and fervour with which Theodore uttered these words interested every person present in his favour. Even Manfred was touched—

yet still possessed with his resemblance to Alfonso, his admiration was dashed with secret horror.

"Rise," said he; "thy life is not my present purpose. But tell me thy history, and how thou camest connected with this old traitor here."

"My Lord," said Jerome eagerly.

"Peace! impostor!" said Manfred; "I will not have him prompted."

"My Lord," said Theodore, "I want no assistance; my story is very brief. I was carried at five years of age to Algiers with my mother, who had been taken by corsairs from the coast of Sicily. She died of grief in less than a twelvemonth;" the tears gushed from Jerome's eyes, on whose countenance a thousand anxious passions stood expressed. "Before she died," continued Theodore, "she bound a writing about my arm under my garments, which told me I was the son of the Count Falconara."

"It is most true," said Jerome; "I am that wretched father."

"Again I enjoin thee silence," said Manfred: "proceed."

"I remained in slavery," said Theodore, "until within these two years, when attending on my master in his cruises, I was delivered by a Christian vessel, which overpowered the pirate; and discovering myself to the captain, he generously put me on shore in Sicily; but alas! instead of finding a father, I learned that his estate, which was situated on the coast, had, during his absence, been laid waste by the Rover who had carried my mother and me into captivity: that his castle had been burnt to the ground, and that my father on his return had sold what remained, and was retired into religion in the kingdom of Naples, but where no man could inform me. Destitute and friendless, hopeless almost of attaining the transport of a parent's embrace, I took the first opportunity of setting sail for Naples, from whence, within these six days, I wandered into this province, still supporting myself by the labour of my hands; nor until yester-morn did I believe that heaven had reserved any lot for me but peace of mind and contented poverty. This, my Lord, is Theodore's story. I am blessed beyond my hope in finding a father; I am unfortunate beyond my desert in having incurred your Highness's displeasure."

He ceased. A murmur of approbation gently arose from the audience.

"This is not all," said Frederic; "I am bound in honour to add what he suppresses. Though he is modest, I must be generous; he is one of the bravest youths on Christian ground. He is warm too; and from the short knowledge I have of him, I will pledge myself for his veracity: if what he reports of himself were not true, he would not utter it—and for me, youth, I honour a frankness which becomes thy birth; but now, and thou didst offend me: yet the noble blood which flows in thy veins, may well be allowed to boil out, when it has so recently traced itself to its source. Come, my Lord," (turning to Manfred), "if I can pardon him, surely you may; it is not the youth's fault, if you took him for a spectre."

This bitter taunt galled the soul of Manfred.

"If beings from another world," replied he haughtily, "have power to impress my mind with awe, it is more than living man can do; nor could a stripling's arm."

"My Lord," interrupted Hippolita, "your guest has occasion for repose: shall we not leave him to his rest?" Saying this, and taking Manfred by the hand, she took leave of Frederic, and led the company forth.

The Prince, not sorry to quit a conversation which recalled to mind the discovery he had made of his most secret sensations, suffered himself to be conducted to his own apartment, after permitting Theodore, though under engagement to return to the castle on the morrow (a condition the young man gladly accepted), to retire with his father to the convent. Matilda and Isabella were too much occupied with their own reflections, and too little content with each other, to wish for farther converse that night. They separated each to her chamber, with more expressions of ceremony and fewer of affection than had passed between them since their childhood.

If they parted with small cordiality, they did but meet with greater impatience, as soon as the sun was risen. Their minds were in a situation that excluded sleep, and each recollected a thousand questions which she wished she had put to the other overnight. Matilda reflected that Isabella had been twice delivered by Theodore in very critical situations, which she could not believe accidental. His eyes, it was true, had been fixed on her in Frederic's chamber; but that might have been to disguise his passion for Isabella from the fathers of both. It were better to clear this up. She wished to know the truth, lest she should wrong her friend by entertaining a passion for Isabella's lover. Thus jealousy prompted, and at the same time borrowed an excuse from friendship to justify its curiosity.

Isabella, not less restless, had better foundation for her suspicions. Both Theodore's tongue and eyes had told her his heart was engaged; it was true—yet, perhaps, Matilda might not correspond to his passion; she had ever appeared insensible to love: all her thoughts were set on heaven.

"Why did I dissuade her?" said Isabella to herself; "I am punished for my generosity; but when did they meet? where? It cannot be; I have deceived myself; perhaps last night was the first time they ever beheld each other; it must be some other object that has prepossessed his affections—if it is, I am not so unhappy as I thought; if it is not my friend Matilda—how! Can I stoop to wish for the affection of a man, who rudely and unnecessarily acquainted me with his indifference? and that at the very moment in which common courtesy demanded at least expressions of civility. I will go to my dear Matilda, who will confirm me in this becoming pride. Man is false—I will advise with her on taking the veil: she will rejoice to find me in this disposition; and I will acquaint her that I no longer oppose her inclination for the cloister."

In this frame of mind, and determined to open her heart entirely to Matilda, she went to that Princess's chamber, whom she found already dressed, and leaning pensively on her arm. This attitude, so correspondent to what she felt herself, revived Isabella's suspicions, and destroyed the confidence she had purposed to place in her friend. They blushed at meeting, and were too much novices to disguise their sensations with address. After some unmeaning questions and replies, Matilda demanded of Isabella the cause of her flight? The latter, who had almost forgotten Manfred's passion, so entirely was she occupied by her own, concluding that Matilda referred to her last escape from the convent, which had occasioned the events of the preceding evening, replied—

"Martelli brought word to the convent that your mother was dead."

"Oh!" said Matilda, interrupting her, "Bianca has explained that mistake to me: on seeing me faint, she cried out, 'The Princess is dead!' and Martelli, who had come for the usual dole to the castle—"

"And what made you faint?" said Isabella, indifferent to the rest. Matilda blushed and stammered—

"My father—he was sitting in judgment on a criminal—"

"What criminal?" said Isabella eagerly.

"A young man," said Matilda; "I believe—I think it was that young man that—"

"What, Theodore?" said Isabella.

"Yes," answered she; "I never saw him before; I do not know how he had offended my father, but as he has been of service to you, I am glad my Lord has pardoned him."

"Served me!" replied Isabella; "do you term it serving me, to wound my father, and almost occasion his death? Though it is but since yesterday that I am blessed with knowing a parent, I hope Matilda does not think I am such a stranger to filial tenderness as not to resent the boldness of that audacious youth, and that it is impossible for me ever to feel any affection for one who dared to lift his arm against the author of my being. No, Matilda, my heart abhors him; and if you still retain the friendship for me that you have vowed from your infancy, you will detest a man who has been on the point of making me miserable for ever."

Matilda held down her head and replied: "I hope my dearest Isabella does not doubt her Matilda's friendship: I never beheld that youth until yesterday; he is almost a stranger to me: but as the surgeons have pronounced your father out of danger, you ought not to harbour uncharitable resentment against one, who I am persuaded did not know the Marquis was related to you."

"You plead his cause very pathetically," said Isabella, "considering he is so much a stranger to you! I am mistaken, or he returns your charity."

"What mean you?" said Matilda.

"Nothing," said Isabella, repenting that she had given Matilda a hint of Theodore's inclination for her. Then changing the discourse, she asked Matilda what occasioned Manfred to take Theodore for a spectre?

"Bless me," said Matilda, "did not you observe his extreme resemblance to the portrait of Alfonso in the gallery? I took notice of it to Bianca even before I saw him in armour; but with the helmet on, he is the very image of that picture."

"I do not much observe pictures," said Isabella: "much less have I examined this young man so attentively as you seem to have done. Ah? Matilda, your heart is in danger, but let me warn you as a friend, he has owned to me that he is in love; it cannot be with you, for yesterday was the first time you ever met—was it not?"

"Certainly," replied Matilda; "but why does my dearest Isabella conclude from anything I have said, that"—she paused—then continuing: "he saw you first, and I am far from having the vanity to think that my little portion of charms could engage a heart devoted to you; may you be happy, Isabella, whatever is the fate of Matilda!"

"My lovely friend," said Isabella, whose heart was too honest to resist a kind expression, "it is you that Theodore admires; I saw it; I am persuaded of it; nor shall a thought of my own happiness suffer me to interfere with yours."

This frankness drew tears from the gentle Matilda; and jealousy that for a moment had raised a coolness between these amiable maidens soon gave way to the natural sincerity and candour of their souls. Each confessed to the other the impression that Theodore had made on her; and this confidence was followed by a struggle of generosity, each insisting on yielding her claim to her friend. At length the dignity of Isabella's virtue reminding her of the preference which Theodore had almost declared for her rival, made her determine to conquer her passion, and cede the beloved object to her friend.

During this contest of amity, Hippolita entered her daughter's chamber.

"Madam," said she to Isabella, "you have so much tenderness for Matilda, and interest yourself so kindly in whatever affects our wretched house, that I can have no secrets with my child which are not proper for you to hear."

The princesses were all attention and anxiety.

"Know then, Madam," continued Hippolita, "and you my dearest Matilda, that being convinced by all the events of these two last ominous days, that heaven purposes the sceptre of Otranto should pass from Manfred's hands into those of the Marquis Frederic, I have been perhaps inspired with the thought of averting our total destruction by the union of our rival houses. With this view I have been proposing to Manfred, my lord, to tender this dear, dear child to Frederic, your father."

"Me to Lord Frederic!" cried Matilda; "good heavens! my gracious mother—and have you named it to my father?"

"I have," said Hippolita; "he listened benignly to my proposal, and is gone to break it to the Marquis."

"Ah! wretched princess!" cried Isabella; "what hast thou done! what ruin has thy inadvertent goodness been preparing for thyself, for me, and for Matilda!"

"Ruin from me to you and to my child!" said Hippolita "what can this mean?"

"Alas!" said Isabella, "the purity of your own heart prevents your seeing the depravity of others. Manfred, your lord, that impious man—"

"Hold," said Hippolita; "you must not in my presence, young lady, mention Manfred with disrespect: he is my lord and husband, and—"

"Will not long be so," said Isabella, "if his wicked purposes can be carried into execution."

"This language amazes me," said Hippolita. "Your feeling, Isabella, is warm; but until this hour I never knew it betray you into intemperance. What deed of Manfred authorises you to treat him as a murderer, an assassin?"

"Thou virtuous, and too credulous Princess!" replied Isabella; "it is not thy life he aims at—it is to separate himself from thee! to divorce thee! to—"

"To divorce me!" "To divorce my mother!" cried Hippolita and Matilda at once.

"Yes," said Isabella; "and to complete his crime, he meditates—I cannot speak it!"

"What can surpass what thou hast already uttered?" said Matilda.

Hippolita was silent. Grief choked her speech; and the recollection of Manfred's late ambiguous discourses confirmed what she heard.

"Excellent, dear lady! madam! mother!" cried Isabella, flinging herself at Hippolita's feet in a transport of passion; "trust me, believe me, I will die a thousand deaths sooner than consent to injure you, than yield to so odious—oh!—"

"This is too much!" cried Hippolita: "What crimes does one crime suggest! Rise, dear Isabella; I do not doubt your virtue. Oh! Matilda, this stroke is too heavy for thee! weep not, my child; and not a murmur, I charge thee. Remember, he is thy father still!"

"But you are my mother too," said Matilda fervently; "and you are virtuous, you are guiltless!—Oh! must not I, must not I complain?"

"You must not," said Hippolita—"come, all will yet be well. Manfred, in the agony for the loss of thy brother, knew not what he said; perhaps Isabella misunderstood him; his heart is good—and, my child, thou knowest not all! There is a destiny hangs over us; the hand of Providence is stretched out; oh! could I but save thee from the wreck! Yes," continued she in a firmer tone, "perhaps the sacrifice of myself may atone for all; I will go and offer myself to this divorce—it boots not what becomes of me. I will withdraw into the neighbouring monastery, and waste the remainder of life in prayers and tears for my child and—the Prince!"

"Thou art as much too good for this world," said Isabella, "as Manfred is execrable; but think not, lady, that thy weakness shall determine for me. I swear, hear me all ye angels—"

"Stop, I adjure thee," cried Hippolita: "remember thou dost not depend on thyself; thou hast a father."

"My father is too pious, too noble," interrupted Isabella, "to command an impious deed. But should he command it; can a father enjoin a cursed act? I was contracted to the son, can I wed the father? No, madam, no; force should not drag me to Manfred's hated bed. I loathe him, I abhor him: divine and human laws forbid—and my friend, my dearest Matilda! would I wound her tender soul by injuring her adored mother? my own mother—I never have known another"—

"Oh! she is the mother of both!" cried Matilda: "can we, can we, Isabella, adore her too much?"

"My lovely children," said the touched Hippolita, "your tenderness overpowers me—but I must not give way to it. It is not ours to make election for ourselves: heaven, our fathers, and our husbands must decide for us. Have patience until you hear what Manfred and Frederic have determined. If the Marquis accepts Matilda's hand, I know she will readily obey. Heaven may interpose and prevent the rest. What means my child?" continued she, seeing Matilda fall at her feet with a flood of speechless tears—"But no; answer me not, my daughter: I must not hear a word against the pleasure of thy father."

"Oh! doubt not my obedience, my dreadful obedience to him and to you!" said Matilda. "But can I, most respected of women, can I experience all this tenderness, this world of goodness, and conceal a thought from the best of mothers?"

"What art thou going to utter?" said Isabella trembling. "Recollect thyself, Matilda."

"No, Isabella," said the Princess, "I should not deserve this incomparable parent, if the inmost recesses of my soul harboured a thought without her permission—nay, I have offended her; I have suffered a passion to enter my heart without her avowal—but here I disclaim it; here I vow to heaven and her—"

"My child! my child," said Hippolita, "what words are these! what new calamities has fate in store for us! Thou, a passion? Thou, in this hour of destruction—"

"Oh! I see all my guilt!" said Matilda. "I abhor myself, if I cost my mother a pang. She is the dearest thing I have on earth—Oh! I will never, never behold him more!"

"Isabella," said Hippolita, "thou art conscious to this unhappy secret, whatever it is. Speak!"

"What!" cried Matilda, "have I so forfeited my mother's love, that she will not permit me even to speak my own guilt? oh! wretched, wretched Matilda!"

"Thou art too cruel," said Isabella to Hippolita: "canst thou behold this anguish of a virtuous mind, and not commiserate it?"

"Not pity my child!" said Hippolita, catching Matilda in her arms—"Oh! I know she is good, she is all virtue, all tenderness, and duty. I do forgive thee, my excellent, my only hope!"

The princesses then revealed to Hippolita their mutual inclination for Theodore, and the purpose of Isabella to resign him to Matilda. Hippolita blamed their imprudence, and showed them the improbability that either father would consent to bestow his heiress on so poor a man, though nobly born. Some comfort it gave her to find their passion of so recent a date, and that Theodore had had but little cause to suspect it in either. She strictly enjoined them to avoid all correspondence with him. This Matilda fervently promised: but Isabella, who flattered herself that she meant no more than to promote his union with her friend, could not determine to avoid him; and made no reply.

"I will go to the convent," said Hippolita, "and order new masses to be said for a deliverance from these calamities."

"Oh! my mother," said Matilda, "you mean to quit us: you mean to take sanctuary, and to give my father an opportunity of pursuing his fatal intention. Alas! on my knees I supplicate you to forbear; will you leave me a prey to Frederic? I will follow you to the convent."

"Be at peace, my child," said Hippolita: "I will return instantly. I will never abandon thee, until I know it is the will of heaven, and for thy benefit."

"Do not deceive me," said Matilda. "I will not marry Frederic until thou commandest it. Alas! what will become of me?"

"Why that exclamation?" said Hippolita. "I have promised thee to return—"

"Ah! my mother," replied Matilda, "stay and save me from myself. A frown from thee can do more than all my father's severity. I have given away my heart, and you alone can make me recall it."

"No more," said Hippolita; "thou must not relapse, Matilda."

"I can quit Theodore," said she, "but must I wed another? let me attend thee to the altar, and shut myself from the world for ever."

"Thy fate depends on thy father," said Hippolita; "I have ill-bestowed my tenderness, if it has taught thee to revere aught beyond him. Adieu! my child: I go to pray for thee."

Hippolita's real purpose was to demand of Jerome, whether in conscience she might not consent to the divorce. She had oft urged Manfred to resign the principality, which the delicacy of her conscience rendered an hourly burthen to her. These scruples concurred to make the separation from her husband appear less dreadful to her than it would have seemed in any other situation.

Jerome, at quitting the castle overnight, had questioned Theodore severely why he had accused him to Manfred of being privy to his escape. Theodore owned it had been with design to prevent Manfred's suspicion from alighting on Matilda; and added, the holiness of Jerome's life and character secured him from the tyrant's wrath. Jerome was heartily grieved to discover his son's inclination for that princess; and leaving him to his rest, promised in the morning to acquaint him with important reasons for conquering his passion.

Theodore, like Isabella, was too recently acquainted with parental authority to submit to its decisions against the impulse of his heart. He had little curiosity to learn the Friar's reasons, and less disposition to obey them. The lovely Matilda had made stronger impressions on him than filial affection. All night he pleased himself with visions of love; and it was not till late after the morning-office, that he recollected the Friar's commands to attend him at Alfonso's tomb.

"Young man," said Jerome, when he saw him, "this tardiness does not please me. Have a father's commands already so little weight?"

Theodore made awkward excuses, and attributed his delay to having overslept himself.

"And on whom were thy dreams employed?" said the Friar sternly. His son blushed. "Come, come," resumed the Friar, "inconsiderate youth, this must not be; eradicate this guilty passion from thy breast—"

"Guilty passion!" cried Theodore: "Can guilt dwell with innocent beauty and virtuous modesty?"

"It is sinful," replied the Friar, "to cherish those whom heaven has doomed to destruction. A tyrant's race must be swept from the earth to the third and fourth generation."

"Will heaven visit the innocent for the crimes of the guilty?" said Theodore. "The fair Matilda has virtues enough—"

"To undo thee:" interrupted Jerome. "Hast thou so soon forgotten that twice the savage Manfred has pronounced thy sentence?"

"Nor have I forgotten, sir," said Theodore, "that the charity of his daughter delivered me from his power. I can forget injuries, but never benefits."

"The injuries thou hast received from Manfred's race," said the Friar, "are beyond what thou canst conceive. Reply not, but view this holy image! Beneath this marble monument rest the ashes of the good Alfonso; a prince adorned with every virtue: the father of his people! the delight of mankind! Kneel, headstrong boy, and list, while a father unfolds a tale of horror that will expel every sentiment from thy soul, but sensations of sacred vengeance—Alfonso! much injured prince! let thy unsatisfied shade sit awful on the troubled air, while these trembling lips—Ha! who comes there?—"

"The most wretched of women!" said Hippolita, entering the choir. "Good Father, art thou at leisure?—but why this kneeling youth? what means the horror imprinted on each countenance? why at this venerable tomb—alas! hast thou seen aught?"

"We were pouring forth our orisons to heaven," replied the Friar, with some confusion, "to put an end to the woes of this deplorable province.

Join with us, Lady! thy spotless soul may obtain an exemption from the judgments which the portents of these days but too speakingly denounce against thy house."

"I pray fervently to heaven to divert them," said the pious Princess. "Thou knowest it has been the occupation of my life to wrest a blessing for my Lord and my harmless children.—One alas! is taken from me! would heaven but hear me for my poor Matilda! Father! intercede for her!"

"Every heart will bless her," cried Theodore with rapture.

"Be dumb, rash youth!" said Jerome. "And thou, fond Princess, contend not with the Powers above! the Lord giveth, and the Lord taketh away: bless His holy name, and submit to his decrees."

"I do most devoutly," said Hippolita; "but will He not spare my only comfort? must Matilda perish too?—ah! Father, I came—but dismiss thy son. No ear but thine must hear what I have to utter."

"May heaven grant thy every wish, most excellent Princess!" said Theodore retiring. Jerome frowned.

Hippolita then acquainted the Friar with the proposal she had suggested to Manfred, his approbation of it, and the tender of Matilda that he was gone to make to Frederic. Jerome could not conceal his dislike of the notion, which he covered under pretence of the improbability that Frederic, the nearest of blood to Alfonso, and who was come to claim his succession, would yield to an alliance with the usurper of his right. But nothing could equal the perplexity of the Friar, when Hippolita confessed her readiness not to oppose the separation, and demanded his opinion on the legality of her acquiescence. The Friar caught eagerly at her request of his advice, and without explaining his aversion to the proposed marriage of Manfred and Isabella, he painted to Hippolita in the most alarming colours the sinfulness of her consent, denounced judgments against her if she complied, and enjoined her in the severest terms to treat any such proposition with every mark of indignation and refusal.

Manfred, in the meantime, had broken his purpose to Frederic, and proposed the double marriage. That weak Prince, who had been struck with the charms of Matilda, listened but too eagerly to the offer. He forgot his enmity to Manfred, whom he saw but little hope of dispossessing by force; and flattering himself that no issue might succeed from the union of his daughter with the tyrant, he looked upon his own succession to the principality as facilitated by wedding Matilda. He made faint opposition to the proposal; affecting, for form only, not to acquiesce unless Hippolita should consent to the divorce. Manfred took that upon himself.

Transported with his success, and impatient to see himself in a situation to expect sons, he hastened to his wife's apartment, determined to extort her compliance. He learned with indignation that she was absent at the convent. His guilt suggested to him that she had probably been informed by Isabella of his purpose. He doubted whether her retirement to the convent did not import an intention of remaining there, until she could raise obstacles to their divorce; and the suspicions he had already entertained of Jerome, made him apprehend that the Friar would not only traverse his views, but might have inspired Hippolita with the resolution of taking sanctuary. Impatient to unravel this clue, and to defeat its success, Manfred hastened to the convent, and arrived there as the Friar was earnestly exhorting the Princess never to yield to the divorce.

"Madam," said Manfred, "what business drew you hither? why did you not await my return from the Marquis?"

"I came to implore a blessing on your councils," replied Hippolita.

"My councils do not need a Friar's intervention," said Manfred; "and of all men living is that hoary traitor the only one whom you delight to confer with?"

"Profane Prince!" said Jerome; "is it at the altar that thou choosest to insult the servants of the altar?—but, Manfred, thy impious schemes are known. Heaven and this virtuous lady know them—nay, frown not, Prince. The Church despises thy menaces. Her thunders will be heard above thy wrath. Dare to proceed in thy cursed purpose of a divorce, until her sentence be known, and here I lance her anathema at thy head."

"Audacious rebel!" said Manfred, endeavouring to conceal the awe with which the Friar's words inspired him. "Dost thou presume to threaten thy lawful Prince?"

"Thou art no lawful Prince," said Jerome; "thou art no Prince—go, discuss thy claim with Frederic; and when that is done—"

"It is done," replied Manfred; "Frederic accepts Matilda's hand, and is content to waive his claim, unless I have no male issue"—as he spoke those words three drops of blood fell from the nose of Alfonso's statue. Manfred turned pale, and the Princess sank on her knees.

"Behold!" said the Friar; "mark this miraculous indication that the blood of Alfonso will never mix with that of Manfred!"

"My gracious Lord," said Hippolita, "let us submit ourselves to heaven. Think not thy ever obedient wife rebels against thy authority. I have no will but that of my Lord and the Church. To that revered tribunal let us appeal. It does not depend on us to burst the bonds that unite us. If the Church shall approve the dissolution of our marriage, be it so—I have but few years, and those of sorrow, to pass. Where can they be worn away so well as at the foot of this altar, in prayers for thine and Matilda's safety?"

"But thou shalt not remain here until then," said Manfred. "Repair with me to the castle, and there I will advise on the proper measures for a divorce;—but this meddling Friar comes not thither; my hospitable roof shall never more harbour a traitor—and for thy Reverence's offspring," continued he, "I banish him from my dominions. He, I ween, is no sacred personage, nor under the protection of the Church. Whoever weds Isabella, it shall not be Father Falconara's started-up son."

"They start up," said the Friar, "who are suddenly beheld in the seat of lawful Princes; but they wither away like the grass, and their place knows them no more."

Manfred, casting a look of scorn at the Friar, led Hippolita forth; but at the door of the church whispered one of his attendants to remain concealed about the convent, and bring him instant notice, if any one from the castle should repair thither.

CHAPTER V

Every reflection which Manfred made on the Friar's behaviour, conspired to persuade him that Jerome was privy to an amour between Isabella and Theodore. But Jerome's new presumption, so dissonant from his former meekness, suggested still deeper apprehensions. The Prince even suspected that the Friar depended on some secret support from Frederic, whose arrival, coinciding with the novel appearance of Theodore, seemed to bespeak a correspondence. Still more was he troubled with the resemblance of Theodore to Alfonso's portrait. The latter he knew had unquestionably died without issue. Frederic had consented to bestow Isabella on him. These contradictions agitated his mind with numberless pangs.

He saw but two methods of extricating himself from his difficulties. The one was to resign his dominions to the Marquis—pride, ambition, and his reliance on ancient prophecies, which had pointed out a possibility of his preserving them to his posterity, combated that thought. The other was to press his marriage with Isabella. After long ruminating on these anxious thoughts, as he marched silently with Hippolita to the castle, he at last discoursed with that Princess on the subject of his disquiet, and used every insinuating and plausible argument to extract her consent to, even her promise of promoting the divorce. Hippolita needed little persuasions to bend her to his pleasure. She endeavoured to win him over to the measure of resigning his dominions; but finding her exhortations fruitless, she assured him, that as far as her conscience would allow, she would raise no opposition to a separation, though without better founded scruples than what he yet alleged, she would not engage to be active in demanding it.

This compliance, though inadequate, was sufficient to raise Manfred's hopes. He trusted that his power and wealth would easily advance his suit at the court of Rome, whither he resolved to engage Frederic to take a journey on purpose. That Prince had discovered so much passion for Matilda, that Manfred hoped to obtain all he wished by holding out or withdrawing his daughter's charms, according as the Marquis should appear more or less disposed to co-operate in his views. Even the absence of Frederic would be a material point gained, until he could take further measures for his security.

Dismissing Hippolita to her apartment, he repaired to that of the Marquis; but crossing the great hall through which he was to pass he met Bianca. The damsel he knew was in the confidence of both the young ladies. It immediately occurred to him to sift her on the subject of Isabella and Theodore. Calling her aside into the recess of the oriel window of the hall, and soothing her with many fair words and promises, he demanded of her whether she knew aught of the state of Isabella's affections.

"I! my Lord! no my Lord—yes my Lord—poor Lady! she is wonderfully alarmed about her father's wounds; but I tell her he will do well; don't your Highness think so?"

"I do not ask you," replied Manfred, "what she thinks about her father; but you are in her secrets. Come, be a good girl and tell me; is there any young man—ha!—you understand me."

"Lord bless me! understand your Highness? no, not I. I told her a few vulnerary herbs and repose—"

"I am not talking," replied the Prince, impatiently, "about her father; I know he will do well."

"Bless me, I rejoice to hear your Highness say so; for though I thought it not right to let my young Lady despond, methought his greatness had a wan look, and a something—I remember when young Ferdinand was wounded by the Venetian—"

"Thou answerest from the point," interrupted Manfred; "but here, take this jewel, perhaps that may fix thy attention—nay, no reverences; my favour shall not stop here—come, tell me truly; how stands Isabella's heart?"

"Well! your Highness has such a way!" said Bianca, "to be sure—but can your Highness keep a secret? if it should ever come out of your lips—"

"It shall not, it shall not," cried Manfred.

"Nay, but swear, your Highness."

"By my halidame, if it should ever be known that I said it—"

"Why, truth is truth, I do not think my Lady Isabella ever much affectioned my young Lord your son; yet he was a sweet youth as one should see; I am sure, if I had been a Princess—but bless me! I must attend my Lady Matilda; she will marvel what is become of me."

"Stay," cried Manfred; "thou hast not satisfied my question. Hast thou ever carried any message, any letter?"

"I! good gracious!" cried Bianca; "I carry a letter? I would not to be a Queen. I hope your Highness thinks, though I am poor, I am honest. Did your Highness never hear what Count Marsigli offered me, when he came a wooing to my Lady Matilda?"

"I have not leisure," said Manfred, "to listen to thy tale. I do not question thy honesty. But it is thy duty to conceal nothing from me. How long has Isabella been acquainted with Theodore?"

"Nay, there is nothing can escape your Highness!" said Bianca; "not that I know any thing of the matter. Theodore, to be sure, is a proper young man, and, as my Lady Matilda says, the very image of good Alfonso. Has not your Highness remarked it?"

"Yes, yes,—No—thou torturest me," said Manfred. "Where did they meet? when?"

"Who! my Lady Matilda?" said Bianca.

"No, no, not Matilda: Isabella; when did Isabella first become acquainted with this Theodore!"

"Virgin Mary!" said Bianca, "how should I know?"

"Thou dost know," said Manfred; "and I must know; I will—"

"Lord! your Highness is not jealous of young Theodore!" said Bianca.

"Jealous! no, no. Why should I be jealous? perhaps I mean to unite them—If I were sure Isabella would have no repugnance."

"Repugnance! no, I'll warrant her," said Bianca; "he is as comely a youth as ever trod on Christian ground. We are all in love with him; there is not a soul in the castle but would be rejoiced to have him for our Prince—I mean, when it shall please heaven to call your Highness to itself."

"Indeed!" said Manfred, "has it gone so far! oh! this cursed Friar!—but I must not lose time—go, Bianca, attend Isabella; but I charge thee, not a word of what has passed. Find out how she is affected towards Theodore; bring me good news, and that ring has a companion. Wait at the foot of the winding staircase: I am going to visit the Marquis, and will talk further with thee at my return."

Manfred, after some general conversation, desired Frederic to dismiss the two Knights, his companions, having to talk with him on urgent affairs.

As soon as they were alone, he began in artful guise to sound the Marquis on the subject of Matilda; and finding him disposed to his wish, he let drop hints on the difficulties that would attend the celebration of their marriage, unless—At that instant Bianca burst into the room with a wildness in her look and gestures that spoke the utmost terror.

"Oh! my Lord, my Lord!" cried she; "we are all undone! it is come again! it is come again!"

"What is come again?" cried Manfred amazed.

"Oh! the hand! the Giant! the hand!—support me! I am terrified out of my senses," cried Bianca. "I will not sleep in the castle to-night. Where shall I go? my things may come after me to-morrow—would I had been content to wed Francesco! this comes of ambition!"

"What has terrified thee thus, young woman?" said the Marquis. "Thou art safe here; be not alarmed."

"Oh! your Greatness is wonderfully good," said Bianca, "but I dare not—no, pray let me go—I had rather leave everything behind me, than stay another hour under this roof."

"Go to, thou hast lost thy senses," said Manfred. "Interrupt us not; we were communing on important matters—My Lord, this wench is subject to fits—Come with me, Bianca."

"Oh! the Saints! No," said Bianca, "for certain it comes to warn your Highness; why should it appear to me else? I say my prayers morning and evening—oh! if your Highness had believed Diego! 'Tis the same hand that he saw the foot to in the gallery-chamber—Father Jerome has often told us the prophecy would be out one of these days—'Bianca,' said he, 'mark my words—'"

"Thou ravest," said Manfred, in a rage; "be gone, and keep these fooleries to frighten thy companions."

"What! my Lord," cried Bianca, "do you think I have seen nothing? go to the foot of the great stairs yourself—as I live I saw it."

"Saw what? tell us, fair maid, what thou hast seen," said Frederic.

"Can your Highness listen," said Manfred, "to the delirium of a silly wench, who has heard stories of apparitions until she believes them?"

"This is more than fancy," said the Marquis; "her terror is too natural and too strongly impressed to be the work of imagination. Tell us, fair maiden, what it is has moved thee thus?"

"Yes, my Lord, thank your Greatness," said Bianca; "I believe I look very pale; I shall be better when I have recovered myself—I was going to my Lady Isabella's chamber, by his Highness's order—"

"We do not want the circumstances," interrupted Manfred. "Since his Highness will have it so, proceed; but be brief."

"Lord! your Highness thwarts one so!" replied Bianca; "I fear my hair—I am sure I never in my life—well! as I was telling your Greatness, I was going by his Highness's order to my Lady Isabella's chamber; she lies in the watchet-coloured chamber, on the right hand, one pair of stairs: so when I came to the great stairs—I was looking on his Highness's present here—"

"Grant me patience!" said Manfred, "will this wench never come to the point? what imports it to the Marquis, that I gave thee a bauble for thy faithful attendance on my daughter? we want to know what thou sawest."

"I was going to tell your Highness," said Bianca, "if you would permit me. So as I was rubbing the ring—I am sure I had not gone up three steps, but I heard the rattling of armour; for all the world such a clatter as Diego says he heard when the Giant turned him about in the gallery-chamber."

"What Giant is this, my Lord?" said the Marquis; "is your castle haunted by giants and goblins?"

"Lord! what, has not your Greatness heard the story of the Giant in the gallery-chamber?" cried Bianca. "I marvel his Highness has not told you; mayhap you do not know there is a prophecy—"

"This trifling is intolerable," interrupted Manfred. "Let us dismiss this silly wench, my Lord! we have more important affairs to discuss."

"By your favour," said Frederic, "these are no trifles. The enormous sabre I was directed to in the wood, yon casque, its fellow—are these visions of this poor maiden's brain?"

"So Jaquez thinks, may it please your Greatness," said Bianca. "He says this moon will not be out without our seeing some strange revolution. For my part, I should not be surprised if it was to happen to-morrow; for, as I was saying, when I heard the clattering of armour, I was all in a cold sweat. I looked up, and, if your Greatness will believe me, I saw upon the uppermost banister of the great stairs a hand in armour as big as big. I thought I should have swooned. I never stopped until I came hither— would I were well out of this castle. My Lady Matilda told me but yester-morning that her Highness Hippolita knows something."

"Thou art an insolent!" cried Manfred. "Lord Marquis, it much misgives me that this scene is concerted to affront me. Are my own domestics suborned to spread tales injurious to my honour? Pursue your claim by manly daring; or let us bury our feuds, as was proposed, by the intermarriage of our children. But trust me, it ill becomes a Prince of your bearing to practise on mercenary wenches."

"I scorn your imputation," said Frederic. "Until this hour I never set eyes on this damsel: I have given her no jewel. My Lord, my Lord, your conscience, your guilt accuses you, and would throw the suspicion on me; but keep your daughter, and think no more of Isabella. The judgments already fallen on your house forbid me matching into it."

Manfred, alarmed at the resolute tone in which Frederic delivered these words, endeavoured to pacify him. Dismissing Bianca, he made such submissions to the Marquis, and threw in such artful encomiums on Matilda, that Frederic was once more staggered. However, as his passion was of so recent a date, it could not at once surmount the scruples he had conceived. He had gathered enough from Bianca's discourse to persuade him that heaven declared itself against Manfred. The proposed marriages too removed his claim to a distance; and the principality of Otranto was a stronger temptation than the contingent reversion of it with Matilda. Still he would not absolutely recede from his engagements; but purposing to gain time, he demanded of Manfred if it was true in fact that Hippolita consented to the divorce. The Prince, transported to find no other obstacle, and depending on his influence over his wife, assured the Marquis it was so, and that he might satisfy himself of the truth from her own mouth.

As they were thus discoursing, word was brought that the banquet was prepared. Manfred conducted Frederic to the great hall, where they were received by Hippolita and the young Princesses. Manfred placed the Marquis next to Matilda, and seated himself between his wife and Isabella. Hippolita comported herself with an easy gravity; but the young ladies were silent and melancholy. Manfred, who was determined to pursue his point with the Marquis in the remainder of the evening, pushed on the feast until it waxed late; affecting unrestrained gaiety, and plying Frederic with repeated goblets of wine. The latter, more upon his guard than Manfred wished, declined his frequent challenges, on pretence of his late loss of blood; while the Prince, to raise his own disordered spirits, and to counterfeit unconcern, indulged himself in plentiful draughts, though not to the intoxication of his senses.

The evening being far advanced, the banquet concluded. Manfred would have withdrawn with Frederic; but the latter pleading weakness and want of repose, retired to his chamber, gallantly telling the Prince that his daughter should amuse his Highness until himself could attend him. Manfred accepted the party, and to the no small grief of Isabella, accompanied her to her apartment. Matilda waited on her mother to enjoy the freshness of the evening on the ramparts of the castle.

Soon as the company were dispersed their several ways, Frederic, quitting his chamber, inquired if Hippolita was alone, and was told by one of her attendants, who had not noticed her going forth, that at that hour she generally withdrew to her oratory, where he probably would find her. The Marquis, during the repast, had beheld Matilda with increase of passion. He now wished to find Hippolita in the disposition her Lord had promised. The portents that had alarmed him were forgotten in his desires. Stealing softly and unobserved to the apartment of Hippolita, he entered it with a resolution to encourage her acquiescence to the divorce, having perceived that Manfred was resolved to make the possession of Isabella an unalterable condition, before he would grant Matilda to his wishes.

The Marquis was not surprised at the silence that reigned in the Princess's apartment. Concluding her, as he had been advertised, in her oratory, he passed on. The door was ajar; the evening gloomy and overcast. Pushing open the door gently, he saw a person kneeling before the altar. As he approached nearer, it seemed not a woman, but one in a long woollen weed, whose back was towards him. The person seemed absorbed in prayer. The Marquis was about to return, when the figure, rising, stood some moments fixed in meditation, without regarding him. The Marquis, expecting the holy person to come forth, and meaning to excuse his uncivil interruption, said,

"Reverend Father, I sought the Lady Hippolita."

"Hippolita!" replied a hollow voice; "camest thou to this castle to seek Hippolita?" and then the figure, turning slowly round, discovered to Frederic the fleshless jaws and empty sockets of a skeleton, wrapt in a hermit's cowl.

"Angels of grace protect me!" cried Frederic, recoiling.

"Deserve their protection!" said the Spectre. Frederic, falling on his knees, adjured the phantom to take pity on him.

"Dost thou not remember me?" said the apparition. "Remember the wood of Joppa!"

"Art thou that holy hermit?" cried Frederic, trembling. "Can I do aught for thy eternal peace?"

"Wast thou delivered from bondage," said the spectre, "to pursue carnal delights? Hast thou forgotten the buried sabre, and the behest of Heaven engraven on it?"

"I have not, I have not," said Frederic; "but say, blest spirit, what is thy errand to me? What remains to be done?"

"To forget Matilda!" said the apparition; and vanished.

Frederic's blood froze in his veins. For some minutes he remained motionless. Then falling prostrate on his face before the altar, he besought the intercession of every saint for pardon. A flood of tears succeeded to this transport; and the image of the beauteous Matilda rushing in spite of him on his thoughts, he lay on the ground in a conflict of penitence and passion. Ere he could recover from this agony of his spirits, the Princess Hippolita with a taper in her hand entered the oratory alone. Seeing a man without motion on the floor, she gave a shriek, concluding him dead. Her fright brought Frederic to himself. Rising suddenly, his face bedewed with tears, he would have rushed from her presence; but Hippolita stopping him, conjured him in the most plaintive accents to explain the cause of his disorder, and by what strange chance she had found him there in that posture.

"Ah, virtuous Princess!" said the Marquis, penetrated with grief, and stopped.

"For the love of Heaven, my Lord," said Hippolita, "disclose the cause of this transport! What mean these doleful sounds, this alarming exclamation on my name? What woes has heaven still in store for the wretched Hippolita? Yet silent! By every pitying angel, I adjure thee, noble Prince," continued she, falling at his feet, "to disclose the purport of what lies at thy heart. I see thou feelest for me; thou feelest the sharp pangs that thou inflictest—speak, for pity! Does aught thou knowest concern my child?"

"I cannot speak," cried Frederic, bursting from her. "Oh, Matilda!"

Quitting the Princess thus abruptly, he hastened to his own apartment. At the door of it he was accosted by Manfred, who flushed by wine and love had come to seek him, and to propose to waste some hours of the night in music and revelling. Frederic, offended at an invitation so dissonant from the mood of his soul, pushed him rudely aside, and entering his chamber, flung the door intemperately against Manfred, and bolted it inwards. The haughty Prince, enraged at this unaccountable behaviour, withdrew in a frame of mind capable of the most fatal excesses. As he crossed the court, he was met by the domestic whom he had planted at the convent as a spy on Jerome and Theodore. This man, almost breathless with the haste he had made, informed his Lord that Theodore, and some lady from the castle were, at that instant, in private conference at the tomb of Alfonso in St. Nicholas's church. He had dogged Theodore thither, but the gloominess of the night had prevented his discovering who the woman was.

Manfred, whose spirits were inflamed, and whom Isabella had driven from her on his urging his passion with too little reserve, did not doubt but the inquietude she had expressed had been occasioned by her impatience to meet Theodore. Provoked by this conjecture, and enraged at her father, he hastened secretly to the great church. Gliding softly between the aisles, and guided by an imperfect gleam of moonshine that shone faintly through the illuminated windows, he stole towards the tomb of Alfonso, to which he was directed by indistinct whispers of the persons he sought. The first sounds he could distinguish were—

"Does it, alas! depend on me? Manfred will never permit our union."

"No, this shall prevent it!" cried the tyrant, drawing his dagger, and plunging it over her shoulder into the bosom of the person that spoke.

"Ah, me, I am slain!" cried Matilda, sinking. "Good heaven, receive my soul!"

"Savage, inhuman monster, what hast thou done!" cried Theodore, rushing on him, and wrenching his dagger from him.

"Stop, stop thy impious hand!" cried Matilda; "it is my father!"

Manfred, waking as from a trance, beat his breast, twisted his hands in his locks, and endeavoured to recover his dagger from Theodore to despatch himself. Theodore, scarce less distracted, and only mastering the transports of his grief to assist Matilda, had now by his cries drawn some of the monks to his aid. While part of them endeavoured, in concert with the afflicted Theodore, to stop the blood of the dying Princess, the rest prevented Manfred from laying violent hands on himself.

Matilda, resigning herself patiently to her fate, acknowledged with looks of grateful love the zeal of Theodore. Yet oft as her faintness would permit her speech its way, she begged the assistants to comfort her father. Jerome, by this time, had learnt the fatal news, and reached the church. His looks seemed to reproach Theodore, but turning to Manfred, he said,

"Now, tyrant! behold the completion of woe fulfilled on thy impious and devoted head! The blood of Alfonso cried to heaven for vengeance; and heaven has permitted its altar to be polluted by assassination, that thou mightest shed thy own blood at the foot of that Prince's sepulchre!"

"Cruel man!" cried Matilda, "to aggravate the woes of a parent; may heaven bless my father, and forgive him as I do! My Lord, my gracious Sire, dost thou forgive thy child? Indeed, I came not hither to meet Theodore. I found him praying at this tomb, whither my mother sent me to intercede for thee, for her—dearest father, bless your child, and say you forgive her."

"Forgive thee! Murderous monster!" cried Manfred, "can assassins forgive? I took thee for Isabella; but heaven directed my bloody hand to the heart of my child. Oh, Matilda!—I cannot utter it—canst thou forgive the blindness of my rage?"

"I can, I do; and may heaven confirm it!" said Matilda; "but while I have life to ask it—oh! my mother! what will she feel? Will you comfort her, my Lord? Will you not put her away? Indeed she loves you! Oh, I am faint! bear me to the castle. Can I live to have her close my eyes?"

Theodore and the monks besought her earnestly to suffer herself to be borne into the convent; but her instances were so pressing to be carried to the castle, that placing her on a litter, they conveyed her thither as she requested. Theodore, supporting her head with his arm, and hanging over her in an agony of despairing love, still endeavoured to inspire her with hopes of life. Jerome, on the other side, comforted her with discourses of heaven, and holding a crucifix before her, which she bathed with innocent tears, prepared her for her passage to immortality. Manfred, plunged in the deepest affliction, followed the litter in despair.

Ere they reached the castle, Hippolita, informed of the dreadful catastrophe, had flown to meet her murdered child; but when she saw the afflicted procession, the mightiness of her grief deprived her of her senses, and she fell lifeless to the earth in a swoon. Isabella and Frederic, who attended her, were overwhelmed in almost equal sorrow. Matilda alone seemed insensible to her own situation: every thought was lost in tenderness for her mother.

Ordering the litter to stop, as soon as Hippolita was brought to herself, she asked for her father. He approached, unable to speak. Matilda, seizing his hand and her mother's, locked them in her own, and then clasped them to her heart. Manfred could not support this act of pathetic piety. He dashed himself on the ground, and cursed the day he was born. Isabella, apprehensive that these struggles of passion were more than Matilda could support, took upon herself to order Manfred to be borne to his apartment, while she caused Matilda to be conveyed to the nearest chamber. Hippolita, scarce more alive than her daughter, was regardless of everything but her; but when the tender Isabella's care would have likewise removed her, while the surgeons examined Matilda's wound, she cried,

"Remove me! never, never! I lived but in her, and will expire with her."

Matilda raised her eyes at her mother's voice, but closed them again without speaking. Her sinking pulse and the damp coldness of her hand soon dispelled all hopes of recovery. Theodore followed the surgeons into the outer chamber, and heard them pronounce the fatal sentence with a transport equal to frenzy.

"Since she cannot live mine," cried he, "at least she shall be mine in death! Father! Jerome! will you not join our hands?" cried he to the Friar, who, with the Marquis, had accompanied the surgeons.

"What means thy distracted rashness?" said Jerome. "Is this an hour for marriage?"

"It is, it is," cried Theodore. "Alas! there is no other!"

"Young man, thou art too unadvised," said Frederic. "Dost thou think we are to listen to thy fond transports in this hour of fate? What pretensions hast thou to the Princess?"

"Those of a Prince," said Theodore; "of the sovereign of Otranto. This reverend man, my father, has informed me who I am."

"Thou ravest," said the Marquis. "There is no Prince of Otranto but myself, now Manfred, by murder, by sacrilegious murder, has forfeited all pretensions."

"My Lord," said Jerome, assuming an air of command, "he tells you true. It was not my purpose the secret should have been divulged so soon, but fate presses onward to its work. What his hot-headed passion has revealed, my tongue confirms. Know, Prince, that when Alfonso set sail for the Holy Land—"

"Is this a season for explanations?" cried Theodore. "Father, come and unite me to the Princess; she shall be mine! In every other thing I will dutifully obey you. My life! my adored Matilda!" continued Theodore, rushing back into the inner chamber, "will you not be mine? Will you not bless your—"

Isabella made signs to him to be silent, apprehending the Princess was near her end.

"What, is she dead?" cried Theodore; "is it possible!"

The violence of his exclamations brought Matilda to herself. Lifting up her eyes, she looked round for her mother.

"Life of my soul, I am here!" cried Hippolita; "think not I will quit thee!"

"Oh! you are too good," said Matilda. "But weep not for me, my mother! I am going where sorrow never dwells—Isabella, thou hast loved me; wouldst thou not supply my fondness to this dear, dear woman? Indeed I am faint!"

"Oh! my child! my child!" said Hippolita in a flood of tears, "can I not withhold thee a moment?"

"It will not be," said Matilda; "commend me to heaven—Where is my father? forgive him, dearest mother—forgive him my death; it was an error. Oh! I had forgotten—dearest mother, I vowed never to see

Theodore more—perhaps that has drawn down this calamity—but it was not intentional—can you pardon me?"

"Oh! wound not my agonising soul!" said Hippolita; "thou never couldst offend me—Alas! she faints! help! help!"

"I would say something more," said Matilda, struggling, "but it cannot be—Isabella—Theodore—for my sake—Oh!—" she expired.

Isabella and her women tore Hippolita from the corse; but Theodore threatened destruction to all who attempted to remove him from it. He printed a thousand kisses on her clay-cold hands, and uttered every expression that despairing love could dictate.

Isabella, in the meantime, was accompanying the afflicted Hippolita to her apartment; but, in the middle of the court, they were met by Manfred, who, distracted with his own thoughts, and anxious once more to behold his daughter, was advancing to the chamber where she lay. As the moon was now at its height, he read in the countenances of this unhappy company the event he dreaded.

"What! is she dead?" cried he in wild confusion. A clap of thunder at that instant shook the castle to its foundations; the earth rocked, and the clank of more than mortal armour was heard behind. Frederic and Jerome thought the last day was at hand. The latter, forcing Theodore along with them, rushed into the court. The moment Theodore appeared, the walls of the castle behind Manfred were thrown down with a mighty force, and the form of Alfonso, dilated to an immense magnitude, appeared in the centre of the ruins.

"Behold in Theodore the true heir of Alfonso!" said the vision: And having pronounced those words, accompanied by a clap of thunder, it ascended solemnly towards heaven, where the clouds parting asunder, the form of St. Nicholas was seen, and receiving Alfonso's shade, they were soon wrapt from mortal eyes in a blaze of glory.

The beholders fell prostrate on their faces, acknowledging the divine will. The first that broke silence was Hippolita.

"My Lord," said she to the desponding Manfred, "behold the vanity of human greatness! Conrad is gone! Matilda is no more! In Theodore we view the true Prince of Otranto. By what miracle he is so I know not—suffice it to us, our doom is pronounced! shall we not, can we but dedicate the few deplorable hours we have to live, in deprecating the further wrath of heaven? heaven ejects us—whither can we fly, but to yon holy cells that yet offer us a retreat."

"Thou guiltless but unhappy woman! unhappy by my crimes!" replied Manfred, "my heart at last is open to thy devout admonitions. Oh! could—but it cannot be—ye are lost in wonder—let me at last do justice on myself! To heap shame on my own head is all the satisfaction I have left to offer to offended heaven. My story has drawn down these judgments: Let my confession atone—but, ah! what can atone for usurpation and a murdered child? a child murdered in a consecrated place? List, sirs, and may this bloody record be a warning to future tyrants!"

"Alfonso, ye all know, died in the Holy Land—ye would interrupt me; ye would say he came not fairly to his end—it is most true—why else this bitter cup which Manfred must drink to the dregs. Ricardo, my grandfather, was his chamberlain—I would draw a veil over my ancestor's crimes—but it is in vain! Alfonso died by poison. A fictitious will declared Ricardo his heir. His crimes pursued him—yet he lost no Conrad, no Matilda! I pay the price of usurpation for all! A storm overtook him. Haunted by his guilt he vowed to St. Nicholas to found a church and two convents, if he lived to reach Otranto. The sacrifice was accepted: the saint appeared to him in a dream, and promised that Ricardo's posterity should reign in Otranto until the rightful owner should be grown too large to inhabit the castle, and as long as issue male from Ricardo's loins should remain to enjoy it—alas! alas! nor male nor female, except myself, remains of all his wretched race! I have done—the woes of these three days speak the rest. How this young man can be Alfonso's heir I know not—yet I do not doubt it. His are these dominions; I resign them—yet I knew not Alfonso had an heir—I question not the will of heaven—poverty and prayer must fill up the woeful space, until Manfred shall be summoned to Ricardo."

"What remains is my part to declare," said Jerome. "When Alfonso set sail for the Holy Land he was driven by a storm to the coast of Sicily. The other vessel, which bore Ricardo and his train, as your Lordship must have heard, was separated from him."

"It is most true," said Manfred; "and the title you give me is more than an outcast can claim—well! be it so—proceed."

Jerome blushed, and continued. "For three months Lord Alfonso was wind-bound in Sicily. There he became enamoured of a fair virgin named

Victoria. He was too pious to tempt her to forbidden pleasures. They were married. Yet deeming this amour incongruous with the holy vow of arms by which he was bound, he determined to conceal their nuptials until his return from the Crusade, when he purposed to seek and acknowledge her for his lawful wife. He left her pregnant. During his absence she was delivered of a daughter. But scarce had she felt a mother's pangs ere she heard the fatal rumour of her Lord's death, and the succession of Ricardo. What could a friendless, helpless woman do? Would her testimony avail?—yet, my lord, I have an authentic writing—"

"It needs not," said Manfred; "the horrors of these days, the vision we have but now seen, all corroborate thy evidence beyond a thousand parchments. Matilda's death and my expulsion—"

"Be composed, my Lord," said Hippolita; "this holy man did not mean to recall your griefs." Jerome proceeded.

"I shall not dwell on what is needless. The daughter of which Victoria was delivered, was at her maturity bestowed in marriage on me. Victoria died; and the secret remained locked in my breast. Theodore's narrative has told the rest."

The Friar ceased. The disconsolate company retired to the remaining part of the castle. In the morning Manfred signed his abdication of the principality, with the approbation of Hippolita, and each took on them the habit of religion in the neighbouring convents. Frederic offered his daughter to the new Prince, which Hippolita's tenderness for Isabella concurred to promote. But Theodore's grief was too fresh to admit the thought of another love; and it was not until after frequent discourses with Isabella of his dear Matilda, that he was persuaded he could know no happiness but in the society of one with whom he could for ever indulge the melancholy that had taken possession of his soul.

The End

REREAD

"THE BODY SNATCHER" BY ROBERT LOUIS STEVENSON, 1884

ROBERT LOUIS STEVENSON'S REPUTATION IS BUILT SOLIDLY ON THREE MASTER-pieces - "Treasure Island," "Strange Case of Dr Jekyll and Mr Hyde," and "Kidnapped," - but that is not the extent of his mastery. Take, for example, his wonderful poetry collection "A Child's Garden of Verses," or the brilliant short story we're discussing here, "The Body Snatcher." They're also masterpieces of their respective genres.

Stevenson was a fascinating person (if you want to know more about him, I suggest reading the recently published biography "A Wilder Shore: The Romantic Odyssey of Fanny and Robert Louis Stevenson") who wrote many fascinating stories, and "The Body Snatcher" is one of his most unforgettable.

Without giving too much away, it's about, well, body snatching. And not in the alien sense. To be clear, this has nothing to do with "Invasion of the Body Snatchers." It's about procuring dead bodies for use in a medical school.

Told in a frame story style where the main tale is related by someone in the introduction - a la "The Princess Bride" or "Frankenstein" or "The Turn of the Screw" - the narrative introduces us to a man named Fettes, who when he encounters an old acquaintance, Dr. Wolfe Macfarlane, begins acting bizarrely. The main story then tells us what happened between the two years ago that caused Fettes to act in such a manner.

The framing device is done very well, as at the conclusion of my reading, I immediately returned to the beginning to reread some key passages.

Overall the book holds up very well for modern audiences. Stevenson has an obvious "old-timey" style - think Poe or Shelley - but all of his works are readable. And if you're like me, you rather enjoy this type of writing. Too, because "The Body Snatcher" is a short story, even if you dislike the style, you'll be done reading the tale before you know it.

Also because it's short, the story doesn't have an extensive plot. I'm writing this before watching the movie, and I don't see how a feature film could be made out of this without some fairly extensive elaborations and additions. (See Rewatch for what I thought after watching it.)

I won't spoil the ending, but it's one of the more memorable endings in literature, and it's fun to discuss it with people who also have read the work.

Again, "The Body Snatcher" is not long enough to be a standalone book, so if you're inspired to read it after this review, look for it in collections of his works; the story often will be paired with "Dr. Jekyll and Mr. Hyde," which is a huge bonus!

Also of note, I came across a graphic novel adaptation of this while researching the story. I haven't read that version yet, but I can imagine "The Body Snatcher" makes a good graphic novel. If you're interested in looking it up, it's called "Body-snatcher" by Vincent Goodwin (adapter) and Rod Espinosa (illustrator).

REWATCH
"THE BODY SNATCHER" DIRECTED BY ROBERT WISE, 1945

IN MY LATE TEENS AND EARLY TWENTIES, I became obsessed with horror stories. Books, TV shows, movies - I loved them all. And I religiously read the horror bible of the time, Fangoria. While I consumed scores of movies I discovered in the magazine, somehow I missed out on "The Body Snatcher."

I'm sorry I did, because it is an exceptionally strong entry in the early horror movie genre.

Directed by Robert Wise and starring legends Boris Karloff and Bela Lugosi,

as well as Henry Daniell, Russell Wade, and Edith Atwater, "The Body Snatcher" does indeed expand on Robert Louis Stevenson's story, as I surmised in Reread.

And as often is NOT the case, the film's changes improve the source material a great deal, and the movie is even better than the book. The film, adapted by Philip MacDonald, keeps the bones of the Stevenson tale intact, but adds more depth and adds a great deal in the character development department, too.

The movie does away with the frame story, which would serve no real purpose in this depiction, and adds a storyline about a paralyzed little girl. There are other changes as well, minor and major, and Stevenson's story is fleshed out to become a short but feels-just-right 78-minute picture.

Sometimes older films - even ones from thirty years ago - can be quite cheesy at points as compared to modern movies, but "The Body Snatcher" skirts that entirely. There's nothing in here that made me groan or laugh. I did get a little annoyed at the amount of the street singer's screen time, but that was remedied in a darkly satisfying manner.

Karloff as Cabman John Gray is suitably creepy and steals the show, despite Henry Daniell being the main character in the film. Lugosi is great in his role, too, and suitably, in their final movie together, the two conduct a fight to the death.

The film ending is almost the same as the book's, but it is more dramatic and arguably better. Both are excellent, though.

Though the digital age might have damaged the popularity of magazines such as Fangoria (which thankfully still exists after a brief death about eight years ago), it is good for being able to find old movies such as "The Body Snatcher." I found it on Amazon Prime and YouTube, and it exists in Blu-Ray/DVD form as well. My library system even has a copy of it in the "Val Lewton Horror Collection."

I highly recommend this film, and I would love to know if you also preferred the movie to the short story. Email us and let us know your thoughts!

-Michael Toeset

An Original Story:

A MILLENNIAL NOËL. IN PROSE. BEING A SPECULATIVELY FICTITIOUS CAROL OF CHRISTMAS

by Ashley K. Frantik

STAVE I

ELZÉAR'S GHOST

Day had yet to break as the lone spacefarer wandered the desolate private platform at the Cañaveral International Cosmodrome and Spaceport. The cold light of dawn was beginning to coax shadows from the metal framework of the launch towers across the concrete expanse; their skeletal appearance reminiscent of the bones of once-grand celestial explorers whose souls still lingered, watching as this new adventurer prepared to take his turn among the stars. He paced aimlessly, trying to escape the chill of the coldest part of the morning that settled upon him like an uncomfortable second skin. He could do nothing else at the moment, since the preparations underway were beyond his ability, and the timing of the launch was beyond his control.

Lorne had been dumped, there was no doubt about that. He had replayed the indicative voicemail far too many times over the past twenty-four hours, as if hearing it again would reveal a loophole he could exploit to rewrite the outcome. He should have seen it coming. His now ex-fiancée had recorded several international hits in multiple languages, comprised of not-so-subtle metaphors about how lonely and unfulfilled she felt on a daily basis. Lorne only spoke one language, and never listened to MiЯka's music. He didn't really see all that much of her, either before or since his elaborate proposal at that haute couture, red-carpet event. He had never been prone to romance, and was not overly invested in starting now, but a high-profile marriage seemed like the kind of thing to do. The next step in his personal development, something to boost his social capital. She had been so enthusiastically committed to the spectacle that he failed to consider that he might have to put in a more nuanced effort to keep her in his life. He didn't care much for relationships, or anything else really, however his holiday plans had depended on her support. Or rather, her physical presence and the media attention that an internationally adored figure such as she effortlessly generated. He now found himself alone, impatiently awaiting his launch window, not because his mission demanded it but because but because MiЯka had chosen to be somewhere other than at his side.

The spaceman-to-be was not a spectacular leader, or a big ideas kind of fellow. He was not a pioneer of thought, nor a brilliant inventor. He had no real friendships or relatives, and while his decisions often made a significant impact on both local consumers and global communities, none of them were exceptionally innovative or universally beloved. What he did have was a whole lot of money.

Lornal Harlon Elzéar was a billionaire. Like all billionaires in those days, he owned a massive corporate empire that did not contribute anything particularly beneficial to society. And, like all billionaires in those days, he was going to space. It had become fashionable for the supremely wealthy to take to the stars, where the majesty of the universe reset their corrupted priorities. The Overview Effect—that magical cognitive shift that astronauts experienced upon seeing Earth—granted them a newfound sense of global unity, humility, and interconnectedness. Allegedly. In the early days, there were executives and socialites who scripted their epiphanies to conveniently support their next business venture, but their words would later be revealed as laughably performative self-promotion; once commercial spacecraft reached orbit, undeniably transformative testimony began to return with the reformed to Earth.

Elzéar had scheduled his cosmological revelation to occur on Christmas Day. He would broadcast his newfound cognisance live, to inspire his fellow citizens in their terrestrial new year. To celebrate his efforts, every American employee of his various companies had been given the day off, with pay, to contemplate his transcendence and the new reflections he would impart upon the spirit of the season. It was cheaper than paying the legally mandated overtime, and Lorne Elzéar was generous like that.

MiЯka had been a critical part of his carefully coordinated pageant. Unlike Lorne, she had a flawless public presence and a reliable, fanatical following. Her popularity as an eclectically eccentric musical artist ensured that his voyage would attract much needed attention, as public interest in private commercial spaceflight was waning from its already feeble regard. She was never going to join him in orbit, but accompanying him to greet the press would make the event more sensational, and her reluctance to leave the troposphere might reflect something resembling bravery or skill onto Lorne.

He tapped around on the screen of his mobile until sufficient funds had been transferred to ensure MiЯka's congenial presence at the launch. She accepted the proposition more readily than he had anticipated, considering she broke off their engagement because she valued her spiritual immateriality over his mindless superficiality. Or something like that. Lorne hadn't really been following. In any case, she agreed to show up, be radiant, and say affirming things for the cameras in exchange for an indecent amount of money.

The launch team had begun to arrive, preparing to fuel the rocket that would begin Elzéar's journey, and ultimate transformation into a sage and admired citizen of humanity. He crossed the launch complex, looking up at the gargantuan propulsion system atop which his comparatively miniscule spacecraft was perched. The physical and conceptual scale of the resources required to put him into orbit might have seemed wasteful or humbling to a more impressionable man. Lorne Elzéar never felt small. He had sufficient assets to make whole nations do whatever was convenient for him; could bankroll an entire land war, if that was what it took to maintain market dominance. Lorne Elzéar was a powerful man. He would remind the world of that today, on one of the few holidays people still seemed to care to celebrate. People didn't take time for themselves anymore. Lorne Elzéar did. He couldn't wait to showcase his earthly success, augmented with his cosmic wisdom that he would earn by reaching low-earth orbit.

The ISS Excelsior had been developed, built, and tested by the astronautics division of LZR Holdings, a conglomerate of seemingly unrelated companies spread out amongst diverse industries. Resource extraction and development, e-commerce, capital intensive manufacturing, and a recently acquired video streaming service were among the most significant in its infinite portfolio. The Excelsior capsule was an automated spacecraft for one, designed to facilitate an intimate and personal revolutionary tour of Earth. Despite dozens of private citizens, including several billionaires, having already reached the appropriate zenith to have their psyches enriched with orbital perspective, Elzéar would be the first to travel in solitude to the Overview Effect. He would market his craft as a more profound setting for astronautic transcendence than being in the conventional shuttle with miscellaneous others. He alone would face the universe, unencumbered by the distractions of human companionship. It wasn't that he disliked people, exactly. He just didn't see the point of them most of the time.

He zipped up his highly decorated flight suit. Nothing about the outfit was necessary. The Excelsior was entirely self-contained and had been constructed to protect its occupant from whatever elements, or lack thereof, might threaten his comfort. The badges and trims had been designed to resemble the official merits issued by ISERRA, the former International Space Exploration, Research, and Regulation Alliance, from a distance, but not so much that he could be accused of forgery should someone get close.

The orbiter had been to space before, but Lorne would be her first human passenger. He preferred to do test runs with lesser vertebrates who demanded fewer rights, compensation, and safety considerations than professional rocketeers. Such beings also lacked the verbal proficiency to usurp from Lorne the attention and praise that came with being the first to accomplish something. However, upon boarding the vessel, and until he revealed his greatest achievement to the world, his role would be entirely passive. The orbiter's systems were not fully autonomous, despite what the marketing claimed, but all the functions that required manual input could be controlled remotely by the ground crew. What was important was that a passenger could take in all the wonder of the universe without the rigorous efforts and specialized competencies required of the cosmonauts, engineers, and technicians who had laid the foundation for this space age of exploration. Lorne didn't need to know anything about piloting a spacecraft. All he needed to do was sit back and let the rocket carry him to enlightenment.

Up Lorne went, ascending the stairs to take his place among the stars. Before ISERRA had been dismantled, amateur space travellers were timed to ensure that they could climb all seven flights to their spacecraft in ninety seconds or less, a demonstration of having the minimum fitness required to traverse the atmosphere. It was a technicality which was even less relevant to Elzéar's autopilot mission than those who had come before him. Clanging up the endless metal-grate steps, he was grateful that there was no longer anyone to monitor his progress. To confirm or deny his capabilities.

Of course, Lorne Elzéar did not need to stop to catch his breath before strolling onto the platform, to give his regards before his life-changing mission, but he paused nonetheless. The gathered press was as sparse as he had expected, yet less than he had hoped. Still, there were cameras and correspondents, scrolling on various cellular instruments that could be used to convey excitement. Could produce stories and images and quotes to be edited, shuffled and shared, until they were interpreted as global envy, awe, and adoration. The event staff had set an unobtrusive stage near a gleaming silver bell where Lorne would announce his departure and bid farewell to mediocrity. Nobody seemed to notice that was where they should be looking. Not yet.

An incredibly familiar song jolted the restless newshounds to life. They scrambled out of flimsy folding chairs to snap photos and document the grand entrance that was unfolding. Accompanied by LZR Holdings' Director of Astronaut and Orbital Sales, MiЯka emerged from the opposite end of the platform from where Lorne was stalling. Thanks to social media, it was common knowledge that the four-time Grammy award winner with three diamond albums to her name, had cancelled her upcoming wedding to the wealthiest man in America. No one had expected her to be there.

Everything about MiЯka was sensational. She looked like no one else on the planet and was a constant performance wherever she went. Her true colour, name, shape, and size was a carefully cultivated mystery. Today, her sparkling celestial cosmetics were more of a kabuki mask than makeup, and her midnight blue hair, striped with white, pink, and green, was more sculpture than coiffure. Her clothing was surreal, counterintuitive, and fascinating. She made her entrance; a starry feathered overcoat billowed in the cold, pre-dawn breeze to expose a tight reflective dress and a priapic space rocket resembling Lorne's own, strapped between her hips. The top-heavy nature and unlikely angles of her theatrical attire suggested that movement would be an obstacle, but MiЯka floated between the cables and lighting with the otherworldly grace of a berezka dancer.

A wave of panic struck Lorne as they locked eyes, and she began to glide toward him. For a second, he forgot that he had arranged this entire affair; had both invited and paid the pop star to be here, until she smiled brilliantly and took his arm. She appeared delighted to play her part and the press eagerly followed their procession.

Bolstered by the self-assurance that an elegant muse imparts upon one who fancies himself a ground-breaking explorer, Elzéar prepared to address those assembled and, more importantly, their recording devices. He momentarily dithered when MiЯka stepped back, but took the wheel from her evocative presence, with the notecards that his publicist had prepared for the occasion.

"Ladies and gentlemen of the press; people of Earth. Internationally acclaimed singer, songwriter, composer, record producer, auteur, and my dear, dear friend MiЯka and I are humbled that you have chosen to join us for the launch of our Millennial Noël." MiЯka charmed the spectators into committing to the speech, and applauding appropriately, by waving to her admirers and clapping as well.

"Today, the latest Overview Orbiter, developed by LZR's aerospace team, will allow me to join in what only God, the dedicated and brave professionals who ushered our planet into this glorious astronomical age, and a very few private citizens have shared. On this momentous holiday mission, I will become a better passenger on our Spaceship Earth through the gift that is known as the Overview Effect."

Lorne strode to the naval-style bell parked en route to the entry hatch of the ISS Excelsior. It clanged abrasively as he rang it with the vigour he deemed necessary to lend sufficient gravitas to his superfluous mission.

"In the nautical tradition," he continued, "a ship's bell is rung when her captain arrives or departs. This powerful and tangible reminder of the history, heritage, and accomplishment of navigation and discovery, was also used to signal the presence of important persons." With a forced and awkwardly demure gesture, he addressed his followers and their cameras.

"Really, I have to thank every one of my employees, every American, my customers all over the world; all of you have paid for this. This cosmic existential endeavour will be transformative for all of us, for the planet. The Earth, it's fragile, it has no borders, and it is in crisis. There are no solutions here; we must find them by going beyond." He smiled and, for emphasis, enthusiastically rang the bell eight more obnoxious times, for one last photo opportunity, before boarding the Excelsior.

A European accent of dubious origins interrupted the modest fanfare of Elzéar taking his leave. Contrary to the conditions that Lorne had included in their informal contract, MiЯka had taken the stage from the podium he had abandoned.

"Today we witness another slave to material wealth searching the cold void of space for human emotional connection," it was hard to detect much expression in MiЯka's heavily made-up face, but she produced an appropriately disdainful sound. "That is not something to find out there, it is a thing you create for yourself, here, in this world of ours."

Elzéar's conviction faltered. He had not expected her to address the public. Without MiЯka by his side, he was no longer the focus of the occasion. Attending bloggers and columnists directed their resources from his departure to the more marketable display.

"Some cannot see that love and beauty are not things that happen to you," MiЯka melodically dunked on Lorne's unimaginative quest, "they are what you make; they are what you share. You cannot gain them by flying to the moon. There is no such quick resolution, no shortcut to enlightenment."

Lorne hadn't taken MiЯka's provocative ensemble seriously enough to really examine her appearance until now. Without the congenial demeanor she had been directing toward him, she looked a lot more formidable than he remembered and she now appeared threatening. Abandoned, he was helpless to do anything but stand there, while his farewell derailed dramatically before him.

"I now have the honour to present you with a superior launch." MiЯka removed the rocket from her waist and balanced it on the podium in front of her. "Not the launch of one who chases the simplistic answers of childhood dreams, but a more meaningful launch for humanity." With this declaration, dazzling projections overshadowed the LZR logos waving on flimsy banners, placed about the staging area in an attempt to provide colour to the event.

"I announce my Christmas gift to all the world, those I love. The past three months have been a trying time for my life. I stifled my creativity to force my soul into mundane domesticity." MiЯka pushed down on her model rocket and it opened itself to reveal an abstractly chromatic square, wrapped in plastic. "But now I have for you a new album." She spoke to her millions of unseen followers, "I sing to you of ideals, realities, and darkness. By no longer trying to please anyone, I can please everyone and free myself from the baggage that Lornal Elzéar absconds to outer space to escape."

Lorne was trapped between MiЯka, some rather absorbed journalists, and the orbiter he was to board. The hatch of the Excelsior was still closed, and he had never learned how it opened. It felt like a bad time to see if he could figure it out, or if he was even physically strong enough to try. He scanned the small crowd for his crew and saw no one able or willing to help him flee the scene.

MiЯka closed the gap between she and Elzéar and pressed her album into his hands. "So that you do not forget what you will be unable to resolve in the heavens from your failures on Earth."

Without an impressive reply or a tasteful exit to make, Lorne scanned the listings on the back of the album cover:

Elzéar's Ghost

1. I Know Him
2. Cashbox
3. Ask Me Who I Was
4. Невір'я «Incrédulité»
5. The Chains Forged in Life
6. Näkymätön
7. Chance of Hope
8. Hjemsøkt
9. I'd Rather Not
10. Shun the Path I Tread

11. When the Bell Tolls

12. Space Won't Set You Free (and You Will Die Alone)

When he looked up, MiЯka had already left and was noiselessly descending the stairs, pursued by reporters clamouring for an exclusive quotation. Any interest spared for Lorne Elzéar had evaporated.

IN AN ENDLESSLY ECHOING WINDOWLESS CAVERN THAT WAS TOO WHITE, UNDER rows of buzzing fluorescent tubes, Dwayne Banks did his job with more urgency than usual. He was accustomed to unreasonable timelines that led to unpaid overtime, but today, even that uninviting option wasn't on the table. It was Christmas, and if it wasn't enough that his workload had dramatically increased with the yuletide volume, the whole complex would be closed in an hour and would not reopen again until his employer had revealed his findings from a costly inspirational tour of the world. Dwayne would somehow have to finish up on time while simultaneously being at the company daycare to pick up his daughter, when they too shut down for the occasion. He was hoping Lindy's mother could get off the floor early so they wouldn't get charged for the kid staying extra, but he hadn't had the chance to text to see how things were going on her end. Their mandatory overnight shift would be coming to a close as Elzéar hurtled through the ionosphere. They planned to sleep through it, so they'd have the energy later to enjoy what remained of the day off, after listening to his semi-mandatory orbital well-wishes. Tuning in was ostensibly optional, but Elzéar had offered every one of his workers logged in a free lifetime subscription to his newly acquired streaming service. Dwayne didn't watch much; there was little original programming anymore. He and Gemma had planned to cancel their account, since the increasing fees were the one expense that they could eliminate to help balance their budget, but their daughter had discovered the reruns of an old children's show that they had grown up with, back when public broadcasting was free to anyone. It seemed unfair to leave her without it when they were around so little. Thirty years of archival footage on the value of friendship, sharing, and caring for each other and the world, for their little girl, seemed worth indulging a CEO's ego.

As it was, they were always living off money that they hadn't made yet. If it wasn't bad enough that they had to build their lives around jobs that only arguably covered their absolute basics, Lorne Elzéar had found a way to make a day off for Christmas more stressful than it should be. The overtime they were missing out on would have been worth far more than the supposed gift of a holiday; some rich man's revelation from the stars was not going to improve their lives in any material way.

STAVE II

A RECKONING OF CHRISTMAS PAST

To recover from his commandeered media event, Lorne had convinced himself that the reality-altering promise of the cosmos would fix everything. No one would judge him after his spiritual awakening, once he shared his illuminating insights with the entire world. Now, however, there was nothing for him to do but ruminate and fantasize.

He sat rigidly, strapped into the command module of his spacecraft. Without windows, or any of the capsule's instruments online yet, he had no way to know how much time had passed or when he could expect things to get interesting. Lorne did not particularly enjoy chatting, unless his ideas were being embraced and shared for public consumption. But since the crew had sealed the entrance to the orbiter above him, the lack of stimulation left him craving interaction. He looked up, which looked like everything else around him. Without any light generated by or penetrating the orbiter, he couldn't count the hull plates above him, even if he had wanted to. He was beginning to want to.

A phone buzzed in the front pocket of his flight suit. The launch team had told him to power down all his gadgets in preparation for lift-off, but he never took direction from anyone, and it could be hours before everything would be ready to go. He blindly fumbled it out to see what message he could be receiving at this hour on Christmas Day. The screen blinked on and flooded the capsule with harsh, HEV lighting and Lorne peered through the irradiating assault to see the memory on his personal feed that triggered the notification. A year ago, he had met the most beloved astronaut in history on live television, where he had also been introduced to MiЯka for the first time. Desperate to alleviate the tedium, Lorne tapped the icon to play the video. A transitional tune from a five-piece orchestra mitigated the seclusion of the grounded command module as it reverberated within the shadowy, claustrophobic chamber. Exaggerated cheers from a captive studio audience parasocially eased him from his solitary confinement.

An unwaveringly congenial emcee worked up the crowd for the next guest to be introduced to his chat-show sofa. He had already interviewed two celebrities, including the recent Eurovision winner and not-yet-to be engaged MiЯka. She unexpectedly complimented the retired parastronaut turned beloved children's program host Commander Chuck Baldwin, who was seated next to her. Baldwin had completed the first emergency spacewalk during which he was struck with his Overview Effect revelation. It inspired him to create *SpaceBuzz*, an internationally co-produced educational series which had been broadcast publicly every day for decades. Anderson White of *That Show, Tonight!* delighted his viewers by mashing together such diverse and talented personalities.

"Welcome back to our celestial, star-studded, Christmastical cosmological special! We've had international musical sensation MiЯka sing an astounding holiday rendition of her very first hit single, and our childhood space hero Chuck Baldwin brought some behind-the-scenes nostalgia for us to share. But enough of the past! Let's look to the future! Our next guest is inventor, entrepreneur, explorer and visionary… Please everyone, let's welcome Mr. Lornal Harlon Elzéar!!"

"Heeeyy!! Thank you, thank you!" Elzéar strode out from backstage, basking in the prompted enthusiasm that ushered him in. It only subsided when he found his place on Anderson's couch and the studio's LED applause signage had gone dark. He had not yet met the highly regarded individuals he now shared the stage with but was pleased to finally take his place among them. "Please, Anderson, call me Lorne," he flashed his best attempt at a genial smile. White clutched his chest in an animated display of infatuation and gratitude, drawing laughter from his audience. "No one calls me by my full name unless I'm in court."

White hopped on the line and elaborated, "have you been dragged into another class-action? Wow, you just can't catch a break, can you?"

"No, no that's all been settled," Lorne truthfully brushed aside Anderson's concern, "another misunderstanding. It happens all the time when you sit on the board of as many firms as I do. Makes it impossible to get the real work done sometimes." He turned to wink at MiЯka, hoping to convey that his discipline was comparable to hers, but she was reading the handmade signs that fans in the audience held up, expressing their undying love, admiration, and the odd marriage proposal. Her artificial beauty intrigued him. He was curious what was under all of her bold, colourful layers and if it was worth the stir that her mere presence consistently produced.

"Right, right. Looks like you've been working extra hard," Lorne laughed when White gestured to the full beard he began sporting recently to prove that he indeed could still grow hair. "You have something pretty ambitious on the go, I hear." The host coaxed Lorne's attention from MiЯka, in her festive and iridescent ensemble, and pressed him to reveal the project that was the entire point of his being there.

"That I am, Anderson," Elzéar stroked his newly iconic facial hair, playing it up for the popstar who was paying him no notice, engrossed in the displays prepared by her supporters. "I'm sorry I won't be able to make your next holiday special; I'm going to be hosting something of my own."

Anderson pouted comically. "Oh no! How can I compete? What kind of show are we talking here? Am I out of a job?"

"Well, it's more of a mission than a show," Lorne unraveled some plans from a tube he had brought with him. "My Excelsior solo orbiter is almost ready. I will be taking her up for an exclusive Overview Effect viewing on December 25th, next year." A masking screen lifted stage left from where White's guests were seated to reveal a full-scale mock-up of the Excelsior flanked by models wearing flashy and sexualized replicas of ISERRA's former dress uniforms. "LZR's Millennial Noël voyage will be the first Christmas broadcasting of an individual's Overview Effect transformation live to the world. Mine."

Their host whistled, "always thinking of the future, that's Lorne Elzéar, alright. It's a bit of a risk though, isn't it Lorne? ISERRA declared low-earth orbit past its critical density for space junk, suspended non-essential crewed spaceflight, discontinued the public space program. How is this mission going to be different?"

"Well now, Anderson," chided Lorne, "I've never been a coward. ISERRA was afraid of risk and too concerned with regulatory red tape. We are at a turning point in the history of astronautic development. Private industry is now able to build up what the public space sector has left neglected. Without their interference, we can explore more exciting human transportation with lower consumer costs. Early space travel chased dreams; we are chasing results." He tried to catch MiЯka's eye, but she was less interested in the market angle than his investors and was not paying attention.

"That's what I keep hearing," said White. "There's been quite a few commercial Overview spaceflights now that the market has opened up. You're going to be, what, the sixth billionaire to make the trip?"

Lorne's demeanor darkened." Something like that," he muttered. Elzéar was fairly bitter about being in such an insignificant placement. He hadn't been aware of how much advanced preparation went into such an endeavor and so, by the time he had heard that his rivals were blasting off in capsules of their own design, it was impossible that he could even be in the top five.

Commander Baldwin always knew when a fellow cadet needed cheering up. "Remember Lorne, it doesn't matter if you come in second, or third, or even sixth. I'm proud of you for finishing, and trying your best. That's what's most important; what we learn in our best efforts about ourselves."

Anyone who had ever tried their very best would always find comfort in the Commander's classic, genuine humility. However, unbeknownst to Baldwin, Lorne had put in very little work into his mission. Beyond demanding it and covering the costs, he hadn't really done anything. The *SpaceBuzz* credo had less impact on the billionaire than it did on the impressionable and sincere children who continued to take such words to heart.

"Yeah, I guess so. Sure." Lorne's confident chattiness had fizzled out now that things were no longer going exactly as he had planned. Anderson steered the conversation to a different guest, so that his audience would not perceive any skipped beats.

"Now MiЯka, I hear there's a track on your new album that was inspired by some of what Lorne's been up to. Can you tell us a bit about that?"

MiЯka artfully turned toward White. Every move she made, if captured by any quality of camera, was fit for the cover of most magazines still available in print. "Well, there was supposed to be, the studio wanted there to be, but I wasn't really able to make it work." MiЯka's command of the English language was pragmatic, and she failed to recognize that it might have been helpful to be politely disingenuous.

"Oh? Why is that? You don't usually give up once inspiration hits." He tried to steer the pop star to describing her mesmerizing and impressive artistic process.

MiЯka remained charming and erratically beautiful, but missed her cue, "well, that's just it, isn't it? Who can waste the time to start something that will not be revolutionary? You do not get a second chance to make an impact on the world; I have never found material wealth to be inspiring."

Lorne was looking at the floor and shuffling his feet, "well it didn't have to be about *money* per se…" He was always hostile to the idea that he had no talents beyond the accumulation of figurative piles of cash.

MiЯka was confused, "oh no, it's not that I was not able to write something meaningful about your fortune; poetry sings to me from every aspect in life. But when you paid the studio to have your song on my next album I —"

Lorne's eyes got wide, and he cut off what MiЯka was implying. "Anderson, it is such a privilege to be sharing the stage with these two. I am so deeply honoured that you invited me to be here."

MiЯka was struggling with an unfamiliar language, concerned she misunderstood the basis of the show they were recording. She was trying to be congenial. "But you wanted this, yes? This special show was your plan?"

Lorne's smile was pasted to his face. He had been caught. He cleared his throat and said pointedly, "I'm not sure what you mean."

"I am so sorry," MiЯka hurried to compensate for her lack of clarity. She blushed, although this was not visible beneath the impressively artistic makeup that she always wore publicly. "I am maybe not expressing this well. My agent, she had told me that was why you are here. Although you are not an entertainer, you own the network, you can be here. We're doing this for you, Mr. Elzéar, are we not? Is that not how this works? You purchase what you admire?"

Anderson was determinedly sorting his notecards, and the set was unnaturally quiet. Everyone but MiЯka was emphatically avoiding eye contact with Elzéar. "I am sorry, is this wrong?" She was uncomfortable with the shadow she had cast over the occasion. She reached over to squeeze Lorne's knee and smiled brightly to dispel the gloom, "what a treasure it is to be here with a man so capable of bringing us all together!" *That Show, Tonight!*'s applause sign illuminated, and sporadic clapping spattered across the awkward moment.

White took command of the show again, "that's right, thank you MiЯka! What a great time of year to bring us all together to celebrate! Why don't we take a quick break to hear from our sponsors? When we come back, Commander Chuck Baldwin has brought a few of his special friends from the *SpaceBuzz* crew to join in our festivities! Remember Quasar and Quark, everyone? Well, they certainly never forgot you…"

Elzéar's attention was mercifully wrenched from the screen by a shudder of motion as the instrument panels in the orbiter bleeped, buzzed, and sparked to life. A crackling voice that came through a speaker more retrospective than he was accustomed to, reminded him that he would soon be leaving the burdens of worldly humiliation and gravity behind.

"Good morning Excelsior; we are ready to launch. You got any last words? We are on standby for count-down."

Lorne powered down his phone as he recognized the prompt to quote *SpaceBuzz* for his mid-launch soundbite. Before reliving the embarrassment of last year's publicity stunt, it had seemed like a rather clever idea. Now, he just wanted to get going. He could see numbers on a timer near his knee flipping back toward zero. The module began to vibrate violently, summoning the velocity required to discharge him from Earth. He spoke directly into a receiver at his shoulder, to be sure that his remarks could be heard above the rattling.

"There is a hero in every one of you, right now on Spaceship Earth…" on the chance that someone was recording his statement for posterity, Elzéar had selected Chuck Baldwin's daily greeting to his viewers, "…but suit up, and reach for the stars!" His excitement grew as the convulsing capsule prepared to make its atmospheric departure, heroically repeating words that began to feel like his own. "Our adventure awaits!" Over the sound of the engines roaring in his ears, through the building momentum that was the beginning of his ascent, he triumphantly shouted, "blast-off, Space Cadets!"

Perhaps it was the thrill of living a boyhood dream. Perhaps it was the anticipation of shedding mortal restrictions to be re-born in space. More likely, it was his failure to partake in any of the recommended training for recreational space travel; as he accelerated through the atmosphere, the blood pressure dropped from his head, and Lorne Elzéar passed out.

STAVE III

A REVELATION OF CHRISTMAS PRESENT

Lorne awakened to an unfamiliar sense of buoyancy and the crackle of mission control addressing him through the command module's speaker system.

"Hello Excelsior, this is Cañaveral." Lorne was barely listening to the Millennial Noël's Capsule Communicator and Success Manager. The rigging that had prevented injury during his launch was especially distracting now that neither the straps nor his body were weighed down by the forces of Earth. "Congratulations, Mr. Elzéar, you have achieved stable orbit. We wish you a very illuminating Overview Effect." The congenial message was followed by a popping sound as Cañaveral severed its communication link.

Lorne had insisted that, contrary to conventional protocol, mission control would disconnect its comms with the Excelsior entirely so that there was no chance of anyone pestering him while underwent his transformation. Without ISERRA governing spaceflight, such things were merely recommendations rather than compulsory, and Lorne didn't like the idea of Cañaveral listening in during his intimate moment. They would re-establish contact in an hour, when he was a changed man, and ready to reveal his radically augmented astronomical perspective. He stopped fiddling with his harness to set a timer. He went to tap the biomonitor and computing device on his wrist, but weightlessness hindered Lorne's coordination, and his hand overshot the mark. He impatiently tried again and again, struggling more and failing harder.

His building frustrations simmered when he remembered that there were no witnesses to his struggle and that since he was in orbit, the LZR voice assist was online.

"Excelsior, set a timer for one hour." His wristwatch, a split-flap display in the command module, and a screen somewhere in the next compartment of the orbiter, displayed how much time remained before Elzéar would address the public. Unstrapping himself from his seat, he allowed microgravity to take over and donned an earpiece and microphone set. He connected them to a power pack he was wearing to facilitate the transmission of his words and vital signs back to ground control as he drifted toward the hatch of Excelsior's observation compartment. As ready as he could be for the final step in his Christmas transformation, Lorne found himself hesitating at the threshold between the service module and his impending breakthrough.

Doubt was somewhat foreign to Lorne Elzéar. Apart from MiЯka backing out from his marriage proposition and the occasional lack of universal adulation from the public, few things in his life worked out less than favourably for him. He was eager for the Overview Effect to bestow him with the sagacity that so many admired in his ex-fiancée. He briefly contemplated the prospect that she may again find him worthy to build a relationship with upon his return. However, given that his inspiring and influential worldview would be derived from an infinitely more sublime source than anything within her strictly Earthly experience, Lorne rationalized he would no longer need her to buttress his reputation. Like others who had ventured this far, he would no longer rely on siphoning prestige from more inspirational individuals. Once he returned to Earth with the profound insights of the Overview Effect, he wouldn't need her— or anyone else—to validate him. He suppressed a chuckle as he considered the general resentment of his low-level employees, and what his company would look like once he earned their approval and respect through this mission. It was all so possible, so close, so simple to win over the masses. His only regret was that he had not been able to achieve it sooner.

He pondered how to best prepare himself for the shock and wonder that was to hit him once he crossed over to look out. Light and infallible, without gravity shackling him, he could not fall. Lorne Elzéar was in control. He turned his back on the bulkhead, "ok, Excelsior, open the orbital hatch." He closed his eyes and pushed himself through to the other side.

The majority of the surface area in the Excelsior's observation deck was transparent, to give its occupant the feeling that he was swimming through space, untethered and at one with the cosmos. Drifting into the new area had already disoriented Lorne spatially, and he was unsure what he would see when he opened his eyes. He cracked them open the slightest bit to squint through his eyelashes, as if he was a boy hiding that he was really awake from his mother while spying on what she might be up to. This was enough for him to see that he was facing the wrong direction and so he swiveled about, only fully opening his eyes when the light of the world came into view. Facing the planet and everyone on it, he blinked at its luminosity and drew a breath. The time had come.

Elzéar stared at the bright, blue disk hanging on the black canvas of the universe through the cabin's bay windows, waiting. Waiting for the epiphany, for the cosmic revelation to strike him with the weight of a thousand insights. He glanced between the planet before him and the Excelsior's displays, alternating between the one on his wrist and the one overhead. He waited for the overwhelming surge of emotion that would affirm his decision to embark on this mission. Five minutes. Ten minutes. A quarter of an hour went by and yet nothing came.

Lorne Elzéar felt nothing.

That is, he felt nothing particularly profound as he watched white swirls of ice and water dance within the definite but invisible barrier between the unique abundance of life on the planet before him and the cold, dead space beyond. No awe. No deep connection to the world or the people below. He had always been somewhat detached from the world around him; took pride in that fact, even. Now, as far removed from society as he could possibly be, he felt a gnawing suspicion that something in this grand yuletide adventure had gone horribly wrong. In preparing for his cosmic epiphany, he had failed to anticipate that the Holy Grail that was to be the culmination of his investments might be unavailable to him. His heart palpitated, not due to any overwhelming metaphysical joy, but rather from the realization that his time to address the people of Earth was nigh, and he had nothing to say.

Lorne caught his reflection in the windows of the observation module, the ghostly watermark of a lone spacefarer hovering awkwardly over a shining circle containing all of humanity. His eyes locked with the fearful lost space cadet, 160 miles from home, with no idea what to do next. He pushed aside the existential dread creeping about the edge of his thoughts and forced his dry mouth to practice something to deliver when he was to reveal, so publicly, his findings in his imminent livestream.

"I—" Lorne croaked. He swallowed and tried again. "I have no words. There are no words." His frozen tongue stumbled over its monosyllabic declaration. "The Earth is fragile; it has no boundaries." His lips were tingling and his voice balked. Perhaps the anxiety could be presented as emotion. "There are... I can't... the water. The blue of the..." His improvised draft speech sputtered out as no metaphor came. Hurtling in orbit at 17,500 miles per hour, Lorne Elzéar began to lose it.

Uncomfortably aware of his breathing, he suddenly couldn't remember how to do it properly. Not being able to firmly anchor himself was not helping. He was icily cold, but also sweating. The capsule's environmental control system must have been failing. "Excelsior, what's the current temperature and oxygen at?" Lorne squeaked. Something was clearly off.

A stilted female voice from the uncanny valley announced that everything was as it should be. *"The ISS Excelsior's observation cabin's internal temperature, humidity, and air quality is set to the specified parameters pre-selected for the sole passenger of the Millennial Noël mission. There are now 20 minutes remaining until communication reconnection and broadcast uplink to Earth."* The last announcement was unprompted, but true. Elzéar's head felt heavy, and the room began to spin. Or was it Lorne himself that was spinning? The motion was nauseating and his heart, which had been fluttering moments ago, was now pounding. The Excelsior's monitors scrambled to keep up with his rising blood pressure and breathing rates and began beeping and buzzing frantically.

Static frizzled through Lorne's earpiece as mission control interrupted his literal and figurative spiral. "Sorry to disturb you, Mr. Elzéar, but we're seeing some concerning changes to your vitals, can you give us a status report?"

The concern in the CapCom's voice was more for the consequences of overriding a direct order from his billionaire CEO, than any specific care for his health or wellbeing. "Excelsior, this is Cañaveral. Do you read? Over."

Lorne no longer trusted himself to speak and the squeezing in his chest would have prevented it anyway.

"Come in, Excelsior. Are you there? Do you copy?"

An alert somewhere behind, above, or below him, was chirping urgently.

"Come in, Mr. Elzéar. Lorne? You there? Come in, man!"

All Lorne could hear was the beep-a-leep of warnings and alarms bouncing off of each other and echoing in his brain as he fought the urge to throw-up and fly into pieces.

IN A DIM APARTMENT THAT WAS NEVER THE RIGHT TEMPERATURE, AND ONLY conveniently located from a transit stop that never got anyone to where they wanted to go quickly enough, an overworked, underpaid, and exhausted Gemma Banks was trying to tune in to the most anticipated Christmas broadcast of the year. She didn't want to watch it, arguably no one did, but it was a simple way to get a free service in a world where everything cost more today than it did yesterday. To make sure that her family didn't miss out on a technicality, she had made sure their passwords were up to date and installed all the required add-ons. But every attempt she made to connect to the server generated an error message and a frustrated reflex to scrunch up her face and scream internally.

Her daughter Lindy had infinitely more positive energy. Not only did she get more sleep at her overnight daycare while her parents had been on shift, but she was further juiced up in her new Christmas jammies and some chocolates that had appeared for her in a stocking she had hung in her bedroom. "Momma, mummy, is it time to watch the thing yet?"

A yawn announced Dwayne's bleary entrance to their kitchen from his own post-shift sleep, still in a t-shirt and sweats.

"Daddy!" Lindy rushed his legs and almost knocked him over. Both of her parents were rarely off work at the same time, and certainly never for a holiday.

"Daddy, daddy. Daddy. It's Christmas and we're all together, it's just like the *movies*. And then we're gonna listen to the thing and then watch Chuck Baldwin and then mummy said we can have grilled cheese."

Dwayne picked Lindy up and shuffled over to Gemma,

"Is it time yet?"

"I don't think so," she was clicking around to see if she'd missed anything, "it's not supposed to be for five minutes. Maybe that's why I can't get in."

Lindy was getting antsy and pestering her overdrawn mother. Dwayne set her up with some *SpaceBuzz* until Elzéar's good tidings began.

Lindy giggled from in front of their television and her parents silently wished they could spend the rest of the day lost in nostalgia with her. They missed the vibrant and inspirational lessons of Commander Chuck's colourful crew. Lindy mimed through a song the Constellation Crustacean was leading, based on her favourite star formations, with more relatable morals than a billionaire CEO could wrench from the stars. Still, they went back to tinkering with the laptop. It was a minor concession to have Lindy have the happiness that such a simple program could provide.

Elzéar's concentration on suppressing the vomit that would have made his entire situation dramatically worse, allowed him to control his breathing to the point where the Excelsior's systems stopped screaming at him.

"Yeah, yeah, I'm here. Cool your tits." He swallowed hard and shook himself to regain control of his body. "You weren't supposed to call in, I was having a moment."

"Apologies, Mr. Elzéar. It's almost time. We are on standby for your scheduled address in five. Orbiter cams activated on your mark, Excelsior."

Lorne wasn't entirely sure what he looked like then, but it was surely worse than the reflection of the clueless space tourist he had seen earlier.

There was nothing he wanted to do less now than attempt a half-assed Christmas speech while looking like death. The mission was over; it was time to go home.

"Forget it, Cañaveral. This is stupid. Dunno why people make such a fuss. It's not so moving."

He thrust himself back into the decent module and shut the hatchway behind him. "Let's blow this popsicle stand," said Lorne, tearing off his headset and grappling for the seat of the orbiter to prepare for landing, "I'm done here."

The CapCom and Success Manager continued through the command module's speakers. "Excelsior, if you're not planning to give your Christmas greetings, we're going to have to wait before authorizing re-entry."

Lorne kicked the instrument panels around him hard, both in frustration and to force himself back into his seat to strap in. "No way, Cañaveral, I'm out. It's dark and boring and I'm finished. Activate the decent thingy; It's over." Lorne pulled out his phone to bring up some of the videos he had saved of his training session.

"I'm sorry, Excelsior, but if you attempt descent now, you will be on the wrong orbital path for landing. We must advise waiting—"

Lorne didn't wait. "Excelsior, activate onboard service module controls."

"Excelsior! Excelsior, Cañaveral does not recommend engaging the descent system at this time—"

But he was already flipping switches and pulling levers to initiate the Excelsior's automatic landing mechanism. "Forget it, Cañaveral, I'm pulling the plug. Lorne Elzéar is out of here." He stowed his mobile in the front pocket of his flight suit, clicked the buckles of his restraint belts into place, and leaned back while the orbiter hummed and shuttered and began to decline.

"Excelsior! Excelsior, you will be off course for retrieval. I repeat, Mr. Elzéar..."

STAVE IV

THE CHRISTMAS NOT YET TO COME

It was unsurprising that Elzéar disregarded the advice of mission control. Equally unsurprising was the rate at which things went awry. A warning bell, a blinking light, then three, then more, alerted him and Cañaveral to multiple critical issues as they emerged. For the first time in his life, the billionaire was personally facing the consequences of his impulsively poor decisions and experiencing the negative effects of disregarding protocol.

"Excelsior, there are some concerning readings regarding your positioning for re-entry, do you copy?"

Lorne wasn't sure if they were asking if he recognized what was happening, or if he was paying attention to what mission control was telling him, so he replied casually. "You don't say?"

"Excelsior, you have entered a precariously hazardous section of the Orbital Debris Belt. You are going to have to be incredibly precise in your manual manoeuvring to avoid a high volume of collision threats in your path. Do you copy?" Cañaveral asked again.

Elzéar blanched and remained uncertain as to what exactly those on the ground were asking of him. "Manual manoeuvring?" He had been under the impression that the most perilous components of the mission would be taken care of by someone else, "is that so, Cañaveral?"

"Apologies Mr. Elzéar, but we're going to have to pick up the pace here, the timing is critical, and you're gathering speed." Some jittering instruments in front Excelsior's ill-equipped pilot that may have been measuring acceleration were already pushed to their red zones, pointers slamming against the demarcation of their meters.

A jarring *whack* rattled the Excelsior and Lorne's brain, but he still made out an impulsive curse from the Success Manager. A siren began to blare, and the orbiter shook with the impact of something striking it again from another angle. More alarms sounded, one after another, building up to a cacophonic symphony for Lorne's return to Earth. He was starting to worry.

GEMMA BANKS WAS ALSO BEGINNING TO WORRY. IT WAS NOW 8 MINUTES PAST the scheduled broadcast, and she still wasn't able to get into the livestream. She had done a hard reset on every piece of hardware she thought relevant, updated every bit of software to ensure compatibility, joined and left every server, and still nothing. She hissed when her phone started buzzing. Its screen lit up: *LZR - Diaz, Chris*. It was a co-worker.

"Babe," she called to Dwayne, "can you get this? I'm still working on our connection."

"Huh?" Dwayne had been popping a drink and missed what she had said.

"It looks like it's Diaz; probably something about the union. Can you take the call?"

Dwayne answered her phone and sat down on the couch behind Lindy who was shouting at the screen; Quark the space-dog puppet had shaken off his bubble helmet and was about to cause some trouble by chewing something he shouldn't. "Hey, s'up."

"Uh… Gemma?" Diaz was confused, "look, we got to talk organizing. Right now. We need this and we gotta…"

"BEHIND YOU CHUCK!" Lindy was heavily invested in protecting the *SpaceBuzz* infrastructure up in orbit from her seat on the carpet of the Banks' apartment, warning The Commander of impending disaster.

Dwayne suppressed a groan and shut his eyes. Unionizing was all anyone on their team would talk about, but it never went anywhere. "Just a sec," he headed to the fire escape to give more attention to Diaz, and to keep Gemma and Lindy from having to witness his irritation should things get heated, "hang on."

Diaz was right, of course. Every day they'd needed to organize a union even more than the one before. But it was so much work with such a high chance of failure that both Dwayne and Gemma were seriously wrestling with whether to support it. It was easier for Diaz; he was younger, with more energy, and no one else who depended on his employment and income. He could still afford to be ideological. Unfortunately, pursuing what was just or necessary was not going to take care of the immediate needs of the Banks family, or those to come. Their current situation was inadequate, but at least it allowed them to stay together. Dwayne wanted to demand more of the life that they had been given but couldn't risk what they already barely had.

He instinctively stepped to clear the extension cord for the fairy lights they had framed their windows with, to get outside. There wasn't space in their apartment for a Christmas tree, their lease didn't permit them anyway, and the display was the compromise they had made to satisfy Lindy's obsession for all things that glittered. In making the effort to avoid tripping, he saw that someone must have already, as the unplugged cord lay straggled across the floor. He plugged it back into the outlet despite the hazard it presented; they could go back to worrying about health and safety in the new year. For now, a small glimmer of holiday cheer seemed more important than an obstacle-free corridor.

He hath cast down the mighty from their seat! A bellowing from the streets below greeted Dwayne as he got out onto the rickety landing. Their local evangelist often expounded his Magnificat until he was hoarse but was especially passionate this time of year. Dwayne did his best to tune out the ranting.

"Yo, Diaz, sorry about that. Gemma's busy trying to log into that LZR speech thing." *Glory be to the Lord, He lifts up the lowly!* Dwayne turned his back on the sermon that was unlikely to end any time soon.

"Ugh, gross," Diaz was always disgusted by their CEO's posturing, "surely you have something better to do. Dwayne, it's Christmas!"

"I know, I know," he wished they could ignore it too, "but Lindy is hooked on *SpaceBuzz*, and we wanted her to have the subscription for the new year."

He fills the hungry with what is good! The fervent Gospel of the neighbourhood's professed minister gained momentum. And volume. *The rich, he sends away! Empty!*

"Come again?" Diaz had caught a snippet of an aggressively hopeful message that was uncharacteristic of Dwayne.

"Nevermind, it's some guy yelling. I'm outside right now." The shouting had shifted to a different, but equally familiar gospel. *Look! The wages you failed to pay the workmen who mowed your fields are crying out against you!*

"Right, anyway, it's Christmas, I'll be quick," Diaz got to his point, "look, he's literally in space, let's get a move on our organizing, while he's gone. This is the only time everyone is off the clock. Let's get those signatures and hold a vote and –" *The cries of the harvesters have reached the ears of the Lord Almighty!*

"Look, Chris, buddy, I get it," Dwayne was sympathetic but tired, "but there's no way we can pull this all together now. You've seen how he's shut it down at other sites. We need way more time, way more planning." *Be patient, then, brothers, until the Lord's coming… be patient! Stand firm!*

"So what is it, Dwayne?" The Banks' waffling was baffling, and frustrated Diaz; they all seemed to be on the same page. He couldn't understand their hesitation, what was holding them up. "You wanna wait until the guy is dead, or what?" *Blessed are those who persevere!*

"We might as well," sighed Dwayne. "Look, I'm going to go see if Gemma needs help. We'll talk about this another day, ok bud?" He ended the call without waiting for a response. He felt guilty dismissing Chris's optimism, but there were other priorities.

The early sunset was one of the more depressing things about that time of year, and Dwayne's heart sank a little with it. The time to organize would never be right. They should have just gone for it. *Next time*, he promised, *next time for sure.* He knew he was lying to himself, perhaps out of shame for abandoning his more enthusiastic co-worker. There was unlikely to be a time that felt safe enough to take a chance.

"Alright Excelsior, you're coming in too steep for a stable entry and you're facing the wrong direction entirely. That last impact altered your trajectory, and there's some kind of internal damage that's preventing us from reorienting the capsule from the ground."

Lorne looked over at the dented panels and protruding wires from when he argued with Cañaveral on initiating his landing and thought he could kick things into submission. "On the *inside* you say, well I don't quite see how—"

The Mission Safety and Success Manager hastily cut him off. "Look Lorne, we don't have time. You've got to get the Excelsior into position and pilot the ballistic re-entry we went over during your landing briefing. If you need clarification, we have to do this now before ionospheric blackout -" Too soon, ground control shorted out.

Every needle on every dial of the Excelsior decent module's control panels spun frantically; every light that could flash red did. Lorne hadn't taken his fourteen hours of training seriously enough to know what any one of the instruments before him meant, but even he could see that, collectively, they signaled that something very bad was about to happen. He scrambled to pull out his phone, the only thing he had ever needed in a high-stakes situation. If it would have been any help at all, it didn't matter; the capricious turbulence of the craft did not allow him to get a grip, and it clattered off to somewhere beyond his reach. As though a visual assessment would have assisted him in any way, he pried open a porthole that was within reach and immediately regretted it; now visible were flying chunks of unidentifiable hardware, breaking up amid plasma and flame. Allowing the cover to snap back shut did not change what he had seen.

In times of mortal distress, it is said that one sees their life flash before the eyes. Whether it was a testament to how little he accomplished on Earth, or a mere reflection of that which he truly feared most, Lorne Elzéar was confronted with his death. Short circuiting with the stress and mounting hysteria, his vision reddened and narrowed to an incorporeal darkness.

Lorne's arms and legs were heavy, wading through a thick, red glow of liminal space, consuming him in darkness and heat. He felt like he was swimming in gelatin that had not quite set. In the indistinct and undulating atmosphere, he could make out subtle openings, infuriatingly beyond his reach. *Matarta. Teloneum.* They were a means to escape a grisly fate. As he clawed forward, whispers swirled about him. *Sin, sin; uncharitable, unmerciful pride.* An archontic force from deep within the nearest exit blew him back to where he started. *Spare no expense; more, more. Insatiable glutton!* The spooked billionaire forced his way to another. Again, particular judgments hissed through his ears.

Usury. Injustice! He was again denied access, driven away by a gust of accusation. *Theft. Sloth. Avarice!* With urgent desperation, he stretched through the viscous yet intangible matter impeding his progress, straining to reach the next waystation. *No prayers for Lorne Elzéar…*

Contemptuous admonishments blew him away: *unrepentant envy! Sins of the tongue! Covetous, Lorne Elzéar. Take all that better and lesser men possess. Obscenity. Hubris! Acedia…*

Gravity righted itself and wrenched Lorne from whatever salvation lay beyond his reach. He pitched backward, plunging through layers of guilt and damnation that would reduce any soul to tears. A colourless sequence of what was surely yet to come stayed his plunge. He found himself suspended among people and consequences he should have considered before this dire moment.

A distant eulogy solemnly announced the untimely and fiery death of an entrepreneurial visionary, and the wealthiest man in American history. It swilled in among scenes of ghoulish and unadulterated joy.

Come weep and howl… The sermon of some street preacher that Lorne might have heard once was the voiceover to the fever dream he found himself in *…ye fraudulent, ye abundantly wealthy.* Elzéar was drowning in waves of tax invoices, marked up to divest him of responsibility to the public who magnified his wealth. Ugly, drunken creditors, investors, and opportunistic shop stewards plundered his assets, swooping and swarming in an incongruous horde of blackflies and vultures. *Your riches are rotten; moths hath eaten your clothes.* Anarchic looting of Lorne's factories and distribution centres left gutted infrastructure razed to the ground. Without him to command his legal team in defending the dubious contracts that tied them to his companies, his employees, domestic and abroad, were poached by other firms. *Your gold has tarnished, your silver, but rust.* Having no will, living relatives, or any formal relationships, Elzéar's remaining property was escheat to the state, a fitting condemnation of a selfish billionaire's unworthy life. *Their corrosion will testify against you…* All around him, everything that represented value to Lorne Elzéar was dismantled *…and eat your flesh like fire.* LZR Holdings was ripped into unrecoverable bits like the overheated shell of its CEO's spaceship, breaking up into a sparkling cascade over the Atlantic, to rival the Star of Bethlehem that lit the sky of a more celebrated Christmas long past.

Amid the horrifying phantasmagoria and strange words of his impending demise, in a bout of terminal lucidity, Lorne feared more what would become of him when it ended. His hands groped about to find the radio transmitter theoretically still connected to someone, somewhere who could hear him. His flustered brain searched for the words to give one last message that might secure himself a better place in the hearts and minds of the citizenry of Earth. But it was too late for pontificating. Lornal Harlon Elzéar was past all hope. Lorne Elzéar was out of time.

STAVE V
THE END OF IT

Elzéar's ears were ringing, and he clawed at a never-ending nylon cover that was suffocating him. He struggled to escape, until he realized that he was still strapped into the seat of the Excelsior's command module. He unbuckled his bindings and tore the sheeting from his face. Hot, intense light hit him, and he squinted in the sun. The sun. *Daylight.* The brightness gave him a headache and the heat was making him sick. In a sweaty, unhinged daze, Lorne rolled out of the seat face first onto a gritty surface, snarled up in what he was beginning to recognize as a parachute. He choked, inhaling a mouthful of sand and, over the ringing of his ears, detected the sloshing sound of waves. He blinked and pushed himself up to kneel on a beach that he concluded he had washed up on, after surviving an emergency splashdown landing. He combed the debris that was scattered about for anything that could be useful when he heard a cough and looked up to see a child filming the wreckage. He stopped when Lorne tried to get up to disentangle himself from the parachute still twisted around him, and failed.

"Hey mister… you okay?"

Lorne touched his face. It was hot and wet and now covered in sand; he had been sobbing violently. "Hey you… kid. Um." He was still uncomfortably hot and addled. "You there… boy," Lorne dragged himself around to see the young videographer better, "what day is it today?"

The incredibly bizarre interaction caught the boy off guard, "the day? It's… why, it's Christmas Day."

Christmas Day. He hadn't missed it. It was a miracle. His very own, personal Christmas miracle.

"You got a signal with that thing?" asked Elzéar, "you online?" The kid nodded. "Okay, okay, great. I need you to post some stuff for me. I need you to tell everyone that I made it. Lorne Elzéar made it. He's sorry and he made it." He was getting choked up but swallowed hard and kept going. "I didn't feel anything, I couldn't feel anything, but it's going to be better now. I'm going to be better now. Lornal Harlon Elzéar is better now, and has work to do.

"I didn't see the light from the Overview Effect; I saw it in death. You can tell them THAT is my holiday message. The life we share here on Earth, it's a miracle, it's precious, and I will no longer take anyone or anything for granted." He sobbed again, but this time his tears were joyful.

"Tell them… tell them Merry Christmas. A happy new year to all the world!" Lorne tittered. He was back on Earth, back among his fellow man. "Hello there, world! Whoop! Hallo!!" He felt giddy; he felt light. Not just from the heatstroke induced by wearing a spacesuit in the open sun, but with all the time that now lay before him. To make amends. To do right.

"Tell them that every LZR employee is getting a raise. Tomorrow. No, no in the New Year. Because they are all on paid vacation until then. And everyone who works for me gets full health benefits for free and… and a full pension when they retire! It's all on me! Everything will be better now. From now on, everything will be okay." In among the wreckage, Lorne spied a bottle.

"Ha ha! Best day ever! Hey kid, kid, get this!" The boy started recording as Lorne popped open the celebratory landing champagne that he had stowed away for his triumphant return. The cork flew as its contents spewed and fizzed everywhere and Lorne drank from the bottle.

"Hallo! Hello World! Whoop! How are you? I am here! You are here! I am here to tell you all… Merry Christmas! A Merry Christmas to everyone! I am now here for the public good! LZR Holdings exists to do good. Whatever you ordered today, yesterday, it's free. You owe me nothing! That streaming service we tricked you all into buying? Forget it, you can have it, everyone can have it, it's free! It's yours!" His tinnitus grew louder as he chugged the champagne. It was making him hot. It was making him dizzy. He was too elated to stop. "Golden sunlight! Heavenly sky! Hey, kid, you want some?" Lorne was rambling.

"Um. I'm nine. You okay, mister?"

"Yeah. Yeah, yeah you're nine. I'm fine, you're nine. Fine…" Elzéar slurred. He was overheating. "Just maybe, maybe too much drinking for a space cadet who's just landed. Maybe a little too much…" Elzéar's speech was garbled, and he sank to his knees again. But he was fine. "From this day…" He was overwhelmed by too many sensations, "Lorne Elzéar will be forever known not for his wealth but…" He had made it, he was back, but his vision was clouding. He fought to remain conscious, rummaging through the scattered landing debris for something to help. There had to be something. "It's fine, it's fine, it's fine…" Elzéar muttered. He had a new lease on life, he had time to make right. He shouted over the increased ringing in his ears, "everything is FINE!"

Lorne clutched a receiver, desperately repeating how fine everything would be as the Excelsior's sirens blared, heralding the end. Radio blackout still prevented Cañaveral from responding to the frenzied shriek, coming through their headsets although there was nothing for them to say anyway. Everything was not fine. Not for Lorne Elzéar. His grand Yuletide redemption had been a delirious multimodal hallucination, the delusions of a dying brain.

A disturbing grinding sound drowned out the last of Lorne's insistence that everything was fine, and the hull of the Excelsior bulged inward from the pressure of its bungled re-entry. The gaskets holding it all together melted away while mission control listened helplessly to propellant tanks exploding in a thermal shockwave that tore the spacecraft and its occupant apart. With its ablative grand finale, the Millennial Noël mission ended.

GEMMA REPEATED THE EXASPERATED NOISES AND TROUBLESHOOTING SHE HAD already tried countless times over. She was running low on steam and patience. Sleep deprivation wasn't all that new to the working mother who put in more than full time hours in the LZR call centre but also as a partner, caregiver, teacher, therapist, housekeeper and technician here at home. Those responsibilities, added to a lifetime of grinding, bore down exponentially with each minute past the hour spent trying to sign in to Elzéar's broadcast. Few things in life are especially easy, but it would have been nice if, just this once, for their first and only family holiday together for the foreseeable future, things would come together without a struggle. Tense and agitated, she barely noticed that Lindy had wormed her way into her lap until she interrupted her with a request. "Mummy – can I have a grilled cheese? The kind in the triangles. Not the squares."

"Later baby, we got to get into this if you want to keep watching Chuck Baldwin" Seemingly unrelated to anything that Gemma had just done, an icon appeared in the middle of a black pop-up window that implied that something was loading. Again.

To complement Gemma's burnout, an abrupt silence erupted from every electronic instrument in the home shutting off simultaneously. The ensuing darkness indicated that an overtaxed fuse had blown.

It can be unpredictable which will be the final straw, and equally so the reaction to it being placed upon one's back. Gemma Banks burst into tears.

"Momma? Mommy?" Lindy put her arms around her mother, trying to squeeze her back together as Gemma had so often done when their roles were reversed. She didn't look up when Dwayne returned from his phone call.

"Shit, shit I'm sorry hun. That was me. My bad. I plugged in some lights. I wasn't thinking." Opening a panel near the door, he unscrewed the blackened cause of their present fiasco. Gemma didn't respond to Dwayne's mea culpa or the slams of him throwing open cupboards and drawers, searching for a replacement that wasn't there. "I'll go get another; someone on the floor will have a spare." Dwayne sprinted off to remedy the situation, leaving Lindy as the only Banks not completely overtaken by the small disaster.

"Shhhh. Shhh, Momma it's ok. Daddy's gonna get the lights back on. It's ok Momma, I like it in the dark. It's fun when the sparkles come in from outside." Lindy applied all the training she had absorbed as a loyal *SpaceBuzz* cadet, despite her inexperience in taking command of a faltering ship.

Gemma was yet to be comforted by her daughter and continued to sputter, "I'm sorry baby. I'm sorry, I tried. I really wanted you to keep your space show. I really did. I am so so sorry baby."

Lindy soldiered on. "It's okay. Mummy, we can watch another time. Let's make grilled cheese. We don't need TV. It's Christmas, Mummy."

"Hunnybear," Gemma miserably pulled it together, "If I can't make this work, there won't be anymore TV. This was going to be your present."

Present. Gifts. Lindy was trying to remember an important lesson that the Commander had taught them. It was the one to solve this crisis. She had to get it right.

"When it pinches to give, it's a good gift, but presents don't have to be things." Lindy mustered the best gift she had on hand and kissed her mother. "We don't need to go to space to be heroes Mummie, you already are."

Commander Balwin's sage advice was less than compelling to her in the moment, but Gemma recovered enough to begin the sandwich preparation that felt like a poor substitute for award-winning multigenerational children's programming. She set a pan on the element and twisted the dial. With a click and a woosh, flames that were less apparent under normal circumstances glowed blue in the unlit flat. The gas range meant an extra bill, and was probably bad for them in other ways, but right now it was a small comfort that something still worked when it was needed.

Dwayne entered as unobtrusively as possible and carefully walked over whatever eggshells may still be scattered about to make his way to the fuse box with his scavenged replacement. Gemma stopped him. "Just a minute. Come help me." She was jittery and trying to get cheese slices, but the packaging wasn't cooperating. Cautiously, Dwayne gave her a squeeze and began peeling them from the plastic wrappers.

"I wanted to make it dark now anyway," said Lindy, trying to bring the mood up, "I want to sit with you and Daddy. I want to look at the lights. Let's eat grilled cheese and have Christmas. I wanna snuggle on the couch and watch the sparklies."

"That's a good idea, baby," Dwayne said, "why don't you go grab one of your stuffies while Momma and I get this sorted out." Lindy shot off to her room at the suggestion and then it was Dwayne's turn to gift Gemma with an embrace. "You good hun? We're gonna be good. We're always good. It'll work out." Like Lindy, Dwayne was repeating assuring words he had often heard himself. But rather than an internationally beloved space hero, it was Gemma who used them so often before. He pivoted to the other pressing issue. "Can I set this right and then we all relax together?" He held up the fuse that would fix one of their troubles. Gemma nodded.

The apartment sparked back to life. Gemma had cranked the volume on their laptop when she had been trying to tune in to Elzéar's broadcast, so the bulletin that blasted from its speakers made everyone jump. "LZR Holdings thanks you for your patience. Due to an unexpected and catastrophic Kessler Syndrome fatality, we regretfully announce…" The grave tone of LZR's Director of Astronaut and Orbital Sales clashed with the cheerful, energetic countdown theme song from the television that welcomed the children of the world to another episode with Chuck Baldwin. Dwayne rushed over to unplug everything before it all blew out again.

"Did you want me to set up the livestream now?" He asked as Gemma flipped sandwiches. "It sounds like it's going."

"No," said Gemma decisively, "I think we've had enough. It's Christmas. And I'll bet what we don't have that Lorne Elzéar isn't thinking about us right now. How about we don't think about him anymore? Shut it down; it's family time." She picked up her phone that Dwayne had dropped in his fury and turned it off to articulate her point. As if it feared being abandoned too, Dwayne's cell vibrated and lit up with the preview of a message from Diaz. *Hey bud you CALLED it!! Looks like we can go ahead after all. A very merry xmas for LZR labour :)*

He left it unread and turned off his phone too, then flicked off the lights in the apartment. Lindy had returned and scrambled up into a window ledge with a stuffed kitty under her arm to look out at the skyline of the city. They had earned one evening to ignore the pinging and buzzing of the outside world, to have one small holiday not defined by employment and stress. Gemma finished with the stove and, with everything else unplugged, powered down, or otherwise switched off, it was as serene as it could be in their downtown apartment. Music bled in from a suite next door to inform them that their neighbours were Dreaming of a White Christmas. Although their state hadn't seen snow at this time of year for decades, with Lindy sitting at the window in her footed pajamas, hugging her favourite plushie, the tune set an appropriately cozy scene. Dwayne washed up and Gemma cut the grilled cheese into the required triangles.

In her corner, looking up and searching for the stars, Lindy was too awestruck to act when she saw a bright streak slash across the sky. *Shooting star*. That hypothetical concept, which had until now been filed away in a part of her brain that she might have labeled 'fiction' if she had the vocabulary, flashed by a lot faster than she might have guessed. She wasn't sure if she had missed her chance; surely one wasn't expected to make a full wish in that fraction of a second. Not wanting to squander the opportunity, but vaguely aware of the risk of making more tangible requests in haste during such magical moments, she whispered what she hoped would cause no harm, if not some good.

"God bless us, every one…"

"What was that babygirl?" Dwayne picked Lindy up from the window ledge so they could all sit together and enjoy what remained of Christmas Day. But Gemma had already handed over her snack, and she was now too preoccupied to clarify.

The skyglow from the city obstructed real stars from being seen, even without the festive lights that twinkled among them at this time of year, but the Banks family were able to see everything that they really cared about.

It was beautiful.

The End

Thank you for reading!

Answers to Riddles:

-A book (spine on the binding, pages like leaves, you open it to read in silence)

-A postage stamp (travels the world stuck to an envelope, gets licked to stick, cancelled/worthless once it reaches its destination)

5	2	6	9	8	3	7	1	4
7	3	8	1	4	2	5	6	9
9	1	4	6	5	7	2	8	3
8	7	9	2	3	5	6	4	1
6	4	3	7	9	1	8	2	5
1	5	2	4	6	8	3	9	7
2	9	5	8	7	4	1	3	6
3	6	1	5	2	9	4	7	8
4	8	7	3	1	6	9	5	2

Issue 19 is coming out in spring!!